Praise for *The*

"Ashe's persuasive behind-the-scenes ballet sections lend heft and authenticity to what could otherwise be mere window dressing, and she transitions her narrative from charming slice of historical fiction to pulse-pounding suspense at an expert pace. It's a fiercely memorable debut from a writer to watch."

—*Publishers Weekly* (starred review)

"Historical-novel fans as well as those who enjoy a bit of gothic intrigue will appreciate this story."

—*Booklist*

"The ballet world sets the stage for this terrifying psychological thriller that takes place in prewar London."

—*Entertainment Weekly*

"Ashe trained with the Royal Ballet School, and she is fascinating on the detail of the girls' lives; on the pain and the bloodied feet that underpin the perfection of the dance; on, as Samuel says, 'this mad life you all live, always on the edge of pain and exhaustion.' A wonderful, eye-opening debut."

—London *Times*

"This unsettling tale . . . is set in 1933 in the poisonously competitive world of ballet. . . . As the story follows the rehearsals for the ballet *Coppélia*, we receive a quick-fire education on how the ballet works and why it inspires obsession. . . . An original thriller with a crafty plot."

—*Daily Mail*

"Based on the real ballet scene in prewar London, this immersive tale will be a delight for historical-fiction fans who like a touch of suspense."

—*Library Journal*

"Dances with historical details, with unease and atmosphere. You can feel the mist of the London canals, hear the ballet shoes touching the stage."

—Abigail Dean, author of *Girl A*

"This book was a joy to read from start to finish. Ashe's writing is razor-sharp with a lyrical edge to it. . . . Rich, mesmerizing, and compelling, *The Dance of the Dolls* heralds the arrival of a bright new voice in literary fiction."

—Awais Khan, author of *No Honour*

"A spellbinding thriller, set against a fascinating background and so beautifully written."

—Frances Quinn, author of *The Smallest Man*

"Lucy has created a mesmerizing atmosphere in her debut novel. This story is one of dreadful, delirious ambition as well as the relentless drive for perfection. . . . Beautiful."

—Sally Oliver, author of *The Weight of Loss*

"*The Dance of the Dolls* is a delight, a book that is at times historical fiction, at times a love story to ballet, and at times even a bit of a thrilling whodunit."

—The Bookbag

"Quite a debut, very assured and confident . . . a wonderfully told story."

—@emreadsthebooks

"Haunting and richly evocative . . . takes the reader on a spellbinding journey through the 1930s London ballet scene, in which the beauty and elegance of the participants is the flip side of a destructive drive for perfection and darkly murderous obsessions. Lucy Ashe's debut is absolutely en pointe."

—Lexie Elliott, author of *How to Kill Your Best Friend*

"Lucy Ashe's debut novel is a clever thriller set in a world which she knows so well, having trained at the Royal Ballet School and being a twin. It's a story of sisterly love, ambition, and obsession. . . . Take a bow, Ms. Ashe."

—*Historical Novel Society*

Also published by Lucy Ashe

The Dance of the Dolls

THE
SLEEPING
BEAUTIES

THE
SLEEPING
BEAUTIES

Lucy Ashe

**UNION
SQUARE
& CO.**

NEW YORK

UNION SQUARE & CO.

NEW YORK

First published in the UK in 2024 in hardcover by Magpie, an imprint of Oneworld. This 2024 paperback edition published by Union Square & Co., LLC.

ISBN 978-1-4549-5125-4
ISBN 978-1-4549-5126-1 (e-book)

For information about custom editions, special sales, and premium purchases, please contact specialsales@unionsquareandco.com.

Printed in Canada
2 4 6 8 10 9 7 5 3 1

unionsquareandco.com

Cover design by Emily Mahon and Patrick Sullivan
Cover images: ClassicStock/Alamy (cars); Iuliia Isaieva/Moment RF/Getty Images (dancer); Shutterstock.com: Magnolija Three (flowers), Timurpix (city)
Interior design by Rich Hazelton
Interior images: gizele/Shutterstock.com (roses)

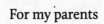

For my parents

Stage Notes

In May 1940, the British Council sent the Sadler's Wells Ballet company across the North Sea to the Netherlands, a country yet to join the war.

After an enthusiastic first-night welcome at the Royal Theatre in The Hague, the mood darkened. Traveling to perform in towns close to the German border, the dancers started noticing signs of war creeping ever closer.

Then, in the early hours of the morning on May 10, Germany invaded. The ballet company was stranded, and it took days of evacuations, and a slow, dangerous journey through the war-torn country, before the dancers finally found their way back home.

Prologue

Thorns catch her dress. The girl ignores the sharp scratch against her wrist, the spike that digs its way beneath her skin. She runs fast through an arch of roses and beneath the heavy scent of summer jasmine, her cheek brushing the faded rot of lilac: she wishes the garden would consume her, grow tall and wild into one giant tangle of branches, roots dug hard into the ground. Tonight, she longs to hide inside a secret garden, to escape for a hundred years between thick forest walls.

She runs farther into the garden. The sounds from the house fade until all that is left is the quiet echo of the wind against the trees, their trunks choked with ivy.

At last she feels safe, her breath gradually easing as she slows her legs and walks. There is a marble seat at the end of the path, its cold silver stone offering a steady glow under the moonlight. It seems to take her an age to reach it, her legs losing their strength now that she is no longer running. When she finally collapses against the marble, her head swims. All evening she has been drinking, and her body is not used to the rising haze of champagne. She knows she should have been more careful, more alert to the dangers around her.

But tonight there was no one to watch over her, no fairy godmother, no mother at all.

Midnight. She can sense time shifting, the night ticking on toward morning. If she can just rest her head, close her eyes for a few minutes, she thinks she will find the strength she needs. She imagines a bedroom, an absurd image of pink silk and tasseled cushions. Instead all she has is a hard marble seat and potted topiary spikes. The summer air thickens around her as though a huge hand is pressing her down. No one can hear her whisper to herself, an incoherent muddle of sighs. Perhaps, she thinks, this is how Princess Aurora felt as the forest groaned and grew, the prick of her finger sending her to sleep.

A man appears at the end of the path, but she doesn't see him. She is nearly asleep, shadows dancing beneath her eyelids, turning trees, shrubs, the red bloom of roses, the bulk of the man, into one eddying monochrome mess.

The man has seen her, though. He walks forward, silent as he pushes a rose away from his face, the thorns shivering into the thicket.

Music scratches in the distance, at the house or farther away in the streets. There are people somewhere, a party, faint shrieks and cries that rise and fall as her eyelids droop. She tries to fight the weight of exhaustion that pulls her body down, but it is no use. The darkness of the garden, the trees that encircle her, the sweet scent of roses: they consume her like the swirling magic of an incantation, a fairy waving her wand.

She falls asleep.

Act I

May 1945

Rosamund Caradon is surrounded by children. Keeping them close, she walks swiftly, a basket of treats for the train journey hanging from her elbow. Inside the basket are the eggs she collected earlier this morning from their garden hens, a task she had lingered over while watching the children run up and down the lawn for the very last time.

As they make their way onto the platform, Rosamund feels the basket press against her, little fingers clutching at the edge. It is Jasmine who peers inside, checking that the eggs, the packet of salt, the sandwiches, the mock marzipan balls of beans, rice, and vanilla essence are exactly where they should be.

Jasmine is the youngest of the little crowd of children that Rosamund hurries farther along the platform, but no one would think it from watching her, seeing how she bubbles with confidence as she hops among them. For she is Rosamund Caradon's daughter. And as her daughter, she takes her hosting responsibilities seriously. Too seriously at times, Rosamund has secretly observed, smiling as her daughter instructs her playmates in the most complex of games and scenarios. The sadness of saying goodbye to the children is only heightened by her worry of how Jasmine will cope without this little army of girls and boys who provide her with endless entertainment and purpose.

Rosamund took in many children during the war, some lasting for less than a month before their parents called for their return, others staying for years. Since the winter of 1939, there has been a steady progress of tears and goodbyes, of children suddenly shy in front of their parents or itching to get back to the familiarity of city living. Rosamund remembers how one little boy hardly recognized the aunt who had come to collect him, hiding behind Jasmine and Rosamund until the poor woman convinced him that she was taking him home. The boy's mother was working all hours at a London hospital, the aunt told Rosamund, but she could no longer stand the pointed questions from the other nurses about when her son was coming home.

Once war was over, everyone wanted to find some normality, to settle and fix their disordered homes. The reality, of course, was that it was impossible. Not with rationing and homes bombed and fathers not yet returned. How could any woman be expected to carry on as before, the aunt exclaimed as Rosamund busied herself in the kitchen making sandwiches for their journey. Rosamund had nodded sagely, thinking how empty the huge house was going to feel with all the children finally gone, just her precious Jasmine left to look after and protect. She would need work, an occupation to keep her busy, make her feel needed and in control of her day. The thought of vacant rooms and acres of empty gardens, silent hallways and the front lawn too smooth without the scuff of balls and cricket bats, made her breathless, as though all the life was being sucked out of her lungs.

The whistle of the train propels the children forward along the platform of Exeter St. David's, Rosamund gathering arms and hands and pushing them into the carriage. Each child has a small suitcase, Jasmine insisting on carrying Eliza's as well as her own, her shoulders straining as she lifts herself up the steps and into the train.

"Come on, Eliza. Time waits for no man." It is a phrase she has picked up from her grandmother, who lives with them at Gittisham Manor and likes to offer clipped words of instruction from her armchair in the front room. Jasmine encourages her friend up into the carriage, keeping the suitcase gripped tightly in her hand.

"You're going to need to give that back to her at some point," Rosamund says, charmed by the effort her daughter is making to look after her friend. Jasmine doesn't reply, a mass of tangled blond hair swishing as she marches forward and finds an empty carriage, the others following obediently.

Behind her is Eliza Matthews, nine years old and declared by Jasmine to be her best friend for life. She is followed by Julia Greene, a fourteen-year-old who goes nowhere without her ballet shoes at her side in a soft cloth bag. She brought a cutout paper theatre with her when she arrived from London, and the children spent hours assembling its pieces and pushing pantomime characters and ballerina fairies in paper tutus around a colorful stage made of cardboard. Then there are the two boys, twin brothers Timothy and John Giles, who were desperately homesick when they arrived, only to become the sole evacuees to stay throughout the war, establishing routines and structures that had settled them and made Gittisham Manor feel like home. Rosamund worries about how they will adjust to London after nearly six years of country living. Her home in Devon is all space and greenery, wide lawns, sturdy old trees to climb, a labyrinthine wood to explore. The Giles brothers live in a tiny flat in Clerkenwell, surrounded by noise. When they boarded a train to the countryside in that first energetic wave of September evacuations, aged just six, London was all they had known. But their memories of London have faded now, replaced with Devon's rolling hills.

The whistle cries out once again and the train starts its slow roll out of Exeter. There are people on the platform, waving with bright smiles as they send children back home to London. Rosamund knows those smiles will lose their certainty once they return to their kitchens and start to accustom themselves to the ordinary simplicity of life without the evacuees, these children that they have found ways to love, nurture, ease their homesickness. They have tried to discover common ground with those who had never seen the sea, never walked through a field of cows, never been the victim of the stinging nettles' rash.

Pulling back from the window, Rosamund settles down to watch the children. She hadn't really wanted to come with them to London, but Jasmine would never agree to waving them off from a platform edge when she could have her own adventure in the big city she has heard so much about. War kept her from it, and now, finally, at the age of eight, she is hurtling through Devon, Somerset, Wiltshire, Berkshire, all these counties she can name on a map, rattling them off like a song. London awaits.

Rosamund has another reason for accompanying the children on the train journey back to London. Her family has a flat in Chelsea, two neglected stories of tired walls and dated furniture that no one has had the energy or inclination to refresh. Her brother Matthew lived there for years, filling it with books and newspapers, piles of notebooks scratched with his attempts at poetry, dusty playbills and signed photographs from actors and opera singers. He left when the war began, moving into a cottage in Somerset with two other bachelors and washing his hands of responsibility for anything to do with the London flat, with Gittisham Manor, with his mother and her endless expectations. He knew that his parents had always judged him, resented how he refused to marry and provide the next generation of men to preserve Gittisham Manor and its acres of farmland. When their father had died two years before the war, Rosamund considered spending some time in London, but life in Devon took on new meaning when Jasmine arrived. Her father was dead, but her husband was gone too, his absence forcing a realignment of what she wanted from her life. Without him, she was nervous about leaving her home in the countryside, of forging her way through unknown and unfamiliar streets.

Alberic's death frightened her, how sudden and unnecessary it was, how easily avoided. He had been at a weekend party in London, a dull event that he felt duty-bound to attend, he'd said before he left: old school friends who insisted they meet once a year for stodgy food and a giddy dose of nostalgic reminiscing. Driving too fast on his way home, Alberic Caradon was killed, his car overturned in a grass ditch, the towering monoliths of Stonehenge impassively watching from across the nearby fields.

Rosamund knows it is time to face London again. Not just for herself, but for Jasmine too. While Rosamund would prefer to keep her safe within the high woodland walls of the Otter Valley, she knows that Jasmine is already outgrowing the smallness of her world. The villages of Devon will not contain her for much longer. Now the war is over, there is nothing left to stop them from getting on the train and starting a new adventure. She just wishes she could have brought her ancient dog Felix along with them, but it wasn't possible. He has stayed behind in Devon, moving from one sunlit spot to another.

Her London lawyer visited the flat last month, reporting back that it had been miraculously saved from bombing while much more loved and cared-for homes on the same street stood in ruins. This was a sign, Rosamund thought, that she must open the flat, flush out its dust and dirt, and start making it into a modern home where she and Jasmine could carve out whatever sort of life they desired. Looking at Jasmine now, hearing her loud chatter as she hands out the sandwiches much earlier than is necessary, Rosamund feels torn between her desire to keep her daughter with her always, protected by the familiar fields of her estate, and her acceptance that this will not be enough. If she could, she'd hide away with Jasmine forever, never venturing beyond the tree-lined border of their home.

Just as the children have settled after the excitement of those first lumbering lurches of the train, a face looms into view at the door. Rosamund inhales and tries to avoid the gaze of the intruder. She wants this compartment for herself and for the children, her last opportunity to take on such a vast maternal role.

A woman is standing in the doorway of their compartment, peering uncertainly inside. When the train staggers, she catches herself against the door, her fingertips pressed white on the wood. "Is there space for one more?" the woman asks. The children stare up at her, momentarily diverted from organizing their bags and sandwiches, the two boys already trying to search for a pack of cards hidden amid their suitcases. Jasmine bares her teeth, smiling at the woman a little aggressively, Rosamund thinks.

"Please," says Rosamund, gesturing to the spare seat opposite her. She cannot risk pretending it is taken, not when Jasmine's disarming honesty would likely have her blurt out the truth. But she wishes they could have the space to themselves without worrying about whether their games are too loud and chaotic. The woman has, however, chosen this carriage when there must, surely, be quieter ones farther along the train: so she will have to put up with them and their chaos.

The woman places her suitcase on the luggage rack, rising high on her toes as she does so. When the train rocks this time, she is steady, her weight shifting gracefully as she slips into her seat. Leaning back, she stretches her legs out in front of her. Rosamund is struck by the agility of the woman's feet, the way they arch over and push against the leather soles of her heeled sandals. She is young, maybe in her mid-twenties, with slim shoulders and hips and a neat waist over which she wears a pretty polka-dotted blue belt that matches her dress. Her hair seems impossibly soft, a light brown wave that bounces against her shoulders.

Rosamund looks down at her own untidy fingernails, the faint smudge of soil beneath them, and closes her hands in her lap. She wishes the woman would go to another carriage. Already the pressure to conform to London fashions and standards is making her anxious, and she finds herself thinking that this young woman has no business looking so pretty and polished when Rosamund is wearing the same old skirt she has patched up many times now. Her mother, back at the manor house, had pursed her lips in disapproval when Rosamund came down this morning, ready for her London trip. A disappointment again, Rosamund knew, her refusal to dress up, fashion her hair smartly, to spend more money on herself than strictly necessary. Rosamund prefers to buy clothes for her daughter—and maybe fresh summer bedding for the garden now that the war is over and she doesn't need to feel guilty taking up precious vegetable space with flowers.

"Are they all yours?" the young woman says to Rosamund, gesturing at the children with a little laugh.

"I sometimes wish they were," Rosamund replies, forcing herself to be friendly. The last thing she wants to do is make polite conversation with this pretty young woman. In her final few hours with these children that she has grown to love, she doesn't want a minute stolen.

"Returning home, are they?" The woman's voice is gentle, and Rosamund can tell she is genuinely interested. But it doesn't stop her from feeling irritated.

"Yes. I took in a lot of evacuees. My home is big, you see, with lots of space for children to play. There have been many coming and going throughout the war. These are the final few."

"Do you live in Exeter?" the woman asks, reaching into her handbag and pulling out a small needle case.

"No, a village about half an hour away. Gittisham."

"Oh, Gittisham is lovely. How lucky for the children," the woman exclaims, setting the sewing kit open on her lap. "I live not far from there. Ottery St. Mary. Well, at least my parents live there, and I return when I can. My home is London now."

"We took the children into Ottery St. Mary a few times. And it's where I do my shopping, there or Honiton, if I can't face driving all the way into Exeter."

"Mama, we're going to play I Spy," calls out Jasmine from the window seat, her voice cutting through the conversation. The woman jumps slightly, turning quickly toward the children.

"Of course, darling," Rosamund replies, smiling apologetically at the woman.

"Oh, please do," the woman says. "Such a fun game for a long journey. Perhaps I can join in?"

"If you want. But don't feel obliged to continue if it gets boring." Rosamund remembers how, before Jasmine arrived, she had longed to be able to play a game of I Spy with a child of her own, watching families enviously on the bus journeys into Exeter when her parents wouldn't let her take the car. She tries to warm to the woman, doing her best to find sympathy for this obvious desire to interact with the children. It is a feeling she understands well.

Jasmine leads, finding a myriad of details to spy, a bright infusion of colors and shapes: the red of the seats; the brown leather of a suitcase; the black and white pattern of a cow as the train rushes by. Even Eliza's blue sailor's collar gets a mention, her loud and surprisingly low laugh rumbling through the carriage when she realizes. When it is the woman's turn, she stumps them all with the letter *B*. They try everything: the banana in Timothy's lunch bag, waiting to be eaten; belts, bags, the floral brooch on Rosamund's collar; the billows of steam from the train engine that occasionally drift past the window. Finally, it is Julia Greene who works it out.

"Ballet shoes!" she exclaims, noticing the pale pink of her own ballet slippers poking their toes out of her bag. A frayed silk ribbon has escaped, and the dusty soles of the shoes are turned up toward the seat.

"And I have my own, too," says the woman. She pulls out from her bag a pair of brand-new pointe shoes. From the reaction of the children, they could be a pair of magic rabbits drawn dramatically out of a hat. The satin shines brightly, so different to the scuffed ends of Julia's. At once all attention is on her, the children forgetting their game and staring intently at this woman who has suddenly become much more interesting. "I need to sew on the ribbons and darn the ends before I reach London," she says, winding a long pink ribbon round and round her hands.

"Are you a ballerina?" asks Jasmine, standing and going right up to her side. Rosamund can see how desperately her daughter wants to reach out and touch the shoes.

"Yes. At Sadler's Wells. I have been dancing all through the war." She waves her arm as she says this. It is a graceful *port de bras*, but it makes Rosamund wince, the warmth she was trying her best to feel gone once again. This will be it now for the rest of the journey, the girls plying this ballet dancer with questions, perhaps an impromptu barre class in the corridor, endless admiration. "You can hold them if you want." The woman passes her shoes to Jasmine, who turns them over in her hands, delicately stroking the satin as though it were a precious pet. Julia has risen to join her, and the two boys are watching with a failed attempt at indifference. They are at that age now where a pretty young woman will capture their interest. Rosamund has noticed them growing and changing, in that awkward space between childhood and puberty. At times she feels some relief that they are returning home before she must navigate them through the uncomfortable passage toward early adulthood.

"Julia is a ballet dancer too," Jasmine announces proudly.

"Yes, I gathered as much from the ballet shoes. Where do you dance?" she asks Julia, her face lighting up with curiosity.

"I'm a student at Sadler's Wells School. At least I was until my parents finally decided it wasn't safe for me to stay in London last year. I've tried to keep up with ballet class in Devon, but it isn't the same without a teacher."

"Oh, she dances every day," interjects Jasmine. "We set up a ballet studio in the library and used the back of the chairs as barres. Julia taught us all how to dance." Jasmine performs a little *arabesque*, her leg stuck out awkwardly behind her. The woman smiles and claps her hands. Rather too generous, Rosamund thinks. While Julia is a talented dancer, working with focus and commitment every day to maintain her flexibility, poise, balance, and grace, Jasmine is more enthusiastic than accurate in her ballet training. She prefers to throw herself energetically across the room, coming dangerously close to knocking books from their shelves with her wild bouncing arms. Her long blond hair, always an impossible bird's nest of tangles, refuses to be tamed into a neat bun on top of her head, wisps of white flying in all directions. Eliza would join in with the ballet classes too, moving solidly through the exercises without any grace to speak of but a charming and unembarrassed strength. Timothy was reluctant to get involved, but John gradually migrated from his position as observer on the armchair at the corner of the room, to timidly mimicking the exercises, to finally taking his place behind a kitchen chair. Julia had coached him kindly and patiently, lifting his elbows when they drooped, showing him how to rotate his legs from the hips, how to get his heels firmly down on the ground when he jumped in *petit allegro*. He found strength through ballet, the pursuit to master every exercise distracting him from sudden bursts of homesickness.

"When will Sadler's Wells open again as a theatre?" Julia asks. She has been longing for information, writing long letters to her friends and to her parents, desperate to know when her ballet training will resume along with its promise of performance and a dancing career. The little paper theatre and its pantomime characters that they had assembled in the hall was not quite an adequate replacement for the real lights of the London stage. She continues, the nostalgia for those missed ballet lessons rekindled. "When I left last year, only the school was still in residence at the theatre. Up there on the top floor, Miss Phillips and Mr. Sergeyev kept the studio open every morning. There could have been bombing all night, but we'd still turn up to class. I suppose you were with the ballet company on tour and at the New Theatre?"

"Yes," the ballet dancer replies, full of animation. "The rest of Sadler's Wells quickly became a soup kitchen and shelter for people who lost their homes in the bombings. We had to find a new home after that, though much of the time we were touring around England, getting used to a different theatre or community hall or even a makeshift stage in an aircraft hangar every few days. I will be glad when we have a space to call our own again." She has taken her shoes back now and is measuring out a stretch of pale pink thread, slipping it through the eye of the needle as she talks.

"What is your name?" asks Julia. "I might have seen you perform."

"I expect you have. I was in the school too, back in the thirties. I joined the company in the spring of 1936. It was wonderful making that transition from the studio at the top of Sadler's Wells to company class and rehearsals." She looks up from the ribbons she is sewing onto her shoes. "My name is Briar Woods. It's lovely to meet you all."

Rosamund watches as Briar speaks brightly with the children, telling dynamic stories about ballet during the war: tales of silk tights drying on the luggage racks of trains as they sped across the country; the parcels of sugar that would arrive in their dressing rooms from fans willing to give up their precious rations to keep the dancers fed; the bored troops sitting through performances of *Les Sylphides* when all they wanted was a music hall number.

But it is Jasmine she seems to smile at the most, her eyes flicking to her even when she is talking to Julia. It is as though she wants to check how the girl is reacting to her, like an actor reading reviews after a show. Perhaps, Rosamund thinks a little cruelly, she is missing the attention of the stage, impatient to get back to performances after a holiday in dull Devon. There is something about Briar Woods that disturbs Rosamund, something she finds hard to define. It could be the way she has centered herself among their group, ruining Rosamund's previous vision of the day. She has taken over, commanded the attention of everyone as she sits there so prettily with her shining pink pointe shoes and neat sewing kit. Rosamund's sewing kit back home is entirely different, she thinks with a grimace, a chaotic mess of threads, all sensible useful colors like black, brown, dark green, and navy. In the first war, when she was just a teenager, she had worked tirelessly with her mother to knit for victory, the two of them recruiting women from the nearby villages to sit in an assembly line of wool and patterns, knitting all sorts of warm clothes for the troops. Pink darning thread for the ends of pointe shoes is a luxury this country cannot afford, she decides, and yet here is this young woman, Briar Woods, telling wide-eyed children about how pointe shoemakers were given special permission during the war to use all the satin and leather they needed.

"Because art and beauty were essential during the war," Briar is telling them, her soft brown hair shaking gently as she speaks. "The country needed something to remind them that culture still existed, that we could do more than fight and survive. Ballet was proof that life carried on."

With tight lips, Rosamund tries not to laugh. She is thinking of her own war, of transforming bedrooms into dormitories, the endless laundry, the children who woke screaming for their parents, the struggle to make rations stretch out and feed all the mouths she had volunteered to take in. But she also knew she wouldn't have had it any other way. The war had given her purpose and direction, a purpose that she felt, with a sudden burst of righteousness, was much worthier than Briar's. While the pointe shoes were pretty, they would be useless if worn outside digging flower beds, replacing roses with onions. Looking at the children now, though, and remembering how happy Julia's ballet lessons had made them, she tries to soften her heart. Briar is just a child herself, an innocent in her blue polka-dot dress, her supple hands moving quickly over the shoes.

Reaching up, Briar tucks a smooth strand of hair behind her ear. Rosamund can't help but mirror her, patting down her own hair, a pointless attempt to tidy the wild bun already tumbling out of the pins she battled with this morning. She made an effort for today's journey into London, despite what her mother thinks, wearing her best hat from the milliner's in Ottery St. Mary and changing out of slacks into a navy pleated skirt and white blouse. She is more comfortable in woolen sweaters and boots, wide-legged slacks that rise high around her waist. With long legs and a strong, lean frame, her default look is a classical statue drowning in gardening clothes, thick sweaters tucked carelessly underneath overalls. And yet today she is even wearing a brooch, a spray of lilacs and jasmine that she found in a jewelry shop in Exeter; it was a gift to herself eight years ago when her daughter arrived and changed her world.

As the train speeds closer to London, the city slowly growing around them, Rosamund feels her stomach knotting with nerves. She is saying goodbye to Eliza and Julia at Paddington, where their parents will be waiting to collect them, but John and Timothy are staying with her all the way to their home in Islington. She is uneasy about seeing where they live, how reluctant she will be to watch them replace their idyllic country existence for a tiny home in the city. When the billeting officer had handed the two boys to her at Exeter St. David's all those years ago, she had warned her that they would be wary of the countryside. So many London parents had to be convinced with a bombardment of persuasive rhetoric that their children would be safer in the country than in the city.

And now they are to be returned, two little boys with not a single item in their suitcases the same as when they left.

At Paddington, Briar helps the children with their bags as they exit the train, refusing to leave them alone. The children are delighted, looking up to her by now as a goddess from another world. But for Julia and Eliza, when they catch sight of their parents waiting anxiously for them at the end of the platform, their attention shifts. Eliza runs into the arms of her mother and father, her suitcase skidding away from her as she reaches them, while Julia offers a cooler embrace to hers. It appears she is yet to forgive them for sending her away from the city where her ballet dreams could be fulfilled.

"Come and watch a rehearsal soon," Briar offers to Rosamund as they say goodbye under the domed roof of the station. The dancer presses Rosamund's hand warmly. "If you give me your address, I can write to you with the details as soon as we have a rehearsal I think Jasmine would enjoy."

It is impossible to refuse, not with her daughter poking her in the waist, even handing her a pencil from her satchel, a firm look fixed on her face. Rosamund hopes her sigh isn't too obvious—she recognizes that look, a little girl who knows her own mind. For a brief second, she thinks she will be saved by the lack of a piece of paper.

But Briar has thought ahead, it seems, drawing an old theatre ticket out of her bag. "It takes me forever to throw out anything," she says, laughing lightly as she hands Rosamund the paper. It is a ticket for *Casse-Noisette* at the New Theatre in 1941, a small cream-and-red booklet with flimsy pages packed with names and advertisements and instructions for what to do if the air raid sirens start during a performance. Rosamund writes down her address, the London flat in South Kensington, squeezing the words in around a cast list of Uncle Drosselmeyer and Clara and Snowflakes. Briar takes it, reads it, then tucks it away inside her bag.

When Briar finally disappears, hugging Jasmine for far longer than Rosamund is happy about, she feels herself start to relax.

All the charm and smiles and stories of the ballet: it had felt like a performance, an unnecessary and self-indulgent one, when Briar could surely have found peace and quiet in another part of the train. And yet she had chosen their carriage, where she could show off her ballet shoes and throw her pretty arms and legs about for a delighted, captive audience.

As they climb into a taxi outside the station, she tries to rationalize it, to push away her unease. Her nerves have been on edge all week, the anxiety of saying goodbye to the children, the journey into London away from the safety of her home, returning to the place she associates with her husband's death, the cruel city that for all she knew would be unrecognizable, a wreckage of war.

But there is something else worrying her. And she knows what it is. She is certain that she has seen Briar Woods before.

Devon, 1937

Rosamund Caradon surrounded herself with dormant branches of lilac. This morning, right after she had settled her mother into the little parlor that looked down to the lake, she escaped out of the house and into the grounds. Her dog, Felix, led the way, knowing instinctively where she was going. She often felt herself drawn to the walled garden, the most beautiful spot on the Gittisham estate, south-facing: a slight slope that caught the sun, flower beds interlaced among small trees, pebbled walkways that led to wrought iron garden furniture, wooden benches, a birdbath in mottled stone, trellises that climbed the rust-red walls.

Dressed in her oldest green sweater and the pair of brown slacks passionately hated by her mother, Rosamund moved purposefully through the sleeping garden, Felix always close by. She tied back the dark leaves of the summer jasmine that had fallen from its trellis before moving on to tidy the yellow blooms of the hardy winter variety that climbed over a sheltered reading spot by the old wall. It was the lilacs that always seemed to draw her attention the most, however, and she studied the dead and rubbing wood, exposed now the flowers had gone, her hands moving swiftly to keep herself warm. Every now and again she jumped up and down on the spot, the large dog at her side prancing excitedly from paw to paw. A strange sight she must make, she thought, the younger mistress of Gittisham Manor dancing around her resting lilacs on a chilly January morning.

This had always been a special place for Rosamund, ever since the end of the Great War, nearly twenty years ago now, when she had been Rosamund Hampton, unmarried and eager for change. Her lilacs and her jasmine, the two shrubs she liked to care for herself, had become a labor of devotion, almost like the children she longed for but which never arrived. The rest of the garden, a huge estate of rolling grasslands, the lake with its pockets of wildflowers lining the water, an orchard at the back of the house next to the potting sheds and glasshouses, rows of vegetables fighting for space between her mother's roses, the orangery beyond the huge cedar trees: all of this she was content to leave to the gardeners. It was the lilac and jasmine in the walled garden that were hers alone to nurture.

Every time one of her plants struggled, Rosamund felt a deep sense of failure. In her more rational moments, she realized that this was silly, her way of coping with the sadness of her past. Then she could shift the blame firmly to her parents: her father, who had never understood her; her mother for saying nothing, a silent, terrible judgment. But her father was gone now, a Christmas Eve death a few weeks ago. His heart had failed, the doctor said. Raymond Hampton, aged sixty-seven, collapsed in the stables on Christmas Eve just before teatime. It was Rosamund who found him as the darkness was starting to settle over the Devonshire hills. Raymond's favorite horse was peering down anxiously at her master, nudging his face with her muzzle.

Rosamund had felt lighter since then, managing her mother's persistent neuroses with a firm but gentle spirit and gradually pushing her father's heavy influence out of her life. Her lilacs, dormant though they were, seemed filled with hopeful anticipation. It would be a good year for them, she thought, as she ran her fingers along the wood.

Midmorning, she broke for tea, finding a sheltered seat underneath an arched trellis of hibernating jasmine. She poured from the flask she had brewed that morning, not so much evidence of organization but so that she could avoid returning inside and facing the demands of her mother. Felix settled himself at her feet, the weight of his body warm against her boots. He shed fur everywhere he went, great bundles of gold in the flower beds, the hallways, the bedrooms. Rosamund brushed him regularly, the two of them seated outside on the grass. It was not a job her mother would ever agree to take on herself. Felix was her second dog. When Flick had died five years ago, at the age of twelve, Rosamund waited a year before deciding she had mourned long enough. She went back to the farm adjacent to her garden and bought another puppy: Flick's great-great-grandson, she liked to think. Mr. Gilbert, one of the farmworkers, who was retired now but still training working dogs, had a home full of retrievers and collies. The old man's son and grandson had both died from war injuries; his dogs filled the lonely gaps of his cottage. It was only from him that Rosamund would think of getting a dog.

Looking around her, she imagined how her garden would look in the early summer, the lilac blooming around her. She had many varieties, a paint box of color. There were the snow-white flowers of 'Madame Lemoine,' her new addition of 'Madame Felix,' with its erect little panicles, the cream-yellow flowers of the primrose variety, the pink and mauve clusters of 'Belle de Nancy,' and the magenta conical trusses of 'Charles X'. It was 'Katherine Havemeyer' that she looked forward to the most, with heart-shaped leaves and lavender-purple flowers that would fade to a soft lilac-pink. This year would be the best they had ever been. She was sure of it.

Rosamund wiggled her toes, feeling the thick wool of her socks press against the leather boots. Coming out here always made her think of the end of the war. She had been eighteen years old, and everything had shone with hope and the promise of change. Her brother was to be on his way home from France before long and her father was already safely back at Gittisham, a broken leg returning him to England a month earlier. Rosamund and her mother had made little attempts at tidying up the library, slowly nudging it toward its prewar state of books and calm. It had been their own war office for the past few years, reams of wool, knitting needles, sewing machines, rolls of brown paper ready to package up their offerings of socks and thermals, hats and sweaters. They had set up a day nursery in the second parlor, Rosamund's old nanny returning from retirement to run a chaotic crèche for the young children of local women who wanted the freedom to join new offers of employment. From early in the morning until the end of the working day, the house would be full of the noise of children and women, Rosamund doing her best to keep track of everyone coming in and out while her mother fretted about the muddy little footprints traipsed through the hall. With her father home from France, it was not so easy for everyone to relax into their work, Raymond appearing every now and again in the door of the library, casting irritated looks at the scraps of wool that littered the smooth wooden floor. It was always a relief to hear the uneven clatter of his crutches fading away as he disappeared back to the sitting room where he had reluctantly agreed to spend his days.

War ended, and her life changed. A deep sadness refused to give her peace.

Rosamund finished her tea and stood, looking down across the garden and toward the line of trees at the edge of her land. She could not see the farm, but that had been a comfort these past eighteen years, protecting her from the pain of memory.

A bird screeched above her and dropped down with startling speed toward the woods. She shivered, wrapping her arms into the sleeves of her sweater. It was impossible to settle today, too many memories surging roughly at the edges of her mind.

When she returned inside, her mother was asleep and the house quiet. They had just one permanent maidservant now, as well as a groundskeeper, the other staff coming in from nearby villages when they were needed to help with laundry and gardening and the odd occasion when her mother decided to entertain. Today, the house felt empty, a hollow shell with no life or noise. How different it could have been, she thought.

Rosamund tiptoed past the parlor and up the stairs to her mother's bedroom. Felix seemed to sense not to follow her this time, instead padding toward the kitchen, where he could sleep next to the warm Georgian range. In her mother's bedroom, the curtains were still drawn, a thin crack of light spilling in and illuminating the heavy mauve fabric on the bed. Wilted gray coals lay cold in the grate, the fire long gone out, and a damp cool air chilled the room.

With nervous hands and a thumping heart, she opened the wooden box at the foot of her mother's bed. It was a mess of papers, note cards, old shopping lists, fragments of dried lavender falling between crumpled letters. It seemed that her mother never threw anything away, rather storing it inside the carved oak of this box in case she ever needed a note card from a grateful guest fifteen years ago or the receipt for a pair of gloves she had discarded years previously. Rosamund rummaged through the chaos, unsurprised by the indifferent confusion of her mother's filing. Still, it didn't take long before she found what she was looking for.

There, hidden among the mess, was a series of tiny navy diaries. There must have been nearly forty of them, one for every year since her mother had been married. She picked through them, reading the dates embossed in gold on the front covers. Finally, she found the one she wanted: the year was 1919. Taking it out of the trunk, she ran her finger over the date, the leather surrounding the numbers soft and worn. She flicked through the pages of the diary, searching for any clue or sign to direct her.

She needed to make a decision.

And it was to those months after the war had ended, that time in her life when everything changed, that she returned to as her guide now.

Maybe, she thought as she gazed at the faded words on the page, it wasn't too late for her. She longed for a child, but she knew there was no hope for her to have one of her own. Her body had refused for so many years, and now it was too late. When adoption had finally established a legal framework eleven years ago, she had thought about it, bringing the conversation around to the topic every few months, a gentle nudging of her husband for him to accept that she simply could not conceive. He had nodded, giving little signs of agreement, of possibility, but never any more than that. Rosamund wasn't convinced that he minded whether he had a child at all. The thought of adoption was simply too complicated for him to take the necessary steps. Alberic Caradon was not a driven man, but apart from this apathy toward starting a family, that had suited Rosamund. Perhaps it was why she had been attracted to him in the first place. It had been the summer of 1922, a season of too many parties and lunches and trips to the shops. They had met at a dance in London, drawn together by their shared desire to escape from the endless rounds of bouncing conversations neither of them felt equipped to navigate. Alberic proposed to her three weeks later, and soon they were married and living together at Gittisham. They found excuses for missing most of the dinner party invitations that came their way, much to the frustration of Rosamund's mother, and soon the number of cards coming up the drive with the postman dwindled to a satisfying trickle. Together the two of them gave each other permission to hide from the world, from society, moving among their garden and estate, happy with the simple security of their life. All except Rosamund's desire for a child, a constant pressure that felt like a cloud forever pressing against the corner of the sun.

When Alberic died, it was as though many doors were slamming shut in her face all at once. She had been numb for months, afraid of venturing outside the grounds of Gittisham, a walking ghost barely finding the energy to tend to her garden. Alberic was gone, and all hope of a child with him.

But perhaps there was another way.

The abbreviated name of a woman: Mrs. A. That was all. But there was an address too, a scribbled few words for a house in Exeter.

Tomorrow, she said to herself. Tomorrow.

May 1945

This is the first time Rosamund has been back to London since her husband died, since before the war. It feels alien to her now, the polluted haze of Euston Road dimming the scene like a smudged painting. Already she feels the pull of the crisp Devon air, the clean lines of rolling green hills, the trees that encircle her home, old Felix sleeping for hours in the cool of the entrance hall. She can sense the tension rising around her neck and into her jaw, the noise of the city working its way insidiously beneath her skin. But she cannot go home yet: there is work to do.

Their taxi driver is oblivious to other vehicles on the road, surging forward with great spurts of acceleration. After the sadness of leaving Eliza and Julia with their parents at Paddington, Rosamund watches Jasmine and the twin boys closely, wishing she could delay the next period of separation. And she is worried one of them will be sick, but they are fixated by the view outside the window, their eyes following the bold advertisement banners on the sides of buses, the mass of people hurrying along the pavements, the groups of workmen clearing rubble into trucks and wheelbarrows. There are signs of war everywhere: piles of broken stone are dumped below damaged buildings; the empty shell of top-floor rooms lies open to the sky, windows cracked and roofs destroyed.

They pass King's Cross station, a steady stream of buses entering and exiting its forecourt, and move on toward Clerkenwell. Rosamund can sense the two boys fidgeting beside her. She cannot imagine how they must feel, whether they will recognize the people they left when they were just six. Their mother had written to her when the war ended, giving a new address a few roads away from her old one, asking Rosamund to delay her sons' return for another week. As a community midwife, she needed time to reorganize her schedule to allow her to become a mother once again after six years of rushing from patients' homes to hospitals, to air raid shelters, to the temporary maternity centers set up on the edges of London. Her husband, she wrote to say, was still not returned from a prisoner-of-war camp and she did not yet know when he would be back. Rosamund had been a little confused by the letter: Did this woman not realize her sons were no longer six years old? They were nearly teenagers, perfectly capable of walking themselves to school and finding amusement at home without their mother. Perhaps she believed time simply had paused for her sons during the war, that they would turn up at her doorstop barely three feet tall, round cheeks and soft arms. How surprised she would be to see two boys probably nearly as tall as her, their long legs and wiry bodies, their love of running, of stories, of digging the garden; John's strong legs as he performed *jetés*, *glissades*, *échappés*, even a *tour en l'air*, through the library of an old country manor. Rosamund has promised John she will speak to his mother about ballet lessons; but she isn't hopeful. This is not going to be a priority for a woman trying to move quickly through packed London streets to deliver the relentless roll call of babies.

But when they round the corner and start driving down Rosebery Avenue, Rosamund feels a spark of hope as she notices Sadler's Wells

Theatre on the right-hand side, a giant poster for Benjamin Britten's *Peter Grimes* looming down in gloomy monochrome from the building wall. With the theatre and Sadler's Wells School just a few streets from the boys' home, perhaps John will find a way to attend class.

They are such gentle boys, always looking out for one another. There was a brief time when Rosamund thought she might have twins of her own, but it was not to be. Saying goodbye to these two is difficult after six years of watching them grow even closer to one another, Timothy guarding his twin brother with protective zeal. She vividly remembers a day when another boy teased John for practicing a *tour en l'air* in the garden. Timothy's usual calm vanished, and he chased the bully into the lake. Rosamund had to have words with them all, finding a sternness she did not really feel.

Their mother is waiting outside her terraced house when they arrive, her eyes flitting anxiously from one direction of the road to the next, unsure from where they will be arriving. Rosamund feels the tension in her neck dissipate when she sees her. She knows she should be less judgmental, more open-minded to the way other people live. But it is a relief to see that Mrs. Giles looks neat and respectable, has made an effort with a window box of flowers off her front room, and has two tiny kittens wrapped up in a basket at her feet. An offering to her sons, an acknowledgment that it is not going to be straightforward assimilating back into London family life.

Jasmine cries in the taxi from Clerkenwell to Chelsea. But her tears dry quickly, and she finds new amusements and new London sights to occupy her. She has become used to children coming and going around her these past six years, but Timothy and John were with them the longest. They are older brothers to her now. She made them promise to write to her regularly, even pressing a set of hand-decorated note cards into their suitcases when they left Gittisham. Now there are no excuses, she told them with a look of strict expectation on her face.

The taxi leaves them on a tired street in South Kensington, wartime rubble still clogging the pavements. When they get inside, somehow surprised that the key even fits in the lock, the flat is a mess, dust choking the furniture and a heavy musk settled over every room. Jasmine shows no dismay at all, though. She sets into action immediately, refusing her mother even a second's rest as she starts rushing around the flat, sending up plumes of dirt from the upholstery.

Rosamund lets her select the room they will start clearing first, their base until they can tackle the rest of the flat. They empty the room of everything except the bed and a few heavy pieces of wooden furniture, carrying piles of linen, old suits left lingering in the wardrobe, books stacked underneath the window ledge, into the second bedroom before shutting the door on the chaos. Jasmine finds a broom and eagerly sweeps the floor, screaming in delight when she sees a dead mouse underneath the bed. Her mother just about gets to her, citing all sorts of concerns about dirt and disease, before Jasmine picks it up with her bare hands. This, she thinks, is a side effect of growing up in the countryside. Dead mice are nothing in comparison to mucking out stables and chasing each other with worms. Rosamund cleans every corner of the room, bringing down the curtains to thrash forcefully. Even then she is not happy, bundling them up to take to the laundry.

At last they have nearly transformed the bedroom into an acceptable space, the few dresses they brought with them from

Devon hanging in the wardrobe and fresh sheets tucked neatly over the bed. Shopping tomorrow, they decide, a treat to venture beyond the limited selection of Ottery St. Mary, even if ration coupons impose a strict measure over their choices.

"Can I still wear my new hat?" Jasmine asks, setting her straw hat with its large green bow on the top shelf of the wardrobe. It is a new purchase from the milliner's in Ottery St. Mary, and Jasmine has tried to wear it daily ever since they bought it. Eliza got a matching one, a farewell gift from her friend. Jasmine's interests are often incongruous, Rosamund has observed. She can switch in seconds from digging in the garden, her knees brown with dirt, to picking out ribbons for a hat. It is the same with ballet, her obsession with the seductive pink of the ballet shoes while her white-blond hair sticks out like a scarecrow's.

"Of course. But you might find something else you want too."

Rosamund enjoyed taking the evacuee children into Ottery St. Mary as a break from the routine she had established at Gittisham Manor. They would bring all their ration books and eat scones at the tearooms by the church before the boys played on the green and the girls followed Rosamund in and out of the shops. They always liked the milliner's the most, its beautiful window displays and colorful lights providing an antidote to war. The owner was a sensible, businesslike woman, but with a natural creative flair that brought women from miles around. Magazines were dotted about the surfaces, glossy bibles of style, and the customers would linger inside for far longer than necessary, reading about the latest fashions that could be re-created for them in a small Devonshire town. It was better, even, than all the hat shops in Exeter. On Silver Street, a finely painted navy-and-gold sign welcomed them into Alice Woods Hats, which was full to the brim with hats of all colors, shapes, and sizes. The milliner divided them up into color schemes, so whole walls shone in shades of pastel pink, fuchsia, mauve, red, scarlet, and burgundy, set against tones of pale blue, aquamarine, turquoise, deep navy, and midnight blue. Even during the war, the milliner found creative ways to bring color to her shop, reclaiming ribbons from Christmas decorations and scraps of felted wool cut carefully from tired old sweaters.

Rosamund gasps, feeling a chill spreading fast along her neck. She stops unpacking, her hand frozen still. An image comes to her, a shop counter, a silver frame. There is a photograph of a young girl in a long net skirt, a Romantic-style tutu, with pointe shoes on her feet. She is leaning forward at the waist a little, her arms crossed in front of her. The girl's shoulders slope elegantly in a costume of satin and feathers.

Her face is clear to Rosamund now, many years younger in the picture certainly, but definitely the same person.

Briar Woods, the girl from the train. She is Alice Woods's daughter.

Rosamund forces herself to resume her unpacking. This realization, the satisfaction of connecting a face with a name, should be enough to remove those lingering feelings of uncertainty about the pretty ballet dancer on the train. But it doesn't have that effect at all. All she can think about is that day when she first saw the photograph, the young ballerina captured in a silver frame. She had been tired, feeling the strain of looking after many children, eight of them at that time. It was exhausting work, endless laundry and cooking, and games to distract them from homesickness with only one girl from the village to help her, and her mother—though usually she was more hindrance than help. The ballerina, her face so serene and her body so beautiful in the classical lines of dance, had briefly taken her away from it all. It was rare for Rosamund to let herself indulge in useless aesthetics, especially when there was so much to do. But there had been something about the girl's face that had drawn her, fascinated her, as though if she picked up the frame and stole it away, the dancer would come alive in her pocket. She remembers how she had stared at the photo, finally asking Mrs. Woods if this was her daughter and whether she lived with them anymore. She remembers her unanswered questions: What was the girl in the picture doing during the war? Was she still a ballet dancer? Where did she dance? The milliner had mumbled something incomprehensible and changed the subject, moving them swiftly on to her own questions about fabrics and colors and delivery details. Rosamund had reflected later that perhaps the girl was dead and that her questions were insensitive and cruel. But she hadn't really believed it. The girl looked far too alive, her eyes dancing in the silver frame.

Today, Rosamund had met her in the flesh. The picture brought to life. She decides that maybe it is the memory of her momentary weakness that disturbs her, that flash of desire to escape from the endurance of work and instead to indulge in beauty.

She shivers, wrapping a shawl around her shoulders. The flat is cold, like a mausoleum that has stood witness to the death and pain from the bombs falling around its walls. Part of her thinks it would have been better if it had been bombed too.

Drawing Jasmine to her protectively, she shivers again. London has unsettled her. She wants nothing more than to get on the train and go back home.

October 1945

The photographer knows how to find the best line of the dancers' legs, the perfect angle to show off the smooth arch of their pointe shoes, the ideal palette of light and shade. His camera rises and falls from the corners of the auditorium, appearing every few minutes at the front of the stalls to seize in time the perpetual dance of the theatre. In the wings, in the dressing rooms, in the slowly growing scenery docks, and in Wardrobe, in the long rabbit-warren corridors where dancers find a space to stretch and warm up, he captures it all. The Royal Opera House, a theatre slowly reclaiming itself after the war, is being transformed. And the photographer, brother of one of the ballet mistresses, records the rebirth, finding beauty in each tiny pocket of creation.

Briar Woods has invited Rosamund and Jasmine to attend company class. Finally, the stage is prepared, stripping it from its wartime use as a mecca dance hall, and the dancers can make the space their own. Rows and rows of red silk chairs have been hauled out of storage, where they sat out the war gathering a protective layer of dust under burlap sheets. The dance floor has gone, along with the jazz bandstands that heaved with musicians at each end, enclosing dancing couples who longed to forget about the dangerous London sky.

* * *

It is Jasmine who opens the post this morning, several months after they first met Briar Woods on the train. They are back in the Chelsea flat for a few weeks, just Rosamund, Jasmine, and Lydia Bailey, a young woman from Gittisham village whom Rosamund persuaded to come with them as a housekeeper-cleaner-laundry maid, with the promise of evenings off to explore London. Rosamund sometimes longs for the days when there was a full house of staff at Gittisham Manor: a cook, several housemaids, a team of gardeners. When the war began the numbers of staff dwindled and now, even with peacetime at last, she must make do with just Miss Bailey and a gardener. Running a large estate has become fraught with complications, a gradual decline that began years ago, long before the war. Rosamund has sold nearly an entire row of the village cottages that her family had thought they would own forever, and now there is pressure to sell some farmland in the Otter Valley: not the Gittisham farm, Rosamund is determined. There are too many memories there, and she cannot quite let them go.

In London they would probably be fine as just the two of them, but Miss Bailey has become invaluable as they try to wrench the flat back into a livable state. There are times, usually in the mornings as the brief song of a bird distorts into the grind of a bus, when Rosamund wishes they could sell the London flat, removing any need to leave the safety of their village. But then she sees Jasmine's excitement every time they step out onto the busy London streets, and her resolve wavers and fades. So mother and daughter spend their days picking out new fabrics within the strict limitations of their ration coupons, as well as searching for paints to rejuvenate the tired old rooms.

Jasmine runs into the kitchen at breakfast time one morning, the note already torn open. There is a tiny sketch of a pair of ballet shoes on the back of the envelope: Briar Woods knew what she was doing, Rosamund thinks wryly, in making sure the note would not escape Jasmine's notice. She wrote that Sadler's Wells Ballet have been invited to make the Royal Opera House, Covent Garden, their home. After the ballet company's energetic work during the war, the Council for the Encouragement of Music and the Arts have decided that they should be the ones to be rewarded with a larger theatre to grow their work. Preparations are in full swing, with a February date set for the opening performance of *The Sleeping Beauty*.

Rosamund and Jasmine are invited to attend morning company ballet class in a week's time. There is to be a small audience of friends and benefactors, a celebration of the slowly emerging theatre. Jasmine, instantly letting her imagination dance in a scatter of excitement, starts planning what time they will get up that morning, the route they will take to get there, what they will wear. She takes to dancing clumsily around the living room, sticking out her arms and feet awkwardly in positions vaguely like the ones Julia had taught her in those wartime ballet classes at Gittisham. Her daughter is not going to be a ballet dancer any time soon, Rosamund thinks with an entirely guilt-free feeling of relief. Unlike John Giles, she found out recently in a note from John and Timothy's mother. Mrs. Giles had written to thank Rosamund for looking after her boys, how grateful she was, but also how sad that she had missed out on all those years of their development. Rosamund could not help her sobs when she read the note; she understood too well how painful it would be to miss even a day of her child's journey through life. But she smiled when she read that

John had started taking ballet classes, wiping her eyes to share the news with Jasmine.

At last, the morning arrives, and they set out early with a determination to walk the entire way. Jasmine hesitates outside the entrance of a school in Kensington, watching as a group of young girls runs up the steps of a pretty, cream Victorian building, satchels bopping against their thighs. She pulls her hand out of Rosamund's as she stares at them, noticing everything: their loud laughter, the white socks falling around their ankles, the pressed white Peter Pan collars, the colorful ribbons in their hair that will of course be confiscated by their teacher as soon as they get into the classroom. Jasmine has never been inside a classroom, not a real one anyway. Her mother dedicates every morning when they are in Gittisham to a busy schedule of homeschooling, notebooks filling quickly with Jasmine's bold, round handwriting, the pencil pressed hard into each page. It was during the war that Jasmine had learned to read and write. A changing roll call of evacuees had filled the space around the table: the books Rosamund had brought home from the library were pushed from one child to the next, older boys and girls helping guide the younger ones as they slowly sounded out the words. It had been strange, that first time after the children had all gone and Rosamund and Jasmine were left alone with their books and pencils and chalkboards.

Rosamund reaches down to her and pulls her along, Jasmine quickening her pace again as they move toward their new favorite places that line the route: Harrods, now restocking its prewar luxury goods; through Green Park; past Buckingham Palace; among the pigeons strutting around the Trafalgar Square fountain; and finally up St. Martin's Lane to Covent Garden. Autumn and winter compete with one another this morning: but the sun makes the final decision, shining brightly and accompanied by the mildest of winds. By the time they arrive at Covent Garden, they are far too warm in their coats and hats. Briar Woods is waiting for them at the stage door. She has specifically asked them to meet her there so she can give them a tour backstage before class. She hugs Jasmine tightly before leaning into Rosamund to give her a quick kiss, not quite meeting her skin. With cheeks pink and glowing from the walk, Jasmine hands the ballerina a little posy of flowers that they bought from the market on their way, and Briar exclaims in delight as she presses the flowers to her nose.

"Come, let me show you around." She holds the door open for them, waving at the stage doorkeeper, who sits behind a desk reading a newspaper. Leading them along a corridor and up some stairs, she points out dressing rooms, rehearsal studios, shoe stores, meeting rooms, kitchens, stacks of crates waiting to find a home. The theatre feels alive, as though everything has been thrown up to the surface and is waiting to find a place to settle.

She takes them to the auditorium and Jasmine looks about in wide-eyed amazement at the endless rows of seats going up and up toward the gods. It is a vast theatre, and without the heavy gold and crimson curtains yet returned to their prewar place of splendor, the stage looks endless, an immense space with depth and height for the cloths, traps, and bridges that conjure the magical settings of each performance. They settle into their seats, behind two older women with immaculately curled white hair and fur collars that rise high around their ears. A group of men lean forward in the front row, cigarettes balanced on their lips, and some members of the orchestra lounge across seats, musical scores resting on their laps. The dancers gradually appear from the wings. They wear layers of woolen sweaters, knitted tights, scarves wrapped about their necks, cloth bags spilling open to reveal the dirty pink of pointe shoe ribbons that have been reused too many times. Jasmine shifts in her seat, staring at the dancers as they start warming up. Some of them are swinging their legs and padding out their feet, while others are sprawled across the floor in impossibly flexible positions.

The ballet mistress calls the dancers to attention, and they find their places along lines of portable wooden barres positioned across the stage. Briar is at a barre at the edge of the stage, sandwiched between a woman with bright red hair and a man who wears a huge cardigan spotted with moth holes. She smiles at Jasmine and Rosamund and waves, before taking hold of the barre and snapping into focus.

Marking out the first exercise with incomprehensible speed, a blur of hand movements and French phrases, the dancers look entirely unfazed by the teacher's instructions. When the music begins, they start to bend and stretch, their arms extending and falling in identical precision. For them, the language of ballet is like breathing, a routine of *pliés, tendus, ports de bras, ronds de jambe* with doubles, triples; *en l'air, en dehors, en dedans*. They follow the class with serene ease, though Rosamund suspects there is a lot of hard work going on beneath the calm. As the class progresses, they remove their layers, revealing powerful muscles and the stain of sweat against leotards and tights. Their shoes are gray with dirt and dust from the stage, the debris of the renovations still coating the ground. But when they dance it is with crisp classical lines, their feet tracing identical patterns across the stage, their arms extending and contracting as they follow the choreography of the teacher. Once the barre exercises are over, they lift the wooden barres to the edge of the stage, stripping off more layers and exchanging long knitted tights for tiny chiffon skirts. The ballet mistress rattles through increasingly complicated combinations, the *petit allegro* an intricate medley of fast footwork. She calls out the words to the rhythm of the piano that thumps out notes from the orchestra pit: *glissade, jeté, jeté, glissade, tombé, pas de bourrée, assemblé derriere, soutenu*. The dancers move forward in waves, the piano continuing until each group has danced twice.

The class comes to an end with *piqué* turns and *chaînés* across the stage, the dancers moving in pairs on a diagonal before finding fourth *croisé* where the proscenium arch begins its ascent toward the ceiling. Rosamund feels dizzy watching them, her mind drifting to all the things she needs to do back at the flat, the paint still to be chosen from the limited supplies available, the walls that need plastering. Jasmine will be useless after this, just wanting to prance outside the living room and mimic as many of the steps as she can remember.

Once Briar has added all her layers again over her leotard and tights, she comes down to the stalls where her guests are seated. "How did you find that? Not too dull, I hope?"

"Not at all," says Rosamund, forcing a smile. She should be grateful for the interest Briar has shown them, bringing her daughter to a treat that many young girls would dream about. The ballet class did interest her, the power in the jumps, the long extensions of the ballet dancers' legs, the way their heads whisked around quickly in the turns. The reality, of course, is that she would like to preserve the adoration of her daughter for herself, create a nest for the two of them without the intrusions of the rest of the world. When the wait for Jasmine to be born was over, it had felt as though all her sadness and disappointments could finally disappear, leaving her with the warm glow of motherhood. And yet she must be honest with herself sometimes, acknowledge that the truth is not so simple. She worries about what will happen when Jasmine grows up and doesn't need her any longer, when the house at Gittisham is empty again. If she could have adopted all those evacuees then she would have, filled the rooms and gardens with friends for Jasmine so she would never want to leave. Rosamund had longed to be a mother for so long. When it had happened at last, she realized that she had replaced one anxiety with another. She became perpetually worried about motherhood being taken away from her, leaving her alone and childless and unneeded.

"Would you like to see Wardrobe?" Briar asks Jasmine. "It's rather a mess still, but the wardrobe department are gradually sorting through it all. We lost a lot when we were on tour in Holland at the start of the war, and rationing isn't helping with sourcing the materials for the new costumes we need, but it's still a magical place."

They start walking back up toward the stage, the auditorium now noisy with the chatter of the guest audience and musicians making their way around to the orchestra pit for a rehearsal.

"So it hasn't been easy preparing for *The Sleeping Beauty* with rationing then?" Rosamund asks, genuinely curious about how they will possibly be able to put on a production of this scale with all the challenges and hardships of war still enduring at every turn.

"If things continue as they are, the entire set for *The Sleeping Beauty* will have to be painted in camouflage colors. It's the only paint that seems to be available these days." Briar doesn't seem too worried, however, her smile never fading as she gestures around her at the vast atrium of the auditorium.

Rosamund nods. This is something she can understand, her own troubles of trying to freshen the flat sabotaged at every turn by ration coupons and empty catalogs.

Jasmine follows eagerly, looking around her with intense curiosity as they make their way through the wings and back out into the labyrinth of corridors. They climb a tired staircase with paint peeling from the steps and move on toward a set of rooms at the top of the theatre where the different wardrobe compartments are stored. In the first room crates are stacked on top of one another, each labeled with the name of a production. Rails of costumes line the center of the room, bagged up and protected from dust and damp.

"There are a lot of old opera costumes from before the war stored here," Briar tells them as they walk. She sounds like an enthusiastic tour guide, all charm and energy. "It's like a precious vault full of artwork. They opened the store of *La traviata* costumes last week. I managed to sneak a look at some of them: gorgeous luxury, all these huge satin skirts with hundreds of chiffon roses. *La bohème* was next: the most magnificent bonnets. Attilio Comelli's designs arisen from their sleep!"

She moves them on to the next room, a shoe store with wooden shelving and compartment boxes lining the walls. There are pointe shoes waiting for collection in some of the boxes; in others, stocks of heeled boots in colors from brown to bright red.

Men's soft ballet shoes are lined up in pairs on a work surface, pots of pigments for dye waiting alongside. In the next room two seamstresses are working on tutus, layers of tulle cut out in huge heaps on the floor and a rail of completed skirts hanging behind them. They smile up at Briar before continuing with their work.

"There are so many costumes to make for *The Sleeping Beauty*," she tells Jasmine and Rosamund. "Oliver Messel is designing the set and costumes and it is going to be wonderfully opulent, if we can get it all done on time. I remember we put on a gala production of *The Sleeping Princess* just before the war, a command performance for the king and the French president. The costumes for that were disappointingly simple, a cardboard crown for Princess Aurora and not a sequin in sight. A good thing the name had been changed from 'beauty' to 'princess' for that production," she laughs. "For this one, there will be a dozen different fairy costumes and even the corps de ballet will be looking spectacular."

A man wanders into the room as she speaks, a Contax II camera held at his side. Rosamund recognizes him from the company class. He had moved between the barres, disappearing in and out of the wings as he took photographs of the dancers.

"This is Gordon," Briar says as he nods at her and lifts his camera toward the tutu currently in creation by one of the seamstresses. She is embroidering deep green and brown thread into a silvery-beige bodice, a spray of branches growing up from the skirt toward the chest. Tiny scarlet birds are waiting to be sewn into the fabric, the thinnest wisps of feathers lining their tails.

"For the songbird fairy," the woman says, aware that the attention is on her creation. The photographer's camera snaps, and Rosamund finds herself longing for the birds to come alive and start flying around the room, wreaking delicious havoc on the tulle and silk piled neatly over the worktop. Jasmine, however, is stroking another deconstructed tutu, feeling the layers of net between her fingers.

"Can you take a photograph of us, Gordon?" Briar says, a charming smile dancing on her lips. "It would be wonderful to have a record of today."

He looks up from his camera, noticing the little girl for the first time. Cocking his head to one side, he seems to be sizing up the potential of the scene, the aesthetic pleasure of a little girl entranced by the magic of the costumes. This is, after all, what he is here to record, these moments of transition from the hardship of war to the joy of theatre. Gesturing to Briar to get in the shot, he stands back and angles his camera toward them.

Briar takes Jasmine's hand, drawing her in abruptly. It catches the girl off guard, and she looks at the camera with wide eyes of surprise. Briar is gripping her hand too tightly, face turned slightly down toward her.

Rosamund feels that uneasy tension spreading sharply across her neck. It is like when they first met Briar on the train and she wanted to get away from her, pull her daughter out of the lure of her smiles. Now, she yearns to reach into the frame of the photograph and tug Jasmine back toward her. She wants to claim her for her own, destroy the camera and all evidence that the photograph was ever taken. "We've got to go," Rosamund hears herself say abruptly. Briar's eyes flick toward her and she is sure she notices a look of resentment: the annoying mother getting in the way of her plans. But then the look vanishes, replaced once again with that pretty smile. Briar leans down to Jasmine and kisses her on the cheek.

When they finally find their way back out onto Floral Street, squinting as they adjust to the natural light, Rosamund grabs Jasmine's hand and starts marching her too quickly away from the theatre. This time they get the bus back toward Chelsea. Rosamund is too impatient to walk, determined to place as much distance as she can between Briar and her daughter.

But the girl doesn't seem to notice. She is lost in her imagination, dancing through a fantasy land of songbird fairies on a path paved with silk, satin, and tulle.

Christmas 1945

Just when Rosamund thinks she has Jasmine all to herself, the house in Devon settles under a fine shimmer of Christmas frost, and that terrible unease returns. It creeps insidiously up from the village, along the drive, and into the thick stone walls of her home. For Briar Woods has arrived in Gittisham, refusing to leave mother and daughter in peace.

Rosamund spies her coming from partway up the drive, the ballet dancer marching fast in her winter boots. An urge to lock the door and bar the windows, to hide Jasmine away up in an attic room where Briar cannot find her, comes over Rosamund. But then her daughter appears at her side, crying out in delight as she recognizes the slim figure striding toward their home.

Jasmine is at the door before Briar arrives, pulling it open and letting in a sharp flood of cold air. Miss Bailey, the housekeeper, emerges from the kitchen but retreats again quickly when she sees Jasmine waving to the woman coming up the drive. The young housekeeper has heard all about Briar Woods: she knows everything about Jasmine's magical day at the theatre, as well as secretly sensing the unenthusiastic reception from her mistress.

The little girl hops from one foot to the other, oblivious to the cold, and waves as Briar approaches. "Hello," she calls out. "Happy Christmas."

"Happy Christmas to you too," Briar calls back, her voice traveling with the winter wind. The temperature has dropped this afternoon, a heavy white cloud is waiting to open over the hills of the Otter Valley, and Briar is dressed warmly in a thick navy coat with a high fur collar. She is wearing an Alice Woods hat, the fabric falling snugly around her ears. Far too fine and fashionable for the villages of Devon, thinks Rosamund, peering down at her own clothes, long beige slacks that she has tucked into a pair of knitted socks.

Briar comes straight in, kicking off her boots and removing her coat. Jasmine takes it from her and hangs it on the hooks alongside the entrance porch, stroking the fabric territorially as she turns back toward the guest. "I hope you don't mind me calling in like this," Briar says, speaking more to Jasmine than to her mother. "I am home for a few days for Christmas and could not resist getting the bus over to see you. Gittisham is such a pretty village. And look at your gorgeous home." She gestures around her, taking in the ornate wooden carving of the staircase with the plush velvet stockings hanging from the banisters, the huge chandelier lighting up the open expanse of the entrance hall, the oil paintings decorating the walls. Briar moves through the room, smiling when she sees the paper theatre, the neat cutout dancers positioned behind the miniature proscenium arch and orchestra pit. Gold and red cardboard edge the stage in pretty, paisley swirls, and a cast of characters are held in motionless splendor as they wait to be pushed and prodded into action.

The dancer looks closely, exclaiming in delight when she sees it is a scene from *The Sleeping Beauty* paused inside the paper walls: there is a princess, a wicked witch, a white cat, an assembly of ballerina fairies. A paper ballerina has fallen over, and Briar reaches inside, restoring her *arabesque*.

Briar turns with a low *arabesque* of her own, her hand sweeping gently past the vast Christmas tree positioned in the window. It is adorned with mini nutcrackers and sugarplum fairies, sparkling golden baubles and tiny gift boxes wrapped in ribbon. Rosamund and Jasmine spent hours decorating the tree, Rosamund's mother calling out instructions from the sofa before falling asleep in the warmth of the fire.

"Do sit down," Rosamund says pointlessly, for Briar is already settling herself on the sofa with Jasmine at her side. Felix senses a change in the room, lifting his head sleepily off the rug and watching Briar with large brown eyes, but the effort is too much, and he lets the warmth of the room send him back to his old dog dreams. Rosamund's mother, Mrs. Beatrice Hampton, wakes from her sleep by the fire, pushing herself up from her throne of pillows. Briar turns to her, all smiles and apologies.

"Oh no, I am so sorry for waking you. It is such a cozy spot here, I am sure I would be fast asleep too if I closed my eyes for a moment. Perhaps Jasmine and I can move elsewhere to talk?" Briar looks around, as if conjuring up a magic portal into another room.

Mrs. Hampton shakes her head as she takes in the scene around her. She has just turned seventy and suffers from osteoporosis, her body shrinking so relentlessly that she looks like a frail Edwardian doll resting on top of the sofa. The cushions barely sink underneath her tiny frame. Sleeping has been her default mode since halfway through the war, the exhaustion of helping Rosamund look after all the evacuee children having taken its toll. Since the children left, she has been in a permanent state of exhaustion, waking every few hours to take small sips of tea from a bone china cup. Her eyes light up now, however, on seeing a pretty visitor dressed elegantly in a pleated scarlet skirt and pristine cream sweater. She wishes her daughter would make more of an effort with clothes, especially on Christmas Eve, rather than insisting on wearing the same beige sweaters and wide-legged slacks every single day. Mrs. Hampton's wardrobe has remained the same for decades, all lace and full sleeves and too many petticoats, a pair of lace gloves in her lap and her silver hair even now piled elegantly atop her head.

Her hand appears from the mound of cushions, and she pats the sofa gently. "Please, my dear, stay where you are. It is always a joy to have visitors bring some brightness to our day." Mrs. Hampton's voice is low and gravelly, barely rising above a whisper, but to Rosamund the words have bite.

"I have brought a few Christmas gifts," Briar says, lifting her bag onto her lap. Rosamund noticed the bag when she arrived, was surprised by its large size: it is nearly a mile's walk from the village bus stop to Gittisham Manor.

Jasmine presses herself closer to Briar's side, while Rosamund stays where she is by the Christmas tree, watching with a feeling of dread as the visitor reaches down into her bag.

"This is for your mother," Briar says, handing a small package, beautifully wrapped, to Jasmine. "Will you give it to her?"

Rosamund bristles, forcing a smile as Jasmine skips over, passing her the gift. "How thoughtful of you. Shall I open it now? Or wait until tomorrow?" She would like to hide the gift far behind the tree and forget about it forever.

"Oh, please now," says her daughter.

"Absolutely. It's nearly Christmas anyway," adds Briar.

Rosamund unties the ribbon and peels off the tissue paper to discover a slim box labeled in the familiar navy-and-gold lettering of Alice Woods Hats. She opens the box. Nestled among matching navy tissue paper is the most elegant of hatpins, long and silver with a cluster of embroidered balls secured to the end. They are woven in soft cotton thread, each a different shade of green; tiny strands of silver are stitched through them like morning frost in moss. Rosamund looks up to see all eyes on her, waiting for her reaction. She lifts the hatpin out of the box and holds it up for everyone to see. "Beautiful," she says. "You really shouldn't have. Is this one of your mother's creations?"

"Yes, that's right. I asked her to make this one especially for my new friend. Green and silver to match your eyes."

Rosamund blinks. No one has commented on the color of her eyes for a long time. But the silver seems like more of a commentary on the streaks of gray starting to spread through her light brown hair. She has given up pulling them out.

"And now something for you."

Jasmine is back at Briar's side, perched expectantly on the edge of the sofa. There are two little parcels for the girl. The first is a pair of white mittens, with matching fur trim around the wrist. Jasmine puts them on immediately, pressing the fur to her face. The second gift is a tiny white cat doll. It is small enough to fit in her palm, a beautiful little two-legged cat wearing a white net tutu. It has pink ribbons around its neck and waist, and white satin ballet shoes on its feet. Briar laughs in excitement as Jasmine turns it over in her hand.

"This is a precise replica of the white cat costume for *The Sleeping Beauty*. One of the seamstresses was making them for her nieces and I persuaded her to make one for us too. Look at the ruff around the neck and all the layers in the skirt."

"I love it." Jasmine makes the cat dance up and down in her palm. "What role does the white cat have in the ballet?" It is a sensible question, thinks Rosamund, hoping that her daughter is able to feel some skepticism about a dancing white cat. Though it is more likely she will develop a new obsession and they'll be looking after a noisy collection of white kittens before they know it. Poor old Felix is unlikely to approve of excitable feline nuisances intruding on his peace.

"At the wedding of Princess Aurora and Prince Florimund," begins Briar, taking the white cat from Jasmine and holding it up in the air, "there is a large guest list, including many characters from French fairy tales. There is Little Red Riding Hood and the wolf, Beauty and the Beast, Bluebeard and his wife, Goldilocks, Puss in Boots. And of course, the white cat. They all come to celebrate the marriage and the end of the curse that sent Princess Aurora and the entire castle to sleep for a hundred years."

"What is the fairy tale of the white cat?" asks Jasmine. "I have never heard it before."

"It's a very long story. A French aristocrat called Madame d'Aulnoy wrote it in the seventeenth century for her literary salon in Paris, hiding all sorts of political criticisms inside her complicated fairy tale."

"A shortened version then?" asks Jasmine, curling her legs under herself on the sofa and removing her mittens. She places them on her lap and strokes the fur.

"Of course. Once upon a time," Briar begins, and Jasmine giggles at the familiar opening. "Once upon a time, there was an old and paranoid king with three sons. He was terrified that they would plot to overthrow him, so he sent them on a complicated and frivolous three-part mission to obstruct them. First, they had to find and bring to him the world's cutest dog."

Rosamund hears herself snort, the others looking up at her in surprise. She comes to join them by the fire, trying at least for Jasmine's sake to show some interest. But as the story progresses, she starts to pay attention, drawn in by the strangeness of the tale.

"The youngest son searches high and low, rejecting many poor little dogs along the way. Eventually he comes across a castle. It is an enchanted castle, and there he meets the most beautiful white cat. She can speak his language, is charming and beguiling, and they live together for a year until he remembers he must find the cutest dog in the world. She hands him an acorn and he holds it up to his ear. Inside is the tiniest dog with an adorable little bow-wow. He takes it back to his father and wins the prize."

Felix, sleeping on the rug, lets out a loud snore, the edges of his nostrils quivering. Rosamund tries to repress the laughter bubbling up inside her, instead reaching down and giving her dog a reassuring scratch behind the ear. Briar smiles prettily, waiting for the dog to settle again before continuing with her tale.

"But this is not enough for the jealous king. He sends his sons out again, this time to find the finest piece of cloth that will fit through the eye of a needle. Once again, the youngest son returns to the white cat and she conjures the most luxurious cloth that, of course, slips easily through the eye of a needle.

"Still the king is not satisfied. The sons must bring him the most beautiful bride. Then he will reward them with the kingdom. He returns to the white cat, and she asks him to do a terrible thing. He must chop off her head and tail and throw them into the fire. Well, how could he possibly do such a thing to this beautiful cat, a cat with whom he has fallen very much in love? But she is persuasive, convincing him that he must do it. And so, with a heavy heart, he chops off her head and tail.

"Suddenly there is a miraculous transformation. The headless cat becomes a stunning woman, a real-life human princess, the prince's beautiful bride."

"Why was she a cat?" asks Jasmine. "And why did he have to cut off her head and tail?"

"She was the victim of a terrible curse," Briar explains, her voice lowering conspiratorially. "A princess trapped as a cat in a castle because of the foolish whims of her evil mother. And why indeed does she have to go through such terrible violence to find love and happiness? Perhaps that is how it has always been for women. We pay a heavy price for joy."

Jasmine doesn't look convinced. She is too young and too protected; everyone she has ever met has made her feel adored. For Rosamund, though, there is something in this. Violence, pain, trauma: she has had to work for her joy too.

Rosamund looks up and catches Briar's eye. What she sees there scares her. It is a look of defiance, of determination. The glow of the fire reflects in the green of her eyes: a white cat who will cut off her head to find joy.

Standing abruptly, Rosamund lets the hatpin box fall from her lap and roll onto the rug. She stares at it for a second too long before she forces herself to pick it up. Leaving the hall quickly, she mutters something about helping Lydia prepare the tea. But Jasmine and Briar don't even acknowledge her departure.

From the kitchen she can hear the laughter of Briar and Jasmine, the clatter of their feet as they prance in front of the fire. When she returns with a tray, Briar is showing Jasmine the white cat dance from *The Sleeping Beauty*. It is a beguiling little dance, usually performed as a *pas de deux* with Puss in Boots, Briar is explaining. It is all *piqué arabesques*, endless *pas de chat*, catlike head rolls, and scratching paws, neat footwork of *pas de bourrée* that Briar performs in her stockings.

At last they collapse back onto the sofa, Jasmine out of breath from trying to mimic the bouncing *pas de chat*. Why it is called *pas de chat*, Rosamund has no idea. She has never seen a cat move that way in her life.

"Can I show Briar the garden?" Jasmine asks, pushing a Christmas biscuit around her plate.

"Yes. But dress up warm. It looks like it might start snowing."

The two of them waste no time in finishing their tea, wrapping up in boots, coats, hats, and scarves. They are out the door and into the garden before Rosamund can say goodbye, a cold blast of wind replacing them. She wishes Felix had the energy to go with them. She would feel happier about the two of them exploring the garden together if her dog was there to chaperone.

Rosamund goes up to her bedroom and uses the time to herself to wrap Christmas presents. She always buys too much for Jasmine, even during the war finding stores in Exeter that would be willing to sell her miniature dolls, ribbons to craft colorful plaited bracelets, books filled with stories and poems. There were serious paper shortages during the war, but some children's books still sold if they were guaranteed to find an audience. This year Rosamund has convinced herself that she has let down the hems and loosened the waists on Jasmine's dresses as much as is possible, and that it is time for new ones. During the last few years, endless piles of clothes for mending and altering have crowded her bedroom and it has not been unusual for Rosamund to fall asleep at night with socks and stockings littering the end of her bed, darning needles balanced precariously within the wool.

This Christmas she has managed to collect enough fabric coupons to buy several dresses. There is also a box of pencils, a gardening shovel, gardening gloves, and the latest Enid Blyton novel: *Five Go to Smuggler's Top*. Rosamund is particularly pleased with this gift. She hopes that the story of boisterous outdoor adventure will divert her daughter from this new obsession with ballet. It was much easier when Jasmine preferred to play in the garden, collecting conkers, riding her bike up and down the long drive. With Julia Greene the ballet was manageable, the classes in the library a welcome break from the mud outside, a physical activity to do when the rain meant that the damp woodland surrounding the house was unappealing. But since meeting Briar, her obsession has grown.

A dull white glow permeates her bedroom. Rosamund looks up from her gift-wrapping, alarmed by the sudden change in the light. From her position, all she can see outside is the heavy white sky and the bare treetops disappearing into cloud. Moving fast to the window, she peers out into the grounds. Snow is falling, a swirling eddy of fat flakes that fly past the window. Instantly the ground is speckled white and a howl from the trees vibrates against the wind.

She pushes open her bedroom door and listens for the voices of Jasmine and Briar. Surely, she thinks, they will be back by now, warming up by the fire. But she can hear nothing, just the whistle of the wind as it swirls around the house.

Running down the stairs, she finds the young housekeeper lingering anxiously by the front door. Felix is next to her, his tail twitching.

"Are they back yet?" Rosamund asks, her words coming out more forcefully than she intended. Lydia shakes her head and continues peering out through the narrow window of the porch. She is looking right down the drive toward the trees. Rosamund notices that she is biting her lip, her hands pressed tightly into one another. "What's the matter? Can you see them?"

Lydia Bailey shakes her head and turns around to Rosamund. "They were in the kitchen garden for a while. I could see them as I was preparing the dinner. But then they walked around to the front of the house and went down the drive together. I came in here to collect the tray and when I looked out the window, I saw them taking a right turn into the wood. I thought maybe Miss Jasmine wanted to show her that tree den she made with the children this summer, but that's not very far and they've been gone for a while now."

"They haven't come out of the wood? Are you sure?"

"Quite sure, ma'am. I've been keeping an eye out. Especially when it started to snow. Though right now it's near impossible to see that far."

She is right. The line of vision from the house to the woodland is entirely swollen with falling snow. They could be anywhere.

Rosamund doesn't hesitate. She pulls on her coat and boots as fast as she can. Running outside, she is immediately covered in weightless snowflakes. From the other side of the door, she can hear Felix barking, an unusual sound in his old age, and his effort makes her move faster down the drive. Her lips turn silver with the cold, and she can taste the frost on her tongue. Long tendrils of swirling snow encircle her, the flakes flying high in the air and refusing to find the ground. She momentarily loses her bearings, the gray sky and whitening grass merging into one painted blur.

This is her house, her grounds, she tells herself. She can find her daughter.

Her boots crunch against the thin layer of snow settling along the driveway and she runs faster toward the line of trees. It is already getting dark, the snow and the sky merging into an obscure gray haze. She blinks as she runs, desperate to see a little girl emerging out of the wood toward her. But there is no one. Just snow and wind and the deepening dark.

The woodland track starts a few hundred yards down the drive. It is a small, nondescript footpath and right now is entirely covered in snow. Quickly the trees thicken around her, what light that is left disappearing into a gloom of wych elm trees, their gnarled and knotted trunks rising high around her. Even without their leaves they map a dense muddle of pathways, with fallen branches creating snow-drenched hazards across the muddy ground. Rosamund goes straight to the den.

The tree den is a collection of branches that Jasmine and the other children had constructed in the summer, a hideaway under which they spread picnic blankets and played games, told stories, imagined themselves as characters from the Enid Blyton books they read together in the evenings. Rosamund had loved to watch them play there. She would use the excuse of bringing them flasks of water so she could keep returning to the spot and absorbing the happy energy of their chatter. Even though there was war and the repetitive effort of closing the blackout blinds, the endless meal planning, the constant darning, Rosamund had been happy then. Now, with the children gone, Jasmine growing up too fast, Briar Woods lingering where she is not wanted, Rosamund feels unsettled, a gnawing discomfort forever in the pit of her stomach. This, now, is her worst nightmare. Without Jasmine, she has lost her balance.

The den is empty, a thin layer of fresh snow blanketing the muddy ground around it. Slim footprints seem to dance through the mud and the snow and the rotting leaves, ghostly imprints that are barely there at all.

Rosamund looks around her wildly; Jasmine must be close by. She calls out, but her voice is absorbed by the snow, her words bouncing back to her among the thick mass of tree trunks.

She runs back to the road, leaving the wood behind her. They could be miles away by now, she thinks, her mind shifting from disaster to disaster. If she goes farther into the trees, she will never find them, the labyrinth of paths too dark and confused.

Back out on the drive, she looks up toward the house. It still surprises her even many months on to see the lights blazing out from the windows. From the middle window she can see the Christmas tree, the glow from the fireplace illuminating the room. In the other direction is the village, its lights just reaching her through the winter spread of trees. It is more than half a mile to the gate; if she goes, she might miss them returning to the house from another direction.

It is the muffled ringing of the bells that forces her to decide. The church of St. Michael's will be calling the parishioners for the Christmas Eve service, the local families making their blissful way to the beautiful medieval church, sitting in rows in the old box pews, singing carols and lighting the little red candles to guide their way home. The Caradon-Hamptons would usually attend, but with her mother so frail, they had decided against it this year. And yet the Christmas Eve service was Jasmine's favorite. She had been Mary one year during the war, something she had liked to remind the other children of whenever she had an opportunity.

Rosamund wraps her coat around her even tighter and starts running down the long, winding drive toward the village. Searching for signs of her daughter, she whips her head from side to side, longing to spy her familiar bright blond hair. Perhaps Jasmine has decided to show Briar the church, to attend the service after all. She should know better, though, than to disappear for so long without telling her.

When she arrives at the church, the snow has stopped and is already melting on the road, disappearing as fast as it arrived. Down here in the village, it feels like a different world, no wind or snow or the cruel emptiness of the wood. Here there are people on the road, women standing in the entrances to the old cob and stone cottages, chatting with their neighbors and handing over Christmas gifts. The church doors are open and there are families heading inside, parents holding their children tightly by the hand. Rosamund stands in the driveway of the vicarage, waiting before she goes through the wooden porch. She feels ashamed, inadequate. While all these people are celebrating their first Christmas without the heavy weight of war, she has failed.

She turns about her, sensing eyes on her from the parishioners arriving for the service. A woman asks her if she is all right, but she waves her off. What can she say without revealing how incapable she feels, how she cannot even look after her own child?

As the doors of the church are about to close, the bells ringing out their final notes, Rosamund slips in and stands at the back. The verger shuffles to her side. He is an older man who lives in an ancient cottage at the edge of the village, and he knows everyone who comes in and out of Gittisham, every child born, the name of every dog and cat that stalks the streets of his village, the day that the first swallow will appear in the skies of the Otter Valley. "This way, Mrs. Caradon," he says, taking her gently by the elbow. She lets him lead her, feeling a terrible urge to cry.

There, in a pew at the front of the church, are Jasmine and Briar. They are standing with the congregation, singing the first verse of "Silent Night." Notes of the organ filter in among the tones of the singers, the low rumble of the men punctuated by the sopranos' arcs of high notes. Jasmine and Briar's heads are close together as they peer down at the hymnbook in the low candlelight of the church.

"She is safe, Mrs. Caradon," the verger whispers to her, guiding her to the pew. He squeezes her hand before he shuffles away. "Such deep green eyes she has, just like your own." The wrinkles around his cheeks sink into the mottled brown of his skin as he smiles. He is trying to reassure her, she knows, his kind words what she needs right now to feel connected to the little girl standing a few feet away.

Rosamund slides into the pew. Jasmine looks up at her and smiles. It is such an open, warm, and innocent smile. She has no idea of the pain she has caused, the panic Rosamund felt in searching for her. It would be easy to scold her, to drag her out of the church and chastise her all the way home. But what would Christmas be then, an upset child and a tension frosting between them?

It is the look on Briar's face that makes her decide. Rosamund just catches sight of it before Briar transforms again: victory metamorphosed into charm. And so Rosamund wraps an arm around her daughter and squeezes her, leaning down to plant a kiss on the side of her head.

Briar Woods will not win this one. Rosamund has no idea why this young woman is trying to infiltrate her way into their relationship, but the one thing she knows is that she is not going to make it easy.

WHEN SHE LEADS ME INTO THE WOOD, I feel a sudden urge to tell her everything. I almost do it at the tree den once we've ducked inside, all those gnarled and ugly old branches snagging against our coats. She trusts me now. I can see it in her movements, how relaxed she is, how comfortable she feels with me. I can see it in the way she gathers tiny balls of snow in her white mittens, the careless way she kicks into the snow-coated mud, dirt clinging to her boots. She tells me about the games they played here in the summer before the others returned to London. With great earnestness, she explains how they found the best fallen branches of elm, the low fork of the tree, the leaves and moss they collected to provide a blanket beneath them.

I am a Devon girl too, but this is so different from my childhood with all those long train journeys from Exeter to London, then while in the city the daily bus ride to Sadler's Wells, the hours of darning pointe shoes, Vivian doing the same a few feet away on her bed. When the local ballet teacher discovered I had some talent, she took me to London and introduced me to Miss de Valois. I enrolled at the ballet school when I was thirteen and moved in with Vivian's family on Pavilion Road in Belgravia, returning home to Ottery St. Mary during the holidays. This woodland, the branches reaching into the dark sky like witches chanting at midnight, it terrifies me. If I look up at the snow falling in silent energy, I might lose my balance among the piercing tendrils of the trees.

She won't stop talking. Even when the trees and the snow seem to thicken the silence around us, she is oblivious to it all. These winter storms, the chill of a darkening wood, she has no fear; this land belongs to her. Jasmine cares nothing for the cold and the distant whistling of the wind in the treetops. But I want her to be serious.

I want to hold her still and make her listen.

This is my chance. I can take her right now, get on a bus and disappear. We will return to London, hide together in the busy streets I know so well. The city is my landscape, my home. I can keep her safe there.

When three notes from the church bell filter in through the trees, the feeling is gone, and I lose my nerve. Then, as suddenly as they began, the bells fall silent again and we are both still, waiting for them to resume their syncopated chimes. A false start, the bell ringers preparing too soon for their call to Christmas Eve.

Jasmine has made a plan, I can tell, and my opportunity is lost. She will not be told what to do.

We walk fast out of the wood, the snow falling more heavily now. When I look behind me, our tracks are already disappearing under a fresh dusting of powder. The drive from the house to the village is long and curved, quickly disappearing from the sight of the manor. Perhaps it is knowing for certain that Rosamund cannot see us, that we are safe from her hard and persistent stare, for I feel a pang of possibility again, that if I am quick and determined, I might get Jasmine on that bus. It will be a while before Rosamund works out where we are.

But when we get to the village, I see the lights of the bus fading away from me. It will be over an hour until the next one. And in truth I know it is too soon. If she comes with me now, she will not understand why it is so important that I get her away from Rosamund Caradon, why she must start afresh with me.

We are early for the service, but Jasmine goes in anyway, leading me straight to the front pew, where we have an excellent view of the Nativity scene that has been set up on a heavy carpet of straw. It has been a while since I went to church. We were touring too much during the war and even my parents, despite the expectations of the parishioners of Ottery St. Mary, avoid going more than they can help it. This old church is beautiful: Christmas foliage decorates the windows and candlelight softens the stone and wood of the interior. It reminds me of the low lighting at the start of the transformation scene in *Casse-Noisette*, Clara making her way downstairs to find her nutcracker brought to life.

The verger speaks to Jasmine, all the while looking me up and down. He is one of those nosy old men, it seems, who needs to know everything about everyone.

"This is Briar," Jasmine tells him after he gives up on his subtle attempts at an introduction and asks her directly who I am.

"Pleased to meet you, Briar," he says, those piercing eyes taking in everything. His gaze lingers a beat too long and makes me shiver.

We nestle close together on the pew. The church provides a respite from the chill outside, but it is still cold. I put an arm around Jasmine, and she shifts even closer to me. "When are you next coming to London?" I ask her.

"Oh soon, I hope," she exclaims. "Though Mama doesn't want to. I don't think she likes London very much. We only go back because she wants to finish renovating the flat in Chelsea. When we first went there in the summer, I think she wanted to spend lots of time there. She seemed quite excited then, making all sorts of plans for what we'd do in London. But it hasn't really worked out that way." Jasmine talks fast, no note of judgment in her voice. She takes everything her mother does with far too much generosity of spirit.

"Why do you think that is?" I tread slowly, steadily. It is too soon to say anything to Jasmine that criticizes her mother. She would not understand.

"She says it's the crowds. And not having her garden to potter around. And she doesn't like getting dressed up," Jasmine adds. "Though I don't really think that's a valid reason, as lots of women in London wear slacks and overalls."

I smile. While she is right about that, most women of Rosamund Caradon's social standing do not wear the type of scruffy woolen clothes she does.

"What about school? Does she want you to go to school in Devon or London?"

"Oh, I would love to go to school. But Mama teaches me herself. We do lessons every morning. It was easier that way during the war rather than trying to squeeze all our guests from London into the village school, and we've just kept going. Though I think it would be much more fun in London in a huge school with lots of other boys and girls."

I take my chance. "Perhaps you should ask her. You could always stay with me in London if she doesn't want to come herself."

There is no way Rosamund will allow this. I have seen the way she stares at Jasmine with such territorial severity. She wants to know where she is every single minute. Right now, I imagine she is frantic, rushing about the gardens looking for us. The thought gives me a little tremor of pleasure.

But before Jasmine has a chance to reply, there she is. The verger is at her side, his hand resting gently on her elbow. Rosamund looks at me with such hostility that I feel my breath rising nervously in my throat. That stare, I think, is hatred.

When she takes her place in the pew, forcing me to slide farther along toward the central aisle, I don't see this as a failure at all. It may be Rosamund's arm now pressed hard into Jasmine's shoulders; but the seeds of doubt have been sown and Jasmine has been forced to recognize that her life could be very different.

She doesn't need to stay here hidden away in the depths of the countryside. She can come home to me.

WHEN THE CHURCH SERVICE ENDS, I give Jasmine a kiss before running to catch the last bus. It is too dark and the ground too wet with melting snow for me to walk the entire way home now, four miles of narrow lanes and not a single streetlight. While I consider missing the bus, therefore needing to stay at Gittisham Manor for the night, I decide I can't do that to my parents. They will be waiting for me at home, wondering what could possibly keep me away for over four hours. I didn't tell them where I was going, instead claiming to be heading out for some last-minute Christmas shopping. They are used to me coming and going, but I know I have been too secretive about my movements recently and I think they are starting to notice.

Mother is in the kitchen when I get home, already preparing the tea. She looks up at me when I come in, her forehead furrowing in frustration. "Where have you been? We've been waiting for you for hours."

There was a time in the past when I would have been silent, ignored her and disappeared upstairs, letting the tension spread uneasily throughout the house. But not now. I have learned how to moderate my moods, my behavior; how to be patient, how to smile when all I want is to run and hide. During those long tours around the country—dancing in drafty town halls, provisional theatres where we changed behind the scenery, freezing aircraft hangars with yawning troops—I practiced how to manage those bubbling feelings of stress and anxiety, instead finding the calm needed to perform *Les Sylphides* or *Les Patineurs* in days-old pairs of pointe shoes. The work was relentless, often eighteen performances a fortnight in one softening pair of shoes. Sometimes bombs fell in the streets outside, the noise intruding on our dance. But we loved our war work, bringing moments of relief to the weary. It was during those years of hardship and beauty, the challenge of living on just four pounds a week allayed by the applause of thousands across the country, that I discovered who I could be.

I go up to Mother and hug her, feeling the solidity of her body relax reluctantly between my arms. "I'm sorry," I say. "I took shelter inside the library when it started to snow and lost track of time exploring the shelves." It is a risk, this lie. The librarians are all Mother's customers, but I doubt she will check.

"We were worried. With the snow coming down so fast, we didn't know if you were safe."

"It's nearly all gone now," I say, trying to change the subject. It is incredible how fast the snow has melted, determined to deny us the white Christmas we all secretly long for. It feels childish, somehow, to say this aloud, not when this Christmas means so much more to us all, the first Christmas since the end of the war. Mother murmurs an agreement and extracts herself from my arms, getting back to the mincemeat she is trying to flavor with our limited supply of brandy. I am yet to win her back fully. There have been too many of these moments recently. She can tell, I think, that I am hiding something. After all, this is not the first time I have buried myself and my troubles from her.

Father joins us in the kitchen, clutching a bottle of Cointreau. He sees Mother carefully pouring the brandy into the mincemeat and exclaims in mock horror, "Don't use it all up. I'm making us our usual."

He means the sidecar, a cocktail recipe he found years ago in one of Mother's magazines. It has become a tradition, Father mixing the drinks and lining them up on the kitchen table among the chaos of our baking.

I hear myself inhale too sharply, a momentary lapse in the cheerful facade I am trying to maintain.

Tonight, with the strain of the day and how close I was to leaving this all behind and starting anew with Jasmine at my side, suddenly everything becomes too much. I excuse myself and run upstairs, peeling off my damp coat as I go. A hot shock of sweat runs along my back and inside my brassiere, the rayon satin sticking to me uncomfortably. In my bedroom, I take off my clothes and stand in front of the mirror, finding stillness in the cool of the room.

I remember everything, how I felt all those years ago, how angry I had been: with myself, with Louis de Manton, the way he slipped in and out of my life as it suited him. I remember how much I wanted to reclaim my body, hating every change, every shift of my skin. Each day felt like I was slipping out of control.

But that was a different person. I close my eyes and try to understand her again. I try to remember why I made that terrible decision on Christmas Eve exactly nine years ago.

Christmas 1936

Before anyone had the chance to notice the undeniable changes to my body, I went home to my parents. Miss de Valois was kind enough not to ask too many questions when I claimed illness and anxiety, signing me off for indefinite leave until I was feeling more myself.

I missed the premiere of *Nocturne*, but Martha sent me newspaper cuttings of the reviews. Upstairs in my bedroom with the large apple tree knocking persistently against the window, I felt like a child again, sulking stubbornly in my room because something hadn't gone my way. It was with a sense of helpless irritation that I unfolded the newspaper pages Martha had sent me, gazing longingly at the photographs of Margot Fonteyn in her gray-and-white dress, the velvet bodice a far too romantic version of loss and poverty. The designs for the costumes had been in the Sadler's Wells Wardrobe back in October, Sophie Fedorovitch's beautiful sketches evoking a nostalgic vision of 1890s Paris. In my bedroom I gazed at them again, but this time they were photographs of the dancers rather than pencil sketches in smudged blocks of color. Sophie Fedorovitch knew how to conjure the period, the style, the character, without blocking the long classical lines of the dancers, a whole world of beauty from which I felt far removed. June Brae had the role of the Rich Girl. I looked at her long white gloves and the ruffles of silk that fell around her shoulders and felt only envy and disappointment. I remembered the rich colors of the dresses hanging ready for fitting in Wardrobe just before I disappeared from London, the folds of bright tulle contrasted with the boldness of white frills and edges. In *The Bystander*, there was a photograph of Margot Fonteyn as the poor innocent flower girl, spurned in love and lying rejected on the ground. Frederick Ashton, dressed in the long black cloak of the Spectator, his tight mustache drawn on in firm lines, leaned down over her trying to bring her some comfort.

Everything made me think of my own tragedy. For that was how it felt, a terrible disaster, my body swelling and angry, my feet longing to dance, my heart wanting nothing more than to be back on the stage, rehearsing and taking ballet class with my friends. It was too quiet in our little country town, the stillness exposing gaps into which Louis and his rich wife crept insidiously, the brightness of their new life together shadowing my shabby failure.

It was Christmas Eve, and I knew Mother was going to force me to talk. I had been silent and sullen for weeks, barely leaving the house except to go for long solitary walks in the hills around Ottery St. Mary. I avoided other people, turning down narrow country lanes or disappearing into the line of the trees if walkers appeared in my path. When a mother went by on the road next to the parish church, one child in a pram and the other rushing along by her side with tiny steps, I felt a wave of panic. Another woman stopped to talk to them, her face brightening as she smiled down at the baby in its crocheted blanket and the little girl in her thick red cape. I pressed my hand to my stomach and tried to imagine the girl as my own, to think what it would be like to dress her in a pretty coat, doing up those big leather buttons and pulling on her tiny gloves.

I tried hard to conjure up a feeling of joy at brushing her ringlets from her eyes, fastening a woolen hat over her ears, stopping on the street to allow other women to coo and smile at my beautiful child. But those feelings refused to rise. Instead, I turned away and rushed back home. Upstairs in my bedroom, surrounded by photographs of ballerinas, programs from Sadler's Wells, pointe shoes and ribbons, the pale pink of darning thread, the silk of my ballet skirt, I could convince myself that this was only temporary, that I would return to London. That I might escape mundanity.

My parents closed early on Christmas Eve, gently ushering out the last-minute shoppers keen to find Mother's popular ready-to-buy hats and headpieces for their wives and daughters. We lived opposite the shop on Silver Street, Mother's beautifully painted navy-and-gold sign for Alice Woods Hats visible from the upstairs landing window. I had recently taken to sitting among piles of cushions in the window seat, finding some distraction in watching people walking up and down the street, listening to the loud bells of the church at the top of the road, counting the number of hatboxes Mother sent out with satisfied customers. A young couple were leaving now, the woman smiling as she clutched her new purchase to her side, the other arm linked through her husband's, the glow of the lights behind them illuminating the cold air of the street. I almost smiled too, but then I remembered Louis buying a hat for his mother, asking my mother's advice with such sincerity while all the time knowing he would never invite me home with him. The milliner's daughter, the ballet girl in her cheap dresses, certainly not a suitable wife for Louis de Manton.

The seamstresses left next, three of them walking fast down the hill and home to whatever Christmas festivities they had planned. They were young and pretty and impatient and Mother knew she wouldn't keep them for long. Young men were often seen dawdling outside, cigarettes dangling from their lips as they waited for their dates to finish work. They took the bus into nearby towns, spending hours watching films at the Gaumont Palace and the Palladium in Exeter, or the Devonia Cinema in Honiton, the girls returning to work the next day full of gossip and hope and plans. Mother tried her best to capture their energy for fashion and innovation, knowing that soon they would be announcing their departure: marriage, starting a family, a life focused on home. This afternoon, with the dark starting to spread along the street, I caught the excitement on their faces as they walked arm in arm toward the cheerful lights of the shops, the pub, the cottages with their Christmas trees framed in the windows.

Finally, the lights dimmed in the shop, a streetlamp's glow striving to illuminate the window display of Mother's finest winter hats. My parents hurried across the street, and I heard the door opening and closing beneath me, a faint breeze sweeping in and up the stairs as they arrived home.

"Briar," I heard Mother call me, her voice cheerful. "Come down and help with the tea." It was our tradition, the Christmas Eve tea, and she knew I usually adored the chance to roll out the pastry, cutting tiny tops in the shape of holly leaves for the mince pies; to glaze the Christmas cake, decorating its golden surface with the miniature figurines of Father Christmas and his sleigh.

Gazing out the window, I noticed a low fog starting to settle among the thickening darkness. Part of me wanted to disappear into my bedroom, to sleep through Christmas, to refuse to acknowledge what was happening to my body and my life, but I knew Mother would not let that happen. I sensed it this morning, the way she looked at me during breakfast, the change in her mood, her refusal to tiptoe around me anymore. Even Father seemed to be aware that today would be different, pushing a fried egg onto my plate and thumping cups of tea in front of me as though he had given up behaving as if I was an invalid. My fragility had gone on long enough, he seemed to say as he splashed milk into my cup and ruffled my hair affectionately when he walked behind me at the table.

I made my way downstairs, my feet taking slow and cautious steps on the wooden staircase. The low voices of my parents spilled out from the kitchen, cupboard doors opening and closing, the kettle starting its whine. Perhaps if I took a few deep breaths and closed my eyes, all would go back to normal. I'd simply be at home for the holiday, an ordinary Christmas before returning to the theatre for the rest of the season.

When I finally entered the kitchen, I thought for an instant that it could be true. Mother handed me an apron and Father emerged out of the pantry with jars of flour and sugar pressed against his chest.

"I'll spruce up the mincemeat while you make the pastry," Mother said, reaching for a bottle of brandy at the top of a cupboard. "Sit here next to your father. He's promised to make the apricot glaze for the cake, haven't you, Dennis?"

My father smiled and shook his head in mock exasperation. "Can't a man make himself a drink on Christmas Eve before getting put to work?"

"You can make us one too then," Mother replied as she sloshed brandy into her bowl of mincemeat. "You'll have a drink, won't you, Briar? One isn't going to do you any harm, and it might just cheer you up."

I stared at her, a stunned silence hovering above the flour and the sugar and the brandy. My parents were both looking at me, two determined faces, a smear of flour staining one tip of my father's mustache. In the growing warmth of the kitchen, the familiar smells of Christmas surrounding me, the table groaning with ingredients, I finally surrendered myself to my parents. They had watched me in silent agony for weeks, trying to find a way to help. There had been no judgment, no words of recrimination, no lectures; just kindness and small gestures of love. But I had ignored them, pushed them away, disappeared into myself. I had walked away every time they tried to come too close.

Mother knew what was happening. She saw it in the quiver of my chin, the tight press of my lips, the shudder in my shoulders. As I started to cry, she was there. I pressed my head against her shoulder, breathing in the reassuring scents of hat leather, fabric dye, the musk of feathers, tea leaves, all infused in the warmth of the brandy. By the time she helped me to a seat at the table, Father was handing me a cocktail glass filled with orange liquid, a swirl of peel decorating the rim. "This will make you feel better," he said, nodding proudly at the drink. "A sidecar. I found the recipe in one of those magazines your mother gets for the shop. Nothing to it, really: Cointreau, brandy, and lemon juice."

I couldn't help but smile at his enthusiasm, the way he stood back and nodded at the three glasses.

We all sat around the kitchen table, slowly working on preparing the food as we sipped our drinks. As I rubbed the pastry between my fingers, I felt all the tension of the last few months falling away. Finally, I was ready to talk, to plan, to let my parents find a way to fix me.

"There is a woman who comes to my shop, a client. I can trust her. I've known her for a long time, over twenty years now. She knows how to manage these things. She'll help us find another family for the baby." Mother held her hands still over the floured pastry. "If that is what you want."

This was the first time anyone had mentioned the future, what would happen when the baby was born. And with Mother saying these words, immediately suggesting an alternative, it was as though an immense weight had been lifted off my chest. I was afraid of voicing this idea, of declaring bluntly and certainly that I did not want the child. This violent revulsion toward my pregnancy, toward motherhood, felt like some primitive and ancient failure as a woman, as though I was betraying a sacred maternal tradition. Since returning to Devon, I had been terrified that my parents were going to say that they would look after the child, bringing it up as their own while I returned to dance in London. I knew that would not do, that the child would tie me to home, anchoring me when what I really wanted was to be free.

I nodded. "Yes, that is what I want."

"Well then," Mother said as she stood from the table to collect the pastry cutter, "that wasn't so hard, was it? We'll go immediately after New Year's and you can meet her." She paused, noting the wave of uncertainty crossing my face. "She's a good woman," she added. "She isn't like those baby farm women from a few decades ago—no checks, babies parceled off to anyone who would pay a few pounds. There are regulations now, and she'll make sure your baby goes to a good, respectable home."

My mother could always solve problems. It was what she did, finding a practical and reasonable solution, making lists, weighing up options with unemotional clarity. She never allowed herself to wallow in difficulty. I was more like Father, with our shared tendency to mull over troubles, reworking them over and over until they became sensational poems rather than lists in a ledger. Father coped by turning life into a joke, an endless merry-go-round of absurdity. Right now, both my mother and father had given me permission to sit back and let them find a solution.

"There will be a woman out there desperate for a child but unable to have one of her own." Mother spoke warmly as she came around the table and placed the pastry cutter next to me. Her hand rested over Father's, their fingers intertwined.

"Your baby will be a gift," Father said, seriousness breaking through his usual jesting frivolity.

I turned to my parents. They were smiling at each other as if far away from this warm kitchen with its clouds of flour and sugar drifting lazily through the air. There was a grainy photograph on the worktop by a stack of recipe books. It was of the three of us, me just four years old and dressed in an oversized winter coat. It would be better, I thought, for the baby to find a home like this one, with parents who were better people than me, selfless and willing to give part of themselves to a child.

There would be a woman out there waiting to become the mother I knew I could never be.

January 1946

I do not visit Gittisham Manor after Christmas. Every morning when I wake, I think about going there, imagining what would happen if I appeared at that heavy oak door and confronted Rosamund. I plan every word of the conversation, my courage, how I will admonish her for the way she keeps Jasmine hidden away from the world. A princess in a tower. But every time I come downstairs to breakfast, I change my mind. Mother will be sketching new designs at the kitchen table or embroidering details onto a hat, tiny lilac petals scattered in silk across the wooden surface. Father will be mumbling into his newspaper, calling out crossword clues every few minutes, which Mother answers without looking up. If I take Jasmine now, I will have to leave all this behind. They won't understand, not yet.

Rehearsals resume soon after Christmas, the opening performance of *The Sleeping Beauty* only a few weeks away. I return to London, relieved to have a break from the quiet of Ottery St. Mary. All those hours of stillness, even the millinery shop closed for the holiday period, have given me too much space to worry. My mind keeps returning to Gittisham.

Train journeys have composed the rhythm of my life for as long as I can remember. Exeter to Paddington, or the slow train from Honiton to London Waterloo; King's Cross to Cambridge;

up and down the country during the war as we found new theatres in new towns to which we could bring our ballet. I love that
feeling as the train pulls out of the station, slowly gathering speed
as it transports its passengers to new adventures. Returning to
London has always been as exciting as visiting my childhood
home in Devon, but today I feel uncertain, pulled both away and
toward that dark old house hidden in the woods of the Otter Valley. Exhaling its shrieking whistle, the train seems to shudder as
it starts to carve its path through the countryside. I am firm with
myself, finding calm with the rise and fall of my needle as I sew an
old set of ribbons onto my new pointe shoes. All I need is patience
and I will find my opportunity.

Martha is still working downstairs in the bookshop when I
arrive. She retired from dancing partway through the war, deciding
that her time could be better used elsewhere. And she was sick of
the constant pain in her feet, an injury from before the war resur-
facing every time we danced on a solid concrete floor or were given
no time and space to warm up before a punishing performance.
She relished the change, casting aside leotards and woolens in favor
of another sort of uniform. On an afternoon off from rehearsals, I
had visited her at the mechanical transport training center in Sur-
rey. I remember not being at all surprised to see ballerina Martha
Brackley looking comfortable in a pair of overalls with a tool bag
at her side. Transitioning from sewing pointe shoes to greasing
engines was easy for her, and I enjoyed watching her emerge from
beneath a truck, a smear of oil across her neck. Once her training
was complete, she moved back to the flat above her father's bookshop on Cecil Court, working as a mechanic repairing ambulances
during the day and managing clients' orders in the evenings when

her father went off to his air raid warden duties. It was, she told me, just swapping one routine for another.

Since 1940, I have lived with Martha in the flat over the shop. Her father doesn't seem to notice me, the rare moments he spends upstairs simply opportunities for him to disappear into his bedroom, an unruly pile of books and journals tumbling from his grip.

"I'm just closing up," Martha says, giving me a quick kiss as I squeeze past the boxes crowding the staircase. The shop and the flat bleed into one another, books finding their way into every available corner. Now that Martha has more time, her duties at the ambulance depot reduced to one shift a week, she is trying to develop her career as a writer. Currently she just does book and theatre reviews for several small journals, but I have seen her working on longer, creative pieces. Her project is to read all the novels she can find that have been published by women in the past few years: research, she calls it. I tell her she should write what she wants, but she taps her nose and tells me that she'll only know what that is once she's found out what everyone else wants too. And so there is a growing pile of Dorothy L. Sayers, Stevie Smith, Nancy Mitford, Elizabeth Bowen, and many more I have never heard of, stacked high around her bed. She lives in what can only be described as a jungle of chaos, and yet somehow she manages to fit more into her days than I can even contemplate. Perhaps that is what I love about her, this pragmatism nestled among creative disorder.

Running up the stairs, I shake my head roughly, pushing these thoughts away. Martha. Jasmine. I know I cannot have them both.

The flat is dark and cold when I get upstairs. Martha will have been too busy to have thought about turning on the heater, and her father is clearly out somewhere. Since the end of his duties as an air raid warden, Mr. Brackley has resumed his literary pursuits, attending book launches and lectures whenever he can persuade Martha to stay late in the shop. Business faded during the war, paper shortages severely limiting his stock, but he is working hard now to recapture his prewar reputation.

I am glad to have time alone before Martha joins me. There is a photograph resting on a bookshelf, propped up by a collection of Edward Thomas poetry and a first edition of Virginia Woolf's *Mrs. Dalloway*. I remember reading both right here on this sofa before we knew the war was coming, though really, if we had been paying attention, we should have worked it out. But it seemed to me then that those books described the aftermath of an old war, a war I assumed would never touch me. Clarissa Dalloway's life was a strange and distant fiction. Back then, when I was so young and thought I knew precisely what I wanted, I let nothing get in the way of the path I had set for myself. I was to dance, perform, progress through the ranks of the ballet company. Everything else was an unnecessary disturbance. Now, in the dullness of the room, only a small table light switched on beside the heavy curtain, I go to stand in front of that photograph, lifting it off the shelf.

There we are: Martha, Vivian, and me, dressed in our snowflake costumes for *Casse-Noisette* in February 1935, before everything changed. Our eyes look huge, black pencil lines drawn heavily over the white shimmer of our makeup. Martha is standing en pointe, but even then, Vivian is taller than her. I am between them, smiling widely. The other two look a little more polished than me, more poised, Vivian with her serene gaze and translucent skin, Martha all precision and style. I remember being a teenager and envying the way they seemed so sure of who they were, effort-lessly fitting in to our ballet-driven lives.

Martha appears in the doorway, and I can sense her watching me as I place the photograph back on the shelf. She knows me better than anyone in the world, but I cannot share this with her. This is for me to do alone. So I hug her and pull her onto the sofa with me and tell her about Christmas at Ottery St. Mary, leaving out everything that matters about Jasmine and Rosamund and the thick stone walls of Gittisham Manor. I briefly let myself be taken back to the past, to the days when everything was easy and I didn't need to pretend.

With Martha, just for tonight, perhaps I can forget about it all and become the Briar Woods I used to be.

Cambridge, 1936

The students were supposed to be revising for their exams, but you wouldn't have known it. As we took ballet class, they kicked a ball before them on their way through St. Edward's Passage, its thud adding a syncopated beat to the music of the piano like a metronome out of time. A bicycle clattered past on the uneven stone street and a loud laugh filtered in through the thick air of the studio. *Plié* and stretch. Lift that elbow. Relax your little finger. Straighten your knee. On and on the exercises went, the sweat dripping down our backs as we glanced out the window when the ballet mistress wasn't looking, longing to join the boys as they headed to a cool stretch of grass by the river.

"Isn't that Louis?" Vivian whispered to me when Miss Moreton wasn't looking. I turned and glanced out the window, feeling a blush creep across my cheeks. Vivian pressed me in the ribs, and I stifled a giggle. We quickly returned to our positions at the barre, a tight fifth position, one arm extended above our heads. Vivian was in front of me, and I watched the muscles in her back tense and release, the skin tight over her shoulder blades. I often found myself staring at her body: how her long arms were patterned with dancing sinews and muscle, the way the bones of her feet seemed to ripple beneath the most delicate skin. Of course I loved her, my best friend, but sometimes her body made me feel mediocre. I was human; she was not.

Martha was across the studio, avoiding any distractions. I glanced at her as we turned to the other side for the *adage*. She held too much tension in her shoulders. Miss Moreton touched her lightly across the back and I saw her relax, her neck less strained as she drew her foot into *retiré*.

When class was over, we spilled out onto the street. It was not yet midday but the air was hot, the sun pressing down over the roofs of the buildings. When we reached King's Parade the heat seemed to intensify, and we squinted from the bright stone glare of King's College across the street. Martha, Vivian, and I had moved into these rooms the week before, our base for a month in Cambridge, dancing at the Cambridge Arts Theatre. We were right opposite the college, giving us the perfect view of the undergraduates as they drifted in and out of the quad, alternating between clutching books and bottles of beer under their arms. There was a row of bike racks in front of the entrance to the college and we enjoyed watching the young men's exclamations of frustration at what must have been a stolen bike, before shrugging and taking someone else's.

The three of us had still been students at the Vic-Wells Ballet School when John Maynard Keynes had opened the Cambridge Arts Theatre in February. We heard about it, how Margot Fonteyn danced a variation from *Façade* and Bobby Helpmann one from *The Rake's Progress*. They were enough of a sensation for us all to be invited back, three weeks of performances that felt like a holiday compared to the daily routine of London. Martha, Vivian, and I graduated into the Vic-Wells Ballet company at the end of the spring season, making the short journey from the school studio at the top of Sadler's Wells Theatre to the rehearsals, the busy dressing rooms and the bright lights of the stage. We were so nervous that first day, the company dancers eyeing us with suspicious superiority, but we found our place quickly, the pace of our routine giving us no time to think about our status.

Cambridge now had dancers dotted about its streets, the girls staying in lodgings and the boys finding digs with college students. Our landlady, Mrs. Mulberry, welcomed us enthusiastically when we arrived with our trunks crammed full of pointe shoes and rehearsal clothes, proudly pointing out her photograph of Anna Pavlova in the hallway. Her enthusiasm quickly waned, however, when she realized our late hours, our long baths, the loud laughter that spilled out of our rooms as we were getting ready to go out. It was no surprise that the Cambridge undergraduates had found us, luring us away from our pointe shoes and our discipline, filling the days between morning practice and evening performances with a heady stream of picnics and parties.

"Bath?" Vivian said as we crept past Mrs. Mulberry's drawing room, where she sat with her knitting and the low murmur of the wireless. She did not approve of us taking baths in the middle of the day, but we ignored her raised eyebrows as we came downstairs early afternoon each day, our makeup fresh and our skin no longer salty from the sweat of ballet class. Our baths were cold, the landlady unwilling to fire up the boiler in such weather: it didn't bother us, though, the cool water a welcome respite from this unusual May heat.

"Yes, definitely," I whispered back, our steps quickening as we went up the stairs and into our little suite of rooms at the top of the house. There was one bedroom with a double and single bed, and a small living room with three tired armchairs, as well as a fireplace that we had no need to light in this heat. Wonderfully, we got the bathroom all to ourselves. This was a luxury compared to my London lodgings, where the bathroom was shared among seven of us, each morning a scramble to get in and out before impatient knocking started up on the door. I lived with Vivian, her mother, father, and three brothers, taking the train home to my parents' cottage in Devon when I had time away from rehearsal and performances. The Grant household was permanently chaotic, her brothers leaving mud and mess in every room. But I loved it there: they made me feel like one of the family.

Martha ran the bath while Vivian and I thrust our heads out the window, watching as the undergraduates cycled past. From our height we could see into the King's College grounds, where a cluster of boys was coming out of the hall. They would have just had lunch, seated in long lines and served large meals with something hearty like cheese and biscuits to finish. All they seemed to do was eat and drink and rush about in those awful black gowns, Vivian commented this morning. I didn't know when they got any work done. Louis had showed me the hall last night and I stood there looking up at the vast ceiling, the ornate carpentry, the somber faces of the old men in the portraits. It made me feel very young, as though I was a child intruding on something ancient and serious, something impossibly aloof from my life of dance. But Louis had shrugged when I said how grand it was. "The food's all right, I guess," he replied, his vowels strangely long and certain, just a hint of a French accent. "Nothing like what I get at home, though."

"Bath's ready," called Martha. Vivian and I drew in our heads from the window, stripping off the tights and leotards that we hadn't bothered removing before putting on our skirts and blouses after class.

Martha was already in the bath, her legs stretched under the water and her skin shivering a little with the shock of the cold. She smiled at us as we came in, a mischievous grin that signaled her transition from the focus of class to the luxury of a free afternoon. She had always been like this, ever since she had joined the ballet school two years ago, an angel in class before transforming into this confident young woman who yearned, instinctively, for a party. She was often at the head of the group of dancers who searched for entertainment after a show, seeking the best dance halls, the best bars, expecting the rest of us to follow obediently, if a little nervously, as she set the pace.

In a tiny flat above a bookshop on Cecil Court, Martha Brackley lived with her father. She had been very young when her mother died, and so her father had taken on the challenge of raising her alone, though perhaps with more enthusiasm than accuracy, trusting almost-strangers to drop her off at ballet studios around London when he was too busy in the shop. She often told us of the parties she came home to after performances, whiskey glasses balancing on tired books and the reek of tobacco drifting into her bedroom. Boldly stealing cigarettes left tottering in ashtrays, she loved to join the curious people he collected at his gatherings, positioning herself on the floor between shelves as she stretched out her legs before bed.

Resting her head back against the end of the bath, she smiled up at us. "There's space for one more."

"You go first," I said to Vivian. "Then I'll swap in."

Vivian extended one long leg as she stepped into the bath, lowering herself gingerly into the cool water. She let out a sigh as she sank down, her toes nearly reaching behind Martha's head. I turned away and went to the mirror, shaking my hair out from its bun. Vivian's naked body was not new to me: for years we had shared baths, a bedroom, theatre dressing rooms. But there was always something about the endless length of her pale limbs, the tightness of her skin over her stomach, that made me ache with envy.

"My feet hurt," Martha said with a gentle whine, pressing her foot into Vivian's shoulder. "Massage them for me, won't you?"

I watched in the mirror as Vivian took Martha's foot and pressed her thumb into the arch. "Gently!" Martha groaned, laughing.

"So demanding," Vivian laughed back, the water swilling over her stomach. I caught Martha's eye in the mirror and her grin grew larger, a wide smile that exposed her bright white teeth. I drew my eyes away and started smearing cream over my cheeks and eyes, its thickness cooling my face, but I could still feel her stare pinned on me.

"Is she going to tell us what happened with that boy?" Martha said loudly to Vivian, knowing full well I could hear.

"It's a good question," Vivian replied. I turned to see her smiling up at me. "Well, Briar," she said, "we know something happened. You left the party with him and finally floated back here, cloudlike, arriving well after Martha and I had brushed our teeth."

"We just walked about a bit. He showed me the college, some of the gardens and the dining hall. Nothing happened."

"Nothing at all?" pressed Martha, reaching out her hand to me. With a grimace, I went to her and knelt by the bath, splashing water up my arms. I liked the way it instantly forced down the temperature of my body, the hairs on my skin rising. Before she could resist, I grabbed Martha under the armpits. She squealed, water sloshing out onto the floor. I released her and she shook her head, laughing. "You know I can't stand being tickled."

"And that's why I do it." I stood, peeling off my undergarments and throwing them into the wash basket. "Come on, it's my turn in the bath now." Martha sighed, water falling away from her as she rose out of the tub.

After handing her one of the stiff mauve towels Mrs. Mulberry provided for us, I stepped into the bath. The water was colder than I'd expected, but I took a breath and ducked my head under the surface, my hair fanning out around my shoulders. When I lifted myself up, I reached for the soap—not the thin, gray lump left for us by our landlady but the shampoo bar that Vivian and I treated ourselves to every few months. It was a regular routine for us, this hair washing, and I twisted around in the bath so I was facing away from her. Vivian took the bar from me and started rubbing my hair, massaging the soap into my scalp. I felt her take up the ends, working hard to get a lather in the cold water. We both inhaled together, enjoying the familiar smell of roses and lemons. Martha watched us, that knowing smile still lurking on her lips.

I sighed. "All right then. But you need to pretend I said nothing to you if we see him later. I don't want to be embarrassed by you two giggling the whole time."

"Of course," Vivian answered, her fingers pressing against my head with just the right firmness. "You know us, always the picture of discretion. So, what happened once you left the party?"

I closed my eyes to stop the soap from running into them. "Louis wanted to show me the college. He said he'd never had a chance to show anyone around in all three years he's been at Cambridge. His family lives in Paris most of the time, but he stays with his uncle sometimes in the holidays. His uncle is an ambassador or something like that—he lives in a residence in London. Louis was so thrilled to be showing me everything, explaining his life as an undergraduate: what the food is like, the tutors—who sound much less terrifying than Miss de Valois—the library. You'd have loved the library, Martha, all those shelves and shelves of books in far neater order than your father's place." I heard Martha laugh a little at that while my eyes were still squeezed shut as Vivian used a jug to rinse the soap from my hair.

"And then?" Vivian prompted.

"Well, it was getting a bit chilly. So we stayed in the library for a while. It was quite thrilling really, because I wasn't supposed to be in there. If the dean found me, Louis would be in big trouble. No women, you see. It was only because it was so late that he could smuggle me in without anyone seeing. We found a little corner with two armchairs, by the poetry section. He got a little nervous when I pulled out a few books from the shelves to take a look. The librarian can smell women, apparently. And so Milton and Meredith had to go back where they came from. We talked and talked. He wanted to know all about me and what it's like to be a ballet dancer, how many hours we train, if the pointe shoes hurt. You know, all the usual questions, but somehow more than that. It felt like he really did want to know, unlike most of those awful men we meet at parties who just want to talk about themselves the whole time. He could have said, "I want to know everything about you," and I'd have believed him."

"So you just talked, then?"

I said nothing, shuffling around to face Vivian and lowering myself into the water, letting the last of the soap rinse from me. I could feel her legs against my hips, endlessly long and slim.

As I stepped out of the bath and wrapped a small towel around my hair, I could sense Martha and Vivian watching me. It made me cold suddenly, strangely exposed. We knew each other's bodies almost as well as our own: Martha's tiny birthmark on the inside of her thigh, Vivian's scar on her knee from when she fell as a child, my left ear that sharpened to a point like a pixie. Their habits had become fixed markers of my daily life: the way Vivian pulled on her hair when she was nervous, Martha's hand tightening into a subconscious fist when she was impatient. I could read them so well and I knew there was nothing I could truly hide from them. But right then my body felt different, shy and young. They waited for me to speak, to tell them about Louis de Manton and how our night had ended. They wanted to know if he had kissed me, if we had embraced in the shadows of the college chapel, if his hands had moved underneath my blouse. I had thought I would tell them, but something held me back. I wanted this for myself, a secret more mine for not being shared.

I picked up another towel and covered my naked body. "He walked me all the way back here, kissed me on the cheek, and said he hoped we'd join them for a picnic today by the river. So can we please hurry up and get ready?"

Martha and Vivian shook their heads, smiling, but I thought they believed me. We got ready, picking out our prettiest day dresses and sandals. Once I was dressed, I went back into the bathroom and stared at my face in the dull smears of the mirror. It was good to be alone at last, to remember what really happened, to replay each moment, to feel it all again.

The lights had gone out in the library, just a few dim table lamps throwing shadows against the leather surfaces. We stood up to leave, both of us reluctant to end the night. But it was late, and I knew I needed to get back before the others started worrying about me. Louis had caught my hand as I squeezed between a bookshelf and a table, gently pulling me back to him. It was such a small, simple movement, nothing compared to the way the boys held us around our waists and hips, their hands under our thighs in a *pas de deux*. But that was just dancing, a classical position designed for stability, strength. With Louis I felt anything but stable, as if my heart might leap out of my chest.

He pressed me into him, my thighs trapped between his legs and the hard wood of the table. His hands wrapped around me, reaching down to below my waist. I shifted and lifted my hands to his face. It was a decisive move, I realized now, a signal that he could continue, even though the sound of my heartbeat was loud in my head, like a warning drum.

Louis kissed me once, a long, deep kiss that made me feel as though I was melting in his arms. It was like nothing I had felt before, so different from the quick, chaste kisses with nervous boys at dances, or that time I'd embarrassed myself by kissing the apprentice in my parents' haberdashery shop.

But then he pulled away, holding me at arm's length. In the gloom of the library, I could just make out the beautiful lines of his face, all angular with a dark shadow masking his eyes. He had thick heavy brows that gave him the look of a serious young god gazing out at his creations, and he seemed to be regarding me with a kind of wonder, as if he'd found something rare and precious.

"Let's get you home before I do something I shouldn't," he said, his voice a low treacly murmur and his French accent creeping in around the clarity of his English. We walked through the college and out onto King's Parade. He kissed me again, a quick peck on the lips, before returning to his rooms. I watched him disappear into the darkness before letting myself in, knowing I wouldn't be able to find calm until I saw him again.

There were already picnic blankets laid out when we arrived at the riverside, some undergraduates lounging on the grass, others wading into the water in their white cotton underpants. Glass bottles of beer, wine, cordial, and lemonade held down the edges of the blankets and there were a few cakes and sausage rolls clustered together on paper plates, the pastry weeping in the heat. Several of the ballet company were there, three girls not far from the water's edge watching the male dancers of the Vic-Wells Ballet with unguarded amusement. The boys had stripped off their shirts and were wrestling in the grass, goading each other to get in the water. It didn't take long for them to cave, and soon the river was filled with young men splashing and laughing. A family went by on a punt, perhaps a day out with their son before his exams began in earnest, and the mother smiled fondly even when a spray of water caught her across the cheek.

"It's easy to tell which are the dancers, isn't it?" murmured Martha. It was true: the undergraduates' pale thin limbs moved awkwardly compared to the grace and energy of the dancers. Vivian waved at one of the men, a dancer in the Vic-Wells called Frank Ellis, with whom she was often partnered in the corps. He waved back before plunging into the water, the muscles on his back strong and lean. They had become close recently; the way they touched one another repeatedly in rehearsals, light little presses of their hands, made it obvious to anyone looking that they were intimate. But it was common knowledge that Frank slept with a new woman every few weeks, the rumors suggesting that he did not confine himself to the opposite sex. Martha and I had warned Vivian not to get too attached, but she had laughed us off, telling us she didn't care what he did. That was the challenge, trying not to take things too seriously, especially being so young and new to the company. We were rushed into a whole labyrinth of sex and flirtation that none of us was equipped to navigate.

Joining the other girls in a patch of dappled shade on the bank of the river, I undid the buckles of my sandals, stretching out my feet into the sun. My legs were pale, and the tender patches of skin on my toes seemed to relax and heal in the light.

I tried to join the conversation of the others, but concentration didn't come easily. Louis wasn't here yet and I was trying hard not to look out for him, not to be seen gazing searchingly across the river, not to be caught waiting for him when he arrived. But I couldn't do it; easy, indifferent nonchalance was simply not me. When Martha made a comment about the book she was reading, I laughed at the wrong moment. She turned to me with a bemused expression, a perfectly arched eyebrow raised. To mask my embarrassment, I pointed out a party drifting past us in a punt, their faces bright in the sun. Margot was among them, her fingers running through the water as a young man stood on the flat wooden surface of the boat, pushing them forward with the long pole. It seemed to me then to be the picture of romance, the water twinkling, the slow slide of the boat, the ease with which the young man fed the pole through his hands, his smile beneath the wildness of his beard.

The reverie was broken when three hissing geese charged toward our picnic. Vivian jumped up in fright. Martha laughed, barely shifting as the geese stalked territorially around us. I watched them with curiosity, wondering how they felt about this invasion of their land.

"Isn't that Louis?" Martha said at last, and I tried to swallow the sausage roll I had just bitten into, licking my teeth to get rid of the pastry flakes. I waited until he was right beside us before turning and looking up at him. He looked younger in the sun, his dark hair flopping about his eyes and his face freshly shaven.

"May I?" he said, before sitting down next to me in the grass and picking up the book that Martha had flung to the side earlier. "Are you reading this? *The House in Paris*, by Elizabeth Bowen." He said the name of the book with genuine curiosity, pronouncing Paris in his French accent, the *s* silent.

"No, it's Martha's. She's always reading something new. Her father owns a bookshop."

"I wonder where this Parisian house is supposed to be." He flicked through the book, skimming the opening pages. "I do miss the Gare du Nord," he said, pointing out the reference on the first page of the story. "But I will be back there for the summer, strolling slowly through the streets and watching the world go by, if my father lets me. It is just not the same in England. No one is ever still for long enough to observe."

"We're still now," I replied, playing with a piece of grass between us.

"Not for long, though. You'll be off soon to put on those pointe shoes and charm all of Cambridge."

"Perhaps not quite all of Cambridge."

"Just the ones that matter, then. I have a ticket for tonight."

I looked up at him, forgetting to be coy and grown-up. "How wonderful! When did you buy it?"

"On the way here just now. I had to flatter the woman at the box office dreadfully to give me a seat close to the front. Apparently they were reserving them for important people in the arts, with a capital A," he said with a wink. "Not for uncultured undergraduates like myself."

"Well, I'm delighted you're coming. I only have a small role, you know, in the corps de ballet. But you aren't only coming to see me, so that doesn't matter," I quickly added, feeling that irritating creep of a blush.

"I will be able to watch only you, though," he said, a little quieter now.

The afternoon disappeared too swiftly, and I wished I could slow the lengthening shadows. We talked and talked, like the night before. He told me about his uncle and aunt who lived in a grand apartment in Kensington at the French embassy, how, when he went to stay with them, they put him to work in the back offices to stop him from wandering into meetings. They approved of Cambridge, though; his uncle was obsessed with all things British and was constantly inviting politicians and writers for dinner. "As long as they are anti-appeasement," Louis added. "He is very specific about that."

But Louis kept returning to me, asking me more and more about my life. It was exhausting, but in a wonderful, powerful way, like that first plunge into the sea in the early summer. "I am far too nosy, that is my problem," he told me when he realized how intense his questions were becoming. "I want to know everything about everyone."

I asked him about Paris and his home there, but he changed the subject. "Let us not talk about that. When I get home it will be all about getting a job that my father thinks is good enough, something dull in politics or law. And my mother, well, she will have all sorts of ideas planned for me." He shuddered before turning back to me with a smile, pushing away a strand of hair that had fallen across his face.

"We need to go," I heard Martha saying to the others. She always knew when our time was up, shifting quickly into the focus of performance. "Come on, Briar," she said, holding out her hand to pull me up.

As we crossed over King's College Bridge, I turned back to see Louis standing among a large crowd of undergraduates, their faces bright in the sun. He was talking, his hands moving energetically as though he was midway through telling a story. The others let out a loud laugh at something he said, and he laughed in return. There was something about it that unsettled me, how different he seemed among the group of young men, their bodies hard all of a sudden. They were like a pack of wolves jostling each other, trying to establish their strength.

He didn't wait for me after the performance. But there was a bouquet at the stage door and a note. I dug the card out of the cluster of delphiniums and gypsophila, turning it around in my hand.

To the beautiful Briar Woods. I only have eyes for you. Yours, Louis de Manton.

It wasn't until I got back to our rooms and the bouquet was in water, the note balanced against the vase, that I remembered the way he had laughed with his friends across the bridge. I fingered the note anxiously, its crisp edges starting to wilt from the damp. Martha was looking at me in that shrewd way she had, watching as I stared uncertainly at the flowers. She came up to me and put her arm around my waist, her familiar smell of vanilla cold cream a comfort.

"I'd try not to let him get too deep in there," she said as I turned around to face her. She pressed her hand against my chest. "I've seen what these men are like, the way they talk about girls when they think we're not listening. The men who come to the shop, they think they can say what they like in front of me because I'm a dancer. When my father isn't in the room to hear them, they make jokes about my legs, how flexible I must be, as though somehow being a performer makes us immune to the heartbreak and the pain of it all."

I gave her a hug before slipping under the sheets and trying to close my eyes. Vivian had already taken the single bed, so Martha climbed in after me. I turned onto my side away from her, as though I could push her words out of my head, refuse to let them settle. But she pulled me to her anyway, her legs pressing into the back of my knees.

"Just enjoy yourself," she whispered. "But have no expectations."

I shifted in her arms. "What expectations?" I whispered back, keeping my voice steady. "I'm not even eighteen and besides, I don't want anyone getting in the way of my dancing."

"Good girl," she murmured into my ear.

But I could already feel him working his way too far into me, a persistent pressure that could only be relieved, I thought, by time and distance. A few weeks more, I told myself. Then I'd make sure I never saw him again.

Act II

January 1946

I am the last to leave the dressing room tonight, and the corridors of the theatre are lit too dimly, and the silence is too wide. We should be used to the dark after nearly six years of groping our way along faint white lines on the road; but somehow that fear of heavy shadows around a corner refuses to leave me.

The smell of neglect is yet to be replaced with new scents of sweat, rosin, leather, the musk of our makeup. Change hangs around us with impatient expectation, paint pots waiting in corners, rolls of linoleum balanced against each other, stacks of timber ready for shaping into scenery. The theatre struggles to wake from its sleep, hovering in a state of exhaustion, like its occupants. Tonight, I try to imagine that the Lilac Fairy is waving her wand, the wreckage of war evaporating to reveal a theatre shimmering with energy, the red and gold curtains quivering in expectation. But it is the wicked fairy Carabosse who creeps at the edges of my vision. My war has only just begun.

Walking quickly to the stage door, I ignore the pull of the empty stage, the vast cavern of the auditorium. It waits, yawning, a deep scarlet mouth poised to expose me, uncover who I am for everyone to see. Every morning on the way to company ballet class, I stand at the edge of the stage, watching as the workmen return the theatre to its prewar state. Gone now is the ballroom dance floor, the sash curtains, the imitation-marble columns, the jazz bandstands. They are packed away and replaced with wings and lighting rigs and an orchestra pit. It makes me think of the paper theatre at Gittisham, how long it must have taken the children to cut out the pieces and assemble them into one unified creation. There is a certain magic to it: Ninette de Valois, Constant Lambert, Oliver Messel, hurrying from meetings to rehearsals to the vast corridors of storage hidden in the attics of the theatre. They salvage what they can from the mothballs and mold and dust, miraculous transformations. It seems there are fairy godmothers everywhere.

We rehearse endlessly, are fitted for costumes, help clear the dressing rooms. While we try to erase war with silks and satins, leather and lace, the shadow is always there, coupons and ration books holding us back from the opulence our production requires. At the edge of all our minds is the fear that our efforts will disintegrate, turn out to be a fragile paper theatre after all.

The date of the first performance is set for February 20, 1946, time charging onward too fast for us to keep up. There is a luxury to the stability of morning ballet class every day in the same studio, so different from the cold halls of our wartime provincial tours, where our feet were too frozen to move inside our pointe shoes. When Miss de Valois announced that we had been invited to move into Covent Garden, taking the Opera House as our home, we felt as though we were finally finding solid ground under our feet. After years of having no theatre of our own, our Sadler's Wells Theatre turned into a sanctuary for Londoners bombed out of their homes, perhaps normality could return. But these weeks have been far from normal. As we rehearse for *The Sleeping Beauty*, I think of Princess Aurora waking from her long sleep, how she must feel replacing a hundred years of darkness for the chaos of an entire castle moving once again. I think of whether she would have changed, waking a different woman from the one who pricked her finger and fell asleep. How could she return to the same life she'd left behind?

It might be less than a decade for me, not the hundred years of Princess Aurora's sleep, and yet it feels like a different age. I let her go so quickly, never let myself mourn. She had no hold over me then, was little more than a nameless stranger. I wanted to purge myself of her, to start afresh as myself, a dancer with my career ahead of me, no one to hold me back. I wanted to perform; I wanted to control my body, return to being beautiful, supple, light. And yet these past months, as I've watched the workmen hammering rhythmically in the scenery docks, the red velvet chairs emerging out of storage, the costumes crafted out of reams of silk, I have struggled to conjure those same feelings. That was a different person. I left her behind in the darkness of war.

I am afraid of change tonight, how it sweeps me along with relentless determination. I try to remember who I was before the war, how easy life was, the clarity of how I understood what I wanted. But that has gone now, an insubstantial memory like petals falling in rain.

I am afraid of what I will do if I cannot have her.

But worse than that, I am afraid of what will happen if I succeed. Carabosse or the Lilac Fairy? Who will I be then?

Mr. Jackson, the stage doorkeeper, looks up from his newspaper as I walk past. "Briar," he exclaims. "I thought everyone had gone. I'd have kept the lights on for you if I'd known."

I shake my head. "I'm sorry, Mr. Jackson. I just wanted to finish darning a pair of pointe shoes before I left. It's so hard to motivate yourself to get out the sewing box when you get home."

"You take care now, Briar," he says, coming around to the door and opening it for me. He knows everyone who comes through the stage door, is on first-name terms with the great ballet and opera stars of the prewar days. He was more relieved than anyone when he heard the theatre was throwing off its dance hall status, reverting to the glory days of the 1930s.

Going out into the night, I find reassurance in the warm laughter that spills out from the public houses on the corners of Floral Street and James Street. I wasn't quite telling the truth about the pointe shoes. But I couldn't explain what I was really doing, why I hadn't left with the other girls after rehearsals had ended. How could I explain that I had been entirely still, seated at my dressing table, my eyes fixed on a small piece of card in black and white? I have taken that photograph from my purse so many times these past few weeks, searching for something in her face that will tell me what to do.

The two of us are captured in front of a rail of tutus, Jasmine's eyes wide, my face turned slightly toward her. I am holding her by the hand, my grip so hard that it looks as though she is trying to draw her arm away from me. It is not how I envisaged our first photograph together.

I imagine photographs of my life laid out before me. Would I recognize myself in the spaces between them, those blocks of time that changed and crafted me? The photograph of the little girl standing between her parents in the silver frame nestled against cookery books on the safety of the kitchen counter; the young ballet dancer preparing to conjure the magic of *Casse-Noisette* in her snowflake costume, two best friends by her side; and then the one that still haunts me. The one I regret.

It was a joke, harmless fun for me, Martha, and Vivian only. No one else was supposed to see those photographs, and yet in my stupid pride I gave one away, signing my name with a kiss. The camera was Martha's, one of the curious gifts left behind by the strange men who lingered at the bookshop late at night, eventually passed on to Martha by her father. She wanted to practice taking photographs. Vivian and I were giggling as we posed in leotards and sheer skirts, our arms held high over our heads. We were drinking cheap wine, the red staining our lips, our bodies relaxing as we drank. Everything had seemed like comedy, the three of us playing at modeling, imagining ourselves famous dancers in front of a photographer like Cecil Beaton or Gordon Anthony. We had nearly finished the bottle when Martha took that photograph, the one where I had removed my skirt, my leotard, everything. I was turned away from the camera, my face in shadow, hair falling over my shoulders. One foot was en pointe, the other crossed behind. My arms were in a closed fourth position, what I had supposed at the time was a swanlike pose, a naked Odette. Perhaps I thought the addition of the pointe shoes would somehow turn it into art, transform erotica into classical dance. But that was ridiculous.

Whenever I thought back to it, my cheeks hot with embarrassment, I remembered finding a novel in among Martha's collection of books, a story of a ballet dancer: it was entitled *Memoirs of a Russian Ballet Girl*. I started reading while I waited for her to be released from duties down in the shop, assuming it would be a delightful coming-of-age story of hard work and tutus on the

Russian stage. It was quickly obvious that this was not the case; the whole concept was of a ballet girl reduced to sex, humiliation, and ballet masters instructing with whips in hand. I flicked through the book in fascinated horror until Martha found me and plucked it from my hand. A private order, she said, for one of her father's more enigmatic clients. The man had never ended up collecting the book, so she'd stolen it away for herself. Even the usually unflappable Martha seemed embarrassed that I had found the book among her things. Both of us, it seemed, had been ignorant to the sexual fantasies a ballet girl could evoke.

The photograph made me look older; there was something sensual about the dark shadows around my face, the curve of my body, the way my legs appeared out of the darkness, white and long. It hadn't looked like me, not really: this was a woman aware of her body's potential, not a nervous child struggling to fit into the bewildering sexual politics of a ballet company. I didn't know what had made me write that note, tucking the photograph inside the envelope. Sending it to Louis had felt wild and liberating. I imagined him picking it up from the porter's lodge at his college, the secret thrill he'd feel on opening it. But almost as soon as I put it in the post, I regretted it. All I could imagine was a group of young men standing on the other side of the bridge on that hot day in Cambridge, laughing as Louis entertained them. Of course, he wouldn't have kept the photograph to himself.

After Cambridge, I thought I wouldn't see him again. But when I went to Paris that same summer and met him in Galeries Lafayette, I let the memories of the photograph fade. It was easier to imagine he had never seen it at all.

Paris, 1936

"What a lot of steps," I heard Mother mumble to herself as we went up yet another flight of the steep iron staircase. Olga Preobrajenska's ballet studio at 69 rue de Douai was at the very top of the Salle Wacker rooms, a treacherous climb leading us up and up, the familiar sounds of piano music floating from the many studios scattered across each floor. It was my first summer in Paris.

It hadn't taken much to persuade Mother that I could join other dancers from the Vic-Wells, spending the summer holiday continuing to train and prepare ourselves for the winter season. The haberdashery and milliner's would cope without her for a few weeks, especially with the new girl she had hired showing such talent. It was her first trip to Paris too, and we intended to fill it with a full schedule of ballet lessons, window shopping, and long walks along the Left Bank. Mother relied on magazines and quick trips into London to keep her small Devon shop up to date with the newest fashions, and she had persuaded Father that Paris would fulfill two purposes: my dancing and her work.

Reaching the fourth floor, we were immediately confronted by a round, monocled man, his neat white mustache twitching. He demanded payment before we had even entered the studio, rummaging briskly in a tray of coins as we handed him a five-franc note.

The studio was already starting to fill with dancers: there were men pressed against the barre, the muscles in their legs pulsing as they kneaded out their feet; beautiful women with long thin arms were tying the ribbons of their shoes, their eyes flicking up and around as they watched for new arrivals; and there were teenagers like myself, none of whom looked quite as nervous and awkward as I felt. I wanted nothing more than to match up to the standard of the professional dancers limbering up at the barre in their casually thrown together outfits of flattering leotards, cardigans, skirts, shawls that rose high around their necks, pink silk tights, or cropped black leggings. I had to remind myself that I was one of them too, a professional dancer now, not just a student in Miss de Valois's school at the top of Sadler's Wells Theatre. Even though I had graduated out of the unattractive mauve tunics we'd had to wear at school, I still felt too young, too inelegant, my pale blue leotard somehow childish among this Parisian collection of ballerinas.

There was a group of mothers jostling for a place next to the piano. The way they leaned in toward one another, their eyes sharp under neatly coiffed hair as they watched their child find a suitable place at the barre, made it clear that they knew one another, were a tight group of territorial matriarchs, their lives dictated by dance. My mother looked uncertain about joining them, and before long she slipped out the door with a quick wave to me. She had never been one for obsessively watching every ballet class, unlike some of the mothers at Sadler's Wells. When Miss de Valois had made it clear that mothers were not welcome in class, she did not mind at all; it was a relief to her, I think, discharging her from a duty she knew she could not fulfill. And besides, Mother hardly ever stayed in London for more than a few nights before hurrying back to Ottery St. Mary and her familiar routines. She had few friends in London, just a young couple who had come to Devon for their honeymoon and happened to visit her shop. The Stewards had recently started their own dressmaking business and Mother became a source of guidance, mentoring them through the ups and downs of the trade. They reminded her of when she and my father were young, slowly seeking the confidence to make their venture a success, their complete belief in each other driving them forward.

I liked the independence my mother allowed me; I couldn't understand how anyone would put up with the constant presence of their mother, this specific breed of woman who never missed a yawn, a neglected meal, a sigh of frustration, a lazy arm in *à la seconde* at the barre. Lodging with Vivian, whose mother lacked the organization and ruthless focus required to meet the fierce role of the ballet mother, made our lives much simpler. Vivian's mother was always in a rush, making packed lunches for her large, loud crowd of boys, cleaning their rugby boots, checking they had done their schoolwork, dropping them off at training and games in muddy playing fields around the country. And there was Martha; for her, mothers were absent, vague ghosts in white lace peering out of silver picture frames, guardian angels who remained forever young and beautiful and silent.

Olga Preobrajenska appeared in the middle of the room, her stick banging against the floor. The chatter died away quickly; a girl in the corner glared at her mother, who hadn't finished her conversation with the woman beside her. Our teacher was famous, a Russian émigré, a celebrated ballerina of those final years before revolution had forced many to leave their country. She was tiny, not quite four foot ten, made even smaller by her rounded back.

But when she stretched out her body to demonstrate a *chassé* into *arabesque*, it was easy to see a glimmer of the great ballerina hidden beneath her age.

After the barre exercises, a fast and complicated medley of endless *dégagé en croix* and *petits battements*, we moved into the center. By then all the shawls and cardigans had been removed, a hot steam of sweat sticking to the mirror that lined the length of one wall. The heat was stifling, and the men had pushed open the windows as far as they would go. Preobrajenska demonstrated the exercises, singing the rhythm for the pianist: she was another émigré woman, older than our teacher and coping admirably with her uneven and chaotic musical expectations. I just about kept up with the others, even in the tricky *petit allegro* with wickedly fast *assemblés* and *soubresauts* in constantly changing direction, unusual flourishes of the arms on each *petit jeté*. The class ended with *fouetté* turns, all of us whipping our arms and legs around and around; I managed eighteen turns before I wobbled, more than many of the older dancers, I was pleased to realize. But still I felt out of place, a little clumsy and unfinished, my feet not springing off the ground fast enough, my arms dull and slow.

It would have been better if Vivian and Martha were here, but they weren't coming to Paris this summer. Martha had to help her father in the bookshop and Vivian's parents couldn't manage it, not with her three younger brothers to look after, unoccupied and looking for trouble during the long summer holiday. I don't think she minded too much, though, instead planning opportunities for assignations with Frank Ellis in dark cinemas and cabaret clubs. She was hoping her mother would simply be too busy to notice her absence. There were some dancers from the Vic-Wells here in Paris, but they were a tight group, and I hadn't yet been accepted into their ranks, though we were similar ages; Pamela May and Laurel Martyn were just two or three years my senior, while Margot Fonteyn and Molly Brown were older by only a few months. What they didn't realize was that I'd do anything to be one of them, that I watched them, copied the inflections of their laughter, stole the flippant jokes they threw between one another, emulated the lightness of their walks, the poise of their necks, the way they stood in fourth position whenever they were still. They owned what I was determined to possess.

Once I made it down the steep flight of steps, my legs shaking from the heat and the intensity of class, I found Mother waiting for me.

"You look like you've melted." She laughed, handing me a handkerchief from her purse. I took it gratefully, wiping away the sweat pooling in the hollows of my throat. "Lunch, then window shopping?" she asked, putting her arm through mine. We were staying at the YWCA on rue de Naples. For less than one pound a week, we had a room to ourselves. It was a short distance to the ballet studio in the mornings, an easy twenty-minute stroll to the displays at Galeries Lafayette in the afternoon, close enough to the Palais Garnier to tempt us to the box office in the evenings, pleading for any returned tickets.

On the ferry over, we had planned and plotted the structure of each day, Mother showing a lightness of heart that hardly ever revealed itself when we were at home in Ottery St. Mary, the routines of running the haberdashery demanding her full attention. My mother was well known in our part of Devon with her beautifully crafted hats, her shop brimming with color and fabric and the busy clatter of sewing machines. With just herself, three girls in the workshop, and Father to organize the orders and deliveries, the milliner's offered the rural lives of the Devonshire women a suitable hint of chic city style. Mother re-created the fashions she found in magazines and movies, making quick and rough sketches as she thumbed the pages of *Miss Modern* and *Vogue*. She recrafted the designs to suit the modest sensibilities of the schoolteacher, the vicar's wife, the farmer's daughter, the shop assistant. Every now and again, a woman would waltz in, newly moved to Devon from a busier, livelier county. A new wife or a young mother, they had no idea of the disapproving looks they would receive if they wore outfits too vibrant and sharp for the likes of the country. Mother knew how to steer them in the right direction, attracting them to the fashionable varieties of her hats, but without the rakish accessories that would make them deeply suspicious in the quiet villages of Devon. They always left satisfied, fitted for a deep green cloche hat that added a touch of mystery against the ordinary cut of their hair, or a wide-brimmed navy style to match their bag, or a set of different-colored lightweight hats that could be changed over each day to suit the rest of the outfit. My parents' millinery business did much better than the dressmaker across the street: while dresses were expensive and usually hidden under a coat, Mother had no trouble persuading her customers that owning multiple hats was an exciting and much cheaper way of revitalizing a well-worn outfit. She was the most practical person I knew, driven by order and reason and a swift packing-away of emotion into something useful and straightforward.

Yet underneath all that, she understood what women desired, how beauty could be captured in a cut of fabric, a posy of flowers, a double plait of ribbon intertwined through felt.

We drifted, arm in arm, toward Galeries Lafayette. The sun seemed to vibrate off the high windows that lined rue de Clichy, and it was a relief to find pockets of shade beneath the shadows of the tall cream buildings. Mother stopped a few times as we walked, her pencil moving quickly over the page of the notebook she always kept with her, in case inspiration struck.

This time two women caught her attention. They were standing above us on a tiny balcony, wrought iron interlaced with ivy and tiny blue flowers. Both women smoked as they talked, fast and high words that sounded nothing like the melody of the only French words I knew, our ballet language of *pliés* and *tendus* and *ronds de jambes*. But it was their heads that interested Mother: they were both wearing straw hats, but different to the ones she made. The crown and brim seemed to blend into one another, flat and wide, and the straw was painted a delicate blue. A light trim of silk forget-me-nots circled the crown, each petal so light it could be real. Mother's sketch flew across the page before we moved on, the sun finding us as we ventured farther down the street.

It was when we were standing before an elaborate display of hats beneath the dazzling glass dome of Galeries Lafayette that I heard my name. A familiar male voice, the French accent rolling across the word.

"Briar."

For a few seconds I could not turn around. I felt the weeks of silence dissolve, the weeks of waiting, of finally accepting that I was nothing to him, a conquest he could boast about to his friends. My anger and indifference vanished, and once more I was back in Cambridge, longing for him to kiss me.

Louis de Manton was right there in front of me, his arms stretched out wide. I didn't think he had noticed my mother, but I could sense her watching him, her head cocked to one side, wondering who this young man stepping toward her daughter could be. I hadn't mentioned him to her after Cambridge, preferring to pack him away, to forget the pain of his ghostlike silence. But now, as he embraced me, kissing me lightly on each cheek, I remembered the note I had sent him from London a week after we returned from Cambridge, the photograph tucked inside the envelope. A hot shock of shame spread across my cheeks.

And yet the way he looked at me now, a wide smile and bright eyes beneath those thick hooded eyebrows, it was easy to forget how I had worried, how I had heard that incessant voice telling me that I had scared him away with a photograph, revealed myself as the stereotype of the brazen dancer, an easy win.

"Briar," he said again, his hands resting on my shoulders as he pulled away from the greeting. "What brings you to Paris? What good luck to have met you like this!"

I had told him I would be coming to Paris. As we had eaten cake by the river in Cambridge, we'd whispered to each other about adventures in his home city, how he was going to show me the Seine at night, how we'd picnic in the Jardin du Luxembourg, eat bread and cheese in tiny cafés in the streets of Montmartre. It seemed that all those stolen hours together had been wiped away as soon as I left Cambridge. With my mother watching, I could only answer his question as if nothing had happened at all.

"I am here to train. I take class each day at the Salle Wacker." I stopped, taking a step toward Mother. "Louis, let me introduce my mother. We are here together for the next few weeks."

His face shifted a little as he turned to Mother. As a young man faced with an older woman, he knew he needed to charm; it was as though he was recalibrating. "*Enchanté de vous rencontrer.*" He took a step toward her, repeating the same tactile greeting he had given me, this time with more formality, a solemn, sensible respect. "I met your daughter in Cambridge. It was such a pleasure to see the performances at the new Arts Theatre. In fact, I met Maynard Keynes just after it opened, back in February. We were lucky that he decided to bring his love of ballet to our little town."

I watched Mother. Despite how he had ignored me for more than two months, I wanted her to like him. He had been mine for three weeks in May and now, as he stood here among the glamour of the hat displays, the handbags that hung like glossy fruit from trees and the glistening glass bottles of perfume, I thought he could be mine again. That perhaps we could start again, create those Paris stories we had crafted along the banks of the river Cam, prove that the photograph was the prologue to romance, not a foolish gesture of my unsuitableness for the nephew of a French diplomat.

Mother smiled, a wary, guarded smile. She turned to me, her eyes searching, trying to find some sign of who this boy was to me. I smiled back, trying my best to give away nothing. "Lovely to meet you too," she replied. "Are you shopping for something in particular?" She gestured into the atrium, her arms taking in the colorful displays of fashion and female accessories. My mother always knew how to find out about people through the simplest of questions. She did it all the time in the shop: a seemingly innocent question about their day, their drive over, their plans later, revealing all she needed to know about the type of hat she would offer them. As always, everything she did had purpose; she never wasted time, never indulged in empty conversation.

Louis nodded. "My mother's birthday. She always asks for the same perfume, but this year I want to get her a surprise. I was thinking a scarf, or a hat perhaps."

This was the right direction for him to take. Mother's smile relaxed and she put her arm around me. "We can help you with that, can't we, Briar?"

I nodded. "Oh yes. I think I told you Mother owns a millinery shop. She can tell you about all the best styles."

If he had forgotten that part of our conversations, he didn't let it show. "*Magnifique.* That would be wonderful."

The three of us turned back to the hat display, Mother pointing out the different styles, the quality of the fabrics, the recency of the fashions. She had no trouble naming the Parisian designers and why a woman such as Louis's mother might be interested in wearing their creations. She jumped directly to the most expensive designs, knowing intuitively that Louis's mother would expect nothing less. She was right, of course. I remembered Louis describing his mother as a woman obsessed with image and appearance, of fitting into the right circles of Paris society, hosting salons, agonizing over the perfect guest list for her dinner parties. And so, he nodded with interest as Mother told him about the surrealist designs of Madame Agnès, the simple shapes of Coco Chanel, the colorful flowers of Lilly Daché, the promising new designs of Rose Valois.

In the end he decided on a cream pillbox hat, elegant with its simple spray of gauze. He asked us to wait while he put in the order with the shop assistant—for Louis de Manton wanted to take us out for tea.

By the time Mother and I returned to our room at the YWCA, we were both a little in love with Louis. He had taken us to a café on a tree-lined street close to Palais Garnier, ordering us iced coffees and sliced baguettes, small plates of tomatoes dripping in oil, and piles of deep red ham. When Mother agreed to letting him order us all small glasses of red wine, followed by the novel indulgence of a Kir Royale, I knew she approved of him. And my own doubts had disappeared, his neglect forgiven, transformed into something justifiable, a sensible, rational decision considering we might never have been able to see one another again. When he had said goodbye at the end of rue de Naples, pressing his hand into mine, I had forgotten about the photograph. Instead, I felt in control once again, a beautiful girl desired and adored.

As July drifted into August, the hot streets of Paris emptying of its residents for the summer holiday, Mother and I knew we too must soon leave. Three weeks of feeling as though my body was permanently alight with excitement would have to, inevitably, come to an end: the morning sweat of ballet class; window shopping with Mother in the summer heat; dinners with Louis as the sun set over the rooftops of Paris; walks through the most romantic cobbled streets, Mother trusting Louis enough now to give me a later and later curfew: it would all disappear too soon. And yet I tried to ignore that lingering feeling of doubt: Louis's family remained an aloof, enigmatic mystery. He had never invited me home to meet any of them. It was easy, though, to push this to the back of my mind, convince myself he was simply keeping me for himself, waiting for the right time to introduce me to his parents. Mother muttered about it every few days, but I quickly changed the subject.

On the final weekend before our ferry back to England, Louis secured the two of us invitations to a garden party at Villa Trianon, a house on the edges of the park of the Palais de Versailles. There lived Lady Mendl, the famous Elsie de Wolfe, who the previous year had been named by Parisian experts as the best-dressed woman in the world. She was nearly eighty but could be found leading the dancing at her extravagant parties until the early hours of the morning.

I had read about her in fashion magazines, her garden fetes and *bals masqués* attracting the brightest and best of society. She was indiscriminating in her choice of guests, and people at both extremes of the political spectrum flocked to her drawing rooms: dancers, musicians, artists, movie stars, and even royalty. She was married to Sir Charles Mendl, the British press attaché in Paris, but they didn't live together. It was well known that Lady Mendl had lived openly with the literary agent and theatre producer Elisabeth Marbury until her death three years ago.

The invitation to Lady Mendl's garden party felt like a bizarre dream, as though I had been transported into the pages of those fashion magazines Mother piled high on the desk in Alice Woods Hats.

"Don't get too excited," Mother told me with a wry smile the night before the party. "These things are always much less enjoyable than how you imagine them, especially when you don't know many people there."

I refused to let her words dull my mood, her sensible wisdom too mundane for a final weekend in Paris. But I was nervous. I would know only Louis and a few other dancers whose invitations had come through the artist Theyre Lee-Elliott. Recently having gained fame from his Speedbird logo for Imperial Airways, the artist had taken an interest in two of the ballet company, Margot and Pamela. I had seen him picking them up after ballet class, him and a quiet young man called Patrick Furse, who was plainly in love with Margot. They would be together in a tight-knit group, but I had no one except Louis. If he left me, I would feel very alone.

It took little time to get ready after Saturday-morning ballet class, and I waited impatiently in the cool of my bedroom, regretting my eagerness. I had rushed back to the YWCA after class, the sweat dripping down my back. It was a relief that there was no queue for the bathroom. Deciding on a dress had preoccupied my week, Louis not particularly helpful, reassuring me that I could wear whatever I wanted as long as it was fashionable. A party that started at five in the afternoon and was likely to seep into the night, even the next morning, was difficult to dress for. Mother and I considered garden party frocks, summer pastels and frills that would look stunning in the light of the afternoon. But we dismissed them quickly, realizing such a dress would be ridiculous as soon as the sun set and the dancing started. And an evening dress seemed too much for traveling through Paris in the middle of the day, even with Louis there to guard against the suspicious stares of the fashionable Paris women, who would never let themselves be seen in the wrong dress at the wrong time of day. Eventually, we found a dress in a boutique on rue Taitbout, a simple silk slip in the lightest gray, thin straps barely visible across the shoulders and the hem falling to the ankles. Mother made a headpiece for me, scraps of silk and lace in cream, gray, silver, and white, all scrunched together into the prettiest roses that hovered above my ear, a band of white around my head holding it all in place and a few imitation pearls sewn into the flowers.

When Louis came to pick me up, he nodded approvingly and told me I looked perfect, kissing me on both cheeks with the warm formality of which Mother approved. Our outfits complemented one another: he wore a light cream suit with a white-gray tie, a pale hat banded by a silver ribbon.

I could not, Louis told me in the taxi to the train station, come to Paris without visiting Versailles. While Villa Trianon was on the outskirts of the Parc de Versailles, he thought he might be able to sneak us into the grounds of the palace through a hidden path in Lady Mendl's vegetable garden. I did long to see Versailles, those halls and salons and gardens that had provided the setting for Louis XIV's ballet lessons and court performances, the very rooms where the Sun King's dancing master had created the five positions of dance. And this, too, was my chance to see the architecture that had inspired the famous designs of Marius Petipa's *The Sleeping Beauty* in the 1890s. The choreographer had commissioned five designers for the ballet, each with their own distinct style. But it was Matvei Shishkov's designs for Act III, an apotheosis entitled *Helios en costume de Louis XIV, éclairé par le soleil entouré des fees*, that mimicked the wonders of Versailles, complete with a Sun King, baroque fairies painted on a clouded backdrop, the carved wood boiserie a nod to the Grand Trianon. I imagined a theatre set of brilliant opulence, gold, the shine of mirrors, baroque architecture that danced in intricate flourishes. Mother shook her head and smiled indulgently at me when I told her, at the last minute, that I would rather visit the palace like a regular tourist than go to the party at Villa Trianon. The nerves and too much waiting were affecting me.

"You'll have a lovely time. Don't listen to all my doom and gloom. You know I'm not one for a party. But you, my darling Briar, you'll be the belle of the ball."

I did, however, notice that she gave me an extra-long hug as I left with Louis.

When we arrived at the station, Louis waved at a group waiting farther down the platform. We hurried to join them. There were two of his Cambridge friends, as well as Theyre Lee-Elliott and Patrick Furse. While Theyre was in his thirties and seemed to know everyone and everything, Patrick was my age. I liked his quiet watchfulness, so different from the noise and chatter of the others. Behind us appeared the other dancers from the Vic-Wells. They smiled at me, Margot Fonteyn giving me a quick hug, and I started to relax. Mother was happy to let me go without her when she found out that Pamela and Laurel were coming, two older girls who could keep an eye on me, as well as Molly and Margot. They had shaken off Margot's mother, Mrs. Hookham—or the Black Queen, as everyone seemed to call her—who was usually reluctant to let her daughter out of her sight.

In the train, Louis drew me to him, the formality he showed in front of Mother disappearing. There was a frivolity to everything we did and said. The hot sun blazed in through the window, streaking the arms and shoulders of the women, bare now we had thrown off the shawls and shrugs that had seemed necessary traveling through Paris. Louis took out the invitation, a thick cream card with an embossed green border. On the back was a map of how to get to Villa Trianon, a red line scratching out the route from the Arc de Triomphe to Versailles, little sketches of Rolls-Royce motorcars lining the road. Louis could not, he explained to me with a laugh, persuade his father to let him have the car for today. He was not trusted to return it in one piece.

Villa Trianon was like nothing I had ever seen before. When we arrived at the house, the taxi pulling up outside the black iron gates, it was as though a curtain had risen on the most elaborate of theatre sets. A stone wall extended from the portico of the villa, flowers and vines tumbling over the wall and railings. Despite the solidity of the stone, it seemed to me like an optical illusion, paints and paper and fabric rather than the real building blocks of a home.

There was something fragile about the entrance, as if it was a castle that might vanish in smoke behind the falling curtain of a stage.

A jazz band was playing outside the *pavillon de musique* designed, Louis told me, in the style of the Louis XV period. The music was light and easy, syncopated rhythms of violin and guitar drifting between the guests steadily flowing in through the wrought iron gates. Topiary shapes patterned the lawn and the most delicate French furniture decorated the terrace, tables set with white flowers and moss-green foliage. I stepped warily through this splendor, these people in their fine dresses like costumes from an opera, afraid that if I looked too closely it would reveal itself to be a makeshift theatre crafted in papier-mâché.

We made our way farther into the garden, gathering cut-glass coupes of champagne, the sun lighting up the silver trays and adding an unearthly sparkle to the scene. Elsie de Wolfe had performed on Broadway for many years, and it was as though she had brought the theatre with her, all color-matched in shades of blue. I could imagine sketches of the villa and the *pavillon de musique* pinned to the wall of a theatre design room: the deep blue window frames, neat borders of summer bedding around fine *arabesques* of water that sprayed from the fountain, sculptures that danced in frozen ivory stone like a corps de ballet. The large lawn, or *tapis vert* as Louis called it, was bordered by gravel pathways and simple white flower beds. A ring of trees created the illusion of an amphitheatre, with clandestine romantic paths leading away from the center as though to a secret backstage world.

Louis led me toward the house, calling out greetings to people he knew along the way. It was an effort to stop myself clinging to his arm, like a *pas de deux* out of time.

In the broad entrance hall, I blinked at the tall vases of cut flowers interlaced with foliage. It was only their deep perfume that convinced me they were real, not elaborate silk props for a play. As we walked across the hall, the sound of my heels was muffled by a long rug, its pattern woven in countless shades of blue. It was a space entirely unencumbered by clutter, so different from all the houses I had lived in where empty corners were instantly lost to the mess of coats, shoes, bags, piles of books and magazines that no one knew where to put. All this space and air—it was like an empty stage waiting for dancers to emerge out of the wings.

"Welcome, my dear Louis." I heard a voice ring out behind us. Even without the New York accent, I would have known that this was Lady Mendl. All in white with a navy sash around her slim waist, it was easy to see why she was called the best-dressed woman in the world. She came toward us with delicate steps, her feet small and tidy in low-heeled shoes. A little dog scrabbled around her ankles, waiting for her with childlike obedience. Her eyes flickered as she took us both in, her gaze lingering over me a little longer. At nearly eighty, she looked remarkable. I had read about her morning routine of exercises, walking on her hands, cartwheels and yoga-style acrobatics that prepared her for the busy schedule of her days. Apparently, she spent an hour each morning on a complex array of face creams and makeup, the effects of which were tastefully displayed right now. On anyone else, the lavender tint of her coiffured hair would look eccentric; but on Lady Mendl it was a work of art.

She kissed Louis on both cheeks. "Please enjoy the party. I am delighted that you could come." She turned to me, her smile warm. I tried not to shift my feet and wriggle in my dress, but it was difficult wondering whether she was judging the cheap pearls in my headpiece and the lack of any recognizable designer for my dress.

"Lady Mendl, this is my friend Briar Woods." Louis took a sideways step toward me, his fingers finding the back of my arm. "She is a dancer at the Vic-Wells and is here in Paris to train at the Salle Wacker."

"I knew you were a dancer just by looking at you, my dear. It's the way you ballerinas stand, feet turned out and your backs so straight. I never managed that poise in my dancing days."

I found myself giving a little bow. "It is wonderful to be here. Your house is gorgeous."

"Thank you, my dear. Now you two go off and enjoy yourselves. And," she added to Louis as she moved away from us, "tell your uncle that he owes me an invitation to dinner next time I'm in London."

"He would be delighted," Louis replied, his voice rolling over the words with delicious French emphasis. "All of London misses you."

"I am not sure that is actually true," Louis whispered to me as we made our way back out to the brightness of the garden. "Rumors are that Wallis Simpson stayed here recently, and you know how the London elite feel about her." I nodded, but this was far beyond any social circle I could possibly hope to understand.

Outside, we joined the others on the terrace. The conversation moved too quickly around me, and I found myself wishing that Martha and Vivian were here, that we could escape into the gardens and explore, dance wildly and childishly among the topiary and the statues and the fountain. But here I must be older than I really was, find a sophistication I knew I did not possess. As the ebb and flow of guests around us drove onward toward the evening, the music grew, and the champagne started to flow faster, the movements of everyone around me merging into one organic dance. I realized I was getting drunk.

"Come on. Let me show you inside," Louis said, standing and pulling me to my feet. I laughed, dragging myself up, the music of the jazz band reaching an unsteady climax before falling to a temporary hush. "Elsie has the most beautiful bathroom you have ever seen."

I followed him inside, his hand holding mine. It felt as though I was bridled to him, and I surrendered myself to the direction he took me. There was laughter coming from every room in the house, great peals ringing out, and the sound of champagne corks popping. We walked through a bedroom. A plush carpet stretched out beneath an iron clamp bed and mirrors with intricately carved frames set in white paneling. I caught a glimpse of my reflection as we moved through the room, an unsteady figure I barely recognized as myself. My eyes looked large, smudged lines of black kohl too dark against my skin, and my lips were a shocking red. I smiled at my reflection, but all I saw was a grimace, a smear of lipstick staining my teeth.

"This is the room everyone really wants to see." He led me onward into an adjoining room. At first glance it looked like a salon. There was a corner fireplace with a mantel of marble in shining black and green. Antique French furniture was dotted around the room and paintings hung within the moss-colored boiserie panels. But then I saw the bath. I heard myself giggle nervously and Louis turned to me in surprise. I was disappointing him, it seemed, with my childish response to such splendor.

It was the most extravagant bathroom I had ever seen, ridiculous even in its beauty. The same black-and-green marble seemed to throb around the gleaming white enamel, and a bath tidy tray was stacked with soaps, jars of bath salts, fluffy white towels, a magazine with crumpled edges, and a book.

With a sudden pang of uncertainty, I felt far away from Louis. I didn't know how to react to this room, whether I should laugh again or coo enthusiastically about the artists and designers I knew nothing about. Once again, I longed for Martha and Vivian, for our whispered laughter, the way we washed each other's hair, massaged each other's scalps, wrapped ourselves together in easy, familiar tenderness.

I went to the window, looking out from between yellow curtains. Night was falling and the party was in full swing, revelers dancing along to the band, the wine still flowing. Food had been brought out at last and laid in a stunning display on a long table beneath the terrace. There were tiered cakes, trays of sandwiches, cut meats, thick rounds of cheese, and jellies and mousses wobbling like fat balloons. Seeing the food made me realize how hungry I was. I had drunk too much, and my head was light, my legs uncertain.

Louis came up behind me and put his arms around my waist. I could feel the heat of his body as he pulled me to him. "How about we stay up here a little longer?" he whispered into my ear, his breath warm against my neck. His legs pressed against mine and I could feel the damp sweat behind my knees bleeding into the silk of my dress.

Before I could think what to reply, we heard a giggle followed by a snort coming from behind a scarlet Chinese screen.

"Who is there?" Louis called out, letting me go and striding toward the screen. I followed him. Right there in front of us, positioned awkwardly on top of a *chaise percée*, were a man and woman. Their clothes were scattered around them, the crumpled silk of the woman's dress glowing in the dim light from the electric candle bulb on the wall. The man's trousers were around his ankles, his shirt open and his tie thrown off, tangled up in the metal chain of the toilet flush. We could not see the woman's face; it was hidden in the shoulder of her lover, her naked back shaking with laughter, the flesh of her buttocks yielding under the man's grip.

I turned and ran, getting out of the room as fast as I could, down the stairs and out onto the terrace. The party swelled around me, and I stopped alongside one of the catering tables, catching my breath next to a giant bowl of dessert, raspberries poking out between the engorged crevices of the cream.

Louis caught up with me. He was laughing, a wild exhilaration in his eyes. "Why did you run away so quickly?" His voice was too loud, his hands grabbing and pinching at my waist. "We could have stayed to watch. They showed no objection."

He was joking, but I did not want to hear it. That photograph came back to me with a heavy lurch, how I had revealed a part of myself to him that I wished so much I could take back. Looking up at him now, I realized he did not know me at all. He had created a different version of me, a dancer with her flexible legs and easy smile, who would dance and perform and expose all parts of herself to the world. A woman he might pluck and consume.

There was nowhere I could go to get away from him. No one would help me, or understand why I longed to leave, to return to the safety of the YWCA, my mother waiting for me, wondering how

I was enjoying the night. I had thought I wanted to be the sophisticated, glamorous dancer, perching on the knees of men and flirting with nonchalant ease. But I did not know how to be that person.

I grabbed another glass of champagne and walked away from the terrace. Sinking farther into the garden and away from the lights of the band and the candlelit terrace, I thought that if I could find somewhere to lie down, to rest my head away from everyone else, I would be all right.

The path, a meandering gravel walkway lined by thorny rosebushes and trees with trunks choked beneath tumbling ivy, led me toward the Parc de Versailles. Absurdly, I imagined making it all the way to the palace, finding a bedroom with a pastel pink bed, falling asleep to the sound of the jazz band far away in the distance. But instead the path came to an end, terminated by a hard marble seat and potted topiary spikes.

With my hands grabbing at the cold marble, I sank down, my head swimming and my legs too weak to hold myself upright any longer. I had never felt so tired before, never longed for sleep the way I did now. The air had become thicker and heavier, as though a huge hand was pressing me down. I mumbled incoherently to myself: perhaps this was how Princess Aurora had felt as the forest groaned and grew, the prick of her finger sending her to sleep.

As my head fell back against the seat, I felt myself wrenched up again. Hands reached around me, lifting me back up and pulling me onto the warm bulk of a body. Louis had followed, finding me just when I wanted to fall asleep and let the night disappear without me.

He kissed me, his mouth strong and wet against the champagne that had stained my lips. Lifting my dress, his hands rose higher, grabbing at my thighs so hard I felt I might bruise. I shifted away from him, forcing myself awake. Although I tried to close my legs and stop the steady ascent of his hands, he jerked my legs open again, his elbow digging into my knee. Jazz music scratched in the distance and the sounds of the guests morphed into faint shrieks and cries.

"Please, Louis, let's return to the party." The whispered words faded on my lips.

Face pressed against my chest, mouth finding my skin, Louis didn't want to hear me. As he pushed his body into me, pressing the breath out of my lungs, for a moment I thought I might die. But I did not. I did not even resist. It was easier to let the alcohol swallow me, like a forest of trees growing up and up in a darkening mass.

I fell asleep.

A lavender pink glow spread across the line of trees. Louis was kneeling beside me, his face all concern and tenderness. The sky rocked above me.

"You are awake at last. Your mother is going to kill me when she knows I let you drink all that champagne." I shifted away from him, the hard marble of the seat digging into my back. My mouth was dry and acidic, my head throbbing.

"What time is it?" I asked, my voice coming out quiet and muffled.

"Time for us to get in a taxi. There are no trains now, so I will just have to persuade the driver to take us all the way to Paris."

On the journey home, we were both silent. When the taxi dropped me off on rue de Naples, Louis stayed inside the car. This time I knew I would never see him again.

SUMMER ENDED AND WE RETURNED TO ROUTINE: bus journeys from Belgravia to Clerkenwell, ballet class to start each day, rehearsals, costume fittings, performances on our familiar Sadler's Wells stage. It was like pulling on a thick warm sweater and feeling safe once again. Only in moments of quiet, in the gaps between class and rehearsals, did I find myself transported back to Paris, Versailles, the marble bench at the end of the path. After Paris, I spent a couple of weeks in Devon before the draw of London, Vivian, and Martha became too hard to resist. Rehearsals started in late August and the regular pattern of the days resumed. As the heat of the summer died, so did my memories of that night. Nightmares that woke me in a flush of feverish sweat gradually drifted away.

With the October winds and deep orange leaves starting to blow around us, I tried to persuade myself that I had finally left Paris and Louis de Manton firmly behind me.

We were preparing to perform a new ballet by Frederick Ashton, called *Nocturne*. The theatre pages expressed excited anticipation and Vivian and I tore through her mother's copies of *The Bystander* to find articles about the Vic-Wells Ballet. Ninette de Valois's *Prometheus* was about to premiere, and *The Bystander* announced that the audience's enthusiasm made our Sadler's Wells Theatre "one of the most alive places in London." I had been cast as a reveler in *Nocturne*: we were twelve dancers who wove our movements around the central characters. Martha was a reveler too, but Vivian was a masker, one of six dancers who seemed to act as a strange chorus, offering a mildly scathing yet ornamental comment on the narrative. I had felt a cold wrench of disappointment when the cast list had gone up on the noticeboard outside the ballet studio. Martha had just shrugged when I'd asked her if she wished she had a bigger part, like Vivian's. There were twelve of us revelers, while only four women performed the masker role, their long arms encased in stylish black silk gloves. I wanted to know why Vivian had been singled out, but I said nothing. None of us ever dared question the cast lists.

Nocturne was about a poor flower seller cast aside by a rich young man in favor of a sophisticated woman. The leading role was Margot Fonteyn's. I found myself obsessively watching her in rehearsals; there was something tragic about the way she portrayed the character of the poor young girl: the line of her neck, the slender curve of her arms, even the way she placed each foot lightly as if her shoes were made of satin alone, no hardness left in their leather and paste. While Ashton seemed to be trying to create a vision of nostalgia for a romanticized poverty, a balletic version of tragedy and loss, when Margot danced she made it real. Her flower girl was not an unrealistic muse. Rather, her sadness and confusion when the young man left her for the rich young woman cut right to how devastating it must feel, refusing an idealized interpretation of destitution. But this still didn't stop Ashton from shouting at her in rehearsals, complaining loudly to Miss de Valois about Margot's "pats of butter" for feet.

Martha found a copy of the ballet's scenario, written by Edward Sackville-West, and we took it back to her flat one evening in mid-October. Vivian joined us late; an unsuccessful dinner at Quaglino's with a boy she'd met at Cambridge, she told us when she arrived. Frank Ellis, it seemed, was no longer a prospect. After an intense summer, he had started ignoring her in class, disappearing too quickly at the end of rehearsals before she could speak to him. Eventually, the rumors spread that he was seeing another dancer over at the Ballet Club, and she forced herself to forget him as best she could. She'd even asked Miss de Valois to try to avoid the two of them dancing together in the next ballet. Miss de Valois had simply raised an eyebrow and told her to keep her drama out of the rehearsal studio. Now, with a string of largely unsuccessful dates, Vivian was doing her best to distract herself.

"He wouldn't stop talking about his mother," she said as she kicked off her shoes, pointing and flexing those slender feet, the bones of her ankles taut beneath her stockings. "I learned all about her horses. One of them just won something, apparently. Though it was hard to tell whether Madame Miriam was the name of the horse or the woman."

"Well, you're here now," I said, throwing open the blanket for her to join us on the sofa. Martha and I were burrowed together on the creaking brown leather cushions, lodged between two towering bookshelves. Brackley Books, the shop in the building below, had spread itself up into the flat, and books were piled on every surface, boxes stacked haphazardly in the corners. Downstairs, new publications jostled for space among Mr. Brackley's favorite old classics, and I had seen young writers subtly push their books forward to replace large leather volumes of Trollope and Dickens, only for Mr. Brackley to reverse them again as soon as they left.

"How did you get away?" This was Martha's default remark when talking about men, an assumption that we should always be looking for an escape route.

"Oh, the usual. Told him I had to get up early for ballet class." She sank down beside me, her long legs folded beneath her. I could feel the solid press of her toes against my thigh. "I had to make a swift exit before he launched into an account of his early-morning rowing program."

"Don't be too harsh," Martha said, laughing. "His rowing shorts are the equivalent of our sweaty leotards. You didn't seem to mind Frank's tights, did you?" I elbowed Martha and shook my head. It was obvious to me that Vivian was not ready to joke about Frank Ellis, sweaty tights or not. When Martha said his name, she grabbed at her hair, pulling anxiously on the long white strands that molted like the fragile finery of dandelion seeds.

Martha opened a bottle of wine, something sticky and sweet she had found balanced behind one of the many stacks of newspapers that her father refused to throw away. I sipped at the wine slowly, but it didn't sit right. My stomach clawed at me, the nerves I had been feeling since Paris refusing to leave me alone tonight. Just when I thought I had forgotten Louis, something returned to bring him back to me again. Tonight, it was Vivian, how hard she was trying not to think about Frank any longer, plunging immediately into dinner dates even if the men were dull and self-obsessed.

Delius's music, the score to *Nocturne*, was playing on the gramophone in the corner of the room, a mournful tone poem called "Paris, Song of a Great City." Perhaps that too was what unsettled me tonight, the sounds of Delius's yearning for the romance of a mysterious city, the slow opening notes that grew into the frenetic fanfare of loud Parisian nightlife. The lyricism of the music playing right now seemed to evoke the first stages of love. I found myself wanting to scream, to end this unreal romance, to tell the ghostly lovers to stop, to go home back to the safety of their own beds. But then the music shifted again, returning to the slow opening, as though Paris was awakening for the routine of the morning. I remembered how I had turned away from Louis in the taxi drive back to Mother, watching Paris yawning awake and the cold midnight blue of night fading into day. I don't know what I'd expected, but my feelings were hurt when Louis did not reach for my hand.

Martha flicked aside Sackville-West's scenario and picked up a copy of *The Bystander*. It was this week's magazine, so I hadn't had a chance to read it yet. Vivian's mother kept them hidden in her handbag until she squeezed out enough reading time between transporting her chaotic sons across London. She must get her shilling's worth, she told us, stuffing the magazine back into her bag when we tried to extract it from her too soon.

"You don't like the wine?" Martha asked me, the magazine falling open to a list of London restaurants. I had barely touched my drink; the sweetness was cloying at my gums. "I can see if we've got something else."

"No, please don't worry. The wine's okay. I just don't feel like drinking much tonight."

I still hadn't found a way to tell Martha about what had happened with Louis. I kept remembering those words of advice she had given me in Cambridge, how insistent she'd been that I not let him dig his way too far into my heart. There was shame, I found now, in admitting how much I had fallen. Vivian knew a version of what had happened, a hollow story about the attentive Louis de Manton falling silent as soon as I left Paris. But I could not tell her the rest, how the trees had seemed to close around me in the gardens of Villa Trianon, a fairy tale transformed into nightmare.

She had guessed some of it, I thought. It was the way she looked at me when she believed I could not see. Living together, sharing a room at her family's home in Belgravia, it was not easy to hide from one another. We knew each other like the closest of sisters. There was love, and trust, but also a wary observation, the fear one of us would outdo the other, become better, more talented, more desired by our ballet masters and mistresses. That tension was building as we found our place in the ballet company. Vivian was growing ever more beautiful, and I knew it wouldn't be long before she surpassed me. In ballet class this morning, we had danced side by side in the *grand allegro* from the corner, our bodies moving in perfect synchronicity. But at the end of the routine, a *piqué arabesque* held in stillness before running off to join the others at the edges of the room, I had wobbled, my torso pushed off balance and my leg bending beneath me. Vivian had smiled sympathetically at me through the reflection of the mirror, and for a second, I had hated her. She had balanced in the most elegant of *arabesques*, Miss Moreton calling out a rare comment of coveted praise. My dancing went unnoticed.

I watched her all the time with an ugly inadequacy, wondering jealously whether she felt the same about me. Every day I seemed to search for more cracks in her perfection. It was how I could tell that Frank Ellis still meant something to her, that she was not ready to forget about him and move on, that her attempts at seeing other men were brave but perfunctory.

My friendship with Martha was different, though, another sort of bond I could not quite define. At times I found myself a little shy around her, catching myself when I was about to blurt out trivial nonsense, recrafting my words into something that would entertain her, impress her. I realized I blushed when she caught me watching her too closely. She'd laugh and squeeze my waist, asking me if I was coveting some new shoes or dress or leotard of hers. But it was not that, not at all. Instead, it was as though there was a part of her I wanted for myself, but whether to possess or to become I did not know.

Her hands had stopped flicking through the magazine. Peering closely at the page, she scrutinized a row of photographs. "Isn't this the boy you met in Cambridge?" Martha's voice seemed to reach me on a delay, her words moving too slowly for me to process.

I turned to her, my brow furrowed. "What boy?"

Of course I knew what boy. But I needed time: time to steel myself before looking across to the open magazine in Martha's hands. Perhaps it would just be the society pages, Louis photographed at a ball or reception. But I knew I was wrong: there was no denying the pictures of women in white dresses I had glimpsed on the open page.

She thrust the page before my eyes. "See for yourself. He definitely didn't seem engaged when we met him in Cambridge."

And there he was, Louis de Manton captured in respectable black and white on his wedding day.

DE MANTON—WEBSTER

Louis de Manton, only son of M. and Mme. Antoine de Manton of rue Bellart, Paris, and Esme Webster, eldest daughter of Sir Bertram and Lady Webster of Hillstead Manor, Hampshire, were married at St. Paul's, Knightsbridge.

Two smiling faces in wedding clothes were framed above the text, just one happy couple of many, printed on the double-page spread of wedding announcements. If I let my eyes blur a little, Louis and his beautiful wife became anonymous strangers, frozen in monochrome. But Louis was staring right at the camera, his eyes dark under those thick eyebrows. His hair looked neat, much more so than usual, with a sharp part across the side of his head. I blinked my eyes closed, trying to forget the last time I had seen him, when the wildness of the night had scattered his hair in disordered strands about his forehead. His wife, the new Mrs. de Manton, was turned slightly from the camera, her body close to Louis's as though she was trying to hide behind him. One arm was thrown behind her, fiddling with the pins, perhaps, that held her veil into place. She was very small, petite, with no visible chest, her dress rising in exquisite lace around her throat. Holding her bouquet high, she looked uncomfortable in front of the camera, a shy smile hovering at her lips.

"God, she looks dull," Martha said. "Why on earth did he marry her?"

"An English title, probably," said Vivian, leaning forward now to get a closer look. "An English virgin he can take home to Paris. She'll be the final prize of his Cambridge education."

Pushing the magazine back to Martha, I left a clammy fingerprint on the page. They were right. She was the perfect wife for Louis: a shy little girl with a baronet for a father; a girl who hid her face and blushed prettily; who wore dresses that covered every inch of her flesh; who would never send a man a nude photograph of herself; who would never drink too much at a party, lose control, fall asleep in a forest at the edge of a palace. Instead, Esme Webster would have been invited to meet his mother, paraded proudly to all her important friends in the salons of Paris. No hiding in the dark for Esme, seduced with false romance and dangerous wine.

I couldn't breathe. My cheeks felt hollow and slack, and I thought I might be sick. The cushions of the sofa crowded me, and a hot sweat dripped down my spine. Standing up too fast, I felt my head spin painfully. My legs shook as I moved to the window, and I pressed my forehead against the cool glass to steady myself.

Martha was right behind me, as was Vivian. I could feel the light touch of their hands against my back.

"Did you ever see him again? After Cambridge?" Martha asked me as I turned around, my eyes blinded by tears.

Vivian shifted uneasily. She knew that I had seen him in Paris. Martha would not like it that I hadn't confided in her.

"Yes. I did. I bumped into him in Paris and we saw each other a few times." I couldn't lie, but I didn't want to talk about it. It wouldn't make it any easier.

"And he never mentioned he had a fiancée?"

"It never came up. I don't know why he should have done."

"Briar." It was Vivian, her voice calm, tender. She pulled her arm around me and pressed me to her. We walked back to the sofa, Vivian and Martha guiding me like a child. "It's okay. You can tell us if something happened. You and Louis were so close in Cambridge."

I was silent, the gnawing pain in my stomach filtering out the confusion and fear. It was only when Martha took my hand, squeezing it in that reassuring way she had, that I decided to tell them everything.

And so, with a feeling of overwhelming release, I did. The way he had charmed me and my mother, the meals in Paris cafés, the walks along the Seine, how interested he was in ballet, music, art. All the things that had drawn me to him. I told them about the party at Villa Trianon, the ridiculous bathroom and how I had longed for my two best friends, the couple wrapped around one another on the hidden toilet seat, the champagne, the jazz, my fraught journey through the garden. How it stopped at the end of the path, Versailles and its parks and palaces behind me. How I woke in the morning, my body frozen, my legs bruised, a dull ache spreading between my thighs, blood spotting the back of my dress. How I hid the dress from Mother, throwing it into the bins at the back of the YWCA when I knew she was asleep, the vigorous way I washed myself in the bathroom until the water ran cold. How Mother had interpreted my silence as tiredness, or sadness at leaving behind Paris and Louis and the ballet classes at the top of the Salle Wacker. How even when we were back in Devon and the aching silence continued, she persuaded me to fill my hollowness with household chores and exercise and helping in the shop, until she willingly sent me back to London to cheer myself up with routine. How, for the first time ever, Mother's sensible reason and order had failed me. She had not taught me about the fickleness of men; she had not guided me when I fell.

Finally, we were silent. The familiar sounds of St. Martin's Lane spilled down Cecil Court and up into the little room above the bookshop. Here we held on to one another, the sweet, sticky wine bottle forgotten.

"When did you have your last monthly?" Martha whispered the words, a question I had refused to ask myself for weeks.

I pulled my knees up toward me, pressing my head against my hands. There was no need to say anything more.

* * *

The next morning in ballet class, I only got as far as *ronds de jambe* and *battements fondu* at the barre before I ran out of the room to be sick. It was as though the pain in my stomach had finally released itself after my three-month attempt to suppress the growth inside me. In the dressing room I turned sideways and scrutinized myself in the mirror. My stomach muscles were strong, firm, flat. But, as I ran my hands over my belly, I felt a change, a small swelling just below the line of my waistband.

When Martha found me, I was kneeling in front of the mirror, my leotard stripped off and discarded beside me. Naked, I clawed at myself, my nails digging angrily into the skin of my stomach. She grabbed me, throwing a towel over my shoulders. Forcing me to sit, she knelt and wrapped her arms about my legs.

"It's going to be okay," she told me, those deep round eyes staring intently. "You'll go home to Devon until this is over, and then you'll be back here with us as if it never happened. You'll be dancing again, and all evidence of Louis will be gone from your life forever."

MARTHA'S WORDS CAME TRUE, at least for a while. By the end of 1937 I was dancing once again, each season progressing with new ballets, new audiences, new opportunities to perform. But it had been a slow journey back to normality, and I found myself a little afraid of my own body, how fast it could swell and shrink with a terrifying mind of its own. I did not feel in control of my skin and still that unease lingered, more than two years after returning to dance. Wrapping myself in layers at the start of class and rehearsals, I sweated under sweaters and scarves and practice skirts until the ballet mistress pinched the back of my leg, checking that I was not hiding poor turnout and sloppy legs underneath the protection of my clothes.

I worked hard, trained my body back into submission, until I found the courage to stand in a leotard in a mirror-lined studio, surrounded by younger dancers with smooth bodies and the taut muscles of unspoiled youth.

And yet I had my reward: for it was at times like this in the first few months of 1939, surrounded by the dancers of the Vic-Wells, the dressing room packed with tutus and pointe shoes, that I knew I had made the right decision. Our second performance of *The Sleeping Princess* was at the Royal Opera House, a special gala command performance in honor of President Lebrun of the French Republic. As we got ready, we enjoyed the space backstage, vast in comparison to our beloved but cramped rooms at Sadler's Wells. Even the newspapers lay discarded in the rubbish bin, our minds too focused on Tchaikovsky, the choreography, the promise of a royal audience waiting for us on the other side of the curtain. Every day there were more fears reaching us from Europe, just this morning news of Hitler taking the Memel Territory from Lithuania. But tonight, we could forget about the world, locking ourselves instead inside the enchanted palace and the sleeping princess of our ballet.

Vivian, Martha, and I shared a dressing room with a dozen other girls, all of us carving out pockets of space in front of the mirrors to sharpen our lipstick and draw long lines of kohl above and below our eyes. In our costumes, the beautiful and elegant designs of Nadia Benois were brought to life against our skin. We had been disappointed the first time we saw the costumes, expecting far more opulence, at least a few sequins and feathers to brighten the stage. Margot was particularly bemused by her cardboard crown. But Ninette de Valois was clear in her direction: she wanted simple and clean lines, a contrast to the great Diaghilev's notoriously disastrous performance in 1921, Léon Bakst's extravagant designs for the Alhambra Theatre too fussy for the tastes of London. We had all heard Miss de Valois repeating the words of Sergei Diaghilev, his lament that he was "fifteen years too early for this ballet." Well, the Vic-Wells was determined that we were precisely on time for the charms of *The Sleeping Princess*.

Tonight, we were performing just Acts I and III, with a rest in-between while the London Philharmonic Orchestra was conducted by Sir Thomas Beecham in Debussy's *Ibéria*. I was a village maiden in Act I and a courtier in Act III. The roles were small, but it didn't matter to me, not when I was here, back with the Vic-Wells Ballet, my body just about my own at last. In my villager's dress with its thick white Romantic-style tutu skirt, red bodice, and loose yellow sleeves, my limbs felt alive, humming with the energy of the ballet.

"Thank goodness it was easier to get here compared to our first performance," Vivian said as she rolled her long blond hair around her hand and started to pin it at the nape of her neck. She was referring to the premiere at Sadler's Wells back in February when London had been choking under the murk of a pea-souper. Even walking along the pavement had been a risk. There was the real danger of a bus veering off its course, the fog dampening all the sounds of the city into an ominous silence. London had struggled to emerge out of cold and foggy weather, but finally this week it was starting to show signs of improvement. For me, though, I was too full of relief that I was dancing and performing, in control of my life once again, to even notice.

Martha rose from the dressing table, her makeup perfect and her dark hair sleek in a tight bun. Kicking shoes and discarded clothes out of the way, she found a space on the floor to stretch. She had a book with her, a translation of Charles Perrault's *La Belle au Bois dormant*, and she opened it, lying on her front with the soles of her feet pressed together to stretch out her hips.

"Every version of this story gets more and more innocent," she said, flipping the pages. "One day it will be nothing more than a pretty fairy tale for children." She pressed her pelvis down into the ground, shifting her weight from side to side. Martha had always struggled with her turnout, spending hours attempting to persuade her hips to find the rotation we all longed to achieve. I knelt next to her and looked at the book. It was a slim, illustrated hardback, the silhouette of a sleeping woman surrounded by roses on the front cover. At first glance it did look like a tale for children, a "once upon a time" story of love and first kisses and happily ever afters.

"Don't be fooled by the pretty pictures," Martha said. "The first version of the story is about a prince who impregnates the princess in her sleep."

I looked at her sharply. Martha returned my gaze for the briefest moment before flicking her eyes back to the book, her cheeks burning. She shifted uncomfortably as she stretched, her thighs pressing harder into the ground. I noticed Vivian staring at us in the mirror, her eyes wide and her lips parted in a small oval of surprise. "Do we really need to hear about this just before the beginners' call?" she objected, coming to my rescue. "I'd prefer to imagine it as all fairies and roses and enchantments."

I was aware of the other girls around us. Their attention had shifted to Martha and her book now that their costumes were fastened and their pointe shoe ribbons stitched in at the ankle.

"It's okay," I whispered, just loud enough for Martha to glance up at me again, an uncertain apology hovering in her eyes.

"It's originally from an anonymous medieval prose romance called *Perceforest*," Martha said. "Troylus gets so frustrated when Zellandine fails to wake up from his kiss that he rapes her. She still doesn't wake up as she's giving birth nine months later. When she finally does emerge out of that sleep, she marries him, but is obviously traumatized for the rest of her life. Then there was an Italian version in the seventeenth century by Giambattista Basile. His was even worse. The princess, named Talia, has twins in her sleep. She stays fast asleep until one of the babies sucks out the cursed splinter of flax from her finger. Then her mother-in-law tries to eat her children, out of jealousy."

"Sun, Moon, and Talia," I said, remembering. Stories from the *Pentamerone*. A red book, gold embossed lettering on the front cover: it was on the bookshelf at home in Devon. I had read the stories with my father when I was younger, the two of us laughing over the wildness of the magic and the improbability of the narratives.

"Perrault's story isn't much better," Martha continued, the noise of the dressing room hushed now to only the low rustle of our skirts. "No rape, thank goodness, but the prince's mother is an ogress who tries very hard to make the cook serve the children for her dinner, before throwing herself into a vat of snakes and toads and lizards in a suicidal rage."

"A lesson for us all," Vivian mumbled under her breath.

"Clearly it is simplest never to marry at all," I said, trying to keep my voice light. These stories, ridiculous fairy tales though they were, had tainted the evening. Like Vivian, I preferred to think of *The Sleeping Princess* as a magical spectacle of fairy godmothers and characters from folklore. But then, we had both learned the hard way about heartbreak and loss: Louis de Manton, Frank Ellis—just boys but with the power to root deep into our self-worth.

With minutes to go before the beginners' call, in ran Moyra Fraser, her costume hidden beneath layers of warm-up woolens. She had joined the company two years ago after a short stint at the school; Bobby Helpmann had befriended her quickly, the two of them sharing a fast wit and vivacious comic energy. She was a village maiden in Act I tonight, followed by Beauty in Act III, as always rushing about the corridors in a mad ecstasy of excitement.

"The king has arrived," she announced, dropping her head in a mock bow. The way she said it, he could be just behind her, but we knew she meant in the foyer of the theatre, no doubt surrounded by a large entourage of family, ambassadors, ministers, and President Lebrun of course. "The theatre looks incredible," she continued, stripping off her woolen layers with a confidence I knew I still lacked, her long slim legs revealed. "I hid myself behind a curtain until one of the ushers shooed me away. I've never seen so many tiaras and diamonds in one place."

"Who else did you see?" asked one of the dancers as we gathered ourselves for the beginners' call.

"Well, it was rather like something out of a storybook. The grand staircase was lined with Yeomen of the Guard, wearing these hilarious scarlet-and-gold uniforms and carrying tasseled halberds."

The sound of feet in pointe shoes tapping along the corridor outside our dressing room hurried our final preparations, and we joined the surge of dancers moving toward the stage.

We were a huge cast, and it was hard to find a free spot in the wings to do my final warm-up exercises. I could see why the stage doorkeeper, Mr. Jackson, had thrown up his hands in a comic display of shock when we'd all arrived for our first rehearsal, so many of us traipsing past him with our heavy bags of pointe shoes and practice tutus as he smoked cigarettes behind his desk. But we all stopped as silence fell in the auditorium, our large numbers coalescing into one uniform, waiting corps. Though Martha and I struggled to stifle our giggles when six trumpets blared out a fanfare from the stage, announcing the arrival of the Royal Family with President Lebrun and his wife.

When the "Marseillaise" followed by the national anthem began, we started moving again, warming up our feet en pointe, bending forward and back to loosen our hamstrings. We had longer than we expected before the performance began, the audience cheering the king and the president for more than five minutes. It was a relief to us all when Constant Lambert lifted his baton and the opening notes of Act I began. As I ran onstage, a flower garland held loosely in one hand, I was stunned by the sight of the audience, usually so dark and faded behind the lights. This audience seemed to sparkle, a twinkling array of medals and jewels, tiaras and necklaces. It was as though women had raided the depths of their jewelry boxes and men had dug through their wardrobes to find uniforms with buttons and sashes that gleamed like new.

The royal box, bordered with yellow velvet draperies, reminded me of a paper theatre I had seen in a shop on Hoxton Street a few years ago, the cutout auditorium decorated in bold primary colors. I remembered how I had stared through the window at the tableau of paper productions, wondering if a door opening and closing too hard would cause the whole display to come tumbling down.

Even though I could not see the faces inside, I knew this royal box held George VI, Queen Elizabeth, and the princesses. It made me smile to imagine how it must feel to be a real princess watching your fairy-tale equivalent dancing on the stage in a cardboard crown, when back at the palace you had drawers full of jewels and crowns of your own. But Margot Fonteyn didn't need a crown to become royalty, and I had to remind myself not to watch her too intensely during her variation. At the end of the performance, the applause felt different than usual, a quieter, muffled sound, as if it couldn't resonate through the space. But then I realized it was because the audience were all wearing gloves, long, white, and elegant for the women, short white goatskin for the men. We had never performed before an audience of such wealth and eminence before tonight.

We dressed quickly at the end of the performance, desperate to get to the reception before all the guests departed. I dabbed uncertainly at my makeup, dulling the lines of kohl and the red of my lipstick, loosening my hair and brushing it roughly to try to make it behave. Martha looked stunning already, her golden skin illuminated by a dark green dress and her hair in perfect curls. Vivian's dress was too loose for her, gaping at her lower back, but it didn't matter; it just accentuated the length of her limbs and the long blond hair that fell chaotically to her waist. In the silver of her dress she looked otherworldly, an ethereal figment of the air too pale for this world. When my body had swollen and expanded, I had been envious of Vivian's never-changing elegance, those long slim ankles that seemed almost without flesh.

Martha came up to me and wrapped her arm about my waist, pouting prettily in the mirror. "You look gorgeous," she told me. "Stop fretting and let's get a drink."

I pulled away from her, shaking my head. "I look completely unremarkable compared to you two."

"Don't be ridiculous," Vivian said. But they knew I would give anything for bigger eyes, longer legs, a smaller, neater waist. My two friends had worked hard in their kindness to me over the past few years, regularly reassuring me how quickly my body had returned to its prepregnancy suppleness and strength. In my less anxious moments, I let myself believe them, recognizing my body's determination in trying to forget a baby had ever grown inside me, but still I found myself staring nervously in the mirror, turning sideways to check my stomach was smooth and hard. I sighed, throwing one last look in the mirror before joining the others and making our way to the reception.

The foyer was decorated with spectacular opulence, towering displays of flowers at every corner and tapestries hanging in splendor at the walls. Guests were dressed in their finest furs, silks, and uniforms, tiaras dazzling in the bright lights of the entrance hall. Vivian was quickly caught up in a group of dancers, but Martha and I kept moving through the space, taking a glass of champagne from a waiter who winked at us, his tray nearly empty.

When I saw him, it was too late to look away. Walking toward us was Louis de Manton. At his side, clutching his arm, was his wife.

The glitter of the foyer seemed to pulse and throb around me, but then it settled again, and I could see him clearly, the crisp white of his shirt, the clean lines of his suit, the smile growing under those familiar dark eyes.

It had crossed my mind that he might be here, a guest of his uncle as part of the French ambassadorial entourage. But I had thrust the thought away, persuaded myself that he wouldn't want to risk encountering me here, his wife on his arm. His expression now, however, suggested he hadn't even considered it would be a problem, that he was genuinely delighted to see me.

"Oh no," Martha whispered. "Take a big sip of that champagne before he gets to us." She took a step toward me.

"Briar!" Louis exclaimed, saying my name exactly as he used to, his tongue rolling over the vowels. "You were wonderful tonight. I spied your name in the cast list and felt far superior to all the old men around me. They are not friends with a ballerina."

I bristled at that, his assumption that we were still friends, his silence for two and a half years glossed over like it was nothing. I heard Martha snort beside me, which made me smile, a small armor of amusement.

"Well, you did always love an opportunity to see us dance," I replied, knocking the last inch of champagne down my throat. The same waiter as before walked toward us, his tray now replenished. I took another glass, as did Martha and Louis. Esme de Manton shook her head, her eyes cast down. She looked like a child, her shoulders narrow inside her duck-egg blue dress, a pretty trim of lace lining her waistband and shoulder straps.

"Let me introduce my wife, Esme." Louis's hand was against her back. He looked as though he was offering her to us on a plate. I watched as she shifted a little, her hands moving instinctively to her stomach. The way she placed her hands against the folds of her dress, the light touch of her fingers, the small swell beneath the blue lace band, I knew she was pregnant. I drew my eyes away from her and back to Louis.

"We are expecting our first child in the summer." Louis announced this with the pride of a man in love, though whether with his wife or his baby, it was unclear. "It will be a boy, we think," he said, taking his wife's hand and kissing it.

"Your first son, then," I said, the champagne making me bold. But he didn't know what I was talking about. Louis had no idea about his daughter, gone far now from his reach. He didn't deserve her, I thought, surprising myself. It was the first time I had expressed such a sentiment, even to myself. Until tonight, I had thought of her as a creature that had grown unwanted inside me, a nameless, faceless being who had simply been waiting to emerge into a world that did not involve me. But standing here now, watching as Louis ushered his wife away to their waiting car, I felt a thread of connection, a tiny, barely visible line that joined me to her in defiance against the man who had tried to ruin my life. For the first time ever, I felt a pang of grief.

Martha and I left immediately, moving quickly through the streets of Covent Garden toward her flat on Cecil Court. I didn't even think of Vivian, left behind at the reception and looking for me, until we were already outside. She would give up eventually and go home, someone telling her that they had seen me leave with Martha. If she, too, caught sight of Louis de Manton and his pregnant wife, she would understand. But in truth I didn't want her right now. Even though she had been there with me every step of the way through my pregnancy and recovery, there was a distance between us that I did not know how to heal. I was angry with her for having kept what I had lost. Her body was a sculpture, crafted to a long, sinewy perfection, while for me every awkward balance in *adage*, every broken *pirouette*, every poor landing from *allegro*, reminded me of my past.

The whole of London seemed to be out tonight, people spilling from restaurants, the sharp scent of cigar smoke hovering at every corner. A couple clung to each other at the end of an alleyway, while actors lingered outside the New Theatre, posters blazing with color above its entrance.

There was a party going on in the shop: we could hear the loud chatter of writers at the end of a book launch. We ignored the people clustered around bottles of wine, their faces pressed close together as they shouted their book news among the endless talk of the war that seemed to creep closer every day despite

Chamberlain's resistance. But all I could think about was getting upstairs and away from everyone, to a place where I could take off my dress, my makeup, strip off the smile I had forced for Louis. Some part of me wished I had confronted him. I should have told him how he had ruined my life, how he had turned me into a different person, made that happy, trusting girl I was vanish. Right there in the foyer of the Opera House, I should have told him everything, how there was a little girl he would never know. The look on his wife's face, the look on his own as his confident cheerfulness dissolved into shock, I tried to imagine it all. I wanted to know how he would feel, realizing his perfect life had its dark corners. I wanted to understand if the Louis I had met in Cambridge, the one who had sought to resist the path his mother had set out for him, had ever existed at all. But all I felt was a fear that saying those words would awaken the pain I had finally laid to rest.

I couldn't tell him. This was my secret, and it had to stay mine if I was to remain in command of my life.

Martha followed me into her bedroom and watched as I untied my dress and slipped it from my shoulders. I realized I was shivering, standing there in my underwear, my bare feet cold and red, the lines from the pointe shoes still marking my skin. I had stopped crying, instead finding resolve in the knowledge that I had done the right thing. Louis had his life, and I had mine. Trying to reconnect them now would only bring more heartache.

"You need to put something on." Martha came toward me, her dressing gown held out. I took it from her and wrapped it around me.

She was right; I felt better with the heavy cotton against my skin, my nakedness hidden, protected. I held out my hand to her and she took it, folding my fingers beneath hers. Her hand was so small and soft and yet it had the strength to carry me.

Pulling me in toward her, we embraced. Her skin smelled sweet—the remnants of the stage, the costumes, powder mixed in with her signature vanilla cold cream—and I inhaled against her neck. She pressed herself in closer to me. We had held each other so many times, me, Martha, Vivian, the three of us finding comfort in the familiarity of each other's bodies. But this was different. The silence around us took on a new meaning, just me and Martha in the safety of her bedroom, our skin warming one another's.

She lifted my hand in hers, our arms stretched out together like the start of a dance. Our eyes met. This was new, the first time either of us had acknowledged that the way we touched each other, the pressure in the air around us when we were close, meant something real. When I was pregnant, I had found myself drawing away from everyone, flinching when anyone touched me. I hated my body, this unfamiliar flesh that refused to do what I wanted. It had been nearly impossible to recover from that feeling once the baby had arrived and gone again and I had started to dance. At first, when the ballet mistress touched me, placing my body back into the strict classical positions, it felt like an electric shock was bouncing through me. In *pas de deux* work, I had to force myself not to jump out of my partner's hands when he supported me by the waist in an *arabesque* or *attitude*. I wanted to shrink so no one would be able to grab on to me at all. Now, for the first time in forever, I needed to feel the full weight of another's arms. I longed for Martha to touch me everywhere.

We faced one another, our heads close. I could hear her breath high in her throat. When we kissed, it was simultaneous, the gap between us closing until there was nothing left.

Before that night, we thought we had known everything there was to know about one another. And yet right then, in the safety of her bedroom, we discovered so much more, how her skin shivered above the birthmark on her thigh, how my body arched when she kissed me, her mouth finding parts of me that I had thought were frozen forever. How she laughed when I kissed her stomach, twisting herself toward me; how I loved the way she wrapped her arms around me.

For a night, we let ourselves forget about everything but ourselves: Louis, the threat of war, the inevitable change it would bring to our lives. Instead, I learned a new way to be touched, just when I had thought I would never let anyone touch me again.

February 19, 1946

Martha kisses me when I leave the flat this morning, but I make myself turn away from her and mutter a quick goodbye. Even though I have no space for her in my plans, I cannot yet find it in me to wrench my life from hers. She must know I am drawing away from her, closing those connections between us that used to be so open and wide. But I have no choice. My priorities have been chosen for me by the pain of loss, war, the guilt of the past.

"I'll be out late," I tell her as I leave. "It's the dress rehearsal."

"Yes, I know." I catch her sigh as she continues dabbing rouge on her cheekbones in front of her bedroom mirror. There is a suitcase open on her bed, a few items already packed inside. I panic, feeling an irrational fear that she is going to leave me. But then I remember. It is me who is leaving her. Her trip is temporary. "I told you I'm away, didn't I? Just for a few days in Edinburgh, to review a new play."

She did tell me, but there had been no need. It was me who had orchestrated the ticket to the play in Edinburgh, forging a note from the press officer to find a reason to get her away for three days. Since repetitive and frustrating injuries forced her to give up dancing two years into the war, her literary career has developed, balancing writing with working in the bookshop. Her father is away this week too, at a literary conference on the south coast at the house of a wealthy patron of the arts. Thankfully that party had already been planned, one of the many events he has been attending since the war ended. He won't return until the weekend, by which time I will be gone too. With the shop closed for a few days, there will be no one to watch as I move in and out, a little girl and suitcases at my side.

Martha and I have separate rooms, as we always have done, me taking a small guest room that used to be full of storage. When I moved out of Vivian's family home during the war, neither Martha nor I had the confidence to share a bedroom. Her father might not have cared—our relationship was far from unusual in his literary world—but we preferred to keep our feelings secret from everyone else, maintaining a facade of simple female friendship. Perhaps, I think as I pull on my coat, this will make it easier. Maybe I can convince myself we were never together at all.

And yet leaving the flat this morning is hard. I can hear Martha moving around in her bedroom, the light patter of her feet as she selects dresses from her wardrobe, pulls stockings from her drawer. Every movement she makes is familiar, and I am afraid of the emptiness when she is no longer in my life, when I can no longer smell the sweet vanilla that follows her. Part of me wants to run back in and hold her, let her carry me through all this pain. But I know that is impossible. Soon it will all be over anyway, and I will be gone. Thinking of Jasmine helps, how she too will be getting ready for a day at the theatre, Rosamund picking out her clothes and brushing her hair for the last time.

I enter the theatre via the stage door and am immediately surrounded by noise. Mr. Jackson is busy signing in visitors and taking deliveries. The lobby that usually provides a respite from the crowds of Covent Garden is this morning an extension of the chaos of the streets. For today is the dress rehearsal of *The Sleeping Beauty*, basically a performance in its own right. For me it has even greater significance; this is not a dress rehearsal but a coda, a swan song just for me.

There will be a small audience, those fortunate few who have managed to get preview tickets. For everyone else, they will need to wait until tomorrow for the grand opening. Tickets have been sold out for weeks and the box office is expecting queues to begin forming outside the theatre tonight, eager hopefuls waiting for last-minute standing tickets to be released.

I go straight to the dressing room, not at all surprised to find it already busy. The other members of the corps de ballet with whom I share the space are talking excitedly about the newspaper articles advertising the opening night, some of which they spotted on their way to the theatre. The reviewers wait with optimism for us to vindicate our right to put on the most splendid and extravagant production since before the war. Two girls are laughing over a cartoon in the *News Chronicle*, a demonic looking Prince Charming in *arabesque* offering a bouquet of flowers labeled COUPON CONCESSIONS to a sleeping princess. The irony of our production's splendor is not, it seems, lost on the London public, not when the front page of the same newspaper announces continued austerity with just the smallest increase in clothing coupons. Unless workers in yarn and cotton mills are back in greater numbers by the summer, it writes, supplies will remain limited. I remember how Rosamund's comments, back in the autumn when they came to watch company class, had revealed that she too disapproved of our theatrical luster.

It is hard to imagine austerity today, though, the rails of costumes hanging heavy with yards of dresses and tutus, opulent headdresses and wigs laid out on the shelves above our dressing tables. The wardrobe department spared no effort in scouring the country for materials for the costumes, fighting their way through rationing. But some costumes have strange sources: Julia Farron's dress as the queen is made from red velvet curtains the designer persuaded an old friend to dig out of her attic, and many dresses are recycled from the skirts of prewar opera costumes, cut up and sewn together anew. Collars and cuffs are purloined from faded fur coats, the seamstresses cutting around the moth holes and ripped linings.

My role in the Prologue is a maid of honor at the christening of Princess Aurora, and afterward I am in the garland waltz at her coming-of-age birthday party in Act I. While it is quick to change in and out of the dresses, the headdresses take longer; one must be unpinned before the next wire frame is fastened into my hair. The first is a wire circlet, green velvet vine leaves nestled among white, pink, and lilac net flowers; as a village maiden in Act I, I have a dark brown straw hat, colorful plastic flowers decorating the rim and two long red ribbons tumbling down the back. I reach up and touch the flowers, feeling how light they are. It makes me smile to think how Jasmine will enjoy exploring the costumes tonight, how amazed she will be by the weightlessness of the headdresses despite their rich vibrancy. This, I think, is the theme of our production: we take what scraps we can from the remnants of our prewar lives and transform them into glory. And perhaps I too can do the same.

Company class has a different energy this morning. We try to let it recenter us, remind us that our bodies need to behave as though it is any ordinary day. To the rhythm of the piano, we must find our center, our balance, go through the familiar routine of barre exercises, stretching, center practice, *allegro*. Most of the company are here, drawn away from their preferred ballet studios across London by a strict word from Miss de Valois. Since the war, the most popular place to take class has been at a tired-looking studio near Cambridge Circus. Classes there, however, are far from shabby, taught by the indomitable Vera Volkova. She draws the best foreign dancers to her as they pass through the city, providing opportunities for them to dance with complete focus for two hours. My attention, though, has been elsewhere and I have not had the courage to attend such star-studded classes, where critics and illustrious guests often find their way in to watch. Perhaps I would have done so years ago, when I was sixteen and desperate to be everywhere and to meet everyone, when Martha and Vivian were still dancing and the three of us thought the world was ours. In Paris, nearly ten years ago, in those classes with Olga Preobrajenska, nothing had stopped me from finding my place among the rows of brilliant ballet dancers. While I sometimes find myself wishing that could still be me, I know it isn't possible. I need to move on to the next stage of my life.

Today I struggle to focus, my mind drifting to the evening and all that it promises. In the *pirouette* exercise, I stumble on a double turn and miss an *assemblé soutenu*, using the wrong leg for the *pirouette en dedans*. I look around nervously to see if anyone has noticed, but it seems everyone is lost in their own thoughts today, with no space to worry about the missteps of others. Miss de Valois is teaching company class this morning, somehow fitting in this duty among her many other priorities. There is still so much to do to prepare for the dress rehearsal: it is hard to imagine the stage, the wings, the dressing rooms, Wardrobe, shifting them-selves into readiness. It is even harder to imagine tomorrow night when the auditorium will be full, more than two thousand in the audience, the king and queen in the royal box. Right now, the red seats look terrifying in their emptiness, a vast space that seems to taunt us with silent echoes. *What if no one turns up?* they seem to say. *We will be here all the same, watching your failure.*

I imagine ghosts watching from those seats now, the young men who jived and danced the jitterbug in those short breaks from armed duty, the women who kept our streets safe, drove ambulances through dangerous London roads as the bombs fell out of the sky. We dance where they found momentary relief during the long endurance of war, our Tchaikovsky replacing their Glenn Miller. There are ghosts everywhere, the people who will never return to dance or sing or play on the Opera House stage, who will never sew a button on a costume, measure out canvas for the sets, pour champagne in the foyer bar. I can feel them all today, their white eyes that stare and shake their heads and say: *We died for you. Don't throw it all away.*

There is one particular ghost who waits for me, her eyes find-ing every fault as I struggle to get my heels down in the *petit alle-gro*, my weight too far back onto the *piqué* turns. She is telling me that it didn't need to be this way, that I could have had it all if I had been less selfish. And she too. She would still be alive if I had thought about what she really wanted, if I had refused to let my envy and fear and self-doubt damage the bonds of our friendship.

I want to stop the class and shout back at her, to tell her that I am trying. Every decision I have made since she died has been because of her and what I did. Tonight, I am going to right the wrongs, make it all worth it again. Vivian Grant, I make this promise to you.

Despite the smallness of the applause, our select audience of balletomanes doing their best to make claps and cheers echo throughout the auditorium, the dress rehearsal feels like a triumph. We make it through with no disasters, Constant Lambert's tempo matching the beat of Margot Fonteyn's step. The costumes hold together, even those dresses on which the final stitches have been sewn just minutes before the beginners' call.

I try to enjoy every step of the ballet, doing my best to ignore the pull of Jasmine in the audience; but it is impossible not to think of her, imagining it all through her eyes. How much more excited she would be if she knew that tonight is to be her liberation, how I will be her knight rescuing her from the tower.

She can dance with me once this is all over; I have already put down my name on a housing waiting list. It is just a small set of rooms in Richmond, but it can be our home, a starting place from where we can build our lives, not too far from the London theatres. I have conjured this moment in my mind so many times now, I can't believe it is here. Tomorrow, we will escape to the train station, spend a few days on the coast where no one will find us, before beginning a slow move into our new lives: a school for Jasmine, ballet teaching for me, theatre in the evenings when we want a trip into the city. Rosamund will be terrified, of course, and maybe she will find us. But Jasmine is my responsibility now. I have the stronger claim.

Jasmine and Rosamund appear in the doorway of my dressing room, pressing themselves to the sides as people move in and out of the room. There are guests coming and going, the dancers doing their best to get changed without crashing, topless, into a friend or relative.

"Come in!" I exclaim in delight, going to the door and taking Jasmine's hand. She looks a little overwhelmed by the noise and bustle of the room, but I find her a seat at a dressing table and kneel next to her. Rosamund stands by the door watching us. She looks so disapproving, the way she glances sideways at the costumes hanging on the rail, her pursed lips as she sees half-naked women slipping out of their ballet tights, their skin exposed and gleaming with sweat. I need to get rid of her, to end this ceaseless watching and control. When I see one of the dancers' mothers, a woman who is helping with the grand floral displays in the auditorium, the evening I have carefully crafted shifts into motion.

Standing, I turn my attention to Rosamund. I need to charm her a little if my plan is to work.

"Would you like to see the flowers for tomorrow's opening night? Jasmine told me about your interest in plants. They are starting to arrange them now and it really will be something wonderful." Before she has a chance to object, I call over to Mrs. Hookham, Margot Fonteyn's mother, who is about to leave with a dress over her arm. "Will you show Mrs. Caradon the flowers for tomorrow? I'm sure she'd love to see your ideas for the arrangements."

"Of course," Mrs. Hookham replies. She has overseen so many details for the opening night, trusted entirely by Miss de Valois. Mrs. Hookham traveled with us on nearly every domestic tour throughout the war, her unflappable devotion to the company making her the ideal mother for us all. Far indeed from the competitive mothers fighting for position around the piano in the studio in Paris, she got on with whatever task was required without once seeing herself, the mother of the prima ballerina, as superior. "Come with me and I'll show you what we have planned."

Rosamund looks trapped: Mrs. Hookham is holding open the door, Jasmine and I smiling up at them. If she refuses to go, she knows she will be making an unnecessary scene, breaking that image of unflappable calm she always tries to maintain. The perfect, practical mother who can look after a household of children through the stress of war. It is only me, it seems, who can see the real Rosamund Caradon beneath that veneer of reason and unshakable competence. I have watched how she controls and constrains Jasmine, hiding her away in that gloomy house in Devon, a child forever young who must not be allowed to experience the world and all it offers. She doesn't understand what Jasmine really wants.

I manage to keep the most innocent of expressions on my face as I turn back to Jasmine and hand her the vine leaf headdress to examine.

"I won't be long, Jasmine," Rosamund says, reluctantly following Mrs. Hookham. But Jasmine has already looked away, engrossed in the details of the headdress. She doesn't hear Rosamund's final plea as she leaves the room. "You wait here for me. Don't go anywhere."

That is supposed to be for me, I assume: a warning. "We'll be right here when you get back," I say. A lie.

Once she is gone, I show Jasmine around the dressing room, pointing out details on the costumes and asking her how she enjoyed the dress rehearsal. "Can I see the evil fairy's costume?" she asks me, looking around her as if it might materialize out of the wall of tutus.

"Carabosse? That's in the men's dressing room, but I expect we can get in there now. Everyone will have finished getting changed." I collect up our coats and we go out into the corridor. Dancers and their guests are leaving quickly now, keen to get out and away before Miss de Valois decides to call everyone together for notes. Once the company is safely tucked into a restaurant, a drink settling their energy after the adrenaline of the rehearsal, not even the ghost of the great choreographer Petipa would be able to drag them back to the theatre.

I knock on the door to the male principals' dressing rooms, but there is no reply. This is Robert Helpmann's room, shared with two other men. Helpmann takes on the impressive role of performing both Carabosse and Prince Florimund. In the space of two hours, he transforms from an evil witch into a handsome prince: from woman to man, malevolent to benign, gothic power to the simple goodness of love.

We step inside, Jasmine ahead of me. She looks terrified, as if Carabosse is going to jump out at her in the darkness. I take her hand and lead her to the costume rail. "This is it."

She reaches forward and touches it, her hand hovering uneasily over the black taffeta skirt. Helpmann wears the costume with immense energy, the strong lines of his makeup standing out even among the heavy layers of black net, taffeta, the deep cuffs of frayed black lace, the red scraps of satin in the skirt that shine out like a pack of glowing evil eyes. His train is vast, decorated with green crinoline cubes and sequins that sparkle in gothic splendor. Diamanté fragments emboss the dark of the bodice like an eddying pit of snakes. Like Jasmine, I too am drawn to this costume, evil and beauty dancing as one.

I stand back to let her feel the bodice and the skirt, my heart beating fast. Somehow it all feels different now that we are here, the gloom of Carabosse swamping the light. I am starting to feel as afraid as Jasmine looks, my imagination flying too fast. Carabosse could be right here waiting for us, an ogress slumped underneath the costume rail ready to surge up and curse us. I have to turn away from the costume, finding something more benevolent on which to focus my attention. It would be easier, I think, if it was the Lilac Fairy's tutu giving me courage, all pink and white and purple. I have cast myself as the fairy godmother, saving a princess from the curse of the past. But when I catch sight of myself in the dressing-table mirror, the stain of my stage makeup still heavy about my eyes, it is not a fairy I see. Shadows have woven their way around my mouth and my hair is scraped back tight against my head, making me look gaunt and unfriendly. My lips have lost their color, the matte of my foundation bleaching them so that it seems as though I have no mouth at all.

"Let's go," I say to Jasmine, my words coming out harsher than I intended.

"Can I see the white cat tutu?" she says, turning back to me, squinting a little as she adjusts her eyes from the darkness of the costume.

"Not now. We don't have time."

I take her hand and lead her out into the corridor. It is so quiet, as though the building has fallen under a spell. There will still be people everywhere, the wardrobe department making lists of the adjustments needed before tomorrow, the technicians turning off the lights and resetting the stage for another performance. Mrs. Hookham and Rosamund will be in the foyer, surrounded by the crates of flowers that wait to be arranged into the most extravagant of blooms. But in this instant it feels like we are the only two left awake beneath this castle of make-believe beauty.

We walk fast, avoiding the stage door and instead moving down toward an exit farther along Floral Street. I can feel the tension in my neck as I drag us forward.

"Where are we going?" Jasmine's voice is too loud, and I squeeze her hand to reassure her. It doesn't work and she stops still, her arm pulling away from mine. I sigh and turn back toward her. We are nearly at the exit I am looking for and I don't have time to explain everything to her now. She just needs to trust me.

I kneel in front of her, trying to show only kindness in my face. The long white tangle of her hair seems to glow like a halo above her, bright against the gloom of the backstage corridor. The door is right there, our escape route into the streets where we can hide among the crowds. "Can you trust me, Jasmine?" I say, loosening my grip on her. She seems to look past me with a vacant expression, as though I am not there at all. "Jasmine," I insist. "Will you come with me?"

She wakes up, looking nervously at her surroundings. The door in front of us is part metal, part wood, and it rattles as I stand and push against it. For a second I think it is locked, that I will have to find another way out. But as I push harder, the metal cackling too loud, it gives way, and we find ourselves out on the street.

Jasmine steps onto Floral Street, blinking at the sudden change in air, noise, light. "Are we meeting Mama?"

"We will do very soon. We're going to walk to my flat and meet her there."

Jasmine seems to accept this. "Is it far?"

"No, not far at all. Just five minutes."

And so it begins. As we walk, she relaxes, pointing out the long queue of people camping out to get a ticket for tomorrow's opening night, laughing as two men cycle down St. Martin's Lane balanced precariously on a single bike, and pressing her face to the window of the pointe shoe shop on the edge of Cecil Court.

When we get inside, the flat quiet and empty, she rushes about trying out the sofa, picking books off the shelves, peering through the window down to the street below. I go into the kitchen to make her a hot drink. But when I return she has fallen asleep, curled up on the sofa where Vivian, Martha, and I used to spend so much time together. The excitement of the evening has exhausted her.

For now, I let her sleep.

Act III

Scene I

I will always remember the first time I saw Jasmine playing on the grounds of Gittisham. It was May 1945, and nearly six years of war were over.

London was celebrating. But for me, I could not find the same joy that seemed to fly from street to street, the parties merging and growing into one great carnival of peace.

I had a different task, a far more important duty. I remember that we were performing a matinee of *Coppélia* at the New Theatre and everyone was impatient for the show to end so we could rush out to Trafalgar Square and join in the celebrations. There had been a last-minute program change to *Coppélia*, Helpmann announcing at the end of the previous night's performance that our VE Day show would be this popular comic ballet. It seemed to suit the mood better than *Lac Act II* and *Comus*. And it certainly had a spirit of celebration, Helpmann as Dr. Coppélius opening the ballet perched on a ladder and tying a Union Jack to a medley of Allied flags, a *V* for victory floating over his front door.

And yet when we spilled out from the stage door onto St. Martin's Lane, I did not follow the others down toward Trafalgar Square. Instead, I turned the other way and got on the first bus I could find that would take me to the house in Belgravia. The house I had been avoiding for the past five years.

I stood on the other side of the street, each detail bringing the past toward me. It was so familiar, the place I had lived with Vivian Grant and her family for all those years. The house where I had grown from a child to an adult, danced, laughed, joined in with the chaos of Vivian's loud and welcoming family, sewn ribbons onto hundreds of pairs of pointe shoes, chatted long into the night with my best friend, shared all of myself. And then I had let it go, betrayed her, turned away from her when I should have been there. Everything that happened to her, every choice she made: it was all my fault.

The curtains were closed, and a silent heaviness seemed to have draped itself over the house. It had always been a quiet road, but now it seemed oppressive in its silence, a house of mourning refusing to join in the exuberant celebrations of the rest of the city. I closed my eyes, trying to remember how it had been when I lived there, the shouts of Vivian's brothers heard from every room of the house, the door constantly opening and closing as friends came and went, the family rushing madly from one activity to the next. A memory came to me: Vivian and I in the kitchen, aged fifteen. We were breaking in pointe shoes, stomping up and down on three-quarter pointe to try to soften the soles. A momentary lapse of concentration meant Vivian had picked up my shoe instead of hers when she moved on to prepare a second pair. She'd laughed when she realized, handing the shoe back to me with a playful grimace. *Far too fat for me*, she'd said, slipping her own longer and slimmer shoe onto her foot. It was a joke, an exaggeration, and I tried to smile. But it had been an effort. Already, I was judging everything about myself against her perfection.

Forcing the memory away, I walked up to the front door. I knocked three times. The noise against the wood startled me, an unwelcome intrusion into the hushed stillness of the street. For a few minutes there was nothing, no change, no noise, no sign that anyone had heard my knock. The house refused to acknowledge me, a stubborn silence telling me I was not welcome back. As I was about to turn away and leave, I heard a noise, a door banging perhaps, a slow swish of clothes, the light tread of footsteps. My stomach tensed as I waited, a clicking and turning of a lock a few feet in front of me announcing that it was too late to change my mind. I was going to have to see this through.

I did not initially recognize the old woman who opened the door. She looked ancient, exhausted, a shrunken shadow drowning in clothes far too big for her. I thought, with a wave of something like relief, that perhaps the family had moved out during the war and that I had missed them. But then I saw those familiar green eyes, the long slim neck that Vivian and all her brothers had inherited, the translucent skin made even whiter and grayer now in her faded body.

Meredith Grant stared at me, her face a blank. "I wondered if we'd ever see you again." Her voice was barely a whisper, tired and strained.

I did not know what to reply. She turned and started to walk away from me. I hesitated, unsure whether to follow.

"Close the door behind you," she said in that difficult whisper. "I was in the garden."

I followed her inside, the memories of the house tumbling around me. The same pictures on the walls, the same muddle of hockey sticks, rugby balls, and cricket bats pressed into the corner of the hallway, the same smears of dirty handprints stamped into the blue-green walls. And yet it was also entirely different, an alien house that had lost its life. The light I remembered as dancing brightly was now choked in dust and dampened by the curtains drawn across the windows. Each room stood empty of noise and laughter, frozen in time and left to decay. But it was when we passed through the kitchen that I felt my throat constrict. I did not recognize anything. It was too tidy, too empty, no toast crumbs covering the table, no stained teapots and half-drunk cups crowding the sideboard. There was no pink ribbon and darning thread waiting to be sewn onto shoes, no pile of muddy laundry, no calendar on the wall with each day crowded full of performances, matches, reminders. Meredith Grant had packed it all away.

By the time I reached the small garden at the back of the house, she was already in her chair, staring out at the shrubs and grass that mingled together untidily. There was hardly a flower to be seen, just the odd violet-blue coloring the rosemary and a few pink chive flowers that had spread, uncared for, in a leggy mess. I hovered uneasily in front of her, waiting for her to offer me a seat. Eventually she turned her eyes to me and gestured to the chair pressed up against the wall. I took it and brought it closer to her, sitting at an angle so she did not need to look at me directly. Her gaze, with those brilliant green eyes, was unsettling. It reminded me of Vivian, the way she had looked at me the last time I saw her, a pained, betrayed look. Then she had died, leaving me with the knowledge that I could never apologize. But now, I thought, maybe I could find a way.

"Mrs. Grant," I said, my voice matching her whisper, my neck tight with nerves. "Meredith," I added. I had always called her

Meredith, ever since I had first moved in with them and she refused to let me stand on ceremony. In those days she was constantly moving through the house, finding it impossible to keep still. *You're one of us now*, she had said. She was to be called Meredith; her husband was Peter. I had accepted this immediately, used to the informality of my own parents. I had exchanged one happy family for another and was lucky to have my mother and father to return to in Devon whenever there was a holiday.

I threw myself into my words, afraid that if I waited my voice would freeze. "I want to say sorry for what happened. About Vivian. I should have come here earlier, but I was afraid. I felt too guilty. I couldn't face you all, when I was alive and she wasn't."

She turned to me sharply. "It was the war," she said. "The war took them from me. You cannot blame yourself for that."

I felt the strain in my neck release a little. But this wasn't what I was here for. I was not ready to be exonerated, forgiven, offered a pass to go on and enjoy my life despite the choices I had made.

She continued, turning back to stare at the green of her garden. "Vivian was the first to die. I had not expected to lose my daughter in the war. But I did. And after that it seemed inevitable that the others would go too. George in 1941. Reggie in 1942."

I did not know about her brothers. Another example of my failure. I had neglected her not only in life, but in death too.

"I'm so sorry. And James? Is he okay?"

James was the youngest of the family, just eleven when war began.

"He is alive." Meredith nodded to herself; it was as though she was reassuring herself that she still had him, that he hadn't died along with the rest of her family. "But it is hard for him, being the only one left, feeling that his brothers and sister died while he waited at home to be old enough to serve. I wanted to freeze time, keep him a child forever."

Again, I did not know how to reply to her. There was both a despair and an acceptance to her words that suggested she had given up trying to find happiness. It was a shock to see her this way, a different person from the busy, energetic, chaotically competent mother I had known.

"You are lucky not to be a mother," she said, breaking the silence that had built around us. "I used to think that all the anxiety and sleepless nights worrying about them was worth it. My children filled my heart to bursting, an intensity that made everything feel real and alive and exciting. I loved it all, the noise, the arguments even, the endless chores, the way they took me for granted. Even that was an affirmation that I made their lives full, that they were happy and did not need to be constantly reminded of what I did for them. My life was loving them, even when it hurt."

She took a deep breath that seemed to rise inside her like a limp balloon inflating. The effort of her words was immense.

"It is difficult now, with James. I want to hold on to him tightly, but he resents it, how I remind him of all we've lost. Peter keeps telling me to give him space, let him find his own way, but I get anxious if I don't know where he is. He left a few hours ago for a party with friends. I tried to make him feel guilty for going. I think I said something unforgivable, reminding him of how lonely I was, how his siblings had gone, how he was all I had left. Even as I said it, I knew it was wrong to throw all my emotions onto him. But it's impossible to stop myself. I can't help but cling to him."

I nodded, wanting to reach out and take her hand, to do something to help her. But I didn't dare. She was unpredictable, an entirely different woman from the one I used to know.

"You and Vivian made the right decision all those years ago."

I bristled. This was not what I had come here for. It would have been easier if she had shouted at me, told me I had been cruel and unnatural to give up my child, that my choice not to be a mother was an abomination, a curse that had led to the deaths of those I had been supposed to protect.

"You escaped the pain that is inevitable as a mother. You gave yourself the freedom not to suffer."

I could not accept this. What did Meredith know of my suffering? How could she assume that the choices I made had led to happiness? If Vivian were still alive, I wonder if she would have regretted what we'd done.

There, I had thought it. And the thought hung between Meredith and me: she knew why I was here.

"No, Briar," Meredith said then, her voice sad. "Vivian made her own decisions. You cannot give yourself that kind of power, nor that responsibility."

But she was wrong. I knew she was wrong with a certainty that made me want to scream, to break the heavy silence of the house and garden.

I had known it since Vivian had gone missing that day in 1940, after we'd argued, after I'd left her alone in a foreign country, too self-obsessed to see why she was angry at me.

I was the reason she had died.

"What do you know about my life, my decisions?" The words came out of my mouth too hard, too loud, and I wanted to claw them back again. The silence of the house taunted me with memories.

"Your decision, Briar, was to give up a child to the first rich woman who would take the responsibility off your hands. You made that decision, and you must live with it. Vivian made her own decisions. They were not because of you."

"But they were because of me," I said, pleading now. I needed her to blame me. How could I even start to forgive myself until I was judged and accused? "What happened to Vivian only happened because she followed me, she trusted me. She could be alive right now, living an entirely different life, if it wasn't for me."

Meredith held up her hand. "Stop, Briar, please. I think you should go now. This isn't helping either of us." She stood, her frail arms shaking as she pushed against the chair. "You can let yourself out. Please."

I rose and started walking to the back door. There was nothing else either of us could say to one another. And yet, when I got to the hallway and started reaching out my hand to open the door, I heard her behind me.

"Briar," she said as I turned back around. "I am sure Rosamund Caradon is providing a fine life for the child at Gittisham Manor. Far better than you or I could offer, especially with what we have both been through. You need to let this go."

With my heart thumping loudly and the blood roaring in my ears, I made it out onto the street. My hands were shaking violently, and as soon as I'd taken a few steps along the pavement I was forced to stop, lightheadedness threatening my vision. I needed to think, to protect those words I had just heard, to lock them deep inside the safety of my memory. Meredith Grant had revealed to me information that I had never heard before. The name of the woman who had adopted a baby girl in the spring of 1937. The house where that girl could be found.

For years, I had not wanted to know. But it was different now; everything had changed. The information had been closed to me, a secret that my parents knew should be hidden, better buried away so everyone could move on and live new, uncomplicated lives.

That Meredith Grant knew the name of the woman who had adopted the child did not surprise me. For it was not only my pregnancy that had turned those months in 1936 and 1937 into a strange, haunting nightmare. Vivian had been pregnant too, her body finally revealing itself one week after my own painful realization. She had latched on to me and our shared disaster, following my every move, making decisions entirely based on what I wanted. Frank Ellis was no more an option for her than Louis de Manton was for me. We turned from them and found strength in our united decisions, our collective grief.

At the time, Vivian's parents had seemed distanced from it all, sending Vivian to stay with me in Devon as though our situation was an inconvenience best left to others to resolve. But I had underestimated Meredith Grant. She was more involved than I realized, digging deeper into the woman who was to adopt our children, keeping a watchful eye from afar. A shadow of a memory came to me as I walked unsteadily away from the house: she had been there after all. I had been too wrapped up in my own pain to remember. I could just about see her: downstairs in the kitchen with my mother, helping Vivian, helping me. When the time came, she made sure she knew exactly what was happening. And now it was thanks to her that I could begin my journey to repair the errors of the past.

The next morning, I took the first train to Exeter, transferring onto the slow bus to Gittisham. As I walked up through the village, the signs of VE Day street parties still visible on the green, I felt a determination I had been lacking for so long. Keeping to the edge of the line of trees, I walked up the long drive toward Gittisham Manor. When I got closer to the house, I disappeared into the woods, hiding behind trees as I made my way up the hill. Soon I could hear the shouts of children playing.

Twin brothers, a teenage girl, a round little infant with a surprisingly low laugh. I knew instantly that none of these children were the girl I was looking for.

Staying close to the trees, I kept moving up the hill. She must be close, and I could not give up now: Vivian's mother had given me the hope I needed. When the woods ended, I stopped, looking around me with a nervous, frantic energy. A long, sloping lawn rose before me, a dark house shadowing the top of the hill. I had to force myself to stay calm.

Then I ran, making a fast dash up through the garden and toward the house. Determined, I ignored the throb of my muscles as I fought against the rise of the hill. The ground beneath me changed to gravel and I threw myself down beneath a window at the side of the house. I could feel my heart beating wildly. Waiting for my breathing to quiet, I pressed my back against the cold stone of the wall.

A door banged from somewhere inside. A woman's voice called out, the words too far away for me to understand. Slowly, I pushed myself up, peering into the window: a hall, large sofas laden with cushions, two armchairs surrounding an empty fireplace, paintings hanging from the walls.

And a girl, her pale hair falling untidily down her back. She was kneeling in front of a paper theatre, pushing a ballerina fairy in and out of the cardboard wings. I froze, holding my breath as I watched.

There she was. And I knew what I had to do. I would need patience, but I could manage that; I had already waited so long. This was how I would atone.

WHEN VIVIAN STORMED OUT of the Hotel du Passage onto the streets of The Hague that fated morning of May 10, 1940, neither Martha nor I could have predicted what would happen. But that was our problem, Martha and I. We thought only of ourselves.

The tour to Holland had started so differently. When Miss de Valois announced that our ballet company had been chosen to travel to The Hague as part of the war effort, a cultural trip to boost international relations, we were thrilled. Finally, it seemed that our wartime endeavors could take on more meaning for the country, ballet becoming its own form of defense against the Nazis. It also delayed the call-up of our male dancers, sending Sadler's Wells to dance for the Dutch in a unique and creative form of cultural propaganda. Later, we found out that the British government had received information just before we left that hinted at the impending German invasion, but they couldn't cancel our trip. It might reveal that the information had been leaked, ruining carefully planned espionage operations. And so we were thrown to the wolves, as it were, ballet dancers, some barely teenagers, dancing in The Hague in May 1940 when the Germans arrived, their parachutes and bombs forcing us to run for our lives.

The company met at King's Cross station, thirty of us with bags stuffed full of pointe shoes, evening dresses, makeup, warm-up clothes, pink silk tights. Many people had come to see us off, members of the British Council who had organized the trip jostling for space among the press officials, friends, anxious family members who did not share the excitement of their dancing sons and daughters. We had all made an effort for the occasion, aware of the cameras following us onto the train, and Martha, Vivian, and I enjoyed picking out the most outrageous hats modeled by the other ballerinas: one dancer, Mary, had gone too far, we felt, with a monstrous baby-blue hat decorated extravagantly with lumps of felt, artificial flowers, and a chiffon veil. My mother would have been appalled. When I think back to that time, I am shocked by our frivolity, how little we understood about what was happening, about the dangers ahead.

Our conductor, Constant Lambert, arrived next, then Ninette de Valois, Bobby Helpmann, Margot Fonteyn, June Brae. It was easy to hide from the more persistent of the press cameramen when celebrated dancers such as Margot eclipsed us all. But just before we left, one of the press huddled us together for a group photograph. I cannot look at that photograph now, the little newspaper clipping I have kept safe among so many others, without feeling something close to anger. There we all are, many of us holding little bouquets of flowers and clutching our handbags, our smiles too bright for the journey we are undertaking. Martha and I are not looking at the camera. Instead, we are smiling at one another, my mouth parted as I laugh at a joke she has made. Vivian is next to us and yet in some way distanced, staring directly at the camera with a focus the rest of us lack. I have wished for years to be able to ask her what she was thinking at that exact instant, whether she knew about Martha and me, whether she felt betrayed by the secret shift in our relationship, whether she sensed she was no longer at the center of our little group. But it is too late now. Those questions can never be answered.

Once we reached Gravesend and embarked on the boat to Rotterdam, the risks of the trip slowly started to present themselves. Helpmann tried to help ease the nerves spreading among us, making a joke about swimming breaststroke to protect his hair if the ship got hit. We laughed, but the chance of the ship sinking in an attack had become more real.

At Gravesend, the customs checks took forever, no one able to agree on whether we should take our gas masks with us, our bags checked for illegal items such as maps and written materials: anything, it seemed, that might be of benefit to the enemy. The costumes and sets had made it through earlier and were already waiting to be loaded onto the boat, the vast rolls of backdrops, crates of dresses and tunics, and the mounds of flat-packed wooden scenery required for *The Rake's Progress*, *The Wise Virgins*, *Checkmate*, *Dante Sonata*, *Façade*, *Les patineurs*, *Horoscope*: we had an ambitious program planned. Lambert nervously checked off the boxes of musical scores, not realizing that most of them would never find their way back to London. We had no idea how much we were to lose on that tour.

Our boat, the *Batavier II*, was older than we had imagined it would be. It was not at all the fearsome war vessel I had expected to usher us safely across the North Sea. Rather, it presented an air of tired reluctance, as though it was sighing in resignation at having to ferry such noisy dancers on a doomed voyage. We sailed off into the evening sky, the sun setting behind us over the land we'd left behind. I couldn't stay on deck for long. As soon as we'd left the calm of the port, the weather darkened, waves rocking our little boat and the wind's whisper growing to howls that shrieked between the double mast and the funnel. Martha stayed out for longer, but Vivian and I found a table inside in a little saloon, taking small sips of wine to try to settle our seasick stomachs. Smoke filled the cabin, dancers chain-smoking as they tried to find a way to pass the time, stay cheerful, forget about the North Sea and the mines that threatened to break up our boat. I hardly ever smoked, but tonight it was essential. I gratefully accepted a cigarette from another dancer seated near us, Vivian refusing with a sharp shake of her head.

I asked Vivian how she was feeling, what she was looking forward to most about Holland. There was something about her that was making me awkward, trying too hard perhaps, as though the easy familiarity we were used to had morphed into a new and strange tension. It was my fault. Martha and I had been hiding our relationship from Vivian. We never spoke about why we didn't tell her. There had been plenty of opportunities when we could have, all the evenings above the bookshop, the lights in the room dim behind the heavy blackout curtains as we drank wine and talked about war, ballet, gossip, anything but our relationship. Or Vivian and I matching our movements through the bedroom as we got ready for sleep in her family home, a gap growing between us that was concealed by our familiar chatter. Martha and I had, without any discussion, decided that we could not include her in this, that she must not know. Perhaps we thought she wouldn't understand, that she'd judge us, find us unnatural, grotesque, laugh at us the way we used to laugh, cruelly, at women in London nightclubs who danced together and kissed under the cover of jazz and seductive lights. While many of the men at Sadler's Wells made little attempt to hide their feelings for others of their own sex from the rest of the company, it was different with women. That part of us was hidden, protected as the most private part of our identity.

But I think we both knew she wouldn't judge us, not really: we just wanted something that was ours alone. Secrecy gave everything a special luster that we were afraid to lose.

"I had a dream last night," Vivian said, looking up from the glass of wine into which she had been staring. "You and I were living in the countryside somewhere. We didn't dance anymore and we'd both got a little fat, all soft arms and hips, and we wore aprons and cooked all the time."

I smiled at that, but her words threw me into the past, a time when I feared that dream might have become my reality. It was impossible to imagine Vivian as fat. She had the longest, leanest limbs of anyone I knew; even when she was pregnant, her body had been serene and smooth, her skin tight over sculpted bones.

She continued, ignoring the tightness of my smile. "And we had two children, both girls, and a dog, a cat that always made you sneeze, and we never left them alone, not ever." She stopped and stared back down at her glass. I could feel my face struggling to find a normal expression. Either I said nothing, smiled at her dream as though it was a simple transference of wartime anxiety, or I could say everything. I could finally have the conversation with her that the two of us had avoided since 1937, since we had made a choice that changed everything.

"Sometimes do you think that it isn't too late?" she whispered, forcing me to lean forward, the two of us finding a different rhythm and intensity to the rest of the noisy, laughing saloon.

"Too late for what?"

I knew what she meant, but I think I needed her to say it. As the sea rocked us, the wine in our glasses swirling unsteadily, I felt as though we were in an in-between state, where nothing would matter or last. We could say what we wanted, and the words would be drowned by the sea, stuck in a space without the weight of land.

"To get married. To be mothers. To be, I don't know, not here. Not on a boat in the North Sea, distracting ourselves from wondering whether we'll make it back to London by smoking too many cigarettes and thinking about how many pointe shoes we managed to squeeze into our bags."

The stench of the cigarettes suddenly became too much, my throat constricting painfully from the bitter smoke that crept through the saloon. What Vivian was asking all in an instant had become cruel, a deliberate attack on my past, my decisions, my relationship with Martha, at which she must have started to guess.

"Not really, Vivian," I said, pushing the smoldering end of the cigarette into the tray. "And even if I did wish for that, it can't happen for me. Not ever. You know that."

"It doesn't have to be that way," she said, reaching her hand toward mine.

I pulled away from her, gripping both hands together in my lap. "Maybe not for you. But for me it's different. I'm happy as I am." I could hear my words coming out hard and coldly defensive. I didn't sound happy at all.

She leaned back in her chair and turned away from me. "Okay," she said, nodding. "But I am not."

I couldn't do this anymore. It felt as though she was blaming me for where she was, for her unhappiness. In all this time, I had never let myself think about whether Vivian had really wanted to give up her child, about why she had done it, why she had followed me to Devon, why she had let my decisions lead hers. Perhaps I had simply refused to see anything other than myself. Or perhaps I wanted the perfect, ethereal Vivian to be human and damaged, like me.

Standing up too quickly, lightheaded from smoking the cigarette too fast, my head rocked. "I'm going to bed. I'm sorry, Vivian, but I can't have this conversation."

I left her there and went to find a bed in the communal cabin, a cramped low-ceilinged room with rows of bunk beds and dark wooden panels. There were already dancers tossing in their beds, trying to find sleep among the threatening surges of the waves. Once I had made an awkward attempt at getting changed and washing my face in the tiny sinks, I hardly slept, too aware of the others as they gradually made their way to bed. Vivian came in soon after me, finding a bed on the other side of the cabin. Martha was one of the last to arrive, giggling with another girl as they lurched unsteadily between bunks to find which ones were still empty. Squeezing my eyes shut, I tried to push out my feelings of frustration. I had been failing to communicate with Vivian while Martha was enjoying herself, drinking too much wine, seeing nothing of the tensions developing between the three of us. She was oblivious to the pain she could cause. But clearly I was too; I had walked away from Vivian when she tried to open up about how she felt.

Just as the cabin was falling silent, I felt the air change above me. Opening my eyes, I saw Martha leaning over me, her face in shadow. Reaching down to me, she brushed my hair away from my cheek, my skin hot and sticky from the cramped stale heat of the cabin. She kissed me, a long, slow kiss that I matched, my lips finding hers.

* * *

We were woken at three in the morning by a loud, terrifying call from the Tannoy system. A bell was ringing and the growing shouts from outside the cabin commanded us to hurry up and get dressed. I pulled on my clothes hastily and followed the others out onto the deck. The wind was high, and a cold gray drizzle sprayed us, whether from the sea or the sky it was impossible to tell. Handing out life jackets, the crew told us that we were crossing a particularly dangerous part of the North Sea, well known for its mines, that had brought down far larger and stronger boats than our modest *Batavier II*. We were to wait on deck until the danger had passed.

There was little shelter and we shivered, walking aimlessly across the deck to keep warm. Under the blue gray of the predawn sky, the world seemed dead, forgotten, as though we were the only people left floating through the desolate waters of the Lethe.

Separating from the others, I made my way to the other side of the deck. I was looking for Martha.

"Briar." I turned around, trying to find where the voice was coming from. Tucked up under the decking of a lifeboat, a blanket she had stolen from the cabin wrapped around her legs and her life jacket being used as a pillow behind her head, she called out to me. "I'm in here." It made me smile to see her, the depressing gray cold of the night forgotten.

I clambered between the wooden beams that held up the lifeboat. My life jacket was too bulky, catching against the wood, so I removed it hastily and clutched it to me as I crawled the last few feet to get to her. It was the most sheltered place on the deck, protected from the wind. She lifted up the blanket for me and I got in next to her, feeling the heat of her legs spreading into me.

Her hand found mine and she pulled me closer to her. I could feel the quiet rise and fall of her chest close to mine. I lifted my chin, my lips pressing lightly against hers.

"What are you doing?"

We froze, our breath suddenly too loud against each other's cheeks.

"Briar, is that you?" The voice stopped, then started again, an exclamation of surprise. "Martha?"

Shifting away from one another, we lifted ourselves up, the life jackets pressed to us as though we could hide behind their buoyant bulk.

"Oh. I see." Then a terrible pause while a long finger of wind seemed to find us even in our sheltered spot.

It was Vivian, peering at us from a few feet away, the dull green and brown of her life jacket making her skin look even paler than normal.

"Don't let me get in the way of whatever this is."

Our embrace and everything it had meant to us changed fast, transforming instantly from romance to an ugly, dirty secret. Martha and I slowly crawled out of our hiding place. We secured the life jackets around us, hiding our shame beneath their weight.

When we arrived in Rotterdam, the boat pulling into a harbor at the end of the long, wide river, Vivian avoided us. She sat next to Molly Brown on the bus to The Hague, chatting to her loudly and cheerfully. It seemed to me like a performance, and not a very good one at that. Martha and I were silent the whole way there, too afraid to touch one another, too anxious to talk even about the sights of Holland building around us, the cyclists with their baskets full, flowers falling brightly from their handlebars. It was so different from London, where we had no time for flowers, no space but for gas masks and the threat of the dark. These people were yet to experience blackouts and bombs. But it was coming, and soon everything was going to change.

Our first performance was to be a double bill of *Checkmate* and *Dante Sonata*. We knew both ballets so well that we didn't need to rehearse when we arrived. Instead, we had a few hours to ourselves, checking in to the hotel and wandering the streets of The Hague until we decided we had better preserve our feet for the evening's performance. Martha and I were sharing a room at the Hotel du Passage, an old building with ornate carpets and winding staircases, half the rooms overlooking an arcade of touristy boutique shops covered by a domed glass roof, the other half opening out toward the Buitenhof. It was much more luxurious than our usual accommodation on tours around the cities and towns of England, but we couldn't find the energy to enjoy ourselves.

It was a relief when we were called to the Royal Theatre, giving us a purpose that lessened the painful agitation of our thoughts. Vivian could no longer avoid me, I hoped, when we were packed into the same dressing room. Both of us were Black Pawns in *Checkmate*, Martha a Red Pawn, and when I entered the dressing room to find Vivian scowling into the mirror as she layered heavy pencil lines around those deep green eyes, I wished I could escape to the bright laughter of the six Red Pawns' dressing room across the corridor. I had been wrong about her not avoiding me. Despite my attempts at conversation, she refused to look at me, pointedly asking one of the other girls to do up the black jacket of her costume. In an act of desperation, I tried asking her if she wanted to come and warm up with me, but she turned away, grabbing her black pointe shoes and disappearing down the corridor to the wings. I was ashamed to acknowledge that I felt lighter, relieved even, the conflict delayed by her departure.

The performance ended with *Dante Sonata*, a new ballet by Frederick Ashton in a modern style. My feet ached and I was grateful to be able to remove my pointe shoes for this one, dancing the role of one of the Children of the Light without the painful addition of pointe work. But it was the curtain call that finally succeeded in lifting my mood.

As we bowed low to a loud and enthusiastic audience, the sparkle of their full evening attire surprising us after the much more practically dressed wartime London and provincial audiences we were used to, a single flower fell at our feet. I looked down: a bright red rose, its petals gleaming under the brilliance of the stage lights. But that was just the start: we gasped, amazed, as a shower of flowers fell upon us. Roses, tulips, carnations, the large pink petals of rhododendrons. This was an extravagance alien to us, even before the war when the prima ballerina alone would graciously accept a bouquet of flowers rushed onto the stage by a nervous stagehand. Looking down at the sea of petals carpeting the front of the stage, I felt as though my life was complete. This, here, was what I wanted. I caught Martha's eye and smiled, laughing as a red tulip caught me across the cheek. Finally, Vivian was smiling too, and I ran over to her as the curtains fell, pressing a crumpled rose into her hands. She didn't throw it away. That, I supposed, was something.

In the dressing rooms, the noise levels bubbled out through the corridors as we prepared for the party hosted at the residence of Sir Nevile Bland, the Envoy Extraordinary to the Netherlands. The thought of the unrationed butter and sugar awaiting us was by far the most thrilling promise of the evening; our lives during the war were dominated by food. One of the dressers had kindly spent time during the performance trying to press the creases out of our evening gowns, and we didn't look too terrible once we'd smoothed out our hair, smudged away the darker lines of our makeup, and pinned a few of the flowers we'd gathered from the stage into posies for our wrists.

It wasn't far to the embassy residence, and we were herded inside, the corps de ballet avoiding the introductions to the important guests, instead heading straight for the buffet. We were not used to the formalities of such an occasion, but thankfully the principal dancers could do most of the work when it came to greetings and presentations. Martha and I found an alcove at the side of the parquet ballroom floor, and we tucked ourselves away with plates of hams, cheese, and thick slices of bread, drinking the champagne with a recklessness that came, no doubt, from the extravagance of the evening. It was the perfect place to watch the party play out, see who danced with whom, which girls managed to avoid the sweaty grip of the diplomats and officials trying to lead them to the dance floor, how many glasses of champagne a group of young ballet boys were seeing away at the edge of the room. They must have known this was one of their last tours with ballet shoes and evening jackets rather than boots and guns packed into their bags.

I stared up, amazed by the curtains that hung wide open against the large glass windows, the lights of the ballroom shining out into the night sky. In London this was impossible, our lives dictated by darkness and the strict rules of the blackout. Here in The Hague it felt as though war was a million miles away, just the few men wearing their military uniforms providing a gentle reminder of what was happening not far away. Three days later, all this was going to come to a terrible and violent end.

Sir Nevile and Lady Bland, our hosts, were doing a vigorous job of introductions, moving swiftly around the rooms like a pair of circus masters trying to maneuver the performers into place. They reminded me, for an instant, of our own leaders: Ninette de Valois and Frederick Ashton at the first stage rehearsal of a new ballet. A group of men in finely tailored evening suits was moving through the ballroom, their wives hovering behind them and chatting in conspiratorial tones. These were the diplomats' wives, drawn together through circumstance, the endless rounds of drinks, parties, and dinners: they looked at ease in this room full of strangers.

One of the women turned toward us, the pale blue lace of her dress swishing in an expensive curve. I felt Martha stiffen beside me.

"Is that who I think it is?" I blinked, trying to place that face, those narrow shoulders and childlike wrists, the way her eyes never settled.

"Louis's wife."

It shocked me to hear that name out loud after trying for so long to forget all about him.

"I knew it. He must be here. Oh god, Briar, shall we hide?"

I grimaced. Hiding from Louis, my halfhearted attempts to get Vivian to talk to me, it was all becoming too much. I wanted simplicity, to enjoy an evening of tulips and sugar, lights and champagne. Tonight all I wanted was to feel I had made the right decisions in my life, that I was allowed to celebrate what I had achieved. But with Vivian judging me, and Louis's wife just a few feet away, I was struggling to find the equilibrium I felt I deserved.

There he was, walking among the group of men in their perfect suits and slicked-back hair, a glass of whiskey glowing in his grip. I watched him with narrowed eyes, Martha's hand resting reassuringly on my arm. In the short time since I had last seen him, he had lost that dark and youthful look and there was a band of flesh thickening around his middle. The heavy weight of his eyebrows still hooded his eyes, but his jawline was looser than I remembered. Too many dinners and events in the embassies of Europe had turned him into the man he had been trying to avoid. It was terrifying how quickly he had changed: it was only fourteen months since I had seen him in the foyer of the Covent Garden opera house.

I wanted to despise him, to forget about the Louis I had met in Cambridge. Tonight, that was easy. Watching him talking to the other men, their wives standing apart in a watercolor of demure pastel dresses, I felt sick to think how easily I had fallen for him. He moved through the room with predatory confidence. A group of young female ballet dancers turned to him nervously as he slipped between them. Congratulating them on their performance, his hands slid down their backs, his kiss as he introduced himself to them lingering a little too long against their cheeks. The Louis I remembered had vanished. The Louis who had dreamed of breaking away from the conventional expectations of his parents, his desire to walk, flaneur-like, through the dusty streets of the cities of Europe, watching, creating, writing, anything to avoid becoming a copy of his celebrated uncle. And yet here he was, working for the Anglo–Netherlands Society, his perfect wife charming the other women with her pretty smile and appropriate conversation. She had learned quickly, it seemed. When I had seen her at the reception after the performance of *The Sleeping Princess* last year, she had seemed terrified, clutching her pregnant belly as though she couldn't quite understand where she was or what she was doing. That nervousness, it had vanished entirely.

"This was always what Louis was destined for," said Martha quietly. It was as though she could read my mind. "I don't think the Louis you thought you knew ever existed at all. That was just a boy playing at something he wasn't." She shifted closer to me, her hand moving around to my waist. "That night in Versailles. He knew what he did to you. That must have been it, don't you think, the moment when his youth and all those idealistic dreams disappeared?"

I had never thought about it like that before, never considered what that night had done to him. I supposed I didn't care. His punishment, if it even was a punishment, was nothing compared to what I had gone through.

I couldn't stay at that party a minute longer. "Come on, let's get out of here."

We slipped away without saying goodbye to anyone, finding our way back through the golden streets of The Hague.

When Vivian and the others returned to the Hotel du Passage later that night, Martha and I were still in the lobby bar, drinking wine and picking through a box of chocolates we had bought from a little shop beneath the domed glass roof of the arcade. I remember we tried to imagine ourselves as cosmopolitan and chic, sitting in our ball gowns and tapping the ash from cheap cigarettes into a faded silver tray. But in reality, we felt drab and tired, tourists longing for bed. Vivian blanched when she saw us and stormed up the staircase with her shoes in her hands. Her long white feet seemed to shine with a strange and translucent light as she flew up toward her room.

Molly, the girl she was sharing a room with, turned to us at the bottom of the stairs. Her face was stony. "Why are you treating her like this?"

Martha froze next to me, her wineglass held too tight in her grip. She didn't like being questioned. But we both knew we were behaving badly, leaving Vivian out, refusing to rectify the tensions growing between us.

Molly sighed, turning away from us as she started to climb the stairs. "You three used to be such good friends. Don't you see that leaving her out like this is really cruel? She was looking for you at the party."

"Not looking very hard then," muttered Martha. I thought her glass was going to shatter in her fist.

"Yes she was," Molly replied, pausing again a few steps up. "When she realized you'd left without her, she looked distraught."

"You don't know what you're talking about, Molly." Martha was on the defensive, her eyes blazing as she leaned forward. "Not everything is about Vivian."

But tonight perhaps it really was all about Vivian. My attempts to talk to her were unconvincing, feeble excuses to persuade myself I was doing something.

And so I made a decision: before the trip was done, I would find a way to talk to her.

As my own war brewed within me, the real war was creeping ever closer. On this doomed cultural tour, we traveled to towns that seemed to be emptying of their residents, all traces of the normality we had enjoyed in The Hague disappearing once we were out on the road. Martha mistook my silence on the bus journey to Hengelo as anxiety about the bleak landscape outside the window. For it was true that as we drove closer to the German border, the signs of war increased. Iron spikes pointed out accusingly from concrete blocks, a cruel mess of barbed wire swelling between them, and wide gray fields had been flooded as a crude form of defense. It was not, however, the depressing grimness of the approaching war that rocked me. It was Vivian and the space that refused to close between us. In ballet class, we stood at opposite ends of the barre; in the dressing rooms we stole furtive, hurried glances in the mirror. Back at the hotel, neither of us would make the journey across the corridor to knock on a bedroom door.

Looking back at that time, I find myself frozen with frustration about how I behaved. But the reality was that I was afraid of myself, of saying all the things I knew I could not say. I was scared that if I opened up to her, I would reveal the cruelty of my thoughts, how glad I'd been when she was pregnant, how it had reduced her, brought her down to my level, made her vulnerable and real. Neither of us knew who we were without ballet: it was our identity, our core. I could not bear to think of Vivian continuing to dance and perform while my very existence was threatened. My misery had been lessened by her fall.

At the theatre at Hengelo there was chaos, the local orchestra refusing to play Constant Lambert's score, some of them walking out in an anti-British display of defiance. Even this drama did not succeed in uniting us.

Hengelo was too close to the German border to be without the influence of Nazi sympathizers and spies. We saw this clearly when we arrived. As I stepped off the bus, a great spray of spittle landed right next to my foot. Looking up, I stood face to face with an angry woman, her skin red and mottled in disgust. Martha grabbed my arm and pulled me along the street to keep up with the others, while I glanced around for Vivian.

The next morning, we traveled to Eindhoven, a long journey across more barren stretches of green land and metal-gray water, barbed wire and roadblocks. Along the dreary traffic-laden roads, we were stopped frequently for our papers to be checked, soldiers in bright blue uniforms momentarily disoriented by the flowers and ribbons and pink satin shoes in our laps. Many of the soldiers were younger than our ballet boys, and I felt a tight sadness in my chest to think of them going off to war while we danced under the relative safety of the stage lights. It didn't feel right that we were readying ourselves to perform again when everything seemed to be closing in around us, but we let the routine of mending tights and darning pointe shoes lull us into a vague notion of reassurance.

We barely registered the newspapers with their great black headlines. Chamberlain, we heard in a faint whisper, was on the way out.

The news felt so far removed from us, and yet we should have been alert to this failure in our government, should have realized this was a sign that everything was changing. Neville Chamberlain's war was over, and it was up to someone new to match the country's shifting emotions: the final sentiments of appeasement, it seemed, were gone.

Our welcome at the theatre in Eindhoven was cold and unenthusiastic, and it was a relief to get back on the bus, falling asleep to the endless moan of army vehicles that drove in the opposite direction toward Germany. The next day we performed in Arnhem, more long bus journeys there and back that left me exhausted and depressed. Those glorious tulips at the theatre in The Hague, the tiaras and evening gowns that adorned the auditorium: it all felt like a dream, hard to fathom alongside the endless roads and army trucks that lined our path. Holland had transformed before our eyes, a glittering party cursed to descend into a darkening nightmare. Martha and I clung to each other in the bus, our heads resting together until one of us would shift, our necks creaking as we tried to find a comfortable position.

Gradually, with every bus journey, every checkpoint, every reluctant smattering of applause, I was forgetting Vivian. Drawing her back in to our little group was no longer a priority; everything had become too tiring and dangerous.

That night, I needed the safe warmth of Martha's arms, not the accusatory stares of my lost friend.

When our bus finally pulled up outside the Hotel du Passage at half past three in the morning on Friday, May 10, I thought my legs would fail to lift me off my seat. My muscles ached heavily from sitting uncomfortably for five hours on a cramped bus. It didn't help that we'd been dancing all evening for an audience that had only turned up out of malevolent curiosity, hostility emanating from their damp clapping and hurried exit from the auditorium during the curtain call. Miss de Valois stood as the bus arrived, turning to us with that same commanding look she always had. Even exhausted, she was equal to the finest general in the British Army. She left no room for doubt or rebellion when she told us she expected us in bed immediately. There was to be no one venturing outside the hotel until we had all met for breakfast in the morning. We knew the atmosphere in the Netherlands was changing, and our ballet mistress was not afraid to treat us like children to keep us safe. Judging by the faces staring back at her, we were simply relieved to be given direction and clarity among the insidious creep of war.

Martha took my hand, and we stepped off the bus, my vision blurring in the strange burnt-yellow lights of the streetlamps and the dull purple of the coming dawn. They still surprised me, these lights, after the relentless blackouts of London.

Reaching the entrance to the arcade, I heard my name called out behind me. At first I thought I had misheard, just one of the company mumbling as they made their way toward the hotel. But then I heard it again, louder this time, with a sharp edge that made me wake abruptly from my drowsy state.

"Briar." I turned. Vivian was standing in the middle of the street, her long legs silhouetted in the streetlamp behind her. She looked to me then like one of the Furies, her fine white hair billowing behind her like wings.

Martha tugged at my waist. "Leave it. Now is not the time for this. You've been trying to talk to her for days and she decides to avoid you until now. She can wait until the morning."

I shrugged her off, stepping out into the street. It seemed to me that Vivian was not going to let me go to bed without a confrontation. Part of me wanted it too; my eyes were wide open, the surface of my skin prickling with anticipation.

"I'll be upstairs. I don't have the energy for this." And so Martha left me there, my heart turning over and over as I watched Vivian's shadow swaying in the pearl light of the dawn. Taking another step toward her, I watched as her face came to life, her eyes flaming. She looked unsteady, her legs not quite still and her waist moving as though a strong wind was billowing about her. And yet there was no wind, just a woman who had found courage and fire.

It only took a second longer for me to spy the bottle of brandy poking out of her bag. As with many of the company, she had been drinking on the bus, sips of brandy to ease the boredom. It had sent most of the dancers to sleep, but Vivian was more awake than ever.

"Let's go inside," I said, moving toward her and holding out my hand. I knew I should talk to her, but not out here. It felt too exposed, too vulnerable, as though we were performing a fraught *pas de deux* on an empty stage.

"No. We need to do this now." She took a step away from me, one hand rising toward her hair.

"Okay. That's good. I want this too. You know I've been trying to talk to you for days." But my words sounded hollow, unconvincing. We both knew my attempts to talk to her had been half-hearted at best.

"I get to decide when we talk, Briar," she said, winding her hair tightly around her fingers. It was her habit when she was nervous, this violent yanking of her ponytail, and I wanted to prise her fingers away from her hair until she relaxed. But the look in her eyes was fierce: she was not going to let me touch her.

"Yes. I realize that now."

She shifted from foot to foot, pulling her hair tighter over her hand. It looked painful, her head rolling back as she wrenched her hair down. "Why didn't you tell me about you and Martha?"

"I don't know, Vivian. I'm sorry, but I didn't mean you to find out that way." Already I heard myself sounding defensive, my voice shaking with tiredness. Martha was right; it was too late for this.

"Don't pretend like it was all a big mistake. Of course you know why you didn't tell me. You must. It can't have been easy hiding it from me, the two of you laughing together as you built this whole world that existed without me."

"It wasn't like that. It just started and began to develop, and we were too afraid of what people would think to let anyone see us that way."

"And I'm just anyone? You didn't trust me? Or worse, you thought I'd judge you? How could you possibly think that of me?"

"No, that wasn't why."

But perhaps it was, I realized, trying desperately to think. Martha and I had never spoken about why we hadn't told Vivian, why we enjoyed the allure of secrecy. But the reality was that we thought we were moving in a different direction to her. Vivian liked to go on long, boring dates with suitable young men who worked for banks and law firms, who transferred to officer training at Sandhurst at the first whiff of war. She went for Sunday lunches with young married women and looked enviously at their babies, tucking herself beneath the solid arm of her army officer date. When her most recent young man had broken it off with her, stating some unconvincing excuse about going off to war and not wanting to get in the way of her dancing career, she had taken it as a direct sign that she would be single forever. Her depression had been unbearable, a griping neediness that shouted her insecurities for anyone to see. She had forgotten, if she ever knew, how to find value in herself. All she wanted was a conventional relationship, a marriage proposal, a child, a reversal of every decision she had made when she was pregnant just a few years ago. Vivian Grant alone was not enough.

So yes, I realized as I stood a few feet from her in the silver glow of the dawn, we had felt superior to her. Martha and I were bohemian and exciting, drawn together by a passion that stood above the dull conventions of society. The secrecy of our relationship made us float above everyone else in our specialness. Vivian was so disappointingly normal, wanting to give up everything in our unstable, theatrical, beautiful lives to get married and have a child. It was only now, seeing the flames in her eyes, that I started to consider that maybe I was wrong.

"I'm so sorry, Vivian," I said, afraid of what I would tell her next, whether I would be able to hide how I had been feeling and protect her from the cruelty of my words. But there was something about the faint dawn light, that timeless zone between night and day, that made me feel invincible, like I could say the truth and it would wash us both clean. I was wrong.

"What is the problem," she hissed, "with sharing your life with me? Just because we want different things doesn't mean I don't understand you. Did you really think I would judge you and Martha?"

"Yes, I suppose I did." I saw her take a step back from me, her body curving forward at the waist. But still I continued. "You've changed, Vivian, lost that passion for dance and art and self-determination.

We went through so much together, you and I. You know I couldn't have survived without you. But now I don't understand who you are. How can you want such a mundane existence? How can you give this up?"

She was shaking her head, refusing to hear me, but I continued. "If you wanted a different life, why didn't you keep your baby? No one was stopping you."

The streets around us were too empty, no sound or motion to swallow up my words. They were spoken and I could not take them back.

"Is that what you think?" The fire in her had gone out. She stared past me, her eyes not able to find mine. It was as though she had crumpled in on herself, her passion burned away. The tiredness and emotion crowded me, and I thought I was going to be sick. Desperately, I wanted to go back in time and try again. I wanted to give her a different version of our friendship, one that didn't drip with the supercilious cruelty I had just thrown at her.

"I'm going for a walk." The words came out in a whisper, and I barely heard her. She turned and started moving away from me into the streets of The Hague.

I have thought about that moment a thousand times. I have replayed it in my head over and over, tried to find an excuse for how I treated her, tried to justify my actions. When that hasn't worked, I have tried fantasy, changing my words, following her into the street, dragging her back to the hotel, where she would be safe.

But I didn't do any of those things. I simply watched her disappearing, the light of the growing morning refining itself around the long lines of her body.

SLEEP REFUSED TO ARRIVE. So when we heard the first planes screaming toward us only an hour after I had made it into bed, I did not move. Gunfire shook the hotel, and the roar of engines shattered the sky, but I stared at the ceiling, hoping this violent noise was my mind finally falling into a fitful sleep. When Martha started shaking me, I felt myself jump into a painful reality.

She was out of bed fast, grabbing at her shoes and coat and throwing a sweater over her nightgown. "Hurry up," she cried at me. "We need to get somewhere safe." It was an instinctive reaction, like when we had first heard the air raid sirens in London, a sound that still made our hearts beat hard against our ribs even though the sirens had not yet materialized into attacks. Here, with the undeniable noise above us, it seemed that the "phony war," as the newspapers kept calling it, had shifted into something real.

A loud bang echoed through our room, and I pushed off the covers and scrambled to where my clothes lay untidily on top of my suitcase.

Out in the corridor, there was chaos, dancers and the other hotel residents clutching at blankets and coats as they rushed uncertainly toward the staircase. The company met in the hotel lobby, our panic growing as the enemy planes and defending gunfire reverberated around us. No one knew what to do. Even Miss de Valois seemed uncertain, her initial understated insistence that this was the Dutch in battle training quickly shifting into a clear realization that the Germans were here.

The hall porter shook his head when one of the men tried to venture out into the square outside the hotel. "You're better in here," he said, closing the door firmly and ushering the young ballet dancer back into the lobby. "You don't want to be out on the streets with all those German planes flying around."

My neck strained and stretched as I looked around the lobby, desperately trying to catch sight of Vivian. It was only an hour since she had walked away from me into the streets, and I was praying that she had come back to the hotel quickly. I longed for her to walk down the staircase, her dressing gown wrapped tight around her. But there was no sign of her anywhere.

"Molly," I called, seeing her roommate pacing anxiously around the lobby, a black smear of forgotten eye makeup clouding her face. "Have you seen Vivian?"

"I was going to ask the same of you. I saw you two talking when we got off the bus."

"She went off. She said she needed to go for a walk."

"How long ago was this?"

There was an ornate Dutch mermaid clock on the wall of the lobby, its face adorned with blue and gold lettering, three pretty mermaid heads peeking out from the edges of the clock. Four thirty in the morning.

"Not much more than an hour ago. She didn't come back?"

"No, she hasn't been in our room."

Our conversation was interrupted by the light ringing of the lobby bell, a persistent note that made all our anxious discussions fade into silence. Miss de Valois stood by the desk, the hotel manager now at her side. "Everyone is instructed to stay in the hotel until further notice."

I could sense the atmosphere changing as she spoke, that voice of calm and order and reason that we had learned to trust instinctively. She could lead us into battle, and we would follow her without question. "We are expecting a call from the British Embassy at any moment. Then we will have a clear plan of how soon we can leave. For now, stay here, keep away from windows, and I suggest you start packing."

A murmur spread as we hesitated, watching each other for signs of action. It was at times like this that our complete dependency on routine and the instructions of a leader were revealed. We were a corps de ballet in everything. One of the soloists announced that he was going back to bed, which started a gradual trickle of dancers winding their way up the staircase to their rooms. Their steps faltered when a loud firing of guns exploded a few streets away and we all looked up, our faces tight with nerves. I longed to search for Vivian, but it was impossible with the German planes circling toward us and the hotel porter standing guard at the door, zealously protecting his domain. He must have felt better having a role to play, unlike the rest of us who were nothing but a nuisance, British ballerinas needing rescuing.

Down in the lobby I felt trapped and helpless. Even though the planes and explosions sounded far too real, without being able to see them I didn't know how to orient myself to my fear. Martha was right by my side, her hand resting on my arm, but even her touch did nothing to relax me.

"I'm telling Miss de Valois," I said at last. I had been watching the clock obsessively, wishing more than anything that I could turn back time and persuade Vivian back into the hotel with me. But time had moved on too fast, and it was now nearly morning, the gray wash of night transforming into day.

Vivian was nowhere to be seen, and while we had been expressly forbidden to leave the hotel, finding her was now more important than hiding her actions from our director. Martha nodded and came with me to where Miss de Valois was waiting by the phone, her foot tapping and her eyes darting from side to side. She was trying to conduct some sort of roll call, I realized, checking that she had seen each of her dancers before they started disappearing back off to bed. When I reported Vivian missing, she shook her head angrily and immediately picked up the telephone, her ear pressed closely to the receiver. I watched as she spoke to an officer at the embassy, describing Vivian in detail, repeating herself with building frustration. At last she put down the phone, turning back to me with sympathy hovering behind those fierce eyes.

"Now we wait. There is nothing you can do by going out into the streets and putting yourself in danger."

Martha and I were silent as we went upstairs, blindly following the others as the lobby cleared. There were just a few of the company left huddled together, too numb to move. They felt safer, perhaps, under the watchful eye of Miss de Valois.

We reached our room and delayed at the entrance, neither of us ready to sit passively and wait: there was a tension hovering between us. Martha sighed and stepped into the room, but I lingered, pressing my hand into the wall.

A small door was open at the end of the top floor corridor. Laughter and light spilled down through it, the wooden rungs of a ladder visible on the other side of the opening. We were drawn to the clarity of the light, how odd it seemed after all the confusion.

Martha followed me willingly. A narrow ladder led up to the roof of the hotel and we climbed awkwardly, unable to naturally judge our tread on the tightly set steps. I made my way out onto the open roof, squinting in the exposing early-morning sun. Below us was another terrace, protected somewhat by the domed glass roof of the arcade.

Up here we were exposed. The sun, the spray of guns from nearby rooftops as soldiers fought to defend their home, the surging planes that attacked from the sky: perhaps we thought we were immune to it all. But it didn't take long for the fear to hit me, a bold thud of realization that this was a dangerous place to be. It was as though a bright stage light had found me in the middle of a faulty *pirouette*.

"We can't be up here," I called out to Martha, all courage I had been feeling dissipating fast.

"It's fine," she replied. "There are loads of people."

I looked around in confusion. Why would anyone decide to stay here, when just a few miles away there was a thick plume of smoke signaling destruction at the hands of the enemy? But she was right. A group of dancers leaned against one another, their legs stretched out and their feet pointed as they watched the sky. They were like a tableau onstage, that stillness before breaking out into the give-and-take of dance. Margot Fonteyn was right in the center, her dressing gown fluttering extravagantly in the wind. Constant Lambert smoked and squinted into the sun at her side.

"Look," Martha cried out, pointing across the rooftops. It always struck me how little fear she had. She refused to worry about Vivian when there was nothing she could do to help. I followed the direction of her gaze. Planes were flying in from the direction of Rotterdam, their wings flashing in the sun. As they approached a field not far from the city, they ducked their noses and rose again, a perfect *balancé* with a sweeping *port de bras*. From the space they left behind in the sky, men were falling, slowed by the parachutes that unfurled above them. They kept on coming, hundreds of them floating down like ballerinas in tutus of silk instead of tulle. It was mesmerizing, the fabric catching the dawn light and the domed air pressing upward like the rich unraveling of a *battement fondu*. It was easy to forget this was the enemy.

The performance ended abruptly. Captivated by the dancing parachutes, we didn't notice the plane until it was nearly upon us. It hurtled fast out of the bright blue sky, the engine roaring with a thick resentment. It was so low that we could see the pilot, his head encased in protective gear that made him look alien, impersonal, a terrifying creature of destruction. The beauty had gone; this was a machine that wanted us dead.

We shrieked as the bullets from a nearby roof started spraying into the sky, running as fast as we could to hide behind the chimneys. The tiny opening from the ladder was blocked with dancers hurrying back down to safety, and Martha and I clung to each other as we covered our ears to block out the deafening noise.

When we looked up again, the plane had gone. Instead, there was a blanket of paper floating lightly on the breeze, leaflets bouncing across the rooftop like falling leaves. Pamphlets fell around us, shot down from the German plane. It seemed to us then like a rather desperate form of warfare, a misguided assumption that the people of the Netherlands could read one flimsy piece of paper scattered by an enemy plane and immediately change their minds about their friends and foe. I couldn't read most of it, the few words of Dutch I had picked up failing me. *"Bekendmaking"* I assumed meant "notice" or "warning," and a few short phrases stood out: *Alle Duitsche troepeneenheden hebben de stad omsingeld.* But I kept one of those pamphlets, a souvenir of war, translating it slowly over the years. It became a self-inflicted punishment, me sitting in the gloom of the London wartime nights with a dictionary and a notepad, trying to atone. I refused to ask for help.

Perhaps, I thought, this was my way of figuring out why it all had to happen that way, why Vivian never returned to the hotel, why I had failed her entirely. But even when I had the words translated, they gave me nothing.

There was only one way I could find the forgiveness that would set me free.

UNDER THE GLASS ARCADE ROOF OF DU PASSAGE, a chocolatier stood waiting. He smiled at the troupe of dancers making their way to the bus, a streak of chocolate staining the white of his apron. His hands were steady as he held out his silver tray of treats. Tiny pyramids of chocolate topped with walnuts nestled between slender fingers of coated candied peel. Sparkling sugar-glazed truffles wobbled next to smooth white domes of glossy delicacies. While we had been cowering inside our hotel waiting to be rescued, he had continued his work, tempering chocolate, measuring sugar, piping fine ribbons onto shining sweets. We traipsed past him now, clutching the few belongings we had been allowed to take with us, and he called out to us, pushing his tray forward into our path. I shook my head and carried on walking.

It had taken two days of waiting that had soured into a desperate boredom, but finally we were on a bus out of The Hague. Martha and I had waited in the hotel lobby for hours on end, drifting in and out of tormented sleep, staring at the door, the telephone, the comings and goings of the soldiers and the embassy staff who were looking after us. All I wanted was news of Vivian.

We were at the whim of officials who finally decided they could not risk us waiting any longer. Rotterdam, only thirty minutes away, was under attack, the death toll growing continually every time the news filtered through to our hotel. Staff from the British Embassy convinced us that they were searching for Vivian and that they would send on news as soon as they had it, but it felt wrong to be leaving The Hague without her. I hesitated as I stepped onto the bus, but a girl behind me nudged my back impatiently and I had no choice but to keep moving.

When the bus finally began its slow drive through the city, we had no idea where we were being taken. The heavily armed young soldier at the front communicated in broken phrases of English, Dutch, German, a medley of fear. A dancer behind me whispered to his friend.

"He's Jewish, that's what he's trying to say. *Juda; nicht aryan.*"

"If only we could take him back to England with us," I heard as the reply. I listened more carefully then, trying to make sense of the words of this young man, his uniform hanging badly over the width of his hips. *Ik bewaar de laste kogel vor Hitler.* Those fragments of conversations came to sit solidly within my memories later, once we were home. But right then my mind refused to settle on anything other than my own pain. All I could think about was Vivian. She had never returned to the hotel—we were leaving without her.

Six hours of a slow crawl along the long, flat road, our tempers rising and falling, arguments brewing and dissipating as we realized the pointlessness of discussion. Everyone felt the same: that we should never have come, that we had been used as pawns of diplomacy and were paying the price of our selfish desire to perform and be adored. No one mentioned Vivian: her absence was too real and terrifying, and perhaps we felt that if we did not speak of it, she would appear before us once again, her long legs wrapped under her as she tried to get comfortable between suitcases on the

cold, cramped bus. It was only me that whispered about it, a mono-
logue of anxiety next to Martha as I endlessly went through the
possibilities of what had happened that early morning, where she
had gone, why she had not returned to us. Martha barely replied,
her face turned toward the window and her eyes cold.

We were stopped frequently for passes to be checked, the entire
bus collectively holding their breath in tense anxiety, until we
finally arrived at a wood, the night crowding thickly between the
wide trunks of the trees. We processed through the bus in a daze,
our few possessions bumping against the seats as we struggled
to make our way forward to the exit. I shivered as I stretched my
legs, struggling to orient myself in this large cold forest. We could
have been anywhere. If a soldier hadn't started leading us forward
through a tangle of roots and nettles, we might have ended up in
a wilderness. Lights from a large house grew as we moved steadily
through the trees, and I wondered who lived there, where they were
now, whether they realized a troupe of ballet dancers were marching in exhaustion toward the welcome solidity of their front door.

Miss de Valois, her face gaunt with the stress and responsibility, led a roll call on the steps of this large country house somewhere in the Netherlands. She skipped Vivian Grant, the absence
easier than silence at the call of her name.

As the murmur of names and replies bounced between us, I
realized I had been in a haze for the whole drive, my mind numb
to the journey, the direction, the hours that had drifted slowly
past us. Everyone looked afraid, but there was a strangeness to us
all, as if we had been lifted out of a storybook and placed in the
pages of the wrong novel. We held our tiny bags of belongings,
but our bodies were swollen with clothes and coats, layer upon

layer of our favorite outfits that we could not bear to leave behind. Martha was wearing thick woolen socks over her stockings, her feet stuffed uncomfortably into high-heeled shoes. The men had all doubled up on two suit jackets, warm-up woolens wrapped around their necks and pullovers bulging beneath them. Their evening jackets could be spotted draped over the shoulders of the women at their sides. We all seemed to cling to one another, finding reassurance in the physical weight of each other's bodies.

Inside was a kind of sleepy chaos, the house already heaving with refugees. We moved through the rooms with sinking acceptance, realizing quickly that there was not a bed to be found. Every room was occupied, every mattress, sofa, armchair, even the stiff wooden kitchen chairs taken up by serious-looking Englishmen who sat stock-still, their suits tracking straight lines down their legs. Martha and I found ourselves outside once again, having moved through the house trying every room on the ground floor. The back garden was vast. Despite the darkness, it was easy to see its beauty, with a long sweeping lawn that traveled all the way down to a dark lake that lay like an oil painting among trees and shrubs. We could have been in a set of *Le Lac des cygnes*, the moonlight throbbing uneasily across the garden and illuminating flashes of movement at the edges of the lawn. I wouldn't have been surprised to see a corps de ballet of swans making their stately way along the lake.

"I need to sleep," Martha said, her voice tense with exhaustion. "We can't stay out here. It's freezing."

I had barely noticed the cold, finding relief in being able to stand up and move after hours in the bus. The thought of trying to find a pocket of space on the ground was far less appealing than a nighttime walk, no matter how cold it was. But I could see that Martha wasn't in the mood.

"You go in. I won't sleep yet." There was something about the garden that made me feel calm, as though all our fears could be frozen for a few hours. How could there be war, I thought, when there was such beauty? I needed this, I realized, after two days of constant anxiety.

"You're going to need sleep eventually. You hardly closed your eyes on the bus." She reached out to touch me, but I instinctively took a step back from her.

"I don't see how I'm supposed to sleep right now. Not without knowing where Vivian is."

"Don't do that, Briar." She was looking at me with exhausted eyes, her skin stretched gray across her usually tanned and neat face.

"Do what?"

"You know. Make it seem as though I don't care, that you are feeling this all so much more than me. This isn't about you. This is Vivian we're talking about: our best friend. You can't take all the responsibility and assume I'm feeling nothing."

I felt myself go rigid, shocked by this attack that seemed to come like an arrow out of the night. "I didn't say that. I know you're feeling this too. But I'm the one she argued with. I'm the one who pushed her away."

"No. We both pushed her away. But you like to think you're the only person who feels any pain. You've been like this since that terrible time with Louis, with your baby. Now with Vivian. You have burdened me and Vivian with your assumption that we've somehow got it all together, that our lives are easy and smooth while yours is complicated and emotional. But we all feel our flaws and insecurities, just the same as you." She stepped toward me again, but this time she did not try to reach out to bridge the gap between us.

"Of course I know that." I stared at her, trying to calm the feelings of rage bubbling within me. Martha was exhausted by the journey, but these words were real. It was obvious that she meant them, that she'd been letting them form and grow within her for longer than a few difficult nights of war. What had happened with Louis was four years ago, four years during which she'd hidden how she really felt behind that flawless face.

Turning away from me, she sighed. "Look, I love you. Of course I do. But sometimes loving you is hard work."

It felt as though someone had punched me in the chest, my whole concept of who I was violently shaken. I saw myself, in that second, through everyone else's eyes: emotional, hard to love, jumping from one drama to the next while perceiving only enviable perfection in my friends. She was right about one thing: I did think Martha and Vivian had it easier than me with their talent and perfect bodies and effortless style. But I had also thought Martha was my escape from pain. Instead, she had resented the role in which I had cast her.

She didn't follow me as I rushed back into the house. Suddenly the anonymous crowds inside felt more attractive than standing with Martha under the exposure of moonlight. My desire to walk through the garden with her felt immature and stupid. But so did everything I had ever said to her, those long nights together when we would talk and talk, dissecting our emotions to the finest thread. It was too much to process all at once. Perhaps it had just been my emotions we scrutinized, a one-sided oration where

I demanded everything, and she indulged my neediness. She had listened, held me, loved me. But I had failed to do the same for her.

I made my way upstairs, stepping over sleeping bodies, a mother and her two young children huddled together on the landing with coats covering their legs. The woman had propped a pillow beneath the heads of her daughters, dark curls falling gently over their eyes. Their bodies were pressed against her, finding comfort from the support of her arms. It didn't seem to matter to her that her head was at an angle, her hips digging into the ground, her feet tucked awkwardly beneath a chest of drawers. I turned away from the pathetic little tableau. It reminded me of my own selfishness. Every decision I had ever made had been for me and my best interests. Even Martha, the person I loved most in the world, knew it.

Opening a door tucked at the end of the landing, I found myself in a small parlor. There were refugees on the two quilted sofas, a few more creating makeshift beds from embroidered cushions. A dim light spread from a tasseled floor lamp in the corner and there was a calm feeling of collective quiet as the occupants settled themselves for sleep. The room looked as though it was stuck in the previous century, stuffed birds perched in bell jars, china ornaments of dancers, milkmaids, fat cupids, and shepherdesses laid out in neat order along the mantelpiece. Inside a glass cabinet, ornate teacups perched daintily on top of saucers, and dried flowers decorated every side table in large plumes of gold and purple and dusky pink. It was the perfect room in which to hide, not a member of the Sadler's Wells Ballet in sight. These people were all strangers to me, three Polish refugees who, we found out later, had escaped from a German labor camp a week earlier, and a Jewish man from Amsterdam, fleeing in the hope of meeting his sister in London. He had a British passport, he told us when we saw him again at the harbor in two days' time. I don't think we processed then how important this journey was for him.

I laid out my coat on the ground by the window, bundling up the clothes from my suitcase as a pillow. The curtains were open, and I lay looking out at the black-and-silver sky. It was a beautiful night and from this nineteenth-century parlor, frozen in time, it felt as though I was floating above my body, the fine lines of my nerves sending a wild, pulsing energy out into the air.

"Are you cold?" It was the man from Amsterdam, his accent a strange mix of English, French, Dutch, even German. He had shuffled closer to me, dragging an eiderdown with him, its blue-and-white embroidered pattern glinting invitingly. I looked up at him, lifting myself onto my elbows. His skin was golden, illuminated by the lamplight, and his features were perfectly defined, sharp and neat. In that instant, he made me think of a beautiful cat that carefully sought out attention but could be scared away with one wrong move. Perhaps it was the war, the long journey, the stress of the day, all the uncertainty of this night in an unknown house. It made me reckless and wild, and all I wanted was for him to touch me. I forgot about Martha, or at least I forgot to care about Martha, and instead I smiled at him and rolled onto my side to trap his gaze in mine.

"A little cold. Are you going to lend me that blanket?"

"How about a compromise and we share it?"

I felt a wave of tension shudder through me and then vanish as I took one edge of the blanket and pulled it over my body. The man slid in next to me, his arm immediately finding the curve of my waist. Responding, I pressed my body into him, the heat between us hidden beneath the thickness of the blanket.

Someone, one of the Poles, switched off the lamp, sending the room into a gorgeous silver darkness, all of us shapes and shadows in the night. I could be anyone and anywhere, free of all responsibility, held in the arms of a man I had spoken fewer than ten words to, his hands tracing circles around my thighs.

When I woke the next morning, sun streaming in through the window and the garden lit up brightly as though for a summer fete, I tried to delay the rush of my thoughts. But they came anyway, a brutal reminder that Vivian was missing, Martha was pulling away from me. And I had betrayed my two best friends.

Two days of waiting, shuffling sleepily from room to room, football games on the grass, the echo of songs around the piano from the Polish men, the sound of guns growing closer at night, and finally we were called out onto the lawn with instructions to depart. I had avoided Martha until it was no longer possible to stay away, but our conversations were brief and cold. She blamed me for abandoning her the previous night and I was not ready to forgive what she had said. Whenever I saw her, I turned away and tried to find another room; she too seemed to stiffen when she saw me. Part of me wanted to enclose her in a tight embrace and sob away my sorrow, but I couldn't let myself. Not when I knew how she judged me. I needed to keep a check on my emotions.

It was impossible to settle. I dreaded bumping into the man from the first night, the memories of that wild hour in the silver darkness souring quickly into regret. That body of mine, the one that had willingly let a stranger explore every inch of my skin, that had let him kiss me on my mouth, against the hard rise of my breasts, his hands traveling between my legs until I longed for him. That body was a stranger too, a traveler in an unknown land of reckless desire. But he seemed to understand how I felt and kept his distance. It turned out, after overhearing members of the company talking, that it wasn't a sister but a wife he was traveling out to join in England. Both of us were ready to pretend that night had never happened.

"Sadler's Wells Ballet company," we heard the soldiers call loudly through the house, and we gathered up our belongings before grouping on the front drive. Two buses were waiting for us, and we pushed our way on impatiently. Martha was already seated, the spaces around her taken, and she didn't even acknowledge me when I walked past her trying to catch her eye.

We were ready to leave, sick with worry and too tired to find romance any longer in the house, the garden, the uncertain drama of our escape from the Netherlands. As we had become accustomed, the bus crept slowly along the road, a journey of barely three miles taking just as many hours. Motorbikes flanked us, their loud engines a reassuring barrier against the guns and planes we could hear reverberating in the skies and fields. Soldiers sat among us, and every time the bus stopped, they pressed their guns tight against the window. Waiting in terror until the all-clear, we flattened ourselves to the ground or ducked our heads as low as we could within the confines of the narrow seats. Eventually the bus would start its halting movement forward and the guns would retreat from the glass.

I tried to reassure myself by imagining that this harbor, IJmuiden, fifty miles north of The Hague, would be a place of safety. We would get to the boat and immediately sail away to the familiar shores of England. When we arrived, though, it quickly became clear that I had been very wrong. Night arrived fast as we queued up along the edge of the quay. I pressed myself into the crowd, for once feeling comfort in numbers, but we were horribly exposed. There were so many of us: the Sadler's Wells Ballet company, English men escaping from their postings across the Netherlands, mothers holding on to their children with tight, nervous grips. If the searchlight of an enemy plane found us, then we'd be helpless, a long snaking line of terrified refugees. We didn't think of ourselves as refugees, we ballet dancers. We clung to the idea of ourselves as servicepeople sent out on a mission, admittedly a failed one. The reality was that our theatrical tour was wasting time and energy, drawing away soldiers from the German invasion to escort us to safety. We were getting in the way, helpless children taking up the space that could have led fifty more deserving and desperate people away from the threat of the Nazis. When I thought of that Jewish soldier guarding our bus two nights ago, I sensed how little we understood about the reality of this war.

Just as this thought crossed my mind, a plane appeared as if materializing out of the vast blankness of space, swooping low toward us. From across the water a loud explosion blasted its golden sparks with an angry roar. We threw ourselves to the ground, panic building. I longed to get onto the ship and for it to sail us back to the relative safety of the Essex shoreline. When the plane vanished back inland, we pulled ourselves up and gathered our belongings. There was a frantic nervousness to our movements now, the queue bunching at the entrance to the ship. A child was crying farther up the line, the mother clutching her little boy to her with a desperate grip. With the ships, the obscure darkness of the water, the rows of sandbags and metal barriers and barbed wires, soldiers patroling with heavy guns, we were stuck in a nightmare we had never thought possible.

The queue moved slowly, inching its way toward an old and imposing cargo ship. The *Dotterel* hardly filled us with confidence, but it was our escape route, and we were grateful for its size and sturdy industrial weight. When we finally reached the front, soldiers lifted us over a narrow metal barrier, casting our suitcases after us with a careless energy. They wanted us on board fast, the threat of the circling planes a constant reminder of our precarious situation.

Once on deck I clambered down a ladder into the main cabin. It felt safer than staying up out in the open air where the black skies and even blacker water merged in a frightening canvas, enemy planes waiting to break toward us like a bold splash of paint.

Underneath the deck was a vast cavernous space, the ground lined with straw and rickety-looking bunks already taken up with men, women, and children, their faces gray with the strain of escape. I stepped over people, searching for a space. Beneath me, I could feel the reeling sway of the water, the ship humming impatiently as it waited to be unleashed out to sea.

The dim light of the cargo ship cast too many shadows to be reassuring, and I paused anxiously in the middle of the hold, looking about me with a growing panic. I had lost everyone, the members of the company I had been queuing with swallowed into the dark. Finally, I caught sight of a group of dancers settling farther back toward one of the corners, their jackets spread out beneath them. Martha was among them, and I watched as she lowered herself to the ground, leaning forward over her legs in a deep stretch. The dancers moved in a canon of shapes, their limbs finding full extensions and their bodies rising and falling like a breath. Joining them, I fell into their rhythm, bending and stretching my legs in a kind of loose *grand plié*, my arms wrapping around my chest before opening wide in an indulgent stretch. Hours of bus journeys over the past few days had stiffened us, and I could sense the shared feeling of claustrophobic strain that bound our bodies.

Even in this dark cavern of a cargo ship, straw packing the ground and shaking hurricane lamps throwing shards of faint golden light, we craved movement. It wasn't much, this impromptu ballet class led by no one but a group compulsion for dance. As I let my muscles release, my hamstrings aching with the pleasure of extension, I felt something else loosen within me. Martha felt it too, I could tell even without looking at her, the slow notes of her breath revealing her to me. Looking up, I waited until she met my gaze, and we drew closer, our hands finding each other under the cover of shadows. Gripping our fingers tight together, I heard her sigh, a long, low exhalation that filled me with life. This distance between us could not be sustained, not when the weight of Vivian's absence was too much to bear alone. A nagging voice persisted, reminding me that Martha and I could not simply return to the way we were after all that had happened during this journey, but for now I was prepared to ignore those doubts and let desire console me.

Eventually the engines were summoned into a noisy roar, and the ship inched its way out into the North Sea. Martha and I drifted away from the others, finding a corner for ourselves where we could lean against one another, our bodies longing for the familiar warmth. We entangled ourselves as though we might become one.

"Girls, can I speak to you both, please?" We looked up instantly, the intrusion shocking through us as we blinked into the gloom. It was Miss de Valois, her face drained of color. In the darkness of the hold, the unsteady lurches of light from the hurricane lamps making her look sick and afraid, I had not recognized this woman who, ever since I had met her all those years ago, had been a rock of reason and order. She was our leader, the ballet mistress, director, choreographer, rule-maker, the woman who held our fate with the care and respect she knew we needed. We had all heard of ballet masters who ignored their dancers when they no longer interested them, a casual indifference or worse, dismissal that ruined careers. We were the lucky ones. And so, seeing her like this now, the strain of the last few days revealing her as human and vulnerable, made my fear undeniably real.

"We've had news from The Hague."

Both Martha and I stared up at her impassively. I was exhausted and preferred to let my brain move slowly, delaying the words she was about to say.

"From the British Embassy. I am so sorry, but they've found Vivian. She was killed during the invasion."

"What do you mean?" The question escaped from my lips, an unthinking response of confusion. How could Vivian, a ballet dancer from Pavilion Road, Belgravia, have been killed in a foreign land?

"A stray bullet from a plane, or maybe a responding soldier, it isn't clear and maybe never will be. It took a while for them to find her because a building had collapsed and they couldn't access the street."

I could tell that our ballet mistress didn't want to say any more, but we waited, expectant, for her to continue.

"She was trapped beneath the rubble, a bullet wound in her thigh."

I closed my eyes. The darkness was too empty. Images of Vivian, the pain of her wound, how afraid she must have been as death consumed her: they all crowded into my vision like an unstoppable nightmare. I pressed my fingers hard into the ground beneath me.

"Are they bringing her home?" I heard Martha whisper, her voice hoarse. I didn't understand her question. Vivian was dead; she could never come home. Those dreams she'd had of marriage, a family, starting a home of her own, those dreams I had sneered at as mediocre and ordinary, they had vanished when she walked away into the streets of The Hague.

"I will tell her family when we get back to London." I knew that her refusal to answer Martha's question meant it wasn't going to happen. It would be a long time before Vivian's body came home.

Looking away from us toward the rest of the company who were huddled together in tight groups around the hold, Miss de Valois's eyes moved swiftly over the grim canvas curtain that hid the urine-soaked communal buckets, its surface stained with the grotesque shadows of those trying to find relief. I could only describe the expression on her face as tormented horror, a shuddering disbelief that it was through her leadership that these young men and women were so afraid. But I took that pain, that responsibility she must have been feeling, and placed it firmly within my own chest. From that instant, I knew I was changed.

In a single second of realization, I had grown up, discarded my selfish, childish dreams of fame under the glittering lights of the stage. A hard core seemed to form within me, distancing me from Martha, from dance, from desire, from the dreams of my youth. All I thought about was how I was going to find the life that Vivian had yearned for, how I was going to make it exist, a memorial of what she had wanted and I had denied her.

When we finally arrived at the East Anglian port outside Harwich, a motorboat taking us to the shore followed by a creeping train journey that transported us in darkness to Liverpool Street, I had made my decision. Vivian's mother was waiting at the station, but I couldn't face her, not yet. I would need to wait until the time was right. As soon as the war was over, I was going to find the little girl that bound together Vivian and me.

When Vivian had realized she was pregnant a week after I had first felt those changes swarming angrily through my body, she was terrified. Frank Ellis, just a boy really, had moved on to new conquests and new flirtations, and she knew it would make him hate her if she told him about the baby growing inside her. We talked about it endlessly in that shared bedroom in Belgravia, throwing our limited options into the air and sifting through them as if we had any control over our path. I led the way, making it clear to both of us that we could not keep these children: they would ruin us, these alien, unwanted creatures that we needed to find a way to remove.

It was up to me to rewrite the past, to make sense of the choices I had made that had pushed Vivian toward her death.

Scene II

February 19, 1946

A startled cry wakes me, and I hurry into the living room. Jasmine is upright on the sofa, looking around her wildly as she tries to remember where she is. I go to her and kneel, taking her hand in mine.

"It's okay, Jasmine. You're with me."

"Where's Mama?"

I wince. It hadn't occurred to me that this could be the first thing she asked. I have imagined this moment so differently, her joy at escaping from the weight of her usurping mother's control, the two of us sharing in the exhilaration of our adventure.

"Jasmine, I need to talk to you about your mother."

She stares back at me, her face crumpling. In this instant she looks so young, her vulnerability exposed. I find it strange to see her this way, very different from the smiling, confident girl I know, the girl who is daunted by nothing, embracing the world with open arms.

"What's happened? Where is she?" A nervous whisper, her voice shaking.

"Mrs. Caradon is fine. You don't need to worry about her."

Jasmine is shivering, wrapping her arms tight around the pretty green fabric of her dress. It is the same dress she wore when she came to watch the open ballet class back in autumn last year, the dress in the photograph that has given me certainty and doubt in equal measure. I reach over to the armchair by the window and grab another blanket, offering it to her. She doesn't respond, so I throw it open and spread it neatly over her legs. Lines of tiredness seem to pattern her youthful face, the white blond of her hair making her look timeless, a creature from another world. The Jasmine I know keeps shifting before me, and I barely recognize her. It shocks me back to reality and I decide I cannot talk to her about this right now, not when the night is still pressing against the windows, the deceptive light of the streetlamps illuminating haphazard details of the room.

"It's the middle of the night. Why don't you try to get some sleep. We can talk in the morning."

"I don't think I can sleep here." Her voice is small, a quiver around her lips giving away how close she is to tears. I sigh. I will have to tell her now. It cannot wait until morning.

Lifting myself up and joining her on the sofa, I reach for her hand again. She lets me take it, but I feel a resistance. There is a barely perceptible recoil as she pulls back and tucks herself into the corner of the sofa.

"Jasmine, what I am going to tell you will come as a shock. And for that I am truly sorry. But once everything becomes clear, you will understand, and I promise it's all going to be so much better than it was before."

She shifts awkwardly, the blanket falling from her legs. Leaning down, I collect it up and pass it back to her, but she doesn't respond.

"I want to tell you a story about a young girl, a girl who has thought about you every day ever since the second you were born."

I press on, determined to say what I have prepared. "Your mother was very young. She didn't realize she was pregnant, and she wasn't married. I don't know if you can understand yet how serious that was, but it was impossible for her to look after you properly." I falter, uncertain how to continue. It dawns on me that perhaps she won't understand. Rosamund was there for her and I was not.

Shaking the thought away, I resume my story. This is, after all, my chance to set right the past.

"So she gave you away. To Rosamund Caradon, with her large house and money and the chance for you to grow up with far more security and opportunity than this young girl could offer you."

"What do you mean? Rosamund is my mother." She is staring right at me now, and it makes my stomach tighten to see the way her eyes blaze. It is as though the ghost of Vivian is possessing her, eyes that transport me back to the Hotel du Passage, our argument before she left and never came back. Now, I let this ghost give me the courage to continue, a reminder of the decision I made on the cargo ship back to England. But the reality is that while all this started for Vivian, as a way to atone, this is also for me. Ever since the first time I saw Jasmine playing in the woods of Gittisham, I knew I was bound to her forever.

"No, Jasmine. She adopted you when you were a baby. Your mother is right here with you now." I wait, letting this sink in. My heart is thumping hard, but I take a breath and say the one sentence that I have been waiting for. "I am your mother."

"I don't think so." Four words, spoken without even a waver in her voice. I blink at her, trying to work out what she means. She is supposed to embrace me, perhaps break into a flood of tears, the relationship the two of us have been building for months realized at last. But she doesn't do either of those things. Instead, she is staring at me with an incredulous look on her face.

"I know it's a lot to understand in one go. And I have so much still to explain to you, about why I couldn't be your mother all those years ago, how I am going to be there for you every day from now on." I let my emotions take over, rushing through the plans I have made. "Tomorrow we'll leave London, stay away for a few days until everything calms down. We'll write to Rosamund from a cottage by the beach. Explain it all. Would you like that, a cottage by the beach?"

She says nothing, her arms folded tight. I continue.

"We'll come back to London soon, of course, live together somewhere not too far from the theatres. And you can go to school as you said you'd love to do. I'll teach ballet, look after you, take you everywhere you've always wanted to go. You can finally have a life outside of that gloomy old house in Devon."

"I like that gloomy old house in Devon. It's my home."

Like a great ball of wool unraveling, I can feel myself losing control of the situation. She should have been so excited by now, imagining her new life with me. Jasmine adores me, I tell myself, the ballerina who gives her so much more than Rosamund is offering. It is too much to process, and I stamp the doubts far back and lean in toward her. "I know it seems that way now, but that's because it's all you've ever known. Imagine a new life with me, your mother." My voice breaks on those last words. *Mother.* It sounds strange, an alien version of myself that I am yet to understand. But I know this is what we both need.

"You're not my mother." She says it louder this time, a defiant shake of the head. "Take me back to my real mother now. I don't want to be here anymore."

"This is where you need to be."

She shakes her head, refusing to look at me now.

"We can talk about this in the morning, when you've had time to process it all. For now, why don't you go back to sleep."

"I can't sleep." Tears have broken, her face wet and glowing. My own are fighting to the surface, tears of frustration and disappointment. But I can't give up. Not when I am so close to making everything right. I stay with her and let her cry, each sob sending a painful shard to my chest. She is exhausted, her small hands fluttering sleepily across her cheeks as she wipes at tears that stick her fine white hair into darker strands. Eventually she falls silent into sleep.

My own sleep is broken, a restless and tormented journey through the past. I dream of a wood, a tangle of branches, my hands scratched by thorns. I fight on, searching for the clearing I know is just ahead. But all I find is a cardboard theatre disintegrating in the damp puddles beneath the trees, its colors fading into gray.

It is early when I wake, the dawn still hidden beneath the stubborn opacity of the dark. In the gloom of my bedroom, I stare hesitantly at the ballet clothes I unpacked from my bag last night: pointe shoes, warm-up woolens, makeup, hairpins. It almost feels like it could be ordinary, a normal day of ballet class, last-minute rehearsals, an opening night. But then I remember the sleeping girl in the next room, her tears, how she refused to accept me as her mother. If only Martha was here, I could ask her what I should do, find certainty in her wisdom.

Always it has been Martha who has pulled me back from my depths and given me the answers I need. During the war, when she had left the ballet company and I was coming home to her here after each provincial tour, it was the thought of her that kept me going through the endless routines of class, rehearsal, long, cold train journeys. We were both so happy when Sadler's Wells Ballet took up temporary residence at the New Theatre, around the corner from the bookshop, and Martha would meet me at the stage door on the nights she wasn't working. The two of us would hurry home in the darkness, my makeup still clinging to my skin. I remember Christmas 1941, when I was a snowflake in *Casse-Noisette*. Everyone dreaded an air raid warning during a performance, but few people actually left. Signs around the theatre discouraged it: "All we ask," the signs said, "is that—if you feel you must go—you will depart quietly and without excitement." That Christmas Eve performance had passed without incident, but I had been longing to get home to Martha. The silver sparkle of my eye makeup seemed to guide us home through the blackout until we were back in her bedroom, Martha kneeling in front of me with cold cream and a face cloth as she cleansed my skin. With her father falling asleep to the sound of the wireless next door, Martha and I stripped away our makeup, our clothes, our fears, until it was just the two of us embracing in the dark.

As I stare at my face in the mirror, dabbing makeup lightly around the darkness of my eyes, I understand that Martha cannot help me this time. I am the one who sent her away. That journey I arranged to take her up to Edinburgh to review a play, that is just the start of our separation. I need to do this alone.

Once I am dressed, I slowly push open my bedroom door and make my way out into the living room. I long to find Jasmine waiting happily for me, everything I told her last night rearranged into joy and excitement.

"Good morning, my sweet one," I say quietly, a gentle call to wake and rise, to prepare for the most important day of both our lives. There is no reply, so I walk farther into the room and around to the sofa.

A shock runs through me. There is no girl sleeping on the sofa. She has vanished.

All that is left is the mess of blankets and the mocking emptiness of the cushion's hollow impression where my daughter should be lying asleep.

THE FLOWERS IN THE THEATRE FOYER are beautiful, huge plumes of tumbling roses mixed with sprays of winter flowers, camellia, hellebore, the long silver-green branches of eucalyptus. Rosamund is almost drawn in by the splendor of it all, these huge bouquets waiting to be tied to the golden frame of the auditorium. The women, a collection of dedicated ballet mothers, fuss around their creations, checking they have the adequate moisture at the stems to keep the flowers fresh for tomorrow's opening night. They remind Rosamund of her own mother before the war, when she would insist on supervising the picking of the flowers from the walled garden at Gittisham, arranging them into exquisite displays in the hallway, the dining room, the guest bedrooms for their many visitors who appeared in motorcars from London and Exeter. It had been a shock to her mother when the roses were replaced with onions, her colorful summer bulbs making way for potatoes and squash. But it had been necessary, beauty making way for utility.

And the same thought comes to her now, an uncomfortable concern that this vibrant extravagance is all too much. She feels a compulsion to run back through the corridors to Jasmine, to collect her from the frills and froth of the dressing room and take her home. Not the London flat that Rosamund is yet to make feel like home, but Gittisham with its solid walls and sweeping lawns.

While Mrs. Hookham and the other mothers are occupied with a final delivery of white roses, Rosamund slips away. The backstage corridors confuse her now that she is on her own, no alarmingly competent ballet mother to lead her. She takes a wrong turn and arrives in the scenery dock to the right of the stage, huge wooden sets sitting in anticipation of the opening night. The gothic carriage of Carabosse glimmers blue and silver at the edge of the dock, fishlike scales decorating its sides, and a giant bed draped in gold and turquoise silks lies incongruously in the center of the space. Everything seems darker now, the stage itself thudded into an eerie obscurity, and she turns quickly before making her way back along the route she came. Onward she goes, peering into each room that isn't locked in the hope it will offer some clue as to her path.

Everything has been left in a state of chaotic readiness, costumes hanging on rails, some cast over chairs with pins holding together last-minute alterations, headdresses flung onto the shelves with sequins and pearls catching the dim lights that lead her through the theatre. Pots of cold cream stand open among hairpins and colorful paints of makeup are strewn across the dressing-room tables. A storeroom full of pointe shoes has been scattered with scraps of pink ribbon, and pots of fabric dye wait in disordered anticipation on a work surface. It is as though the residents of the theatre have been snatched away amid their tasks, a magic wand waving them into nothingness.

At last there is a sign on a wall pointing her to the dressing rooms. She hurries on, a gnawing fear surging through her belly. Everything is too quiet and empty, the frantic energy from the end of the dress rehearsal dissipated into an unsettling silence. Only the pipes in the walls seem to speak to her, straining and groaning as they push their elements around the vast spaces of the theatre.

She doesn't knock, bursting into the dressing room with a fierce determination. It angers her that she let herself be separated from Jasmine even for an hour, giving in to the manipulations of Briar Woods. The dressing room is in near darkness, one set of table lights left on in the corner. Hurrying toward the light, she is surprised to see a single figure seated at the dressing table, brushing her sleek black hair into a long ponytail that runs down her back. It is not Briar, and Jasmine is nowhere to be seen.

"Have you seen Briar and Jasmine?" Rosamund blurts out, startling the ballerina who had been lost in her own thoughts. It is the lead dancer, the one who had performed as Princess Aurora in the dress rehearsal, and she looks as though her mind is still onstage. Seeing her now in a simple black jersey rather than the pink tulle of her tutu awakens Rosamund to the human toil behind this whole pretty world of make-believe.

The dancer looks at her through the reflection in the dressing-room mirror. "Briar Woods? She left a while ago. I heard her mention something about Carabosse's costume." She returns to brushing her hair before asking, "Are you her mother?"

"Yes, that's right. I need to find where Briar has taken her."

"Oh, I see." The dancer blushes, her eyes darting back to her hairbrush. Rosamund stares at her in confusion before realizing she thought Briar was her daughter. While she is just about old enough, it is a shock to realize she might actually look that old, even though she knows she has neglected her graying hair and the fine lines that have started to deepen around her eyes and lips. Tall and bony, her face has become slimmer and tauter over the years, her nose more angular and her cheekbones jutting out in profile. With the light of the dressing-room table exposing every detail of her image, she feels herself shudder at the sight of her reflection. In contrast to this beautiful ballerina sitting before her, she looks ancient, giant, too tall and clumsy, with her long limbs that will not glide in elegant ease like all these dancers. Even her slenderness is imposing, too many angles and bones showing through the loose fit of her dress.

"Do you know where I can find the Carabosse costume then?" Rosamund says, trying to keep her voice steady.

"Bobby's room. Down the hall."

When Rosamund doesn't respond, the woman looks up again with a sigh. She has huge, deep eyes, capable of capturing an auditorium. Even without her stage makeup she is beautiful, the way she stares with such a concentrated gaze that reminds Rosamund of that photograph of Briar Woods in the hatmaker's shop, the one that had struck Rosamund so powerfully the first time she saw it. Little did she know the girl in the photograph would bring such relentless torment.

"Robert Helpmann. It will be labeled on the door."

Rosamund turns without thanking her, her mind too focused on finding Jasmine. Pushing her way into the dressing room labeled with Helpmann's name, she is horrified to find the room in complete darkness. There is no one there.

Panic rises in her throat, and she has to force herself to slow her breathing and think. Walking fast, she goes straight to the stage door, where the doorkeeper leans against the exit with a cigarette balanced between his lips. He nods at Rosamund, pushing open the door for her to leave. She shakes her head and comes close to him, smoke embracing her. Breathing it in, she lets it calm her, reminding her of those stolen moments of her youth when everything was easy, when she smoked secret indulgent cigarettes behind the barn of the local farm, when there hadn't been two wars and so much loss and death and struggle. Jasmine had been her salvation, and for the second time she doesn't know where she is. After Christmas Eve, when Briar had forced her way into their lives and put Rosamund through that terrible stress, she had been determined never to let this happen again.

"Have you seen Briar Woods leave here with a little girl? I've lost my daughter." The doorkeeper cocks his head at her, processing slowly. She adds a clarification, her confidence shaken after the ballerina's mistake in the dressing room. "A little girl called Jasmine Caradon. She is my daughter and I think Briar has taken her somewhere."

"I've not seen them. Sorry, my dear. If they've left, it's not through the stage door. I don't miss anyone who comes in and out of here. Have you tried the foyer?"

"Yes, I've been there. But maybe I missed them. Can I leave a note for them with you, so they know where to find me if they do come this way?"

"Of course." He walks around to the other side of his desk, the cigarette balanced between his lips. Rummaging through a pile of papers, he pulls out a notebook. Rosamund shifts from foot to foot, impatiently waiting for him to dig through another pile to retrieve a pencil. He passes them to her and she scribbles down a note, trying to think sensibly about a place to meet. She can't go home, not yet.

To Jasmine and Briar, I could not find you in the dressing rooms. I am going to check the foyer now, but if you aren't there, I will go to the Salisbury Stores pub down the street on St. Martin's Lane and wait there until you find this note and come to meet me. From your mother/Rosamund.

As she hands it back to the stage doorkeeper, she has a thought. Perhaps they have gone to Briar's flat. She knows it isn't far from here, but she doesn't know where. Her living arrangements have never come up in their conversations, Briar always somehow bringing everything back to Jasmine and ballet.

"Can you tell me where Briar lives?" she asks the man. "Perhaps they have gone there together."

He looks at the ceiling, as if sifting through a great pile of mental information. Eventually, he looks back to her and shakes his head. "She used to live in Belgravia, with her friend Vivian Grant. I expect you've heard the story. Such a tragedy." He continues, ignoring Rosamund's shake of the head and impatient sigh. "I only met Vivian once, back in 1939 when they came here for a gala performance of *The Sleeping Princess*, as it was called then. A beautiful girl, with this long white hair that you'd never forget once you'd seen it. But she was killed during the war. In The Hague while on tour."

"So do you know where she lives now?" Rosamund presses him again, too wound up to feel the slightest interest in this story of Vivian Grant and her death. All she cares about is Briar and where she has taken her daughter.

"That's what I'm thinking. There was another girl they were both friends with who danced for Sadler's Wells Ballet a while back. She lives with her now, but where exactly I don't know. The other girl isn't a dancer anymore and I can't remember her name."

Rosamund manages to mutter a brief thank-you as she passes him the note. "You won't forget to give them this?"

The doorkeeper looks offended, taking a long drag on his cigarette. "I've never forgotten to pass on a note in all the years I've worked here. And that's nearly as long as you've been alive."

"Of course. Thank you." Rosamund escapes and runs around to the Bow Street entrance, jostling awkwardly past the nighttime revelers who linger at the corner of Floral Street. Nearly stumbling over the row of young people who have camped out along the edge of the theatre in the hope of acquiring a last-minute standing ticket for the performance, Rosamund doesn't have time to feel anything but annoyance for their overexuberant commitment. But then she notices some of them are in uniform, servicepeople still working to bring the country back to normality after the war, and her frustration diminishes.

The cold evening air is picking up into an angry wind, and Rosamund presses herself against the front doors of the theatre, hitting her hip hard when they fail to budge. The entrance is locked, the lights inside switched off. Peering through the glass doors, she can make out the piles of flowers in their extravagant arrangements, a few escaped roses and eucalyptus branches strewn across the floor. Tomorrow they will be strung up in the auditorium, decorating the royal box, but for tonight they wait like the rest of the theatre: a chaotic display of near readiness, time frozen in anticipation of the awakening.

With a sinking heart she realizes the foyer is empty. The theatre has fallen asleep for the night, a spell of slumber cast over the bricks. Everyone has gone, and her daughter has vanished.

It is a short walk to the Salisbury Stores pub, back along Floral Street, Garrick Street, and St. Martin's Lane. But she knows she cannot just go there and wait. Rosamund needs to be moving, searching, actively hunting for the woman she knows has stolen her child.

On Bow Street, the police station is still awake, golden lights shining out behind heavy windows. She hesitates, gathering her thoughts, planning her words, but then an impulse of urgency surges through her and she starts to run toward the entrance. Almost tripping as she climbs the steps, she pushes firmly against the front door of the police station. It opens easily and she is thrown inside. A blast of wind follows her, the February night seeking its way off the street.

A policeman looks at her from behind the front desk, his eyebrows furrowed in concern. Rosamund pulls herself together and approaches the desk, comforted by the friendly face of the man with his graying beard and skin wrinkled with age. Perhaps, she thinks, he will understand why she cannot wait for the theatre to wake in the morning and her search to resume. "How can I help you?" he says, leaning toward her over the desk.

"My daughter. She has gone. Taken." Rosamund tries to slow her breathing, collect her words.

The policeman is staring at her, his concern shifting into a wary suspicion. "Gone where?" he asks, sitting back in his chair.

"We were at the theatre, the opera house, backstage. My daughter, Jasmine, was in the dressing rooms with one of the dancers. I went to look at the flowers, and when I came back she was gone."

"Have you asked the dancers if they've seen her? She can't have gone far. It's a big theatre, that one. Easy to get lost inside."

"She's taken her. I know it. She's been planning this all along." Rosamund can hear her voice rising in a terrified whine.

"Okay, slow down," the policeman says, and Rosamund can make out the smallest of smirks creeping around the edge of his lips. "Who has taken her?"

"Briar Woods. She has been haunting us, befriending my daughter, and now she's got her."

"How long has she been gone for?"

Rosamund's gaze rises to the clock behind the policeman's desk. It is almost eleven o'clock. "I last saw her an hour ago."

The policeman raises an eyebrow. "So let me see if I've got this straight. Your daughter is with someone she thinks is a friend, a dancer at the opera house. You leave them together for a short while, and when you come back they've gone?"

Rosamund lets out a groan, wringing her hands in frustration. He should have rallied the other men by now. They should have started searching the streets.

The policeman continues, his voice slowing as though talking to a child. "You left them together in the dressing room? Perhaps they didn't know how to find you so have gone home to meet you there?"

"No. That's not possible."

"Look, it sounds like this girl, Briar did you say, is simply a friend of your daughter. They're probably having a lovely time somewhere and you'll see them when you get home."

Rosamund is shaking her head, her fingers gripping the edge of the desk with fierce strength. "My daughter is eight years old. She won't know what to do without me."

The policeman takes a step back, registering the desperation in her voice. "I'll talk to the PCs on the beat, tell them to keep an eye out. I suggest you go home, and if they aren't there, then come back in the morning. If they still haven't appeared in the theatre together then, which I expect they will have done, come here and I'll get more of the men out on the streets looking for them."

Rosamund stares at him in shock. He doesn't understand; he has no idea of the anguish she is feeling. Or perhaps he does, she realizes, and thinks she is mad, a crazy mother, overprotective, paranoid. The expression on his face has changed from concern to a thinly veiled amusement. And yet in truth she knows that even with every police constable in London roaming the streets, Briar will be hiding Jasmine out of their reach.

"I will be here first thing in the morning," Rosamund says, turning abruptly to leave. The tap of her heels echoes noisily through the hall as she hurries to the door and goes out once more onto the street.

The wind has picked up and her hair blows wildly around her face. Rosamund looks crazed, terrified, her head jerking from left to right as she runs. She is desperate for some sign of Jasmine and Briar. But there is no one, just strangers continuing their nighttime business. They are dreamers in their own worlds, caring nothing for Rosamund Caradon and her pain.

The Salisbury Stores is still open, a girl behind the bar stacking glasses and wiping down the glossy wooden surface. A group chats loudly in the corner, their drinks lined up along the table. Actors from the many theatres that dominate this neighborhood dissect the night's performance, their nearly missed cues, the props gone awry, the enthusiasm of the audience's reaction, the noise of the crowds at the stage door. There is something grating about their laughter, Rosamund finds as she tucks herself behind a table near the door, hidden from their curious stares as they wonder why this woman is alone in a pub late at night. Her isolation makes her conspicuous, a strange woman out of place. After the emptiness of the opera house, she feels mocked by the loudness of the actors, the careless way they light cigarettes from one another and empty their glasses in long, thirsty gulps. At least their noise drowns out the fast rise and fall of her breath as she tries to compose herself.

She needs the best view of the street in case Briar and Jasmine come this way without seeing her note. Across the mahogany wood of the table, her hands flutter nervously. The carved woodwork and etchings that crowd the walls unsettle her, their patterns making her nauseous. Looking up at the golden candelabra and the ornate staircase that swirls above her to unknown private floors, she feels awkward, an uncomfortable, incongruous figure. The last time she sat in a London pub, she had only just met her husband. That is a lifetime ago now.

The girl at the bar looks over to her with curiosity and a touch of impatience. She wants to take this woman's drink order, to clean up the empty glasses, to end her shift, her eyes flicking to the clock above the door. But Rosamund knows she can't drink anything, not when her mind is rushing from place to place, trying to work out where Jasmine could be.

Ever since that first day she met Briar Woods on the train from Exeter to London, she has been conflicted about her. Both drawn and repulsed by her, as though her presence is a threat she desires and detests, it has been difficult seeing the way her daughter latched on to her so fast, falling in love with the magical world she offered. At her more rational moments, usually when she has Jasmine safely by her side, the two of them reading a book together or playing in the gardens of Gittisham, she can appreciate the importance of Jasmine having interests beyond the boundaries of the walls of her estate, that this friendship is a positive step in her development. But the reality is that Rosamund had enjoyed the war and the way it kept them tucked away together in Devon, the evacuee children providing all the stimulation Jasmine needed to be satisfied with her life. She wonders whether it would be different if Jasmine was biologically her own, if somehow the physical differences between them have created a layer of insecurity that Rosamund can't overcome. Holding on to her daughter is all the more important, a declaration that they belong to one another. All her failures as a mother are sharpened by this one undeniable reminder. She has never told Jasmine she is adopted because every time she considers it, she finds herself shuddering with an anxious fear. She cannot risk any change to their tightly wound mother-daughter bond.

She thinks back to the train in the summer, when Briar had appeared in the doorway of their carriage, settling down in the one remaining seat despite the empty carriages farther up. How it had been like a childish courtship, drawing out her pointe shoes, enchanting the children with tales of the ballet, how she invited them to see the open class at Covent Garden. There was a deliberateness to it, one carefully planned move at a time to bring Jasmine to this moment.

Rosamund sits up, her knee knocking roughly into the table.

This suspicion has come to her before, though she expelled it from her mind as too ridiculous to be true. But now she isn't so sure. When she adopted Jasmine as a tiny newborn baby, she hadn't wanted to know the name of the birth mother. It was easier to deny her existence entirely; the less she knew about her the better. The agency in Exeter had been in a state of change, chaotic and disordered, and they'd accepted her wish without question. The manager was in the process of taking over the business from her mother, who had recently died, and Rosamund had been given the impression that the previous owner had run the operation without much care for paperwork and policies and the changing adoption rules that had started to filter in since it had become regulated back in 1926. Rosamund had found the agency through that cryptic note in her mother's diary, the illusive "Mrs. A" and her scribbled address. She knew why her mother had that name recorded; it was a period from both of their pasts that they never spoke about. That time had gone, and with the help of Jasmine's arrival in their lives, they had moved on.

Miss Allen had described herself and her mother as adoption facilitators when they had met all those years ago, the woman smiling with that large, toothy grin and gesticulating broadly as she spoke. Her mother, the elder Mrs. Allen, had found her first client in the final years of the Great War, and her work had spread by word of mouth ever since then. Priding themselves on challenging outdated attitudes to the pressures placed on unmarried mothers, Miss Allen spoke with conviction about the need to weed out the corrupt practices of those offering to organize adoptions. She despised this hidden and dirty system, vulnerable young women forced into giving up their children, the promise of money and the influence of their parents leading them to accept situations they did not want or understand. There was no guarantee when they handed their baby over to a stranger that their child would even be granted a home at all. So many of the babies languished in unsanitary conditions, the care that had been promised failing to arrive.

The Allens were different. They refused to take any babies until the adopting parents had been found. They would accommodate no screaming rows of abandoned children, no hurried exchanges of babies for a few grubby coins.

Miss Allen had been thorough in assessing Rosamund's home and questioning her about parenthood. However, she'd not batted an eyelid when Rosamund wrote "widow" on the marital status line of the form, and Rosamund felt a strange mixture of relief and sadness. She had waited so long to take this step, assuming her lack of a husband would prevent her from being accepted as an eligible candidate for adopting. But it seemed the Allens did not concern themselves with this, even in 1937 when more and more rules and regulations were complicating the path.

Rosamund is at the bar, tapping her fingers anxiously on the sticky wood while she waits for the girl to return from collecting the empty glasses of the actors in the corner. She knows what she needs to do, and it cannot wait until the morning.

"Do you have a telephone I can use?"

The girl nods, a small raise of her eyebrows as she accepts that the night's shift is far from over. "It's behind the bar. You're lucky it's me here and not Eric. He never lets anyone touch that telephone." She smiles at Rosamund as she lets her through. "I can tell you're not going to accept a no from anyone today, though."

The black box is attached to the wall, a rough brown cable running from it to the ground. Rosamund rotates the dial to call the operator, her other hand fiddling anxiously, prying open the three strands of cable cord until the girl coughs meaningfully at her and she lets go. It is a relief when the operator puts her through to Gittisham and Lydia picks up. Only at the last minute had Rosamund considered how disastrous it would have been if it was her frail mother making her slow and fumbling way to the phone late at night.

"Lydia, hello. It's me."

"Is everything okay, ma'am? Why are you calling so late?"

"I need you to do something for me. Go upstairs to the desk in my bedroom and bring down the blue address book. There's a phone number in there that I need."

The wait for Lydia to go up the stairs, fetch the notebook, and make it back down again to the telephone seems to take an age, and Rosamund worries about not being able to see out onto the street from her position behind the bar.

At last a voice cracks through the earpiece. "I've got it. What is it that you need?"

"Allen. The area code and number, please."

Rosamund doesn't linger to say thank you, just presses the phone down hard and picks it up again to call the number. This time, however, there is no speedy answer once the operator puts her through. With the telephone ringing on and on, Rosamund can feel this final idea slipping away. It's been a long time since she has felt so helpless, and she rests her head against the wall to steady herself.

"Can I help you?"

The voice shocks her after the endless ringing. Interrupted from her sleep by the persistent cry of the phone, the woman sounds unimpressed. Miss Claudia Allen makes it clear to her clients that they do not need to call her in the middle of the night. An adoption should take place in daylight with paperwork and clear heads and a baby that has been washed and fed. But many of the young women she supports understand the concept of self-preservation, how quickly their sensibly made decisions could fall apart in that one simple moment at their breast. Even though late-night telephone calls have come to be expected, she still resents them. Her mother was different, establishing herself as the great savior of women, offering them an alternative to the misery of unplanned or poverty-stricken parenthood. This zeal made up for her complete lack of organization and Miss Allen still finds herself sighing over the chaos of her mother's paperwork, records lost forever or perhaps never kept at all.

"Yes, I think so. It's Rosamund Caradon. I adopted a baby with your help in 1937. Her name is Jasmine."

"I remember." How could she forget, thinks Claudia: 1937, the year her mother had died and she was left to pick up the pieces, dragging the agency unwillingly into the modern age. She remembers Rosamund Caradon, how she'd arrived at her doorstep one January morning with a look of grim determination, as though she was prepared to fight for what she wanted. It had come as a surprise to the woman, Claudia reflects now, that the request to adopt a child had been approved. Claudia had even suggested she adopt two babies, give them the chance to grow up as siblings in that huge house in the Otter Valley. She had visited the house to check all was in order, and she'd thought how lucky they would be to have so much space and fresh air for themselves. But in the end one of the babies died just hours after it was born, and Rosamund Caradon took a single little girl home with her, signing her name as Jasmine.

"I need to know the name of the birth mother."

Silence as Claudia closes her eyes and tries to prevent a sigh from escaping her lips.

"It's important," continues Rosamund. "I think she has found my daughter and wants to take her back. All you need to do is confirm with me. Is the birth mother named Briar Woods?"

This barrage of information comes out fast and frenzied, each sentence bleeding into the next. Briar Woods. The name knocks into Claudia, the familiarity confusing her. She pauses, and Rosamund latches on to the hope of discovery. Claudia recovers quickly.

"You know this is not something I can tell you over the phone. Perhaps we can arrange a meeting here next week and we can go through it all then. There were, I remember, confidentiality agreements. I can't just go giving you the name without checking all the files."

Rosamund stiffens, Claudia Allen's words suspended uncomfortably across the miles and miles of open country. She can almost imagine the telephone wire hanging still above the Devonshire hills, a taut tension of anticipation.

"All I need you to do is say yes or no. Is the birth mother of my child named Briar Woods?"

"Wait a moment, please." Claudia places the headset on the desk and walks to her filing cabinet. Everything is arranged neatly now, the names of the adopting parents and pregnant mothers in alphabetical order, each with their own folder of documents. She opens the A–C drawer, flicking through with fast hands. It is yet unclear to her how much she is going to tell Rosamund, but it is better to have all the facts in front of her before she proceeds. A sudden thought, a desire for thoroughness, makes her also open the W–Z drawer. Briar Woods has a file too, but she knows for certain that Rosamund did not adopt Briar's daughter. Leafing through the file quickly, she is about to place it back with her knowledge confirmed. But as she does so, she sees something else in there. A sealed envelope yellowed with age, the pen faded. She cannot remember ever noticing it before, but then there was so much to sort and clear when her mother died; she couldn't read everything. But she does so now, ripping open the envelope.

A few minutes later she returns to the telephone and picks it up, her ear immediately attuned to the anxious breathing on the other end.

"I'm sorry for keeping you waiting. I can confirm that Briar Woods is not Jasmine's birth mother." A sharp intake of breath at the other end of the line. Claudia continues speaking, not hearing the click on the line. "However, there are some irregularities in the file that we should discuss in person."

There is silence. Rosamund has hung up.

Rosamund tries the operator again, her hands slipping as she turns the dial. One last chance to find out who Briar really is and why she has taken her daughter.

"Is there a telephone number registered under the name of Briar Woods?" She forces herself to speak slowly and clearly.

A silence on the other end of the line. Finally, a voice emerges. "Do you know the address?"

"No. No address."

Silence again. "Sorry. There is no number registered under that name."

Leaving the pub, she starts to walk south toward Trafalgar Square but then stops abruptly and turns north. That Briar Woods is not Jasmine's birth mother is both reassuring and terrifying, this revelation making her mind swerve painfully from one scenario to the next. A taxi rushes past too fast, the wheels screeching close to her feet. The noise and speed take her breath away and she must lean against the solid rise of a streetlamp to steady herself. She is afraid for her daughter, a girl who knows nothing of London beyond the few journeys made with Rosamund at her side, carefully chosen streets that reveal no evidence of the city's underbelly. There is, she finds, a reluctant reassurance in knowing Jasmine is with Briar, this young woman who must understand London and how to stay safe among the traffic and strangers and nighttime crowds. But another thought pushes its way in: that if Briar isn't Jasmine's mother, will she really give up everything to protect her, keep her safe even as she steals her away? Knowing they have no biological connection at all deepens the nightmare.

The opera house is in darkness, even the stage door now locked for the night. Rosamund cannot go home; she needs to be close by, watching and waiting at the last place she saw her daughter. She considers going to the police again, begging the man to take her seriously, but she knows he won't listen. How can she explain that a friend of her daughter, a beautiful ballerina, has stolen away her child?

Back on Bow Street, the queue of young men and women is pressed against the wall of the opera house, sleepily waiting for the morning to come and the box office to open. They have prepared for the night, blankets wrapped around their legs and shoulders, thermos flasks and paper bags of sandwiches lined up ready at their sides. A girl leans against her boyfriend, and he folds his arms around her, keeping out the cold wind as they wait like pilgrims before the great wall of an ancient city. Rosamund moves along the line, speaking fast as she asks them if they've seen a woman with a little girl come by here tonight. The people stare at her blankly, pulling their blankets higher around their shoulders.

Rosamund feels a wave of panic, her legs weak and her stomach churning painfully. It is as though a lead weight is slowly dropping through her bones. There is nothing she can do but join these young people, finding a place at the end of the queue and sinking down to the ground with her coat tight around her.

She will remain here until the morning comes and she can start her search once again.

I CALL FOR HER AS I MOVE FAST through the flat, trying every corner in which she could have hidden herself away. Going into Martha's room is painful; the bed is unmade, and her makeup brushes are scattered untidily along the top of the chest of drawers. So many times have I lain on that bed, watching her as she paints on her makeup, an artist of pale pinks and bronze and the deep black of kohl. I leave her room quickly: it hurts too much to think that I have lost her too. My priority is finding Jasmine.

The first timid rays of morning light filter through the closed curtains and I go to them, wrenching them open. The room shifts, bookshelves shimmering behind a floating film of dust and the sagging fabric of the sofa slowly returning to plumpness. With the daylight filling the room, I feel the reality of her loss even more. I need to find her.

When I realize the flat door is unlocked, the surprise travels through me with a jolt. Last night seems like an age ago, and I cannot remember whether I locked it in the thrill of getting Jasmine here at last. The staircase creaks in all the familiar places as I run down it, avoiding the boxes of deliveries that Martha's father stacks precariously up the stairs when he runs out of space in his storeroom. I make my way into the shop, fumbling by the back entrance for the light switch. The shutters are down across the windows and the high shelves of books darken the air. It feels like a maze to me now, hurdles of furniture and display cases to navigate.

The low temperature confuses me, and I shiver. Everything feels different, as though I am standing in the wrong bookshop, a sleep-walker waking out of place. A cold draft creeps through the shelves and a persistent banging from the doorway startles me into action.

I run to the door, horrified to find it ajar: the cold air of Cecil Court presses inside and the CLOSED sign strikes the glass in angry repetitions.

Stepping out on the street, I am desperate to catch sight of Jasmine. But as I turn around and around, a broken chaos of contorted pirouettes, I see nothing but the rows of shops and the rise of the bricks looming down from the morning sky. I struggle to focus, a fear creeping between my eyes and darkening the narrow street.

Returning inside, I force myself to slow down, to think. I cannot lose her now. My first night as a mother, and I have failed.

But then I hear something, a sound behind one of the shelves, a tiny cough followed by muffled sniffing.

I freeze, unsure how I should approach. My first thought is relief, but then a nervousness starts to dominate as I realize how afraid Jasmine must have been, running off into the London streets only to return here again, hiding among the books. But at least I have found her.

"Jasmine," I say, trying to soften my voice, removing all the anxiety that I know will only make her more afraid. "It's okay. I'm here now."

I find her curled up near the window, a display of poetry books balanced on the shelf above her. Kneeling, I smile and remove a long strand of blond hair sticking wetly to her face.

"Where did you go?" I say to her when she refuses to look up at me. There is a smear of mud on her long white socks.

"I don't know."

Finally she is speaking to me, her lip quivering. I move closer to her and give her hand a reassuring squeeze.

"I wanted to find my mama. But I couldn't remember the way home and when I asked a woman which way it was to South Kensington, she laughed at me. She leaned down toward me and grabbed my cheek and I saw she only had two teeth and her eyes were bright red."

I shudder, imagining what it must have been like for her to make her way through the London drunks.

Jasmine continues, her words faster now. She stares at me with an earnest intensity. "And I saw a policeman so I ran toward him, but then I stopped and hid because he was dragging a horrible man with him, who was shouting and pushing and had blood all over his chin. So I came back here and I was going to try again when it got light, but I was too afraid to leave." She sighs, pulling her hand out of mine. "I want to go home." She whispers the words, exhausted from lack of sleep and fear. I feel terrible, but she will understand soon. Steeling myself, I refuse to be swayed from the path we both need.

"I know you do. But can you just give me more time to help you see why it is so important you stay with me now?"

One strong shake of her head, her nose wet from crying. But I continue, desperate to find a way to make her accept me.

"Rosamund isn't your mother. It is up to me now to look after you and make sure you are happy. Rosamund wants to shut you away forever and keep you all to herself. I want you to live and experience everything you've ever dreamed about."

She doesn't answer me, her eyes glazing over with a new film of tears. I try again, reaching to her and taking her hand. Her skin is cold and wet, and she gives nothing back to me but the limp, indifferent weight of her touch. I realize I cannot take her away from London right now; she is too tired to make a journey.

"Why don't we stay here today and get some sleep. We'll leave together later, when you're ready? I know it doesn't feel like it right now, but I promise you I'm going to be the best mother you could imagine, better even than a fairy godmother with her magic spells." I try to make her smile, but she doesn't respond, ignoring my attempt to lighten the mood with magic and fairies. The adoration she felt when I was a pretty ballerina with my pointe shoes and my ballet skirts and my elaborate floral headdresses has disappeared. Perhaps, soon, we will need to return to the theatre, remind her of the feelings she used to have. "Let's get you back upstairs." I stand and reach down to her.

That is when she screams. It is so loud, piercing through the shop and bouncing angrily between the shelves of books. Her hands are pressed to her ears and her mouth is wide like the great opening of a cave, the pink of her tongue pressed taut. I panic, holding on to her and pleading with her to stop, but the scream continues growing and growing, her face bright red with the effort. After the quiet of the night, I imagine the whole world can hear her, the echoes of her cry traveling fast through the London streets.

"Jasmine, please." She turns her head and stares right at me, her scream building again and throwing itself violently between my eyes. I flinch, the pitch of her cry hitting me hard. There is something terrifying about her fury, all this energy unleashing itself like a torrent of rain and noise and thunder. I feel an echo of her cry growing within me, deep inside. My own guilt and loss and tragedy have been loosened by this primeval scream, unlocking an anger I have been trying to keep pressed down for years. I stare back at her, seeing myself reflected, a distorted warping of time flashing in those bright green eyes: Louis de Manton, the marble bench at the end of the garden, the swelling of my womb, war, death, Vivian turning from me and walking away, the enemy planes, the house in the forest outside The Hague, Martha.

We stare at one another, eyes locked. Perhaps she can see something within me, something that rivals her rage. She silences her scream and cocks her head, waiting. I find myself afraid of her, as though she has revealed unexpected layers that I had not thought existed, far from the docile princess who will be charmed by a white cat doll and a pair of satin gloves.

All my plans keep shifting, like new choreography that refuses to settle into our bodies. I will have to take her to the opera house, keep her hidden until she is ready to leave, ready to accept me. Maybe once she is back among the magic of costumes and the-atre, everything will start to dance into place. Once she sees me as the ballerina she used to trust and admire, our relationship will be repaired. It seems I cannot shed my ballerina identity so easily after all.

Jasmine will think I am taking her back to Rosamund, but it is a small deception and I know she will forgive me for it once she accepts the truth. Standing, I reach down to help her up. "Fine. The two of us will go to the theatre today. But I don't want you disappearing like this again. I need to know where you are at all times." I must sound like Rosamund Caradon. But for now, this is necessary.

She nods and stands, brushing her crumpled dress from between her legs. I admire how quickly she has recovered, content now she has got her way. It is a risk, taking her to the theatre, but I know where I can keep her hidden and entertained. I, too, will need to stay away from Rosamund, who must be searching for us both. As soon as Jasmine has slept long enough, we will leave. By then I know she will be starting to understand, her loyalties shifting in my favor.

We return upstairs, but Jasmine stops at the top of the steps. She stands stubbornly by the door, her coat in her hands.

"We'll have breakfast first," I say, taking her coat from her and leading her into the kitchen. "I'll make you some porridge and you can pretend you are Goldilocks about to meet the three bears." Her lips tighten; no fairy tales will work on her this morning, it seems.

I pour her a glass of milk while I go to the stove, collecting up a pan, oats, water. She sits upright on the chair, refusing to relax, her foot tapping a jumbled beat beneath the table.

As the porridge starts to bubble, steam loosening the chill of the room, I know what I must do. I reach into the cupboard above the stove, standing on my toes as I search through the clutter of mismatched teacups and chipped saucers. Eventually I find what I am looking for.

The bottle of brandy Martha and I relied on to help us sleep in those difficult days after Vivian's death is not quite empty. I pour Jasmine another glass of milk, this time stirring in the remaining measure of brandy. It is just enough to quiet her, to calm her nerves so I can get her into the theatre without the threat of another tantrum. For now, I need Jasmine to think that I am taking her back to the place where she last saw Rosamund, that she will be reunited with her once again.

Handing her the bowl of porridge, I replace her glass with the new one. She picks at her food, but it is a relief to see her drink the milk, a white line of froth settling above her lip.

Looking up at me, she pushes her bowl into the center of the table. "Let's go now," she says, her words an order. She will not tolerate any more delays.

Although only just past eight thirty in the morning, the streets are alive with Londoners walking swiftly toward their work. Vendors' carts lurch unsteadily over the muck of the ground, and bicycles weave in and out of the trucks and buses and motorcars that lumber into the day. I hold tightly on to Jasmine's hand as we head along St. Martin's Lane, and she keeps up eagerly, all her fears forgotten now that we are outside and on our way to the Opera House.

I peer down Floral Street and see that the stage door is opening. Mr. Jackson is standing in the doorway, greeting the first arriving dancers and theatre crew in his loud and friendly way. It is impossible to enter through there, not with Jasmine by my side. Continuing down James Street, we find a door wedged open in anticipation of the deliveries being unloaded from a catering cart a few feet away. We slip inside unnoticed, the theatre staff too busy with counting out the many crates of wine required for interval drinks. I know exactly where to go, and I drive us forward as fast as I can.

The staircase to the top floor storage rooms is old and tired, far down the list of priorities for renovation and redecoration. An acrid smell of mothballs filters toward us as we reach the top, combined with a pungent mix of leather, musk, and vinegar.

Jasmine wrinkles her nose and falters on the last step, her hand pulling out of mine.

"It's okay, Jasmine. It's safe and quiet up here, and you can rest for a bit. I know you didn't get much sleep."

"Why can't I stay down in the dressing room with you? Or in the auditorium?" There is a whine to her voice, so different to the defiant scream of before. Tiredness is consuming her, the brandy starting to send her toward sleep.

"There is too much going on today. It isn't a good idea for you to be in among all that noise and chaos when you need to sleep. I'll come to check on you in a few hours."

"I don't want to." She has stopped still and is glancing around her anxiously. I sigh, my own frustration threatening to bubble to the surface.

"Rosamund will be here soon," I lie. "She knows you're here and will come to find you as soon as she arrives." Jasmine looks at me with suspicion, but then her face relaxes. I feel terrible lying to her, but the way she clings on to the hope of seeing Rosamund again is even worse.

Leading her along the corridor, I glance into each storage room, the crates of costumes packed tightly with large labels scrawled in black ink. Memories of so many prewar productions are stacked up here, notes, arias, recitatives, great choral ensembles caught and boxed and sleeping inside the fabric of the costumes. I find the perfect room, a small alcove that has been half unpacked, dresses, shoes, and thick velvet cloaks spilling out of the crates. The costumes will entertain her until she falls asleep, and I am pleased to see a rail of tutus pressed against the edge of the room, mountains of satin and tulle. They need repair, stored up here to clear space in Wardrobe downstairs while the hundreds of costume items for *The Sleeping Beauty* are created. I fashion a bed for her out of a large brown cloak, its label cataloging it as *Faust, Marguerite, Act III*. Over her legs I place a dress from the same store box, a gray gown with a lace bodice, a faded label scribbling the illegible name of an opera singer from the past. Another dress lies underneath, and I reach for it, pressing the fabric between my fingers. This one feels more delicate, a ragged gray-and-brown shift with the name penciled faintly into the label: *Marguerite, Act IV*. A memory comes to me from my childhood: 1933, freshly arrived in London and training at Miss de Valois's school at Sadler's Wells. Vivian and I are watching a rehearsal for the opera *Faust* at the Old Vic, waiting for our own role as dancers in the Walpurgisnacht *scènes de ballet*. Marguerite, alone onstage, sits at a spinning wheel singing the most haunting of arias: "Il ne revient pas." She has gone mad, imprisoned for murdering her child and waiting for Mephistopheles to damn her forever. But it was the spinning wheel that had struck me then, why she would choose fiber and yarn and thread, the repetitive turning of that relentless wheel at this tragic crux of her life. Did she hope the wheel would continue its motion forever, binding her to this world? Or was she trying to change the fabric of time, relive her choices and find a new and better path?

Jasmine is almost asleep, her hand clutching the edge of the dress. I kiss her on the forehead and smooth down her hair. "Will you come back soon?" she whispers, her eyes drooping.

"Of course. Look, why don't you take these?" I hand her a new pair of pointe shoes, the ribbons not yet sewn. "Hold these and you'll know I'm just downstairs taking ballet class, thinking of you the whole time."

* * *

I make my way to the dressing room, joining the other girls who have arrived early: it is a day of new beginnings for us all. But as I get changed into my practice clothes, I feel so removed from them, their excitement small and trivial compared to all the decisions that have led me to this. I peer at them in the mirror as I pin my hair above my head.

It is only when I start peeling off my woolen stockings, replacing them with the pink of my ballet tights, that a shiver snakes through my skin. I will need to find a new identity now, one no longer defined by dance. As I listen to the chatter of the others, I am drawn into the eager anticipation of performance: perhaps, after all, I need to dance today, my final goodbye to the stage.

And yet while the girls talk of rehearsals and costume fittings and a busy schedule of last-minute preparations, I think of Jasmine falling asleep up in the attic of the theatre, ballet shoes clutched tight against her chest.

A SCREAM WAKES HER, the sound driving its way between the fragments of her feverish sleep. Rosamund's dreams were loud, cacophonies that drowned out the true sounds of the city. The woods surrounding her home in Devon were calling out to her, the branches singing in sighs. Among their lament, she was sure she could hear the terrible wail of a baby retreating from her, the engine of a car, wheels rolling heavily over wet ground. But she was trapped inside the house, the front door bricked over and the windows clamped shut with iron bars: every exit she tried seemed to tighten like the thick cords of a knotted rope.

Rosamund lurches awake, her eyes searching frantically for the source of the cry that woke her. But she must have still been dreaming: no one has reacted, the young people who have been sleeping beside her slowly stirring from their uncomfortable night against the wall of the Covent Garden Royal Opera House.

A red-and-yellow poster has fallen to the ground before her, the ballet advertised in large black letters. She peels it off the pavement, her eyes adjusting to the dullness of the morning as she picks out the words: *Covent Garden*; *The Sadler's Wells Ballet*; *The Sleeping Beauty*. The reality of this nightmare hits her hard as she stumbles up to her knees. Across the road, Bow Street Magistrates Court shifts slowly into life and the station next door shakes itself awake as policemen arrive on their bicycles. A few more hours, then she will march in there and demand to be taken seriously.

Pulling herself off the ground, she groans at the ache in her back. Frozen and sore, she stretches her arms above herself and starts walking swiftly in the direction of the stage door. She is disappointed to find it still locked, the day not yet far enough advanced for anyone to have arrived. Staying still is impossible, not with the cold of the night creeping painfully though her bones and her thoughts aching for news of Jasmine, so she walks around to the market, where the early-morning hour beckons a hive of activity and movement, the noise spilling out toward her. It is only just past seven and she cannot believe the energy of the market already, women tottering toward their counters with impossibly huge sacks of onions in their arms, a man pulling a cart of carrots, the green foliage of their tops shaking as he makes his steady way onward. Two old women sit smoking on top of bags of potatoes and a woman in a long fur coat selects bright carnations from a row of crates. Rosamund tucks herself inside the covered market and reaches into her purse. A pang of hunger shudders through her, only now revealing itself after the endless night of impatient sleep.

A market seller looks up at her with amused curiosity when she asks for a single apple. "It's been a long night," she says, taking it from him and turning away. She knows she looks a mess, her hair falling wildly about her shoulders, but conversation is the last thing she wants.

"Try the Nag's Head on James Street," she hears him call after her. "They open early for the traders and will be sure to give you a hot drink."

Turning back to him, she nods thankfully, holding the apple to her chest in a gesture of gratitude. The Nag's Head and the promise of a hot coffee are what she needs.

Once inside, she goes straight to the bar, where a woman is stacking clean glasses on the shelves. She throws the briefest glance at Rosamund before pushing a steaming coffee across the bar. Her fingers are long and bony, the stain of tobacco darkening her nails. Immediately she returns to her task, settling into the slow rhythm of placing each glass on the shelf. Rosamund waits anxiously, hoping this woman might be willing to break out of her morning routine to help her. When there is no sign she is going to turn back around, Rosamund starts to speak, a loud and anxious plea.

"Have you seen a woman and young girl come by here recently? The girl, she's eight years old with very blond hair."

"I can't say I have." The woman doesn't even look at her, pausing from her task only to let out three sickly coughs.

Rosamund persists, leaning her body into the bar as she tries to make the woman listen. She can feel the heat of the coffee rising toward her skin.

"I was supposed to be meeting her here, but she's not arrived." It is a version of the truth, the only one she can bring herself to say out loud right now.

The proprietor is tired of listening to her customers pour their secrets and their fears across the bar, treating her like an empty vessel waiting to be filled with their failures. She will not tolerate it, even for this sad woman with the exhausted eyes. Picking up the empty crate, she disappears into the kitchen behind the bar.

Her silence seems to mock Rosamund, an empty, insidious echo that follows her as she leaves the pub and makes a hurried path back to the theatre.

Another hour of anxious waiting, Rosamund marching briskly around the streets of Covent Garden with her eyes alert to any sign of her daughter, and at last the theatre opens. She is relieved to find the same stage doorkeeper from last night guarding the entrance.

"Haven't seen them, I'm afraid," he says, barely looking up from his newspaper as she walks in. "You still not managed to get in touch?" He glances up, taking in Rosamund's disheveled state. "Tough night, eh?"

She nods, trying to keep a firm check on the quiver at the back of her throat. The first word of kindness from anyone and she might dissolve into tears.

"Why don't you come in and use the bathroom, freshen up. You'll feel more yourself. There must be enough hairpins in this building to style an army." He chuckles to himself, pulling a cigarette out of his jacket pocket.

Rosamund thanks him and moves through toward the dressing rooms. She can just about remember the route from the night before, and coming back here now gives her a sudden burst of hope that maybe she will find Jasmine and Briar exactly as they were when she left them, playing with feathers and pearls on a headdress.

The corridors are quiet, just a few dancers dressed in practice clothes moving toward the rehearsal rooms to warm up for class. But the noise builds as she reaches the dressing rooms, peals of excited laughter escaping as the doors open and close. Waiting until the door she thinks she wants is flung open, she slips inside and glances quickly around her. There are young women drawing on their leotards and tights, cardigans and thick woolen leggings pulled over the top. A woman stands topless in front of the mirror, her breasts pulled tight and her arms above her, pinning her hair into a chignon. On a different day Rosamund knows she would have turned away, embarrassed by this unguarded display of flesh, clothes hugging the lines of their bodies with unashamed precision. But today she doesn't care. All her thoughts are on finding Jasmine.

"Has anyone seen Briar Woods?" she calls out in the room. A few heads turn toward her with looks of mild surprise at this woman with her disordered hair and crumpled clothes. But most of them ignore her.

Eventually one of the girls nearer the door takes pity on Rosamund, looking up from the floor where she crouches to shave leather off the sole of her pointe shoe with a utility knife. "Briar's dressing room is down the hall. Last door on the left."

As Rosamund walks back out to the corridor, she takes a deep breath and tells herself to stay calm. She has made enough mistakes already.

The door to the dressing room opens and she thinks she is hallucinating, her exhausted mind playing tricks. But no, there she is. Briar Woods is bursting out of the room. She moves fast, colliding directly with Rosamund. The dancer takes a step back, her feet sliding awkwardly in her ballet tights, and the two women stare at one another. Skin pale and breath hard, Briar looks as if she has seen a ghost. Stillness, time suspended, the confrontation that has been lying in wait is finally hovering between them.

Rosamund breaks the silence. "Where is Jasmine?"

"I can't do this now, Mrs. Caradon." Briar tries to break past her, pushing her away with a rough crashing of shoulders.

"Yes you can. Is Jasmine in there? You need to take me to her right now."

Briar is panicking, her body taut and ready to run. She steps forward again, this time with more force, but Rosamund grabs her by the shoulders, her grip fierce.

Rosamund can feel the words bubbling, ready to pour out, all her suspicions and fears finally surfacing. A terrible desire to crush this woman surges through her, a hot pumping in her ears building and building. The time for silence and waiting is over.

"Why are you doing this? Jasmine is not yours to take. She is my daughter and she's not going to leave with you, no matter what delusions you have convinced yourself of."

Briar struggles, but her shoulders ache from the pressure and she cannot escape. Rosamund's words bite into her, and she turns her head, refusing to listen.

"Maybe you found out that Jasmine was adopted, maybe you have always wanted a child of your own. I don't know and I really don't care. What I do know is that Jasmine is not your daughter. For a while I thought maybe she was, that you were the birth mother coming to take her back. But that's just not true, is it? You have no connection to Jasmine whatsoever. So who are you? And what do you want with my daughter?"

"You're wrong." Briar turns back to her and fixes her firmly in her gaze. "Jasmine is everything to me. I am connected to her in love, life, even death. You have no idea what I've had to go through to get to this moment. Jasmine belongs with me, even if you can't see it. Perhaps taking her from you would be more difficult if you were the perfect mother, giving Jasmine everything she needs to grow up happy and healthy. But you're not, are you? You control every minute of her life, keep her hidden away in that big old house, not letting her out of your sight. You suffocate her. Can't you see who she is? A girl waiting to grow up, whereas you want to keep her a child forever."

Rosamund almost laughs at the absurdity of this version of who she is, who her daughter is. But then she sees the conviction in Briar's delusions, and she feels her chest tightening with fear. "This simply isn't true. You have no idea what you're talking about. Do you realize she is eight years old? That's all. A child, needing protection. Why are you trying to treat her like a young woman needing to find her way in the world? You're mistaking what Jasmine needs for some complicated, twisted version of your own life. And frankly, that doesn't interest me in the slightest." Rosamund tightens her grip on Briar's shoulders, her fingers pressing hard into the bones. "Go and take your troubled past far away from me and my family."

"I can't do that, Rosamund. I need this, and Jasmine needs this too."

Rosamund feels the ground lurching beneath her. The girl before her is terrifying in her obstinance, creating a twisted narrative so far from the truth. Briar has described her as a person that she cannot recognize as herself. She has been cast as the villain, a witch holding a princess captive. That is not who she is, and she refuses to let Briar's words torment her. There is only one way forward.

Without letting go of Briar's shoulders, Rosamund takes a step toward the dancer and raises her leg. With a sharp stamp, she digs the heel of her shoe into the top of Briar's foot. The cry that follows vibrates down the corridor, Briar doubling over in pain, dressing-room doors opening, heads appearing with a growing murmur of alarm. Rosamund pulls herself away and runs into the dressing room Briar had come from, calling out for her daughter. The dancers notice her this time, her loud cries interrupting the pace of their routines. But Jasmine is not there.

Back in the corridor, Briar is crouched on the ground holding her foot, the bruising spreading fast.

"Where is she?" Rosamund screams the words at her. She is desperate, a powerful urgency traveling quickly through her. Briar looks up, gripping her foot tight. She stares at Rosamund stubbornly, her lips sealed shut.

Rosamund cannot wait any longer. She knows her daughter is here somewhere, and she knows she can find her.

When Rosamund moves past her, Briar stands and tries to keep up, but her foot is throbbing. Blood seeps along the arch of her foot, staining the pink silk of her tights. She closes her eyes, trying to control the pain, but by the time she has found the strength to continue, Rosamund has gone.

Rosamund feels a compulsion driving her onward. She flings open doors to dressing rooms, store cupboards, rehearsal spaces, the large scenery docks with the painted flats and cut cloths waiting for each act of the ballet. She can sense her daughter close by, somewhere in this labyrinthine theatre, and she keeps moving, breaking through each obstacle, each door, each startled stage-hand, musician, dancer, as though they are tangled and thorny weeds that only she can cut down. Running too close to the metal frame of an unused stage light, she feels her skirt tearing, the rip spreading fast down the plaid wool. She wrenches herself free and continues forward. Nothing can stop her this time.

A staircase, chipped paint, the steps worn. She can feel a change in the air as she climbs, the smells of leather and musk creeping toward her. Here sleeps the past. Not just the collections of old costumes, the crates of musical scores, notation books, props from productions long forgotten. She lets those lie, moving onward, drawn by visions of another time, another life, another Rosamund before Jasmine arrived in her life. It is time to face the past and trust the present, she whispers to herself. But what it will require from her is going to need a giant leap of faith.

Jasmine.

She is asleep, a pointe shoe rolled onto the ground next to her. Instantly, her mother closes the distance between them; she needs to embrace her, to feel that she is really there. It has always been this way, this instinctive desire to hold her, to reassure herself that her daughter exists, is not some trick of the imagination, a cruel illusion sent to mock her.

Rosamund takes her daughter's hand, leaning forward to feel the peaceful rise and fall of her breath. Jasmine's cheek is flushed, one leg thrown on top of the piles of fabric, a gray-and-brown dress crumpled at her feet. An urge to bundle her up and take her home dominates Rosamund's thoughts. How she longs to be back in Devon, her garden waiting, simple jobs to do about the house, the fire lit for lazy evenings together with a storybook between them, Felix sleeping on their feet. How could Briar see this as anything but the safety of childhood, a mother providing protection and love?

A sudden memory, Jasmine several months after the end of the war. They have returned from a trip to London, all the children long gone. She asks about school. When is she going to join a classroom, buy a brown leather satchel, the uniform white socks and a pinafore dress? It was the girls she had seen in Kensington, all of them skipping along the pavement toward the school entrance, their voices high and loud echoing between the Victorian porticos that framed the building. Jasmine had stopped and watched them, pulling her hand out of Rosamund's. Two days later, when they were back in Devon, Jasmine asked the question and Rosamund dismissed it with a wave. What can you get at school that you can't get here with me, she'd said, pulling out the arithmetic exercise books and spelling charts and the big atlas from the library. Rosamund had ignored her daughter's disappointment, settling at the table with her and starting on their morning lessons. But later that evening she'd found a drawing in Jasmine's sketch pad, all rough lines and blotches of colored chalk, but the sentiment was clear. Two young girls, one with long white hair, the other a brunette, holding hands as they walked up the steps into a large cream building, satchels hanging by their sides. Rosamund had closed the pad and pushed the image to the back of her mind.

Staying at home had always been the plan, and Jasmine never seemed to mind. But now, as she watches her sleep, she thinks that perhaps the dynamics of their relationship have shifted recently, that Jasmine has been pushing away from her, wanting to do more, see more, is no longer satisfied with the high green forest that borders their home. There has been a restlessness in her, as though she senses that the beginning of her life came from somewhere beyond the contours of the Otter Valley. This is Rosamund's fear, that Jasmine will find out she is adopted and pull away from her, search for those hidden roots. She has been delaying that day ever since Jasmine came into this world.

Jasmine stirs, her eyes blinking open.

"It's okay, darling, I'm here now." Rosamund takes her in her arms and the two of them hold on to each other as though their breath has become one. Jasmine wraps her arms around her mother's shoulders, squeezing tight. Neither of them moves, the bonds between them re-forming anew. If Rosamund could freeze time forever, she would do so, her daughter safely at her side, the questions she knows are coming still below the surface.

But then Jasmine seems to harden, the warmth gone. Pulling back, she reaches for the pointe shoe at her side. She fiddles with it nervously, bending the sole back and forth and rubbing the satin of the toe. Without looking up, she lets a sob escape her lips, before gathering herself and saying the words Rosamund has been dreading.

"Briar told me you aren't my mother. What did she mean by that?"

There it is. Rosamund isn't prepared and she can feel a tightness spreading through her chest. Looking at Jasmine now, the determination on her face, that certainty that something has been hidden from her, Rosamund knows her time is up. Kneeling, she takes Jasmine's hand, gently removing the pointe shoe from her grip. It seems to bite her as she takes it, a bead of blood immediately surfacing on the tip of her finger. She exclaims, raising her finger to her lips. It is only a darning needle resting in the end of the shoe. Pushing it away from her, she turns her attention to her daughter. The weight of what she is about to do seems to lighten, and she feels a surge of hope and courage.

"I *am* your mother. I have been your mother since the day you were born. But it is true I didn't give birth to you. A girl, whose name I do not know, couldn't keep you. She was very young and knew you would have a better, happier life if your mother could dedicate her life to loving you and looking after you. And that is what I have done. I have loved you every moment of every day, from before you were born, when I found out that I could adopt you. When you were growing inside someone else's womb, I loved you even then, waiting for the day you would arrive and we could be together."

Jasmine is looking at the ground as her mother speaks, the significance of these words dancing in a new and strange arrangement, shifting the version of her life she had believed to be true.

"What about my father?" she whispers, her voice uncertain. "You said he died."

"Yes, my husband died, the man who would have been your father had he lived. But he wasn't your father. I don't know who your father was, and whether he is still alive. For that I am very sorry."

Silence hangs between them, the noises of the theatre far away from this tiny room on the top floor. Finally, when Rosamund thinks she can no longer bear the strain of silence, Jasmine speaks.

"Briar said to me that you weren't my mother because *she* was my mother."

Rosamund starts to speak, to explain that isn't true. But Jasmine shakes her head, a plea for Rosamund to slow down, to wait for what she wants to say. There is a strength to the girl, as though the strangeness of the last twelve hours has shown her that she too can have a say in the stories of her past.

"I said to her that I didn't care. That even if what she said was true, that she gave birth to me and you adopted me, that you were still my mother and that I love you."

Rosamund cannot speak. All she can do is hug Jasmine again, hiding the tears streaming down her face. She has never even let herself dream that Jasmine would say those words. This, she thinks as she kisses her daughter on the cheek, is the most powerful declaration of love her daughter can ever give her.

"Let's get out of here," Rosamund says as she rises. "Can you stand?"

Smiling wryly at her mother, Jasmine gets up to her feet and shakes out her crumpled skirt. "Of course I can stand." It is a relief to see that familiar energy returning to her daughter.

"Feeling rested then?" Rosamund laughs, wrapping her arm around the girl's shoulders. Jasmine has grown this year, not for a long while now the tiny child she has watched running circles around the gardens at Gittisham. For the first time ever, Rosamund lets herself enjoy this realization, accepting the promise of her daughter's growth into the assured young girl she is becoming. "I'm sure there are more comfortable places to sleep than among all these smelly old costumes."

They make their way down the staircase, the life of the theatre filtering toward them as they reach the ground floor. Moving swiftly along the corridors, they search for the exit, stepping out of the way of the busy men and women preparing for the opening night. Music and voices and the echo of pointe shoes all mix in an orchestra of energy, until Jasmine and Rosamund find themselves at the side of the stage in the props and scenery dock. The huge painted cloths of the set seem fragmented and strange from back here, the large brushstrokes of the trees, the wobbling columns, the thick paint of the winding river and large round of a silver moon struggling to conjure the magic of an enchanted castle and forest. A rail of quick-change costumes has been prepared at the side of the space, screens marking out a small area for the dancers to change between roles, and a proper-ties table is blocked into squares with thick white lines of chalk. The illusion of theatre is laid bare, its building blocks exposed. They spy a door at the other side of the dock and walk quickly toward it, feeling vulnerable beneath the high ceilings that seem to disappear above them. Slipping through the door, they are led into another narrow corridor before this opens out into the auditorium.

Now they stop in stunned silence, amazed by the contrast between the tired jumble of backstage and the sleek calm of the auditorium. Standing at the back of the stalls circle, they gaze at the empty red velvet seats, the golden house lights illuminat-ing the vast cavern of the auditorium. Flowers are strung up along the front of the grand tier boxes and a stagehand walks slowly beneath each arrangement collecting up stray fallen petals. There is just one dancer rehearsing onstage, the set for the Prologue hanging ready behind him. From the audience's perspective it looks entirely different, the layers of the painted cloth rich and real, a forest springing to life and a fountain spurting up in blue and silver sprays of frozen motion.

"That's Robert Helpmann," whispers Jasmine. It is like watch-ing a sacred moment of privacy, the dancer concentrating hard as he flies across the stage. "He is the evil fairy Carabosse at the start before becoming Prince Florimund for the rest of the ballet.

Imagine having to take off all that evil witch makeup and change into a handsome young prince."

"That's quite a transformation," replies Rosamund, watching the powerful ripples of energy as the man bounds and turns, making the space his own. She wonders how he can find the inspiration to switch in the space of a few minutes from evil to good, cruel to kind, a witch to a prince. One character sends the princess to sleep; the other kisses her awake.

"Who's that?" Jasmine is tugging on her sleeve, pointing at a woman seated in the orchestra stalls. Rosamund turns abruptly, following the line of Jasmine's gaze. Her stomach jolts strangely when she sees her, a middle-aged woman sitting patiently in the center of the stalls. A navy Alice Woods hat is perched elegantly over the gray of her hair.

"I think we need to speak to her," Rosamund whispers, trying to calm the building anxiety of her thoughts. She doesn't understand why this woman is here, the familiar face of the Devonshire hatmaker so strange among the golden glamour of the auditorium. Slipping clumsily along the seats until they are next to her, it seems to take them an age to make their way down to the stalls.

The woman turns to them and nods, placing her hand lightly on Rosamund's. "Mrs. Caradon. I had a telephone call late last night. You and I need to talk."

"A telephone call?"

"From Miss Claudia Allen. Well, from my husband Dennis. Claudia called our home in Ottery St. Mary, but I was already in a hotel in London. I traveled up yesterday afternoon, for the opening night."

Rosamund looks at her in confusion. She doesn't understand why Alice Woods is here, why Claudia Allen wanted to speak to her. Rosamund had been preparing to confront Alice about her daughter's delusions, but it seems she has her own story to tell. Alice continues, her voice composed.

"What Claudia had to tell me took us right back to 1919, when a woman arrived at Mrs. Allen's house. Claudia was just a child then, but she has a record of that night among her mother's files."

Alice fixes her gaze on Rosamund.

"This woman had a baby girl in her arms and strict instructions to never tell anyone where the baby came from." She leans in toward Rosamund. "That woman, Mrs. Caradon, was your mother, and the baby girl was yours."

Rosamund feels a sharp pain of memory slicing through her, a baby she thought had died, a child she had buried deep within the sadness of the past.

Alice Woods takes a deep breath and turns her gaze back to the stage. What neither Alice, Rosamund, nor Jasmine realize is that Briar has made her way into the auditorium through the front of the house grand tier corridors, slipping past the stagehands who are tidying the flowers and finding a hiding place in the shade of the darkened seats. She sits in a box above them as she listens.

ALICE WOODS DID NOT THINK the day would ever come where she needed to tell this story. It has been hidden and forgotten for so long, better that way rather than drag confusion into their lives. But she has no choice now: she needs to straighten out the tangled threads of their past.

"When Briar arrived in our lives, we felt as though we had been blessed by a dozen fairy godmothers," she begins, folding her hands neatly in her lap. Rosamund bristles at hearing Briar's name, but Alice ignores her and continues.

"My husband and I tried for a baby for many years. Everyone around us was having children, babies arriving, growing up so fast, all in the space of our emptiness. Women would bring their children into the milliner's shop in Exeter where I worked as an apprentice, and I would go home to Dennis with an aching longing and a steadily sinking acceptance that it was never going to happen for us. We had already been married nine years when the war began, and Dennis went off to France. I missed him every day, but there was a relief somehow in knowing the pressure to conceive was gone. Our focus was on ourselves and survival and the surge of hope I felt every time a letter arrived from him.

"When the war ended, we expected nothing. We'd given up trying to make our bodies bring us a child and had settled into a different sort of peace, a quiet existence for the two of us. I opened the milliner's in the final years of the war, a tiny burst of color and life in our little village. I started small, the hats developing slowly among the sewing and knitting I did for the war effort. As a new shop, I had to tread carefully. Anything new, especially during war, was suspicious, and I worked hard to build connections in Ottery St. Mary. I sourced everything I could locally, sought the advice of the women who seemed to run the village, made them feel essential to my venture. I even designed a hat for the vicar's wife, and once she'd committed to me, the others followed. Soon I had people flocking to me, and when the war ended my business grew fast. A new hat among the terrible onslaught of unwanted news and endless tragedy was small but it was something. I hosted events in the evenings, a Women's Institute talk, discussions on women's suffrage, craft workshops, flower arrangement in the summer, the interior transformed as women created posies that matched their latest millinery purchase. Dennis didn't go back to his office job in Exeter after the war. He worked with me, managing the orders, balancing the books, traveling around the county to find new materials.

"This was enough for us. We were happy crafting our lives together, building a community, making a name for ourselves. Alice Woods Hats had customers from all over Devon and our lives were full. But still I felt a tug deep within me when young women came in with their perambulators, rocking babies on their hip as I showed them my latest designs. I knew that feeling would never go away entirely.

"I had a friend called Margaret Allen. She liked to be called Peggy or Mrs. A. She'd flap her hand with a loud laugh when I tried to use her full name. *We're not so fine in my corner of Exeter*, she'd say.

I enjoyed her company. She wanted to break all the rules, throw away everything we'd accepted about how we were supposed to live. I met her in 1910 at the first meeting of the NUWSS in Ottery St. Mary. We were a small group then, but our numbers grew quickly. The most vocal of anyone at our suffrage meetings, she organized marches and protests in Exeter, making rather a name for herself with the local police force. During the war, when Dennis was away, she was my rock, turning up as the shop was closing with two bottles of beer, a newspaper, and some pamphlets she wanted me to put up among my hat displays. No doubt I lost a few customers from those, women who were terrified of freedom and change, but I didn't mind. There were enough of us to drown out their disapproving stares."

Rosamund feels a pang of familiarity with this version of the local women, that clash of generations and beliefs. Her own mother was of the traditional ilk, often muttering disapproving remarks about any change to the balance of households, men and women each in their proper place.

Alice continues, delving back farther into the intimacy of her past. There is something about the timelessness of the theatre's auditorium that conjures her story with ease.

"Peggy would bring her little girl, Claudia, who'd sit behind the desk with scraps of cloth and a sketchbook, filling the page with colorful pictures. Claudia was five years old at the end of the war; Peggy was over forty. She was an old mother for those days. If you hadn't had a child by the time you were thirty, everyone assumed that was it for you. But Peggy said she hadn't been ready to give up her independence and waited for as long as she could. Eventually, when uncertainty across Europe merged into an inevitable threat of war, and her fifty-year-old husband said he could wait no longer, Claudia was born. The addition of a child curbed none of Peggy's determination to fight for women's rights. She went to just as many marches, NUWSS events, committee meetings around Exeter and Honiton, galvanizing councils into action, all with Claudia strapped to her chest.

"There was one issue that remained closest to her heart: that of women's rights over their bodies and their futures. No one seemed interested when she brought discussions around to this at the end of the committee meetings. Instead, women who moments before had been cheering loudly in support of women's suffrage were firing looks of shock at her. Her proposals were too radical, too modern. It seemed the women of Devon were not yet ready for her ideas. Nothing could deter her, though, and in 1916 she started her agency. One evening, when I'd just signed the lease on the shop and was starting to design the interior, she arrived with the two bottles of beer and a new look of defiance.

"I remember how determined she was. The Mrs. A Adoption Agency, she wanted to call it. I raised an eyebrow. Unmarried mothers, if they could get themselves into that situation, so the feeling went, should either take on the responsibility of motherhood without fuss or be grateful for the first opportunity to quietly hand over their child. I knew Peggy did not see it that way. She'd told me many times of the heartbreaking homes in the poorest parts of Exeter, young girls watching their bodies change, their terror as they held their babies, no support in place, judgment from the community, hopes of an apprenticeship, a career, all gone. And the few places that would help were corrupt, babies packed into dirty nurseries and women paying to buy a child of their own.

"Peggy had spoken about it with real passion. I remember she'd said to me that women were more educated than they had ever been, had more employment opportunities, were on the cusp of the vote. But what was the point of all that if they had no control over their bodies. Yes, she said, we need not to get pregnant, we need men to stop assuming they can do what they want with a woman's body, we need cheaper doctors. But if all that fails, we also need to give women choice, an alternative to trying to soldier on with a baby they never wanted.

"I told her that I understood, that I agreed. But she couldn't go around advertising the Mrs. A Adoption Agency. Not in 1916. She didn't like being told no. Her face was like thunder when I challenged her. Eventually I convinced her that she needed to build it up gradually, starting with word of mouth, just a few cases as people learned to respect the work she was doing.

"And so she did. The name disappeared. It was just Mrs. A and an address. That was it. And word did spread, how she made magic happen for women, for children, for the couples who longed for a child of their own. Her work traveled through the villages of Devon, spreading into Cornwall, Dorset, Somerset. I saw less of her then. She was busy traveling across the counties, interviewing couples, inspecting their homes. An anonymous woman from an estate near Dartmoor donated a sum of money to support her work and Peggy bought herself a Ford Model T, enabling her to make many more visits, her efforts growing.

"One day at the end of the war, she asked about me, if I'd adopt a child. I shook my head and said the time for that had passed. We had made our peace."

Alice stops speaking, looking up toward the stage with a small smile. She takes a deep breath before continuing.

"But then everything changed."

Rosamund shifts uneasily, the velvet seat hot beneath her. She can sense the direction of the story turning, building to something new and strange, something she is struggling to fit within the neat boundaries of her thoughts. Jasmine is falling asleep at her side, and Rosamund pulls her in closer, feeling the soft strands of the girl's hair between her fingers.

"Dennis and I were both over at Peggy's house one humid and heavy evening in the summer of 1919. We were having dinner. Peggy's husband Lionel was a writer and was reading us a hilariously damning review of his latest novel. I remember I'd brought an armful of summer red roses from the market in Ottery St. Mary, the flowers tightly closed. Something about them had caught my eye that day and I'd been drawn back to the flower stall, a rare purchase of indulgence. They were in a vase at the center of the table, vibrant buds matching our open bottle of red wine.

"It had started to rain, a loud relieving torrent, and we nearly missed the frantic knocking on the door downstairs.

"Peggy went down to see who it was. The heat of the August day had almost broken, and a warm rain was lashing the pavements in a heavy downpour. Opening the door, the first thing she saw was a large Ford car parked across the street, a man hurrying back to the driver's seat. It had been him who had knocked on the door, and now that Peggy had opened it, a woman emerged from the back of the car. She was dressed in the fashions of ten years previous, a high collar grazing her jaw and the fabric of her dress far too layered for the season. With her hair pinned firmly above her head, her face looked stretched and severe. We watched from the upstairs window, knowing exactly what was in the woman's arms. The conversation between them seemed to grow frantic, an argument brewing. All we could see were the exclamations of Peggy's arms, the woman shaking her head with a grim, determined stare. Eventually the woman pressed the bundle to Peggy's chest and disappeared inside the car. It roared off into the wet night."

Rosamund presses her hands into her skirt, her palms hot and damp. She recognizes the description of her mother: Mrs. Hampton in her old-fashioned skirts ordering the chauffeur to do her bidding.

"When Peggy came back upstairs, the rain dripping from her hair, she was all business and order. She handed the baby to Dennis while she and I rushed around warming water, finding clean cloths, heating cow's milk on the stove. A tiny baby girl, no more than a few hours old, her fingers bright red and wrinkled, her eyes pressed tightly closed. When she cried, which she did loudly and persistently, her whole body seemed to quiver with life. Lionel called for a doctor, and he came promptly, promising discretion and confirming to our great relief that the baby girl was healthy. Refusing payment, Lionel Allen gave him a signed copy of his latest book and Peggy handed him a red rose from the display in the kitchen. Mr. and Mrs. Allen knew how to make friends—with a generous ease, they seemed to draw people into helping them. Dennis and I were soon to find out how strong this compulsion could be.

"At last, we settled into a rhythm for the night, Peggy with the feeding bottle, me preparing fresh cloths and napkins. When the baby finally fell asleep, Peggy whispered to me. She said that this wasn't how it was supposed to be: she should have new parents ready to take the baby, all organized in advance. Her business was not a nursery. I questioned her about what had happened, who the woman was who had appeared at her door, but she refused to answer me. She claimed not to know, that the woman hadn't given her name or any details about why the baby needed a home. But I think she did know, or at least suspected. Perhaps she felt it was her duty now to find the child a home where it would be safe and desired.

"When morning arrived and none of us had found more than a few hours of sleep, we sat around the kitchen table, the baby swaddled in cotton and moving from one set of arms to the next. The red roses surprised us all when the sun made its blazing way into the room. Overnight the buds had sprung open to their fullest glory. Peggy handed the baby to me, and I could feel the warmth of the tiny body, all soft and small and precious. I'll never forget what happened next.

"*You know what I'm going to ask you*, she said. That was all. And I remember Dennis, how he was looking at us, a smile hovering at his lips.

"It was Dennis who said it first. *We'll do it.* That was it. The words that changed our lives. But of course we would. Ever since Peggy had walked up those stairs, the bundle in her arms, I had known."

"How did you decide what to call her?" Rosamund says, her voice barely a whisper. She knows how this story ends now, but she can't quite bring herself to the conclusion.

"Lionel suggested we name her Rose. It was because of that vase of them on the table, and a writer jumping immediately to his storybook world of names and metaphors and symbols. But I didn't think she was a Rose. I remember staring down at the fierce look on her face, her mouth puckered in a small circle of protest. I paused, as her miniature fingers grabbed mine. *Briar*, I said. *That's what we'll call her. Briar Woods.*"

THE STAGE IS EMPTY, the auditorium silent. The only sounds come from that secret world behind the proscenium arch: the murmur of the stage manager talking backstage, a dancer knocking her pointe shoes against a step somewhere not too far away, the rustle of tutus as the Wardrobe mistress shakes out the skirts for the final time.

Rosamund finds herself far away, another time, another life. She has her own story of that summer. August 1919, just eighteen and oblivious to the journey her mother takes through the hot summer rain. Her memories untangle.

It all started on November 11, 1918. Rosamund sent everyone home at lunchtime. It was not possible to work, not with the excitement of the Armistice, the people of Gittisham readying themselves for celebrations. Her parents didn't even wave goodbye as they rushed to the car, her mother wrapped in ancient furs and her father stuffed uncomfortably into the only suit that would fit over the bandaging of his leg. Their chauffeur drove them off in their large Ford car to a party with friends at Killerton House, leaving Rosamund free to do exactly as she wished.

Getting changed into warm outdoor clothes as quickly as possible, she left the house and ran along the drive toward the village. The path wound down the hill, a long and meandering road that their groundsman battled endlessly to keep clear from mud. Even with the house set up on a hill, the village was not visible from their windows, and when Rosamund was younger, she often found that she resented this distance, the thick line of trees closing them off from the cottages, the church, the farm, the village hall and its pretty lawn. And yet the real reason was not the village green or the medieval church with its precious wagon roof and sixteenth-century glass or the small stream that ran delicately under a stone bridge. The real reason was Felix.

She knew she would find Felix Gilbert at the farm. Since his injury in France, he had kept himself hidden away, hardly ever joining the other farmhands for a drink after work, burying himself in the dark of the barn to eat his lunch. But Rosamund always knew where to find him, refusing to let him avoid her, denying him the chance to turn away his scarred face and the glazed white of his damaged eye. She would run her hands over his skin, press her lips to his jaw, feel the thickness of his sandy blond hair between her fingers. And he had given up resisting her, stopped trying to persuade her to turn her attention elsewhere, to someone she could walk with on the street, someone her parents would accept at their dinner table. For it was not the scars of war on his face that kept their relationship a secret. Felix worked on the farm; Rosamund was the daughter of a landowner, a wealthy girl with a second house in London where she was soon to be sent for a season of parties and appointments, chaperoned meetings with suitable young men and their suitably sized wallets.

When she found him, she pulled him to her, inhaling the rich smells of the barn, the leather of his jacket, the animal musk that clung to him. He kissed her, finding the small of her back and wrapping his arms around her. The end of the war made him forget the impossible reality of their love; today they could feel invincible.

Felix and Rosamund had been friends since they were children. They had spent hours together at every opportunity, finding each other at village fetes, Sunday school, or simply playing in the grounds of the Gittisham estate on clear, sunny days. Rosamund's brother Matthew, keenly feeling the absence of another boy in the family with whom he could play boyish games, dragged Felix up to the house whenever he could, instructing him in a myriad of ball games and muddy outdoor pursuits, until he went to boarding school and returned with a strong sense of social hierarchies and his own superior place at the top of the hill. Matthew had given up on games by then and instead fixated on literature and theatre, vanishing to London as often as he could to meet his sophisticated thespian friends. Felix was not invited after that, but it was too late to prevent Rosamund from taking her brother's place, her friendship with Felix growing and shifting and expanding.

It had been a slow journey of discovery. They were children holding hands as they pulled each other through the play dens of the forest, and then, one day, they weren't. Rosamund and Felix both sensed the change in the way it felt when they touched, that different energy that seemed to hover between them. Smoking together behind the barn, they wanted to grow up fast. Rosamund brought matches secreted away from the kitchen, Felix sneaking cigarettes from his grandfather's coat pockets.

Felix was sixteen and Rosamund fourteen when the war began. If only they could have stayed that age for the duration.

When Felix went to France in 1916, Rosamund thought her heart would break. Her wish for adulthood was halted; she wanted more than anything for Felix to be just a year younger, protected from the pain of conscription. Her family assumed her tears were for her dear big brother Matthew, but it was Felix's departure that affected her most. Nearly a year later, the news of Felix's injury filtered to her slowly, a girl from the village whispering it to her one morning when she came to drop off her toddler at their community nursery. It was another five months before he finally arrived back home, his face wrapped in bandages. But for Rosamund, it was a relief. He was home, safe, the blindness in one eye keeping him far from the battlefields forever.

Rosamund reluctantly shifted out of his embrace, fixing the scarf tied loosely around her hair. "Let's go up to the house," she said, taking him by the hand. "My parents have gone to a party. They won't be back until late."

Felix nodded, a shy smile breaking through the lines of his face. Still, he found himself nervous around her sometimes, this beautiful woman who had emerged, swanlike, from the awkward and skinny child he had played with innocently before the war. Then she had been like a boy, her knees permanently grazed and bony, her fingernails dirty from playing in the forest, her hair tangled in an unruly bird's nest. Now he wanted to explore every part of her anew, finding all the secrets of her body, the new curves at her waist, the smooth line of her jaw, the long and graceful lines of her hands. He wanted to trace her outline, find where the girl he had known had transformed into this woman.

They ran up through the fields behind the farm and into the grounds of the Gittisham estate. When they got to the front of the house, they stood still with their shoulders touching, looking up at the impenetrable stone of the facade and the tight rectangles of the windows. A few faint lights filtered toward them, but otherwise it looked cold and uninviting. Without speaking, they kept on moving until they reached the entrance to the walled garden.

Felix and Rosamund took slow steps between the flower beds, ducked their heads underneath the trellised arches, circled around the small trees with their falling golden leaves. When they reached a hidden corner of the garden, protected and sheltered by the brick wall, an archway of rose plants, a thick shrub of sleeping jasmine, they lay down on the dampening grass, Felix throwing his jacket underneath them. Rosamund turned onto her side and nestled herself against him, breathing in the freshness of the grass and the physical aroma of hay and soil that lingered against his skin. As they slowly started moving against one another, their kisses hardened and changed. A new urgency bound their bodies into the grass and leaves and dirt.

When that evening Felix finally returned to the cottage where he lived with his grandfather, Rosamund could not bring herself to run a bath. She clung to herself, remembering everything, wanting him again and again. A branch of old lilac was entangled in her hair, a jasmine leaf stuck between the folds of her skirt. But when, two months later, she found out she was pregnant, there was no Felix to run to at the farm. She could not share the news with the one person who would understand why she was so unbearably happy, why her heart felt full to burst with the joy of his child growing inside her.

His war injuries had lingered and grown. The damage to his eye was not, it appeared, confined to the superficial limitations of sight. A brain hemorrhage killed him one morning as he walked to work at the farm, and he would never know of the child conceived among the sleeping lilac and jasmine of Rosamund's garden. His grandfather had been the one to tell her. He knew she would come to the farm in search of Felix, and he waited for her by the gate while his dogs explored familiar scents close by. But when he saw her coming across the field, he had to fight back the urge to retreat to his cottage. The four dogs returned and sat patiently at his feet as he told her, collies and retrievers who had the intelligence to sense the gravity of the conversation going on above them.

Rosamund was sick throughout her pregnancy. The wild confusion of a mind devastated by loss jarred against a body teeming with life: it shocked her into a dangerous illness that refused to mend. Her mother told her that she was arranging for the baby to be adopted, but Rosamund refused to hear it. She insisted, even when delirious with nausea, that she was going to keep the child. Her baby was born in August 1919, a terrible tearing into the world that left Rosamund perilously ill, too tired and weak to resist as her parents took her child away from her. By the time she emerged from the rank gloom of her bedroom, the heat of summer had faded, and the leaves were already changing to red and gold and brown. She moved slowly through the house and garden, finding memories of Felix in every corner, feeling the loss of her baby in each falling leaf.

By the time Armistice memorial celebrations began in November, she had given up asking her parents where her baby was buried, given up her useless pleas as her mother shut the door in silence. She could find no comfort from her brother either. He drove off to London one day, the quiet of Devon too empty and echoing after his harrowing experiences of war. She was alone, and it was only when she married that she found relief from her loneliness.

Then Jasmine came along, and her world shifted once again, this time with the wheel of fortune placing her firmly up toward the skies.

Rosamund brings herself back to the present, the sounds of the theatre sharpening once again. It feels to her like the ending of a performance when the curtain falls and the house lights rise on reality. She turns to Alice, prepared to share with her only the shortest chapter of her past.

"My mother told me that my baby died, and I never questioned her. But I can see now that was what she wanted me to think. She was terrified of me ruining my life, my chance of a good marriage, my future, all because I refused to give up my baby. She floated the idea of adoption several times, talking with enthusiasm about the industrious Mrs. A to see my reaction, but I wouldn't listen. She must have realized it would never work, that there'd be no closure, too many questions, too many opportunities for me to search. I remember that she did make an appointment with Mrs. Allen, but I persuaded her to cancel it. I suppose she took advantage of this, as well as how sick I was at the end of my pregnancy, to come up with a plan that would shut down all questions forever."

Rosamund shivers, drawing Jasmine closer. The young girl murmurs sleepily and presses her head against her mother's shoulder. Her daughter has always been an amulet against the tragedy of her past.

"I barely remember the birth. I was very sick, and I accepted my mother's story too easily. I believed my child had died. My mother would have felt no guilt in paying our chauffeur to drive her to Mrs. Allen's house, as you described."

Alice nods, reaching out her hand toward her, but Rosamund pulls away. She is not ready to find comfort in this woman. Alice doesn't give up, determined to connect with Rosamund and her pain. "You did nothing wrong. There is no judgment. What we need to do now is work out how we move on from here."

Rosamund shakes her head. She cannot think about Briar anew, not yet. The Briar she knows, the woman who tried to steal her child, cannot be consolidated into that baby she believed had died so many years ago. They are two different people: the fierceness of the love she feels for Jasmine will not let her heart soften.

All she sees is a dangerous woman, and she does not want her in their life.

Up in the grand tier, hidden among the red curtains, the roses and camellia, the long silver branches of eucalyptus, Briar grips the seat, straining to hear every word spoken between the two women in the stalls.

HERE IN THE THEATRE with the heavy curtains open, the set for
The Sleeping Beauty ready onstage, the auditorium decked in flowers, it looks and feels like a fantasy land, a world of make-believe
and strange fictions. Rosamund can sense her thoughts trying to
deny the reality of Alice's story, reframing it into a terrible fairy tale,
words that would fit easily alongside narratives of Rumpelstiltskin,
Snow White, Red Riding Hood, Hansel and Gretel. She wants to
find a way out, a small flaw that will let her challenge Alice Woods
and keep Briar away from her and Jasmine forever.

"How did Claudia Allen find all of this out?" Rosamund snaps,
turning to Alice accusingly. "You said that my mother told Peggy
Allen never to reveal this to anyone."

"There are two notes in Briar's file that make it obvious what
happened. Even though Peggy never kept many records, there were
some, and Claudia has spent years organizing them. But she never
looked at these two notes, other than to file them away without
reading them, until your telephone call last night."

Rosamund is hostile, her gaze cold and hard. But Alice keeps
talking.

"It seems Beatrice Hampton did likely pay her chauffeur to stay
silent about that drive to the house in Exeter that night, the baby
wrapped up in her arms. What she didn't know was that someone,

years later, sent an anonymous note to Mrs. Allen. All it said was *Mrs. Hampton's daughter from Gittisham Manor. That night in August 1919.* It must have been the chauffeur. Who knows why he sent it: perhaps he had retired from service by then, perhaps he was unmarried, childless, lonely, regretting the part he had played in the deception. Such few words scribbled on the back of a postcard, the picture a shadowy print of the river Exe. A cryptic plea for forgiveness perhaps. But for Peggy Allen it must have opened too many questions, making her doubt the decisions she made that night.

"She filed it away with the records of the secret adoption of Briar Woods, certain it would never be seen again. As she got older and the discussions about adoption rights started changing around her, I expect that the image of the postcard kept reappearing in her mind, a nagging message of uncertainty. And so, a year before she died, she forced herself to sit at her desk and put pen to paper. Yesterday, Claudia found and read her mother's account of the night, a memento to the truth in the permanence of ink. For there was nothing else Peggy could have done. The birth certificate had been signed by me and Dennis. To reveal the truth then would have ruined us. I know Peggy. She wouldn't have been able to do it, not to her closest friends. Briar was our daughter, and she couldn't take that away from us."

Alice tries again to draw Rosamund to her, leaning in and tilting her chin toward Jasmine. The girl cannot keep up with the conversation, her eyes drooping as she tucks herself under her mother's arm.

"I know that is something you can understand too," Alice says. "Some secrets, Peggy must have thought as she sealed the envelope and placed it in the bottom of her desk, are better left undiscovered.

"When you called Claudia last night, she looked in your file. But she also looked in Briar's file. She knows Briar, of course. With the Allens being old family friends, you saying her name like that got her thinking. Apparently, you hung up before she could explain what she had found. She was concerned, and contacted Dennis, who then called me at my hotel."

The sounds of the theatre are rising: piano music drifts in from the side of the stage and there is the singsong echo of a ballet mistress calling out instructions for the start of class. Jasmine is by her mother's side, her attention drifting drowsily between the words of the two women and the dancing shadows that move across the stage. The theatre is trembling with anticipation, every minute bringing them closer to opening night.

Rosamund closes her eyes, sees the years dancing wildly into new patterns and shapes under the pink of her eyelids. When she opens them again, Alice Woods is looking at her anxiously, her hands pressed together in her lap.

Alice feels as though she is holding her breath, her chest tight as she looks up at the tumbling displays of flowers that decorate the grand tier boxes. She knows she is the only one who can pull together the unraveling threads of their lives. The story is not yet complete.

"You see, Mrs. Caradon, there are two sets of records about Briar in the Allen office. From when my husband and I claimed her in 1919, taking a baby that you, her birth mother, had been told was dead, a child that we had no idea was yours, or that you wanted her. And from 1937, when Briar was pregnant and knew she couldn't keep the child. She was so young then, just eighteen, and the father was not a man any of us ever wanted to see again."

Alice lowers her voice, glancing uncertainly at Jasmine. But the girl is too tired to process the story building around her.

Alice sighs, uncertain. But she knows she must continue. Hard though it is, Rosamund needs to know the full story about Briar and Louis.

"He raped her, discarded her, married a rich young woman." The words hang between them a beat too long.

"So Jasmine *is* her child?" Rosamund grabs the seat in front of her, the vast ceiling of the auditorium terrifying in its height. Jasmine is suddenly awake, her eyes dry and red.

"No. Jasmine is not Briar's child."

A shape is moving forward from the back of the stalls, slipping between the aisles of red velvet and golden light until she is standing right there, a row of seats between them. Her eyes blaze. Three women, one young girl. They take in one another, staring as though seeing these faces for the first time.

All four of them have changed, the connections between them reforming, rooting themselves afresh in new ground.

Rosamund sees Felix walking toward her and wonders why she hasn't noticed before how the handsome lines of his face are traced onto Briar's.

Alice lets her heart bleed for Rosamund, how she suffered, oblivious to the fact that her daughter was living a few miles away. While Rosamund had been fitted for hats in the shop on Silver Street, her daughter was just across the road, growing up without her.

Jasmine can sense her own story slipping slowly between the revelations of these women. But she remains determined that her mother, her true mother no matter how she was born, is Rosamund Caradon. And Rosamund knows this too, finally awake to the strength of the bond she shares with Jasmine.

Only Briar refuses to let the twisted visions of her past unravel.

But something is changing. When she looks at Jasmine, the ghost of Vivian dances before her, reaching out with those bright green eyes. Her white-blond hair shivers and she seems to speak to her through the mottled clouds of memory. *You need to let her go*, the ghost says, her voice a whisper in the chords of piano music that float out from behind the stage. *Vivian made her decision; you made yours.*

When Vivian turned up at Ottery St. Mary one January day in 1937, her stomach matching the swell of Briar's, the Woods family took her under their wing. Vivian's mother had come with her to Devon but left swiftly, relieved that someone else could deal with the confusion of her daughter's situation. She longed to get back to the simple chaos of her sons with their sports and mess and oversleeping. Vivian was a burden she did not understand, and she refused to listen when Vivian told her about Frank Ellis. She did not want to know about his endless flirtations, how he moved through the ballet dancers, men as well as women, so quickly that he barely remembered the roll call of his promiscuities, how impossible it would be to marry him.

And so it was decided. Alice Woods went to see her old friend's daughter, relieved that the agency was still running even after Peggy's death. Both babies would be adopted, and Claudia would organize it all. There was no need for the girls to worry. She had found the perfect home for them, and Alice was happy to trust her.

Meredith Grant appeared at the last minute: too many nights of broken sleep worrying about her daughter meant she was unable to stay away. She met Claudia Allen, found out the plans for her granddaughter's adoption, and was there to hold Vivian's hand in those painful moments of separation. She has thought about that day so many times over the years, replaying it over and over and wondering if Vivian might still be alive if she had offered to look after the child herself, a decision that would have rerouted the tragedy of their lives. Meredith Grant and Briar Woods have both suffered with the agony of being unable to change the past.

Briar went into labor first. The midwife tried to save the baby, but the silence made its persistent journey through the house as they waited for the cry that never came. Vivian, a week later, gave birth to a healthy baby girl, white hair already springing energetically from her head. Claudia took her away and Vivian turned from the loss. There was a strange liberation, she found, in joining her friend in grief.

"Vivian knew what she was doing," Alice says, holding out her arm to Briar. "It is time for you to move on. Leave all that death behind and move forward into life."

Curtain

WITH MY FOOT STRAPPED UP in bandages beneath the pink silk of my tights, I take my place at the barre. There is an ache when I rise en pointe and the usual adrenaline of performance does nothing to ease the pain. Tonight my body will not find rhythm and routine in the clockwork preparation of performance. I missed morning class, but the ballet mistress didn't comment when we all met onstage later for final notes and last-minute rehearsals; there was too much to prepare to notice one missing member of the corps de ballet. Miss de Valois, however, stared at me with narrowed eyes when I stumbled in a landing during a rehearsal of the Garland Waltz. A shock of pain spread through my foot, and I forced myself to continue dancing the rocking *balancé*, my arms aching as they held the floral garland high.

Twenty minutes until the curtains open. I falter as I start my warm-up, my mind refusing to settle even as I work through the familiar repetitions of *pliés* and *tendus*, a *cambré* forward and back, a long, slow *développé passé*. Above me, the huge ceiling of the scenery dock seems to disappear into a disorientating expanse of too much space. I feel exposed, as though all the lights of the stage are about to turn on me and reveal who I am for everyone to see.

The assistant stage manager makes the call for beginners and the wings start to fill. I strip off my warm-up woolens and check that the ribbons on my pointe shoes are secure, my hands moving uneasily over my costume and headdress. When the music starts, those dramatic opening notes that set up the motifs of good and evil, I need to forget about the details of costumes, shoes, hair, makeup. But tonight this seems like an impossible task: nothing is taking on its usual fairy-tale hue.

There is a hush in the auditorium, and I can imagine the royal box filling, the orchestra pausing the chords of their warm-up as the king and queen take their seats. There it is, the slow tune of the national anthem that takes me back to the year before the war when Vivian, Martha, and I stood in this very spot, waiting to dance. It is a relief when those notes come to an end and the memory of my loss can fade.

Applause, Constant Lambert taking his place at the podium, those powerful first three notes. And then there they are, the two musical themes. The ballet starts with the strong, violent rhythms of Carabosse, her anger at being excluded from the christening of Princess Aurora casting a cruel curse across the castle. But then the music changes and the notes become gentle, the mellow tones of the cor anglais finding their way forward. The motif of the Lilac Fairy returns again and again throughout the ballet, a promise that love and hope can be found among tragedy. I long for those notes to speak to me tonight, but I feel nothing.

My feet seem to freeze inside my shoes as the music shifts to the opening march and the curtains draw open. A dancer has to push me onstage, and I find myself swaying with a vertiginous nausea as the bright lights find me. Looking out, everything feels wrong, distorted into shapes of grotesque proportions. Glittering jewels from the audience throb in angry rhythm and behind me the painted cloths of grand columns and green woodland sway dangerously. The set reminds me of the forest surrounding Gittisham Manor, how I watched Jasmine playing with a sensation of utter conviction in the truth of my mission. Now the memory makes me feel sick. It is a gross reminder of what I've done.

The fairies make their entrance, these six beautiful fairy god-mothers offering their gifts, blessings of virtue and goodness. I struggle to watch them from my place among the courtiers and maids of honor. Each one is a mockery of who I failed to be: there is the fairy of the crystal fountain, the enchanted garden, the woodland glades; of the songbirds and of the golden vine, each offering a charming classical solo with light feet en pointe and lively *port de bras*. But it is the entrance of Carabosse I dread most, her dramatic carriage and envious anger. The darkness of her gothic dress and black veil exudes far more power than the pink and purple and golden-edged fairy tutus and I find myself shuddering at Carabosse's fierce mime, how she relishes every stage of her curse.

This is how Rosamund sees me. My birth mother. I lost her as soon as I saw her.

The Prologue ends at last, and I have a brief respite from the glare of the stage lights while I prepare for Act I. Lining up at the side of the stage with my garland of flowers wound between my fingers, I notice two women watching from farther back in the wings. I look again, praying, hoping, that there are two more beside them, a girl, a new mother. But they are not there. I feel foolish for ever thinking they could be.

But my mother is there.

And Martha. She sees me and waves. She is smiling.

I turn away quickly, my eyes blurry with tears as I try to focus on the stage. Martha's love hurts too much: I do not deserve it, not yet. Perhaps the anonymity of the corps de ballet is what I desire, scrutiny directed only to the sharpness of our lines, the angle of our arms, the rhythm of our feet.

My mother. Martha. I cannot go to them yet. I want to hide from how they must see me, how everyone must see me. But soon the curtains will close, the house lights will brighten, and there can be no more hiding from the reality of what I have done.

Back in the safety of the Otter Valley, the rhythms of their lives do not settle easily. Jasmine struggles to focus on her lessons and Rosamund finds herself peering nervously down the driveway and out toward the thickening green of the forest, as though a face will appear to haunt them.

But no one comes, and as spring establishes itself more firmly throughout the grounds of Gittisham Manor, Rosamund can sense a pressure building inside her. And the source of it all, her mother: Beatrice Hampton, who sleeps all day downstairs by the fire, her eyes flickering open as one of them brings her weak cups of tea that she discards, a cold film of milk pooling on the surface.

When Rosamund and Jasmine arrived home after that terrible February day, they had found the old woman asleep on the sofa. Rosamund had slipped past her, guiding her daughter upstairs to get ready for bed. They were both exhausted, shaken from the events of the last few days. She could not find the strength to confront her mother, to demand an explanation for that cruel decision she made at the end of the war, all those years ago. Every day she woke thinking today would be the day: today she would find the courage to speak, to churn up the past, assert her right to the truth. But still she cannot do it. Instead, an icy barrier has built between them, hardening and sharpening until her mother is invisible, a frail shape disappearing into the cushions of the sofa. It is just Lydia, the housekeeper, who hovers around Mrs. Hampton, guiding her up and down the stairs at the start and end of each day, or Jasmine who lingers nervously, afraid of disturbing the delicate balance of the silent house.

The last day of March. Mother and daughter walk up the long drive from the village, the church bells ringing out into the bold blue sky. Spring has settled, and for several days now there has been a warmth in the air, the trees filling out with handsome abundance. The church was busy this morning, women clutching the fragrant posies of flowers that their children gathered under the patient guidance of the vicar's wife. Mothering Sunday has taken on a new fragility since the war, and for Rosamund too: she feels on edge today, as though the brightness of the morning might darken at any moment.

As the house comes into sharper view up the hill in front of them, Rosamund can sense herself speeding up, a strange urgency pulling her forward. There is something vanishing from her, an opportunity soon to fade forever.

She starts to run, letting go of Jasmine's hand as she covers the last stretch of the drive. The door is open, a pair of gardening gloves discarded next to a basket outside. Lydia collecting herbs for their lunch, she thinks, pressing onward and into the empty stillness of the house.

Beatrice Hampton makes only the smallest imprint on the cushions. A cup of tea has fallen from her hand and her eyes are open, their gaze fixed on some invisible memory, a moment conjured in this house that has been hers to shape and define. Does she remember, Rosamund finds herself thinking as she stares at Beatrice's dead body, plucking a baby from a mother's arms? Does she remember that drive through the rain?

It is too late to ask the questions that have been building inside her. It is too late to speak, to listen, to seek understanding, to forgive. All she has now, on this Mothering Sunday morning, is a silence that can never be breached.

Jasmine is by her side, reaching for her hand. Her daughter has never seen death before, but she understands what this is. "We didn't get to say goodbye," Jasmine whispers.

And just like that, ten minutes too late, the barriers that Rosamund had erected come tumbling down.

That evening, once Jasmine is in bed and the undertakers have gone, Rosamund pulls on a sweater and goes out into the garden. Her old dog follows, a slow lumbering gait through the grounds he knows so well. Twilight blurs the edges of the forest, and the grass deepens into a graphite green. Rosamund moves slowly, her body heavy. She feels the weight of her mother's death, the unresolved anger that hovered between them.

Her walled garden beckons, and she feels calmer once inside its stone walls, the narrow pebbled walkways firm beneath her feet. At last, after the difficulty of the day, she can think.

Rosamund knows she cannot let this happen again, this cycle of silence and recriminations and secrets: it has to end. Tomorrow, she says to herself as she tidies away a sprawling branch of slowly waking lilac.

Tomorrow: a train to London, a new beginning, a journey started afresh.

Historical Note

On February 20, 1946, the Royal Opera House, Covent Garden, reopened after years of war. It seems entirely fitting that the Sadler's Wells Ballet chose to put on *The Sleeping Beauty*, a story of reawakening, hope, and new beginnings, a symbol of a country emerging out of the austerity of World War II. It is clear from reviews of the production that while many were excited about the prospect of returning Covent Garden to its prewar use as a theatre, others felt that the extravagance of *The Sleeping Beauty*, with its exquisite new sets and costumes by Oliver Messel, was out of touch with the hardship many in the country were facing. This conflict is a familiar one, and centers around the value we give to the arts in times of difficulty. In researching for this novel, I was encouraged by the energy of ballet during those war years, as well as the decision made in 1945 by CEMA (the Council for the Encouragement of Music and the Arts, renamed the Arts Council in 1946), led by Lord Maynard Keynes, to make the Opera House a home for a resident opera and resident ballet company. It was time to remove the bandstands and mecca dance floor that had covered the entire stage and auditorium during the war, and bring in a new era of music and dance.

The story of the Sadler's Wells Ballet in the war years is a remarkable one, and I have not been able to do justice to their courageous and dedicated work in continuing to bring ballet to so many corners of the country. There were many challenges: male dancers conscripted into the armed forces; limited costumes and sets; the lack of an orchestra for most of their tours; unsuitable conditions for performing, such as freezing aircraft hangars; long nights in slow sleeper trains; the endless round of finding new digs; air raids interrupting performances. (Karen Eliot's 2008 article "Starved for Beauty: British Ballet and Public Morale during the Second World War" is an excellent source of information on the efforts of dance companies to continue throughout the war.) It was the company's tour to Holland in May 1940 that led the dancers into the most danger, and I am very grateful for Annabel Farjeon's detailed account of those days in The Hague, the bus journeys between performances, the evacuation from the Hotel du Passage after Germany invaded on May 10, nervous conversations with soldiers, and rooftop encounters with the enemy. Thanks to the diaries kept by Farjeon, a dancer in the company who later became a writer, I have found it possible to be true to many details of those fraught few days, incorporating precise moments from her account into Briar's story. Farjeon writes of Ninette de Valois's determined resolve to keep the company safe, her tireless work in getting them home, the stress she must have faced in being responsible for so many young dancers in the middle of a violent and dangerous invasion. While there were many times they came close to disaster, the company all journeyed home safely, although some musical scores, costumes, and sets were lost forever.

While Briar and Rosamund's stories are fictional, they move through the lives of many real events, people, and places. In research, I was particularly drawn to Lady Mendl, born Elsie de Wolfe, and her parties at the fantastically decorated Villa Trianon. I was surprised to find out that Margot Fonteyn herself had visited Villa Trianon for a garden party in the summer of 1937 during a Paris tour performing Ninette de Valois's ballet *Checkmate*—a wonderful coincidence and one I could not neglect. Fonteyn and her mother stayed in the Paris YWCA for one pound per week, and Fonteyn attended ballet class in Paris at Salle Wacker with Olga Preobrajenska. The ballerina writes fondly of these classes in her 1976 autobiography. I am thankful to Meredith Daneman's excellent 2004 biography of Margot Fonteyn for insights into the prewar and war years of the Sadler's Wells Ballet, as well as Ninette de Valois's autobiography *Come Dance with Me*. A source of particular significance is Mary Clarke's important book *The Sadler's Wells Ballet: A History and an Appreciation* (1955), which is one of the most thorough accounts of the development of the company.

I have taken details from ballets created and performed in the years the novel is set, in particular *Nocturne*, choreographed by Frederick Ashton and first performed in November 1936. For this, I have tried to be as accurate as possible about the rehearsal process, the designs by Sophie Federovitch, and the reviews. I was inspired by the designs in the V&A online archives, as well as paintings of the ballet by Theyre Lee-Elliott and photographs by Gordon Anthony. There is no doubt that in every year since the founding of the Vic-Wells Ballet in 1931 (later renamed Sadler's Wells Ballet, then the Royal Ballet), audiences and artists were falling more and more in love with the growing dynamism of British ballet. There is a strong argument to suggest that it was the company's efforts during the war that cemented their success: by 1942, audiences were packed, and enthusiastic fans were leaving packets of precious rations (butter, steak, eggs, sugar) at the stage door.

Petipa and Tchaikovsky's version of *The Sleeping Beauty* differs significantly from the source texts, and I have included echoes of these darker stories in my novel. I explored the courtly medieval romance *Perceforest*, which tells the tale of Zellandine and Troylus, Giambattista Basile's Italian fairy tale "Sun, Moon and Talia," Charles Perrault's *La belle au Bois dormant*, and the Brothers' Grimm tale "Little Briar Rose." All of these have moments of horror, whether it is a prince raping a sleeping princess, the princess giving birth in her sleep, or an ogress trying to eat the children. These tales are very different from the Disney version of true love's kiss so familiar today. My novel was particularly inspired by a version of the ballet called *Les Beaux dormants*, created by the Canadian choreographer Hélène Blackburn and performed at the Linbury Theatre by the Ballet of the Opera National du Rhin in 2019. The ballet is a deconstruction of the traditional version, and it was the portrayal of Carabosse that I found most fascinating. The role is played by a man, topless, with a Romantic-style tutu skirt of black sparkling chiffon. On one foot is a pointe shoe, on the other a soft black dance shoe. This is a Carabosse who refuses to conform to the stereotype of the evil fairy. Integral to the character are dichotomies of power and vulnerability, a desire to curse and a fear of being cursed, ugliness and beauty. I was interested in the complexities of good and evil, the symbolic characters of Carabosse, and the Lilac Fairy changing as the different versions of the characters' stories unravel. In fact, perhaps Tchaikovsky had the same idea: when the Lilac Fairy sends the court to sleep, her familiar gentle leitmotif transforms into the dynamic musical theme of Carabosse.

Both this novel and the ballet of *The Sleeping Beauty* explore motherhood: in the ballet we have the queen, the fairy godmothers, the evil Carabosse. In my novel there are Alice, Rosamund, Briar. And for any reader who has danced or has a child who has danced, they will know what I mean when I talk about the ballet mother. Margot Fonteyn's mother—Mrs. Hilda Hookham, or the Black Queen, as she became known by the company—plays a small role in the novel, but in reality, she was integral to the life of the Sadler's Wells Ballet throughout Fonteyn's career. She regularly traveled with the company on tour and became a surrogate mother to many of the dancers, helping in Wardrobe, making lunches and teas, sourcing materials for the costumes. There are many accounts of the relationship between Margot Fonteyn and her immensely involved mother, most of them remarkably positive. For readers interested in learning more, I recommend Meredith Daneman's biography of Fonteyn. Or, for a shorter read, Alastair Macaulay's 2021 Women's History Month essay "The Ballet Mother," which is highly informative.

My own years of training at the Royal Ballet School have given me a special insight into the way ballet can put immense stress on the roles of motherhood. My mother tells me stories of her conversations with fellow ballet mothers struggling to cope with the anxiety of their child trying to make it in the competitive world of classical ballet.

In my novel, motherhood is complicated by adoption. Rules and regulations for adoption gradually developed in the first half of the twentieth century, with attitudes to adoption, secrecy, and the responsibilities of pregnant women changing at the same time. I am indebted to the research by Jenny Keating in her 2009 book *A Child for Keeps: The History of Adoption in England, 1918–45*, in which she writes about the significant changes during these years. It wasn't until 1926, with the Adoption of Children Act, that adopting parents gained any legal rights. In fact, before that year legal adoption did not exist in the United Kingdom. And for those wanting to adopt a child there were no regulations: Keating provides anecdotes of children picked from adoption societies, only to be returned if the parents weren't satisfied with their choice. The agency run by the Allens in my novel is entirely fictional, but I have tried to provide a sense of the changing practices and discourses surrounding adoption in the years between 1919 and 1937.

This is a novel about storytelling, fairy tales, and the narratives we follow to try to achieve our dreams. I hope readers will enjoy finding fragments of different stories throughout the novel, whether of a sleeping beauty and a prince, a beguiling white cat, the tales that inspired the ballets of Frederick Ashton and Ninette de Valois, or the story of the Sadler's Wells Ballet in those challenging years of war. The tale of a sleeping beauty has inspired so many creations over the centuries: my version is about celebrating all of life's joys and challenges. It is about waking up and embracing life.

Ballet Movements

adage—section of a ballet class with slow movements of the legs to improve balance, extension, and coordination.

allegro—section of a ballet class with jumping steps.

arabesque—one leg extended behind the body with the knee straight and the foot pointed.

assemblé—a jump from one leg during which the legs assemble and land together.

attitude—the working leg is lifted either in front (devant), side (à la seconde), or back (derrière), with the knee bent.

balancé—a swaying, rocking step in any direction to a waltz rhythm.

barre exercises—in the first part of a ballet class, dancers run through a series of exercises. These take place at the barre, a bar on which the dancer places their hand while dancing. These exercises include, in the order in which they are carried out:

> *pliés*—to bend and stretch both legs at the same time.
>
> *battements tendus or dégagé*—one foot slides out smoothly along the floor to a full pointe of the toe. They can be performed in any direction, including en croix (in the shape of a cross—front, side, back, side).
>
> *battements jetés or glissés*—as with tendu but with the toe just lifting off the floor.
>
> *ronds de jambe*—the leg makes a circle, front, side, then back, either on the ground (à terre) or lifted off the ground (en l'air). They can be performed en dedans (inward) or en dehors (outward).

battements fondus—smoothly unfolding the leg into the air, with the supporting leg bending and then extending.

battements frappés—a raised, flexed foot touches the ankle, then springs out with great energy to a pointed position.

petits battements—the foot moves quickly around the ankle, with the knee bent.

développés—drawing one foot up to the knee and then unfolding the leg into the air. In a développé passé, the foot is passed from the front to the back, or the reverse.

grands battements—exercises that usually finish the barre work; throwing the leg high and controlling the movement as it lowers. For grands battements en cloche, the leg is thrown forward, then back alternately.

cambré—a bend of the body from the waist in any direction.

chaînés—quick, traveling half-turns with the feet in a tight first position.

croisé—a position of the body: toward the corner and crossed, with the front leg closest to the audience.

demi-bras—arms held low, extended on either side of the body.

échappé—the legs spring out at the same time to either side, front or back. Sur les pointes is onto the toes.

en pointe—dancing on the tips of the toes while wearing pointe shoes.

épaulement—turning the body from the waist so one shoulder comes forward and the other goes back.

fouetté—with many variations, it is often a quick whipping movement of the leg accompanied by a turn.

grand jeté—a large jump with the legs split in the air.

pas de bourrée—three small steps, with many variations of style and position of the feet.

pas de chat—a jump in which both feet come up, one by one, underneath the body, with the knees bent.

pas de deux—partner dancing, traditionally where the female dancer is supported or lifted by the male dancer.

petit allegro—small jumps, including jumps such as échappés, glissades, and jetés.

piqué turns—a turn, often performed in a series, with a sharp step up onto the pointe or ball of the foot of the straight leg.

pirouette—a full turn on one leg. They can be performed en dedans (inward) or en dehors (outward).

port de bras—arm movements, literally meaning "carriage of the arms."

retiré—keeping contact with the supporting leg, drawing one foot up to the knee.

soubresaut—a jump straight up into the air during which the legs do not change.

soutenu—sustained movement, often used to describe a turn in which the legs assemble tight together on the toes of both feet (assemblé soutenu en tournant).

tombé—a "fall" from one leg to the other, in any direction, with the legs either bent or straight.

tour en l'air—a jump straight up into the air, with one or more full turns.

Historical Figures

Anthony, Gordon (1902–89)—photographer whose work documents many productions and dancers in the early years of the company. His sister was Dame Ninette de Valois.

Ashton, Frederick (1904–88)—dancer and choreographer integral to the development of British ballet, and chief choreographer for the Vic-Wells Ballet, later called the Sadler's Wells Ballet and then the Royal Ballet. Some of his most famous work includes *Façade* (1931), *Nocturne* (1936), *Dante Sonata* (1940), *Cinderella* (1948), and *La Fille mal gardée* (1960).

Bakst, Léon (1866–1924)—Russian artist who designed costumes and sets for the Ballets Russes, including *The Sleeping Princess* in 1921.

Beaton, Cecil (1904–80)—British photographer who photographed dancers from the Sadler's Wells Ballet, including Margot Fonteyn and Frederick Ashton.

Benois, Nadia (1896–1975)—painter, stage designer, and writer, born in Russia. She designed the scenery and costumes for the 1939 Vic-Wells Ballet production of *The Sleeping Princess*.

Bland, Sir George Nevile Maltby (1886–1972)—served as Envoy Extraordinary and Minister Plenipotentiary to the Netherlands during World War II.

Bland, Lady Portia (1885–1968)—wife of Sir George Nevile Maltby Bland.

Brae, June (1917–2000)—British ballerina, born June Bear. She lived in Shanghai for the first part of her life, training with Margot Fonteyn. She joined the school of the Vic-Wells Ballet in 1933 and was admitted into the company in 1935. She took on many leading roles, including the Rich Girl in *Nocturne* (1936) and the Lilac Fairy in *The Sleeping Princess* (1939).

Brown, Molly (lifespan unknown)—dancer with the Vic-Wells Ballet, a contemporary of Margot Fonteyn. She is often seen in photographs and cast lists from the 1930s and 1940s.

Comelli, Attilio (1858–1925)—Italian costume designer, responsible for the creation of many costumes for productions at the Royal Opera House in the early twentieth century. The designs remained in wardrobe stores during the war and are now part of the Royal Opera House Collections.

Diaghilev, Serge (1872–1929)—founder of the Ballets Russes.

Farron, Julia (1922–2019)—ballerina at the Vic-Wells Ballet, becoming the company's youngest member when she joined, aged fourteen, in 1936. She was the queen in the 1946 opening performance of *The Sleeping Beauty*. Later in her life she served as the director of the Royal Academy of Dance.

Federovitch, Sophie (1893–1953)—costume designer who frequently collaborated with Frederick Ashton, including designing the costumes for *Nocturne* (1936) and *Dante Sonata* (1940).

Fonteyn, Margot (1919–91)—born Margaret Hookham, she joined the school of the Vic-Wells Ballet and quickly became a leading member of the company. She was eventually appointed prima ballerina assoluta in 1979, a rare and prestigious title.

Fraser, Moyra (1923–2009)—ballet dancer who later became an actor. She joined the Sadler's Wells Ballet school when she was fourteen and became a close friend of Robert Helpmann.

Furse, Patrick (1918–2005)—artist whose work includes studies of dancers drawn backstage at Sadler's Wells theatre. He was a friend of Margot Fonteyn: the Royal Opera House collection holds letters from Fonteyn to Furse written during World War II.

Helpmann, Robert (1909–86)—Australian ballet dancer who joined the Vic-Wells Ballet in 1932 and quickly became a star of the company. He took on an intense performing schedule during the war years. Because of his nationality, he was one of the few male dancers not conscripted into service.

Hookham, Hilda (1894–1988)—née Fontes, she was the mother of Margot Fonteyn. She was committed to her daughter's career and often helped on tour and backstage.

Jackson, Mr. (lifespan unknown)—Mr. Jackson was the stage doorkeeper at the Covent Garden Royal Opera House for many years before and after World War II. He is mentioned fondly in several memoirs and autobiographies of performers from those years.

Lambert, Constant (1905–51)—composer and conductor, he was the music director of the Vic-Wells Ballet. His work was central to the development of British ballet in the 1930s and 1940s, and he conducted *The Sleeping Beauty* on the opening night of the postwar Royal Opera House in February 1946.

Lee-Elliott, Theyre (1903–88)—artist most famous for his Art Deco logos, such as the Speedbird. He also worked on the scenery at Sadler's Wells Theatre and painted ballet dancers. His book *Paintings of the Ballet* was published in 1947.

Martyn, Laurel (1916–2013)—Australian ballerina who joined the Vic-Wells Ballet in December 1935, and by 1938 she was a soloist. She joined Margot Fonteyn on a trip to Paris in the summer of 1936.

May, Pamela (1917–2005)—born Doris May, Ninette de Valois asked her to change her name to Pamela around 1934, when she joined the Vic-Wells Ballet. She was a principal dancer at the Royal Ballet, then a character dancer, before becoming a teacher at the Royal Ballet School.

Maynard Keynes, John (1883–1946)—economist with a keen interest in the arts; married to the ballerina Lydia Lopokova. He gave financial support to the Cambridge Arts Theatre, which opened in 1936. He was a member of CEMA (the Council for the Encouragement of Music and the Arts), and a founding member of the Arts Council, which was instrumental in the reopening of the Royal Opera House and providing a new home for the Sadler's Wells Ballet.

Messel, Oliver (1904–78)—artist and stage designer who designed the sets and costumes for the production of *The Sleeping Beauty* in 1946. Previous work includes a production for Diaghilev in 1925 and designs for Cochran's revues in the later 1920s and early 1930s.

Moreton, Ursula (1903–73)—ballet dancer who was one of the six founding members of the Vic-Wells Ballet. She worked closely with Ninette de Valois and was ballet mistress for the Vic-Wells Ballet from its early days in 1931. Later, she was assistant director of the Sadler's Wells Theatre Ballet, and then director of the Royal Ballet School.

Petipa, Marius (1818–1910)—a famous French-Russian choreographer. He choreographed *The Sleeping Princess*, now known as *The Sleeping Beauty*, in 1890.

Phillips, Ailne (1905–92)—dancer and teacher for the Sadler's Wells Ballet. She was one of the first members of the company when it was founded in 1931 as the Vic-Wells Ballet. She taught at Sadler's Wells Ballet School during the war, maintaining the school's work even when the theatre itself was repurposed as a shelter for those affected by bombing.

Preobrajenska, Olga (1871–1962)—ballerina of the Russian Imperial Ballet, she emigrated in 1921 and eventually settled in Paris along with many others who had left Russia in the wake of the Russian Revolution. She was a popular teacher, drawing many famous dancers to her studio at the Salle Wacker near Montmartre.

Sackville-West, Edward (1901–65)—music critic and novelist, he wrote the scenario for the ballet *Nocturne* (1936), which was choreographed by Frederick Ashton to Delius's *Paris: The Song of a Great City* (1899).

Sergeyev, Nicholas (1876–1951)—regisseur of the Imperial Ballet at the Mariinsky Theatre, he fled Russia after the 1917 Revolution. He took with him trunks containing the written records of many of the great ballets of Marius Petipa and Lev Ivanov. The classical repertoire of ballets, including *Coppélia*, *Giselle*, *Swan Lake* (*Le Lac des cygnes*), *The Nutcracker* (*Casse-Noisette*), and *The Sleeping Princess*, is known as the Sergeyev Collection.

de Valois, Dame Ninette (1898–2001)—founder of the Vic-Wells Ballet, which evolved into Sadler's Wells Ballet, then the Royal Ballet and Birmingham Royal Ballet. She is known in the ballet world simply as Madam.

Volkova, Vera (1905–75)—Russian ballet dancer who defected in 1929. In 1943 she retired from dancing and became a ballet teacher. Her classes at a studio in Knightsbridge (then the West End) were popular with many dancers.

de Wolfe, Elsie (Lady Mendl) (1859–1950)—American actress who became an important interior designer. She married the English diplomat Sir Charles Mendl in 1926, but it was a marriage of convenience; she was in a lifelong relationship with Elisabeth Marbury, her theatre agent. She was a socialite and hosted large parties at Villa Trianon, her house in France.

Acknowledgments

Writing a second novel is a very different experience to a debut, and I am so grateful for the guidance and advice I have been given since the conception of this book. I have so many people to thank for supporting me throughout the writing, production, and publication of *The Sleeping Beauties*.

Thank you to my agent, Antony Topping. His early guidance on the story was invaluable, as well as his comments on each draft. I am grateful to everyone at Greene and Heaton and to the US agency JVNLA. Jennifer Weltz has been wonderfully supportive, both in my writing and in welcoming me to a new city.

I am lucky to have two brilliant editors: Jenny Parrott at Oneworld and Claire Wachtel at Union Square & Co. Their editorial guidance has brought depth and precision to the writing, and I am so grateful for their enthusiasm.

The team in the UK at Oneworld are exceptional champions of their writers, and I am fortunate to work with such a talented group. Thank you to Julian Ball, Anne Bihan, Beth Marshall Brown, Lucy Cooper, Laura McFarlane, Paul Nash, Mark Rusher, Hayley Warnham, Matilda Warner, and Margot Weale. Thank you to Sarah Terry and Diane João (in the US) for copyediting with such attention to detail. Producing a book is a huge team effort and I am privileged to also work with an amazing US publisher, Union Square & Co. Thank you to Barbara Berger, Alison Skrabek, Kevin Ullrich, Elizabeth Lindy, Lisa Forde, Daniel Denning, Jenny Lu, Nathan Siegel, and Chris Vaccari. My visits to

New York City have been all the more exciting because of meetings at Union Square.

In researching the history of the Sadler's Wells Ballet, now the Royal Ballet, I have connected with experts in the field who have generously given of their time. I have loved my conversations with Anna Meadmore, the Manager of Special Collections at The Royal Ballet School, and I am grateful to her for allowing me to explore the archives. Thank you also to Rachel Hollings at the Royal Opera House for her kindness, as well as to Maud Stiegler.

I started writing this book at a time of significant life change: my husband had recently moved to New York City while I continued to teach English in London. *The Sleeping Beauties* was written in two cities, and in the sky between them, and it was the creation of this book that gave me direction when I felt rootless or lonely. Thank you to my wonderful husband, Erik, for his support, even across the ocean, and for reading each draft with such enthusiasm and kindness.

Thank you to friends and family who gave me so much of their love, time, and support as I wrote this book, understanding the challenges of such long stretches of time without Erik. Special mention must go to Beth Armstrong, who always listened and understood.

My friends and family have been such enthusiastic cheerleaders since the publication of my first novel, *The Dance of the Dolls* (or *Clara & Olivia* as it is called in the UK). Their words of encouragement have been a source of great joy. Thank you especially to Brittany Ashworth, Natasha Bassett, Jo Bratten, Jim Buckland, Will Goldsmith, Rob Green, Rivka Jacobson, Ashley Hickson-Lovence, Bryerly Long, Tom and Elisa Moy, Daira

Szostak, Susie Wallat-Vago, Wolfgang Wallat, and all my relatives here in the UK and in South Africa. Thank you to my London book club friends—I will miss you all so much. Thank you to my fellow English teachers, the best colleagues I could ever ask for. I am so fortunate to have had my friend and colleague Alison O'Neill supporting me every day. Thank you to the wonderful Debut 2023 group. Connecting with you all has brought laughter, reassurance, and shared joy. I hope to meet more of you in person soon, but particular thanks to Amita Parikh and Rachel Corsini for welcoming me when I first came to the US.

A special thank-you to my grandfather, Patrick Ashe. He died many years ago, but his memories live on. The Cambridge sections of the novel are partly inspired by Grandpa's stories of his time studying at St. John's College, Cambridge, in the 1930s, recorded in his memoir entitled *Dust and Ashes*.

Thank you to my parents, John and Shelagh, and to my sisters, Suzie Lambert and Jo Ashe. They all read early drafts of *The Sleeping Beauties* and their feedback was tremendously helpful, providing a range of perspectives that helped to refine the story. I believe it is rare to have a family who is so willing to read everything (several times in my case), so I hope they know how grateful I am.

Finally, thank you to the dancers past and present who inspire me. I left ballet years ago, but returning to dance through my writing has been the most fulfilling decision of my life.

Reading Group Guide

TOPICS AND QUESTIONS FOR DISCUSSION

1. Rosamund and Briar's war years were very different: Rosamund took in evacuees, while Briar toured with Sadler's Wells Ballet company. What did you think about their attitudes to their own and each other's work during the war?

2. Elements of the fairy tale of the Sleeping Beauty appear in many ways throughout the novel. For example, awakening from a long curse as a metaphor for the end of the war; the transitional stages of growing up reflected in sleeping and waking; the house in Devon surrounded by a forest; the ballet performances of *The Sleeping Princess* in 1939 and *The Sleeping Beauty* in 1946. Were there any Sleeping Beauty moments that resonated with you most strongly?

3. Briar, Martha, and Vivian are close friends, but their friendship changes as the novel develops. What do you think led to those changes, and how might some of their conflicts have been avoided?

4. Briar's determination to atone for what she felt were her mistakes before and during the war takes her down a dangerous path. She starts to lose her grip on reality, as well as her understanding of right and wrong. How did you react to her actions and decisions?

5. Both this novel and the ballet of *The Sleeping Beauty* explore motherhood. The ballet has the queen, the fairy godmothers, and the evil fairy Carabosse. In the novel, there are Alice, Rosamund, Briar, Beatrice, and some "ballet mothers." What was your impression of the different types of mothers and ways of being a mother depicted in the novel?

6. Motherhood in the novel is also explored through the complexities of adoption. Page 322 of the Historical Note provides some context for this, and the changing attitudes and regulations surrounding adoption. What anxieties about adoption did some of the characters express, and how did they overcome these?

7. What did you think about the men in the novel? How did the fathers take on different responsibilities compared to the mothers?

8. Rosamund's mother, Beatrice Hampton, makes a decision about her daughter's pregnancy that is shocking and invasive. Why did she do this, and do you think Rosamund ever forgives her? Likewise, do you think Rosamund will be able to forgive Briar and start a new relationship with her? If so, how might this come about?

ENHANCE YOUR BOOK CLUB

1. Explore the story of the Sleeping Beauty and the way the narrative has changed over the centuries. There are many excellent online videos and resources for this. The book *Sleeping Beauty and Other Tales of Slumbering Princesses* by Amelia Carruthers is a good starting place for exploring the changing versions of the story.

2. Watch a recorded version of the ballet *The Sleeping Beauty*. The Royal Opera House, Covent Garden, London, has an online streaming service with several recordings of the ballet.

3. Read about the history of the Royal Ballet and their work during the war. Ninette de Valois's memoir *Come Dance With Me* and Meredith Daneman's 2004 biography of Margot Fonteyn provide excellent accounts of this time.

A CONVERSATION WITH LUCY ASHE

What inspired you to write *The Sleeping Beauties*?

My first novel, *The Dance of the Dolls*, ends with twin sisters Clara and Olivia rehearsing the famous and challenging "Rose Adagio" from *The Sleeping Beauty*. That novel was set in 1933, a time of new beginnings for British ballet, with the Vic-Wells Ballet (now known as the Royal Ballet) still in its infancy. I decided I wanted to write a novel set at another pivotal moment for ballet: the years surrounding World War II.

When I was researching the work of the Sadler's Wells Ballet company during the war, it was fascinating to learn about the reopening of the Royal Opera House, Covent Garden, after its use as a dance hall during the war. It was a performance of *The Sleeping Beauty* that reopened the theater in February 1946, with Margot Fonteyn in the leading role. When I was planning the novel, the more I read about this time, the more certain I became that I would set the climactic scenes of the novel on this opening night.

However, my greatest inspiration for writing the novel is my love of ballet. I trained at the Royal Ballet School in London for eight years, first as a Junior Associate, and then at the boarding school, White Lodge, in Richmond Park. To say my goal at that stage of my life was to be a ballet dancer is an understatement: my life then was devoted to dance, and it took many years to come to terms with the fact that my career took a different direction. I continued to dance and perform, but I also went to Oxford University to study English literature, and then I became an English teacher. Returning to ballet through my writing, first with my debut novel, *The Dance of the Dolls*, and then with *The Sleeping Beauties*, has been a wonderfully fulfilling way of bringing dance back into my life.

What are your favorite moments in the ballet of *The Sleeping Beauty*?

The Sleeping Beauty has been one of my favorite ballets ever since I was a student at the Royal Ballet School. We learned and danced all the fairy solos in repertoire class, as well as the famous garland waltz. In researching for this novel, it was wonderful to return to the choreography once again, and to explore the history of the ballet. My favorite solo to dance was the Fairy of the Golden Vine, as well as the Princess Florine variation. These are challenging dances, requiring immense control and strong pointe work, and we were lucky to be coached by highly experienced teachers at the Royal Ballet School, many of whom had performed these roles themselves.

I was also inspired by the ballet's music, composed by Tchaikovsky. It is a stunning score, and I listened to it on repeat while writing the novel. The music is filled with motifs that represent the different characters; for example, the gentle leitmotif of the Lilac Fairy contrasts with the dynamism of the music for the arrival of Carabosse. There are, however, moments when the motifs intertwine: when the Lilac Fairy sends the castle to sleep, the gentle music transforms into the darker theme of Carabosse, complicating the simple binary of good and evil. This inspired me to think more deeply about the ways in which we look for good and evil in people, and yet how often it is impossible to make such simple characterizations.

What is it about the tale of the Sleeping Beauty that you found most compelling when writing *The Sleeping Beauties*?

In the fairy tale of the Sleeping Beauty, a castle reawakens after a long curse. The dark forest of thorns is transformed into roses, true love, a happily ever after. It fascinates me, therefore, that it was a performance of *The Sleeping Beauty* that reopened the Royal Opera House, Covent Garden, after the Second World War, in February 1946. The directors of the Sadler's Wells Ballet company must have felt that this was an appropriate metaphor to celebrate the change from the darkness and endurance of war, to the hope of peace. However, alongside the metaphors of hope, escapism, growing up, and the transitions from childhood to adolescence, the story of the Sleeping Beauty is a story about change.

Psychologists have frequently turned to fairy tales when trying to explain the challenges of growing up and the important but difficult journey of leaving behind the safety of childhood. The tale of the Sleeping Beauty is a useful narrative for examining this transition. The princess falls asleep just as she is reaching adulthood. The spinning wheel, a metaphor for the relentless nature of time, is unwelcome, the needle that pricks her finger provoking the next stage of her life: adolescence, menstruation, maturity.

We could see the Sleeping Beauty's curse as a reflection of life's transitions, how each one is fraught with difficulty, leading to a desire to retreat and to sleep. The Lilac Fairy's spell keeps the princess frozen in time with no aging or pain or fear, but also none of the joys of life. The fairy tale teaches us that change is essential, and that without it we are merely sleeping through life.

The novel is a combination of fact and fiction. How did you approach the research for the novel?

As with many novels set during times of real conflict, such as the Second World War, *The Sleeping Beauties* is a fictional story set within real historical events. I was inspired by those real events when researching for the novel, and I allowed my explorations to guide the creation of the novel's synopsis. I hope this has led to a unique approach to the Second World War novel, integrating the real ballet wartime tour to The Hague, Holland, with an emotive fictional narrative of a woman's attempt to find meaning in her past.

While the story of Briar, Rosamund, and Jasmine is entirely fictional, every performance I mention in the novel is historically researched, from the 1936 production of *Nocturne* to the 1939 performance of *The Sleeping Princess*, as well as all the touring performances in Holland in 1940, and *Casse-Noisette* in London at the New Theatre that continued despite the threat of air raids. I wanted the setting of the novel to be as historically accurate as possible, and I drew on a large range of sources to build my knowledge of this specific slice of 1930s and 1940s history.

My starting point was reading memoirs and biographies by and about dancers or those connected to the dance world from this time; for example, Dame Ninette de Valois, Margot Fonteyn, Hilda Hookham (Margot Fonteyn's mother), Mary Clarke, and Annabel Farjeon. The British Newspaper Archive was also helpful in providing reviews of the performances I write about in the novel. Visual resources helped inspire the descriptions and mood of the book, and I loved looking through backstage and performance photographs by Gordon Anthony (in *Shadowland: 1926–52*), as well as a wonderful collection of paintings of the ballet by Theyre Lee-Elliott, an artist best known for his Art Deco Speedbird logo. The V&A and the Royal Opera House online archives provided details about Oliver Messel's designs for *The Sleeping Beauty* costumes, and I was fortunate to be able to visit the Royal Ballet School archives as part of my research, a memorable day that took me back to the place I had spent so many years as a teenager.

Many historical figures make brief appearances in the novel. Who did you find most interesting to research, and how did you go about integrating them into this fictional story?

It was reading about the early career of Margot Fonteyn that inspired me the most when I was researching for *The Sleeping Beauties*. Her memoir (published in 1976), as well as the biography by Meredith Daneman (published in 2004), give full and fascinating accounts of the challenges she faced in becoming the ballet company's star at such a young age. She was just twenty years old when the war began, and already she was a ballet celebrity. The responsibility of this when touring and traveling amid the threat of war, in particular the fraught 1940 tour to The Hague that I write about in *The Sleeping Beauties*, was a heavy burden. Fonteyn was thrown into a world that was both glamorous and ruthless, and she had to learn quickly how to navigate the challenges of growing up, war, fame, the pressures of adult relationships, and the attention of men. And yet close by her side was her mother, Mrs. Hilda Hookham, keeping a close eye on her daughter while also allowing her to find her own way. It was this relationship between a mother and daughter, a relationship made complex through the pressures of a ballet career, that I was drawn to again and again when writing *The Sleeping Beauties*.

Another historical figure who inspired me when I was writing was my grandfather, Patrick Ashe. Grandpa died many years ago, but his memories live on. I feel honored that I was able to draw on parts of his life in my book. He wrote a memoir called *Dust and Ashes* that includes accounts of his time studying at Cambridge in the 1930s. He remembers the ballet coming to the newly opened Arts Theatre, and there is a story he tells about a punting outing with some of the dancers. One of the girls in his punt was Margot Fonteyn. He writes: "We had no idea then that she was to become one of the best ballet dancers in the world."

Your debut novel, *The Dance of the Dolls*, is set at a similar time and features the same ballet company as in *The Sleeping Beauties*. Are the two novels linked in any other ways?

The Dance of the Dolls is set in 1933, two years after the founding of the Vic-Wells Ballet, the company that went on to become the Sadler's Wells Ballet, and then the Royal Ballet. Many of the same historical figures feature in both books; for example, Ninette de Valois, Constant Lambert, Robert Helpmann, Ursula Moreton, and John Maynard Keynes. For anyone keen to learn about the development of British ballet in the 1930s and '40s, reading the two novels in chronological order would offer an interesting perspective on the early years of the Royal Ballet. However, the two books are separate stories and do not feature the same fictional characters.

What do you hope readers will take from the novel?
I hope readers will enjoy reading about the Second World War from an unusual perspective, and that it will offer an opportunity to explore questions about the value we give to the arts in times of conflict.

Each character has a different experience of war, of motherhood, of dance, of love. Likewise, I imagine that readers will have different experiences of reading *The Sleeping Beauties*, some finding themselves drawn to Rosamund, others to Briar, while still others might find something in each character that resonates with them, perhaps because of—rather than despite—the flaws, insecurities, and challenges the characters face.

Mostly, I hope readers will enjoy being swept between theaters, towns, countries, dance studios, and bookshops, escaping into a historical setting that combines the uncertainties of war with the magic of ballet.